D0455780

INVITATION
TO DIE

BOOKS BY THE AUTHOR

The Joe Sandilands Investigations
The Last Kashmiri Rose
Ragtime in Simla
The Damascened Blade
The Palace Tiger
The Bee's Kiss
Tug of War
Folly du Jour
Strange Images of Death
The Blood Royal
Not My Blood
A Spider in the Cup
Enter Pale Death
Diana's Altar

The Detective Inspector Redfyre Investigations
Fall of Angels
Invitation to Die

INVITATION
TO DIE

Barbara Cleverly

SOHO
CRIME

Published by
Soho Press, Inc.
853 Broadway
New York, NY 10003

Library of Congress Cataloging-in-Publication Data

Cleverly, Barbara, author.
Invitation to die / Barbara Cleverly.
Series: An Inspector Redfyre mystery ; 2

ISBN 978-1-64129-027-2
eISBN 978-1-64129-028-9
I. Title

PR6103.L48 I58 2019 823'.92—dc23 2018060875

Interior design by Janine Agro, Soho Press, Inc.

Printed in the United States of America

10 9 8 7 6 5 4 3 2 1

With many thanks to my friend Polly who inspired this Cambridge story.

~⌒

And dedicated to the memory of ancestor Mark Cooper,
a fifteen year old cavalryman in the South African War.
"A gentleman in khaki ordered south."

CHAPTER 1

S truck by a rare lapse in confidence, Rupert Rendlesham pulled up sharply in the middle of the King's Parade on his way down to the market square. At half past eleven on a Friday in May, the street was almost deserted. Examination papers and desperate last-minute revision had cleared undergraduates from the streets, and there was no one about to raise an eyebrow at the sudden break in the stride, the fleeting frown of indecision. Nevertheless, he looked furtively from side to side before turning to check on his reflection in the window of the gents' outfitters he was passing. Vanity? No. "Judicious self-awareness," he would have called his decision to indulge in a little light preening. Rupert was too vain ever to suspect himself of vanity.

There was another, less shaming trigger for his sudden spasm of doubt. This was no everyday expedition into the realms of the Great Unwashed he was undertaking. He was on a mission. A manhunt. His mind, steeped in medieval literature, dared to add: *a quest*. And he was running out of time. He had one hour to secure the trophy that would see him garlanded in praise by his fellows before the day was out. Amused by his own whimsy, Rupert twirled the end of an imaginary moustache and shared a flirtatious leer with his reflection.

A cheeky wolf whistle caught him in midpose. A further rude comment on his parentage from a butcher's boy pedalling by on a bike distracted and annoyed him.

"You ignoramus!" he hurled back. It occurred to Rupert that his choice of insult, if indeed apt, would be incomprehensible to the target. "Oik!" he added for clarity. "And your granny!"

Mild enough, but he regretted at once descending into mindless repartee. What the hell! He could do better than indulge in surreptitious self-examination for the entertainment of the lower classes.

With a swirl of the academic gown he'd chosen to retain as protective camouflage for his foray into the market, he breezed into the shop.

"Dr. Rendlesham! May I be of assistance, sir?"

"Ah, Blandish!" Rupert returned the greeting of the salesman who stepped forward at once to attend him. "You certainly can! I was just passing and felt the need to check the length of my gown in your—"

Before he could finish the sentence, a tall mirror was being pushed towards him and angled correctly. Rupert twirled in front of it, peering critically at his own elegant figure.

"Tell me now, Blandish . . . It's being whispered around college that the longer length of gown, like this one you sold me last year, is somewhat passé. I invite you to share your thoughts. I like to have these things straight from the horse's mouth." He turned again, adjusted his tie and smoothed down his short fair hair. At that moment, Rupert caught Blandish's sardonic eye, and a flash of skittish humour prompted him to grasp the two sides of his gown at heart level, elbows out, in a parody of a lecturer's stance. He tilted his head to offer the mirror an inspiring profile. He'd do! By George, he'd do! If the goddess Britannia had had a son and that son had been admitted as a scholar to St. Jude's, he'd surely have presented just such an image. Clean-cut. Direct gaze. Yet sporting a nose that would have provoked an envious Duke of Wellington into calling *en garde!*

Nerves calmed, he could now go on his way. Complete his mission. But Blandish appeared to be taking this nonsense at face value; he was giving the matter serious consideration.

"All is perfection, Dr. Rendlesham. I assure you the hemline rests where it has rested for seven hundred years. Halfway between hock and heel, just brushing the fetlock. But . . ." A reproving finger was raised. "If you will permit me, sir."

From heaven knew where, the man had suddenly conjured up a tailor's sponge and was dabbing at a fold in the back of his gown, tutting all the while. "Eve's pudding for supper last night, sir? You must have been seated in front of a clumsy custard-eater. There, that's better. I'll just give the shoulders a brushing and you'll be ready to take tea with the queen."

"Ah! Tea with the queen?" Rupert snorted with amusement. "Dinner with the devil is more what I have in mind! Thank you, Blandish. I'll be on my way."

"Give His Satanic Majesty my regards, sir."

Rupert just made out the words murmured behind his back as he returned to the hubbub of the street. Yon Blandish would bear watching, he decided. Hidden depths? A possibility there? No. Too useful in his capacity of outfitter to the university and gentry of the town. Rupert's nephew would be coming up next term, and he'd planned on confiding the boy to this establishment for his sartorial needs. Never curdle the cream and never foul your own nest—those were the rules. He must seek his prey farther afield.

HE STRODE THROUGH the market square, surveying the midday crowd from his formidable six-foot-two stature. It had been a good idea to wear his gown. At worst, it cloaked him in anonymity; at best, it granted him ease of passage. People moved out of his way, demonstrating their mistrust and dislike of academe. He scanned the mass of housewives and traders, lounging townies and the sprinkling of students desperate for fresh air and a change of scene. Checking, scorning and ultimately rejecting the lot of them. A predictable and boring collection with nothing more interesting on their minds than the size of Sunday's ham joint and the freshness of the cauliflower. Nothing here remotely resembling his target.

Had he missed him? Mistimed his sortie? Rendlesham was growing anxious. His afternoon meeting was due to start at one; there was little time to spare. After a very brief consideration, Rupert forgave himself. He would have to suggest a postponement. But his pride would be eternally dented if he let down the chaps. This was his first quest, and he'd volunteered, after all. What's more, the selection had been made for him—the scented lure had been pressed to his nostrils by Fanshawe himself. He merely had to follow where it led. He could not be seen to fail. He'd have to calm down, put a lid on the cauldron of conflicting emotions bubbling over and put his nose to the ground.

Testily, he wondered whether Fanshawe had been ill-advised. Surely there were more fruitful hunting grounds than the market square? The sunny green banks of the Cam? No, not during exam season. The only people lurking discreetly below the trailing green foliage of the willows were students. Swotting, sweating, occasionally throwing themselves off bridges. The bar of the Eagle? Packed with unintelligible science-wallahs. Drunk or boring. Frequently both. To be used only as a last resort.

Where in this city did one find a genuine civilian? Someone unconnected with the university? A socially negligible stranger? Rupert realised that in his six years here as a student and graduate researcher and lecturer, he'd scarcely set foot on non-university territory. Where was that to be found? The

Alhambra cinema came first to mind. Ugh! Flea-infested and full of copulating couples. Anyone who would pay a shilling to sit in the dark watching Rudolph Valentino sneer his way through something called *Blood and Sand* for an hour and a half was automatically disqualified. They weren't looking for a grunting Neanderthaler, after all.

He looked about, preparing to leave the square. He gave a final check to the impeccable fascia and gleaming vitrine of Aunty's Tea Rooms. A watering hole popular with both Town and Gown, who were to be seen, if not sharing a table, at least sitting peaceably at adjacent tables. There might be a few early tourists about, taking a cup of tea and a bun. Fanshawe had marked his card: *Our man is said to frequent— if that's the right word, though I'd suggest—infest—the environs of the café at lunchtime, when the place is at its busiest. People with enough cash to waste at "Aunty's" are likely to feel a frisson of guilt at the sight of a beggar when they step out, bloated on cakes and ham sandwiches. In the act of putting away their wallets and their purses, it's no trouble to hand over their small change to whoever asks for it. That's where you'll find the parasite.*

There was no beggar lurking about here at the entrance to put anyone off his lunch today, however. Could he return empty-handed? *Faute de mieux*, would a tourist suffice? Rupert rather liked the notion. By their nature, tourists could be expected to vanish from the scene. Transients moved on and were less predictable. They didn't come home for tea and a gossip at a regular time each day. They had no truck with the local forces of law or the organs of information. And there was precedent. Hadn't there been a visiting foreign person a few years ago? Yes! The older members still spoke of it, tears of laughter in their eyes. Garlic-eater, they would remember with an exaggerated shudder. Almost a caricature, danced the tango, chattered a lot in hilarious English. He'd provided good sport. And no repercussions.

But as he scanned the tearoom, Aunty's seemed to explode.

Rupert could have sworn the genteel façade had suffered a kaleidoscopic shift. The wide front door burst open noisily, accompanied by a bellow of outrage. The bellower himself erupted onto the street. Chintz drapes, which harked back to the more spacious days of William Morris, were in motion. They were being tweaked aside, and the wondering faces of the clientele appeared, jostling for the best position to view the events developing on the pavement outside. The door had been opened to its widest extent to allow space for the manager—a cumbersome fellow in a dark suit—to manhandle and eject from the café a bundle of old clothes enveloping the skinny frame of what Rupert took to be a down-and-out. His tramp?

"Ah, there you are! So that's where you were skulking!" Rupert's attention was instantly caught. Occasionally, driven by hunger or despair, one of these all-too-numerous unfortunates would make a hopeless attempt to invade the premises of one of the city's establishments by the front door instead of creeping round to the back, where he would be treated with furtive generosity by the serving staff if he was lucky.

Embarrassing little spat! Townies at play. Kinder not to look? Rupert would normally have grimaced and prepared to move on. But today he stayed put, observing the struggling pair. The portly grotesque, watch chain now straining across his silk-waistcoated abdomen, intrigued him. He widened the focus of his huntsman's stare to take in the broader picture. Who was this? Rupert had taken him for the manager, but he corrected himself. No salaried employee would have taken the liberty of creating such a public scene. This lardy gent carried himself with all the assurance of . . . the owner. Rupert chuckled. He'd seen much the same whipped up, noisy aggression in a male robin establishing its proprietorial rights in the springtime nest-building frenzy. Well, well! Many had speculated on the identity of "Aunty," and now, before his eyes, the mask seemed to have slipped off.

Rupert moved closer. He wanted to judge the quality of the verbal exchange that was now occurring between the two badly matched adversaries. Was his target articulate? Educated? The chairman had rather stressed that quality in his briefing. "Bear in mind that a modicum of resilience in the subject is to be preferred. We need a touch of steel to strike a spark!" It hardly mattered; the bell of Great St. Mary's Church was banging out twelve. This man would have to do.

The sweating incarnation of "Aunty" was holding forth: "Git yer ugly carcass out of my tearoom or I'll call the coppers! 'oo the 'ell do you think you are, coming in 'ere, all la-di-dah and taking the mickey, you old scarecrow?"

Oh dear. Rupert heard the bombastic tone of a London air-raid warden and sighed. This was some upstart Cockney war profiteer, no doubt having invested his ill-gotten pile in a nice little business. A jaw-cracking bore. His interest was reclaimed on noticing the scarecrow resisting the manhandling. What a fool! *His* best course would be to wriggle out from under the clasp of the beefy paws and show a clean pair of heels.

One abrupt upwards slashing, a cavalryman's flourish of the right arm, was all it took for the tramp to free himself from Aunty's clutches. Immediately following that, the bony fellow, stiff with indignation, pulled himself to his full height and rounded on Aunty. He attacked his tormentor with words, delivered in a ringing baritone. And yes, "la-di-dah" just about described his tone, which was, might one say . . . almost gentlemanly? Hard to tell when the sentiments being expressed were decidedly *un*gentlemanly.

"Mind your manners, you overstuffed little cream puff! I'd smack you plumb in the watch chain if I didn't fear the resulting explosion would contaminate the market square. But, what the hell . . . In for a penny!" His second attack came swiftly as his bunched left fist punched into the distended target with surprising vigour. Aunty doubled up, gasping and heaving, eyes popping.

An audience was hurrying to get a ringside seat. *Fight! Fight!* Where had they all come from, swarming up from nowhere like a plague of self-generating frogs?

For a sickening moment, Rupert was back in a prep-school playground, hearing both jeers and shouts of encouragement. From the same throat, in certain instances. A soggy tomato launched with pinpoint accuracy from the nearest stall added further decoration to Aunty's waistcoat. So, predictably, the English townsfolk had chosen to take the side of the underdog, Rupert noted. He thought he heard a police whistle somewhere in the distance. He would have to act fast. Having found his prey, he didn't want it carted off from under his nose by the local bobbies. No time for niceties.

He stepped forward, imperious in his black gown, calming and authoritative. A Cambridge crowd always appreciated instant judgement and swift retribution. Rupert was aware that, until quite recently, public hangings outside the Castle Street jail had drawn shamefully large audiences. He looked with a shudder at the overbright eyes and gawping mouths. Probably these people's grandparents, he calculated. But, however reprehensible, a crowd was easily manipulated. Mark Antony had played on the emotions of the mob over the bloodied corpse of Caesar in the Roman forum. He, Rupert Rendlesham, could perform the same trick with a scattering of idlers enjoying a rumpus amongst the vegetables in the Cambridge market.

With a dramatic swing of the folds of his gown over one shoulder, he became a toga-clad senator. Better still—a blue-eyed, fair-haired authority figure with a short back-and-sides. Trustworthy. If he'd stuck out a finger and barked, "Your country needs you!" they would have formed an orderly queue to sign up. Instead of the hoots and catcalls he'd feared, the crowd fell silent and attentive.

For a shameful moment, the thrill of exercising a dark power had him in its grip. He knew that, impressed by a commanding presence and oratorical skills, a mischief-seeking rabble could be roused to the point of stringing either of these idiots up from the nearest lamppost.

Rupert didn't hesitate.

"You!" he announced, pointing a headmasterly finger at Aunty, "You, my man, have just received the trouncing you deserved! A disgraceful display, sir! You set a poor example for the youth of the town."

The youth of the town concurred. "Yer! We saw ya!"

"Knocking six bells out of a poor old bummer!"

"Bullyraggin' an old man! Shame on yer!"

Ale-drinkers to a man, Rupert decided—they would have no truck with Aunty's expensive refreshments. The man appeared, indeed, to be already an unpopular figure with the crowd. Rupert had backed the winner. Before it occurred to anyone to demand further and better retribution involving ropes and lampposts, he spoke again to the still-speechless loser. "Now go back inside and make your apologies to your customers. Miss! Step forward!" A waitress who had crept close, wide-eyed with dismay and excitement, obeyed his beckoning gesture and helped her boss back indoors.

"Storm in a teacup, eh?" Rupert shared a joke with the crowd and allowed a judicious pause for the laughter to roll away. "You can all move on now. The tavern's that way!" A black-sleeved arm extended to indicate the way to the nearest pub. To the lingerers, he added, "I shall remain. Be assured, I shall present myself as a witness to this, er, contretemps, should a witness for something so trivial be required. That will be all. Thank you for your concern."

The last bystanders ambled away, tut-tutting or laughing. Rupert turned his attention to the tramp, who was now clowning about in the fashion of Charlie Chaplin, doing a surprisingly nimble boxer's victory dance around an imaginary ring. A fit of coughing brought that to a halt and he took to doffing his cap and giving a doddering salute to the ones who were pausing to drop pennies at his feet. He made no move to pick up the coins or hurry away.

Search over. Rupert had found his man.

"Good left jab! Where did you learn that? Military man, are you?"

"I've a matching right one! Want to sample it?" His eyes flashed with the pathetic challenge of a cornered mongrel.

"Sir! I asked a polite question."

"So you did. Sir. And delivered a compliment. At least I *think* it was a compliment." The tramp paused, then added, "King's Own Yorkshire Light Infantry. Once upon a time."

Rupert surveyed his target from head to toe with fresh eyes. Even he was aware of the fire-eating reputation of the regiment. "KOYLIs, eh? Well, the king would be looking at you a long time before he recognised one of his own, I'm afraid. Down on your luck, you're going to tell me? But I'm puzzled. Help me out . . . What on earth were you doing, mounting an incursion into a douce tea shop by the front door?" He wrinkled his nose. "Your feral odour risked overpowering the fragrance of the Earl Grey, wouldn't you say?"

The sharp features hardened as the tramp studied his face, and Rupert understood that, unusually, he was being regarded with dislike, and—more disturbingly—his prey was about to break loose. Pity. For a moment, there had been something promising, even intriguing, in his manner. Rupert acknowledged that he'd gone too far. The fish was off the hook. He'd have to take a step back and select a different, more attractive lure.

"I mean to say—*Aunty's* of all places! Whatever possessed you? You couldn't drag me in there to join *that* clientele even with the promise of a pot of Lapsang Souchong and a petite madeleine to soak it up. Just look at the hats!" He pointed through the window. "All feathers and frills nodding at one another over the china."

He'd chosen the right tack, it seemed. The scruffy gent was nodding. Even producing a grudging response. "Right. I haven't seen so many pink frou-frous outside a tart's boudoir."

A comment calculated to challenge and silence a monastic academic, Rupert judged, but he replied anyway. "And the conversation!" he said heartily. "The conversation, if similarly elevated, would render us catatonic in thirty seconds, eh?"

The man had not made off into the crowds, but the scorn in his eyes told Rupert that his attempt at comradeship was despised. "It's none of your business, sir, but I happened to see a soldier from my old regiment going in there for a cuppa. Stupid, but I wanted to see him again. Make sure he was all right. He was in a pretty bad state last time I clapped eyes on him. Being stretchered off a Transvaal battlefield, covered in blood. Shrapnel bullet, they said."

"Ah. The Transvaal? That bloody business in South Africa? He was your officer?" Rupert asked, spinning out the conversation, reeling in the line and wondering how long it took for a bobby to run from Parker's Piece to the marketplace.

"No, he was my sergeant. And—yes, that bloody business."
The man's eyes flicked back regretfully to the shop window.
"Still—as I say—stupid of me. I was probably mistaken." He
shrugged. "He couldn't possibly have survived. And he'd never
recognise me after all these years anyway. It was just that feeling of someone walking over my grave . . ." He gave an
exaggerated shudder to illustrate his thought, then, "I'd best be
off. But thank you for your kind intervention, sir. Truly—it was
much appreciated."

Rupert seized him by the arm. "Look here . . . when did you
last eat?" he asked bluntly.

"Lord! Dunno!" The tramp frowned in mock concentration,
then: "Ah! How could I have forgotten the unctuous *tripes à la
mode de Caen*? Washed down with a tankard of *eau du robinet*.
Last week, courtesy of the Sally Bash down the Mill Road
Shelter. Tripe. Familiar with tripe, are you? The lining of a
cow's stomach, stewed up with onions and washed down with
a measure of best Cambridge tap water. They know how to
treat a bloke with respect, the Sally."

Rupert took the jibe on the chin and managed to produce
a sympathetic smile. "You've earned a damn good meal, I
think. And I don't have a Bath Bun in mind. I say . . ." Head
cocked on one side as though the thought had just occurred
to him, he added, "What about a slap-up dinner in congenial
company this very evening? There'll be a couple of pals. We
always treat ourselves to something special on a Friday evening. Accompanied by fine wines, of course." His eyes gleamed
as he added his ultimate temptation: "A refined hock and a
hearty burgundy? You'd be very welcome, frisky chap like you.
Here." He fished about in an inside pocket and took out a
printed card.

The tramp took it between grimy fingers, looked at it in
disbelief and read:

INVITATION TO DINE.

You are cordially invited
to break bread with the Amici Apicii.
Please bring this card with you
when you attend.

"Well, I never . . . ! Sure you didn't mean a refined cock and a hearty buggery?"

"Oh! I say!"

The tramp grinned, enjoying the embarrassment and indignation his crude observation had caused. He handed the card back to the spluttering don. "Well . . . bit vague, isn't it? No names, no pack-drill, no rendezvous. What sort of a mug do you take me for? And who the hell is this crew? Body snatchers? White slavers? Or just a bunch of tosspots who can't manage to get a fourth for a hand of bridge?" He leered unpleasantly. "Seems to me I risk being boiled up for glue, shafted or bored out of my brains."

"Sir! May I remind you that this is Cambridge! We are not savages. Quite the reverse. We take our name from an ancient Roman cook whose lavish yet refined cuisine has come down to us through the Middle Ages. One of our members is even now working on a translation into English of the original text. The . . . erm, Amici—the Friends—are a group of *bons viveurs*—aesthetes. Our group is fastidious regarding the choice of dinner guests for our intimate soirées," Rupert objected, stiff with shock and anger. He hesitated, and his eyes glazed over as he remembered whom he was addressing. Had he made himself clear?

"Toffs, are you saying, Your Honour? Afficionados of the

philosopher Epicurus? I thought they'd all died out, what with the recent privations. Or don't you suffer from food rationing like the common man if you know a bit of Latin?"

Oh joy! They'd caught themselves a socialist! And a pretentious word-juggler at that. This was promising. Could Fanshawe have been aware? His shock and anger were somewhat mollified as he persisted with his explanation. "Our guests are carefully selected—and not for the pecuniary value of their various body parts." He ran a scathing eye over the pathetic figure in front of him. "For bones, buggery or bridge, be assured I should be seeking plumper prey," he said haughtily. The man's appearance was certainly a drawback. Rendlesham couldn't be certain whether he resembled Coleridge's Ancient Mariner—the greybeard loon—or one of the more disreputable Vikings of the Sagas. Ulf the Unwashed, perhaps? Had they, after all, wasted precious time on a nonstarter? Perhaps he ought now to abandon this squalid scene and move on? He added a rehearsed mechanical formula, distancing himself as he spoke. "The invitation stands. Were you to decide to accept, it would be for sherry at six, knives and forks at seven. Over by ten in case you have plans to go on somewhere."

The tramp uttered a guffaw instead of the snarl of derision Rupert had expected. With some aplomb, he stood upright, shoulders back, grasped the lapel of his greatcoat with one hand and extended the other in an affected gesture he'd most probably seen on a page of the Gamages catalogue. "Frightfully sorry, old man," he said, "I didn't pack an evening suit. Hadn't realised Cambridge was so hospitable . . . so socially experimental. I'm dressed, as you see, for the Salvation Army shelter. I believe we're to have jellied eels tonight, and I may even go on afterward to the dog races down the Newmarket Road if I can charm sixpence out of the hatched-faced old dears in bonnets who dispense the hospitality. So—ta, but no ta!"

He handed back the card.

"Very good. Well understood," Rupert said hurriedly. "A man like you is not to be tempted by food and wine. I had rather been thinking you might have been starved over this last bit of something more essential to your well-being. A convivial and uncensored exchange of views and experience between equal minds? Intelligent conversation! You could tell us how—and, perhaps more pertinently, *why*—you defeated the Zulus. Or was it the Boers?" he finished with an engaging smile.

His remark had certainly caught the man's attention. Rupert flinched at the sharpness of the glare launched in his direction. Two deadly, steel-grey eyes locked on to his with the menace of a Lee Metford or whatever blunderbusses those pre–Great War riflemen had used. Aware that he had said something deeply annoying, Rupert looked away, bit his lip and came to a decision. "Listen carefully." He could not prevent himself from looking shiftily to the right and left to ensure they were not being overheard. "Should you change your mind, present yourself on the steps of the Wren Chapel in Trumpington Street at six this evening and show this card to the man who will greet you."

Ignoring the man's smile of disbelief and the scathing comments of the "Coo, er! What? No password? Shall I carry a copy of the *Times* under my left arm and a carnation in my teeth?" style, he slipped the card back into the tramp's hand and pressed on. A dislike and suspicion of this subject was taking hold in Rupert's normally insensitive bosom. He tried, with not much success, to hold back his distaste and his growing desire to see the man squirm. "Come exactly as you are. We don't stand on ceremony. Though you may well, er, feel more comfortable in company if you were to spend this sixpence at the slipper baths." He produced a handful of change from the bottom of his sleeve, selected a sixpenny coin and handed it over.

Too late, Rupert sensed that he had again misjudged the situation. The tramp, icily polite, took the coin and looked at it carefully. "I usually find the fee for a hot bath including soap and towel on a Friday afternoon is twopence. Extra-special Derbac nit soap costs a further penny. Why not? Let's push the boat out! I'm sure delousing is a prerequisite for the entertainment on offer. So—that'll be threepence change." He bent and picked up three pennies from the pavement and put them in Rupert's hand.

The don flinched at the insult and his hand quivered at the contact with coins from the gutter, but he decided to go down fighting, with his flag—though beginning to look a bit tattered—still flying.

"That's the spirit! May I further suggest you take a postbath stroll down King Street and seek out a barber's shop?" A quick assessment of the tramp's shaggy beard and overgrown thatch prompted him to add a half crown to the sixpence. "Raymond at the Select Salon should be equal to the task, but . . . um . . . no need to . . ."

"Mention your name, sir? Wouldn't dream of it. Even if I knew it," the man replied briskly, pocketing the coin. "You haven't introduced yourself." He frowned. "And evidently your dining club friends are equally incurious concerning the names of their guests. Odd, that . . . Something of a breach in etiquette, one might say? Don't you want to know who I am? Even the angels down at the shelter are particular as to the identity of their guests. I usually sign in as 'Charlie Chaplin' or 'Kaiser Bill.'"

Rendlesham gave him a strained smile. "I had already assumed you were Noël Coward, dear boy. The ready wit, the insouciance, the insistence on the social niceties . . . Commendable attributes, but a dead giveaway!" He reined in his flash of petulance and produced an inviting smile. "Come now! Don't disappoint me."

His smile could not quite mask the uneasy realisation that he was now himself being played. "Noël Coward" was eyeing him with, yes, a twinkling mischief.

"Mmm . . . the Friends of Apicius, eh?" the tramp drawled. He was studying the invitation card with a raised eyebrow. "Well, just as long as you can guarantee that you've not got your old Roman mate with his pinny on, officiating in the kitchens . . . I can't be doing with larks' tongues. And ostrich ragout— believe one who has experienced it—is vastly overrated."

Seeing, from the corner of his eye, a policeman turn the corner of Peas Hill and come running towards the tea shop, Rendlesham's target came to a swift decision. He tucked the card away carefully into an inside pocket of his greatcoat, saluted and shot off.

AS THEY WENT their separate ways, neither man was aware of the watchful presence, standing half-hidden by the curtains in the back corner of the tea shop. Dismissing Rendle-sham, the watcher focused his attention on the tramp until he was lost to view, heading straight through the market crowds in the direction of King Street.

A flustered waitress approached the table bearing a tray of toasted tea cakes and a pot of tea. He waved away the tray impatiently and spoke urgently to his female companion. "Get your coat, Edith. Sod the tea cakes! We have to leave. *Now*, Edith!"

CHAPTER 2

"Your usual chair, sir?"

Stanley's Barber Shop was conveniently quiet between the busy morning session and the late afternoon rush to spruce up for a Friday night on the tiles. The proprietor himself was at the shop this afternoon and alone in the parlour, his sole assistant taking a minute off in the back room to brew up a pot of tea. Stan greeted his customer with a grin, allowing him to remove his greatcoat and hang it up on the hat stand himself with the ease of one familiar with the routine.

He settled his customer and made a face at him in the mirror. "And not before time, Your Hairiness! Dickie! Where the hell have you been? Just look at the state of you! I've seen less luxuriant quiffs on Highland cattle! You haven't set foot in a cutting shop since I last had the pleasure sometime last year."

"I've been away, tramping the Yorkshire Moors. Cold, wet and unwelcoming. The people, ditto," was the smiling response. "Glad to be back where the cash is! And the open pockets! I put on a lunchtime concert in the market square just now. Did well! So—give it your best shot, Stan! I can cover it. And pay what I owe you. I think I've got two bob on the slate, but you're too polite to mention it."

The tramp settled into his favourite chair, sighing with anticipation as the warm towel was tucked about his shoulders and under his chin. "Hold back on the scent spray, Stan! I've just left the baths. I'm neat and sweet and smelling faintly of coal tar soap and I don't want your eau de hammam Turc spoiling the effect. Only a shearing needed to civilise me. Hair first, then a shave."

"Right-oh. From haystack to gigolo in twenty minutes. Tell me where to stop. I wouldn't want to oversteer. Any special requirements?"

"Yes, I do have a special request . . . Just for fun, why don't you use all your expertise and turn me into Noël Coward? If you know who I mean?"

He looked along a display of current heartthrobs of stage and screen, offered as inspiration to the customers. His eye lit on a signed publicity photograph of a pale, smooth-faced young man whose dark hair gleamed with the sleek perfection of a raven's wing. The unsmiling subject was wearing a white dinner jacket, a carnation in his buttonhole and he was smoking a cigarette in a short ebony holder.

"There he is! Third from the left between Gilbert Roland and Adolphe Menjou."

"Gerraway, man! That'd take more than skill—that'd take magic. You're twenty years too old and far too butch. And, anyway, you've just not got the essentials." He held up a springy lock of salt-and-pepper hair. "This is wire wool, not patent leather I have to work with. How about a Harpo Marx?"

"It's what I want."

"You sure? That's full shave, short back and sides, left parting, heavy on the bay rum. Touch of brilliantine to catch the stage lights if you're auditioning for something? I can even supply the buttonhole, but you'll have to provide your own Balkan Sobranie."

"Best you can do, Stan."

Stan smirked. "Well, the last client who asked for that look was well pleased with the result! Take a look at this!" With a pantomime of modesty he plucked the photograph from the shelf and put it in front of the nose of the tramp, who at once burst out laughing.

He read out the inscription in blue ink written sideways over the lower part of the white jacket: "'For Stan, *coiffeur sans pareil*! From Noël, *artiste sans pareil*!' Well, well!"

"He was down here on tour last year, starring in his own play, *The Young Idea*. Fast, witty stuff! I sat through two shows, matinée and evening. Full of bounce—it went down well in Cambridge, where 'young' is the *only* idea. Lovely bloke! Barrel of laughs and no airs and graces. We were Stan and Noël before you could say 'razor.' Elegant bloke, too! Shame about the ears. Now then, face first. Shears, I think for the preliminaries, then I'll close in with the old cutthroat."

He worked away with deft fingers and soothing chatter, conscious that his client's mind was elsewhere and that his eyes never left the mirror that reflected the scene in the street behind him. Probably watching out for the local rozzers. The boys in blue always harassed the vagrants at this time of year. Bastards! Always on the lookout for an easy target or an easy mark. Stan felt his client's slight twitch of alarm when the doorbell tinkled and a customer strolled in.

"Good afternoon, sir!" Stan greeted him. "Take a seat. Someone will be with you directly. Ambrose!" he called, summoning his assistant from his tea break. "Forward, please! Client for chair three." Swiftly assessing the quality of the man's blazer and flannel bags and deciding between rich tourist and Maurice Chevalier slumming it, he added in a teasing, fluting tone, "Take care of the gentleman's *canotier*, would you, Ambrose?"

With a smile of appreciation at the gentle joke, the newcomer handed over a straw boater sporting a Cambridge-blue grosgrain ribbon around the crown readily enough, but he confidently overruled Ambrose, who was attempting to steer him towards a chair near the door. He elected, oddly, to seat himself right next to the tramp. Ah well . . . as in the Roman baths of old, a visit to the barber's shop was a social occasion for some. Men came in for the chat, the gossip. In his trade, Stan had heard all sorts of secrets and scandals. Some of the raciest, he'd invented himself. He'd seen contacts made, friendships develop, quarrels break out. He'd heard his own stories told back to him within the hour as the "gospel truth." Nothing could surprise him. But the new bloke appeared not to be seeking conversation. He sat quietly, monosyllabic in his responses to Ambrose's overtures, allowing him to lather him up for a shave of what looked to be an already immaculate face.

Unconcerned, Stan worked away on his own client with the cutthroat, stretching the skin expertly this way and that to whisk away every scrap of stubble.

It happened so swiftly, Stan could never untangle the series of moves that led to the appalling tableau now startling him into speechless rigidity.

In midshave, with the sinuous speed of an adder striking from the bracken, Dickie had snatched the razor from him, whipped aside the towels, shot from his chair and elbowed Ambrose out of the way. While Ambrose sat reeling on the floor clutching his left ear, the tramp was now standing menacingly over the customer with the blade of the razor glinting through a lather of soap exactly at the point where Stan had always been taught that the jugular vein lay throbbing.

Stan breathed in wheezily, unable even to shout a warning as the blade sank below the foam and moved in a delicate slicing movement across the skin. A trickle of blood oozed up and spread out to marble the shaving foam with red streaks under the horrified eyes gazing into the mirror.

"Be still! Be very still!" the tramp hissed, quite unnecessarily as the realisation that he was a tenth of an inch from death had paralysed his victim.

"Dickie! What the hell!" Stan found his voice and yelled. "Put the soddin' razor down, you berk! It's fresh-stropped! Sharp as hell! One slip and you could do some serious damage—"

"Damage? He should be so lucky! It's *destruction* I've got in mind. Unless I get a straight answer to my question from this chancer."

Stan was recovering his wits. "Question? Eh? What question? Look, the thing about questions is, first you've got to *ask* them, you daft 'erbert! Next—a bloke can't answer while you're squeezing the breath out of him with your great paw on his gizzard. Give me the blade, Dickie! Ambrose! On your feet, lad. Go and fetch that teapot in. We could all do with a cup."

"Ambrose, lock the door! Stay where I can see you!" Such was the cold authority behind the snapped orders, Ambrose hurried to obey him rather than his boss.

The victim of the assault gurgled in what might have been interpreted as approval of Stan's suggestion, staring eyes never leaving the grotesquely half-shaven, angry face that lowered over him.

Again, Stan tried to get a handle on events. "Hear that? He's agreeing to your terms . . . whatever they are . . . Go on, then, Dickie dear! Ask away! You've got everybody's attention. What do you want him to tell you that's so urgent? The winner of today's three-thirty at Newmarket? The name of his tailor? Who killed Cock Robin?"

"Shut it, Stan! He knows the question. He knows the answer."

He released the pressure he'd been exerting on his victim's throat, though the blade remained in place.

The answer, when it came, was little more than a croak. "They're here in town. It's on for tonight."

The tramp nodded briefly in acknowledgement.

Sensing a lightening of the atmosphere, Stan leapt in with both feet. "Well, there you are, then, Dickie! You've got a green light for the party! Couldn't you just have asked nicely? Don't you think you'd better come back to the chair for the second half? You two could go over the guest list and talk about what you're going to wear . . ."

Dickie ignored him and looked at the wall clock, then addressed the man in the chair. "Listen, you! It's nearly four. Not much time. I wouldn't want to contaminate Stan's nice linoleum with blood spatter. We'll continue this conversation somewhere more spit and sawdust, and you can explain why you're trawling around Cambridge dogging my every step. Meet me at the Salvation Army shelter—know where that is?—at five. Be there or you'll regret it! You wouldn't want me to come calling for you at the Regent."

"What shall I tell Edith?" came the wailing complaint.

This was greeted with exasperation, a trace of pity and wilful misunderstanding. "Just say you cut yourself shaving."

Stonily, at last he removed the razor from the throat and handed him his towel. "Here, tidy yourself up. Get rid of the strawberry sundae—it's not a good advert for Stan's business."

He stood aside as the customer sprang to his feet like a jackrabbit and ran for the door, dabbing at his face.

All his courtesy training coming to the fore, Ambrose was there before him to unlock and hand him his boater as he ran out, turned left, turned about, then shot off to the right in the direction of the town centre.

"Thank you, Ambrose," the tramp said coolly. "Did someone mention a cup of tea?"

"Good idea! Steady the nerves," Stan breathed. "The way my hands are twitching, you wouldn't want them anywhere near your throat, mate, not when I've half the face left to do. And if you were thinking of inviting *me* to your party tonight, please forget it! I think the entertainment might be a touch overstimulating for me."

CHAPTER 3

The guest arrived looking about himself warily, seeking amongst the untidy row of run-down Victorian villas the number of the hostel he'd been given by the receptionist at his hotel. He'd called in at the Regent to clean up, apply a plaster to his neck and change his clothes. Edith hadn't been there, thank God, and he'd left in good time for his dubious assignation with mad Dickie.

The tramp stepped forward from the concealing embrasure of a neighbouring door. "Glad to see you, Oily!" Dickie greeted him by his army nickname.

Was that meant to be reassuring? Oily thought not, but he didn't raise an objection or demand to be addressed by his real name. Dickie was on a short fuse these days, he'd heard it rumoured . . . skittish, quick to take offence—nervous! But, then, who could blame him? They all had good reason to be nervous, though Oily preferred to think of it as alert and prepared for danger. He corrected himself: not *all* of them. One of their number did not need to go about in fear, looking over his shoulder. *His* was the face the others feared seeing.

Best, anyway, to handle the bloke with kid gloves. He touched the sticking plaster on his neck to remind himself of the man's bad-tempered bursts of violence. Any mention of the difference in their present social standing and financial status might well wind him up. He assessed the tramp's getup. Still wearing that old greatcoat, swaggering about like an officer. Though with his new haircut and shave he could just about get away with it, Oily conceded. If you didn't despise ancient eccentricity. Oily did. But at least the man was dressed correctly for the time and place—unlike himself. Oily's London suit, his stylish hat and polished shoes would get him stopped at the doorway of this den if he attempted to go inside. Too bad. It was all he had in his suitcase. He could hardly have told Edith to pack a scarecrow outfit on the off chance he'd be invited to a down-and-outs' tea party.

"Don't be concerned! You'll do very well! I see you made time to change for dinner . . ." Dickie said reassuringly, taking him by the elbow. The arsehole had always been able to read their minds. "Now come and meet some of my friends." He gave one of his affected pauses, then: "I say, I hope you don't mind if I give a little advice, habitué that I am, concerning the correct social etiquette. *You*, my boy, are taking *me* out to dinner. It's a set meal of two courses, you'll find, and when asked you're to pay in cash—sixpence for each diner. If you would like to pay extra to sponsor other indigent guests, do feel free to do that—the boater would seem to signal such magnanimity. And—most important—when you encounter the ladies who officiate, do not try to get alongside with compliments on their beauty and kindness. However angelic they may appear to you, you must resist. Remember that they are, for the most part, the wives, sisters and daughters of the volunteer army that saves the lives and occasionally the souls of the poor of Cambridge. These gentlemen are frequently on hand and have a short way with troublemakers. Shall we?"

The sourpuss in a bonnet who kept the door looked him up and down with suspicion and held up a hand to bar his entry. After a minute or two of Dickie's blarney, so fulsome and apparently endless even Eliza grew weary of it, she agreed to accept

Oily as a twice-paying, philanthropic Friend of the Army, held out a hand for a two-shilling piece and entered it into a cash book. Their signatures were required in a second ledger, and she allowed Dickie to sign in for them both. Oily noted that for this evening they were Noël Coward and Maurice Money-bags. Finally, she tore off four dockets from a pad—two red for mains (bread included)—two yellow for puddings and let them through.

"Gawd!" Oily exclaimed with relief. "I had less trouble getting into Suzie's Sporting Salon in Cape Town! Cheaper, too! And at least there were some pretty girls there. I'm still looking for your 'angels.' His eye roamed very briefly over the lineup of capacious pinnied bosoms and muscular arms officiating over the evening's handout. "Ah! You were having me on. Lord! Do you expect me to eat that muck they're dishing out?"

"Just take your plate, smile and say thank you," Dickie muttered. "Mrs. Campion! My favourite again! How *do* you know when to expect me? Thank you so much! We will savour it! And apple pie for afters."

Without a word exchanged, they both headed with their plates towards the furthest corner of the room and chose a table where they could keep an eye on both the door and on each other. Dickie smiled. "I see neither of us has forgotten the old safety-first techniques."

"We're still alive, aren't we?" said Oily with a shrug. "Tells you something. At this moment, Cambridge is a more dangerous place to be wandering about in than the Transvaal veldt. Though we have the same problem with the enemy—where the bloody hell is he? Is he sitting right in my sights, with the camouflage of a leopard, unmoving? Which one is he? By the time you spot him, it's too late. For a moment back there in the barber's, I thought I'd gotten it all arsy-tarsy and *you* were the one coming for me. Sorry about that! From your hair-trigger reaction, I'd guess that you're likewise aware we're all in a spot of bother this weekend? I was about to lean over and warn you in a hissing stage whisper when you came over all Sweeney Todd."

"I've been back from the wilderness a week, mate. I've caught up. And, Oily, old man, I could have topped you six times since you arrived on the steps of the Regent Hotel at five past ten if I'd wanted."

Oily grunted. "And I thought I was tailing *you*."

"You don't have a network of people who will report things they've seen. I've got eyes and ears in every backyard." He grinned evilly. "And in some front parlours. I'm at home here. After years of wandering, a spell in Yorkshire finally cured me of wanderlust."

Oily shuddered his sympathy. "That would cure you of most things . . . torpid liver, impoverished blood, will to live. But here you are once more in your fiefdom!" He looked about him at the clattering, masticating mass of no-hopers and added, "Nirvana? You were always searching! Have you found it?"

Dickie weathered the insult calmly. "Nirvana. To a Hindu: peace. To a Buddhist: emptiness. I'm not a man who can endure either of those for long. If you're reaching for the classical, try: Eridu, the Sumerian Garden of the Gods. Complete with singing nymphs, golden apples and sunsets by Turner. If there's a lusty dragon for me to slay, all the better. I'm still seeking knowledge. Acquiring experience. Eridu"—he pointed to his head—"is up here."

"Pity you couldn't have used your knowledge and experience to put a stop to all this earthly and very real unpleasantness. Cleared up a corrosive misunderstanding before five lives were put at risk."

"A misunderstanding? Is that what you'd call it? I'd say it was plain bloody vengeful evil. And what do you mean, 'before someone gets hurt'? Haven't you heard? One of *us* is more than hurt already—he's dead. As I see it, we were a group of one murderer with a deadly gripe against five of his ex-mates. Now those mates number four."

"Four? Hang on a minute, Dickie—who've we lost?"

"We're down by a corporal. Ernest's a goner. It happened two years ago, right here in town. It was in the local paper, but it didn't make the London *Times*, so you probably missed it."

Oily listened as Dickie filled him in on events in Cambridge two years before and gave a moment's respect for the dead before responding. "Poor old Ernest! Still . . . two years back, you say? Why the gap? It's more than twenty years since . . . since—"

"Our little spot of bother?"

Oily grunted. "If you like. And why the sudden rush? I doubt his death's connected. Look, leave this with me. I can have it all verified and examined. I have the expertise and the secretaries to sit for hours with their ears to the telephone. Ernest, eh? Can't say I'm surprised to hear he's *not* the man responsible for all this hysteria. He never had the belly for killing when it was legitimate—he's hardly a likely candidate to have set up as a self-appointed slaughterer once the Queen stopped paying his wages! Though there were bits of army life he didn't despise. Something of a spit-and-polish merchant, I seem to remember. Obeyed every rule you could chuck at him to the letter. He was always meticulous about observing the Armistice and joined the Royal British Legion when it was set up in . . ."

"1921, it was. The only one of us who bothered to sign on. I checked the lists at the library. You should start frequenting the public libraries, Oily. It's splendid for keeping tabs on world and local events while keeping warm and dry. It's a good way of keeping track of old friends."

"You say the police found no one they could pin it on?"

"No, his death remains a mystery. His murder, rather. There were clear indications that he'd been done in. I had a quiet word with one of the PCs on the case. Somebody'd grabbed him by the ears and bashed his head against the nearest hard surface."

"Sounds like a drunken altercation to me."

"Except that he wasn't drunk and hadn't been in a fight. It was neat and sweet, Oily. Just like we were taught. His private life was a bit messy, apparently. Unsatisfactory wife he wanted to be rid of and who would have been glad to be rid of him. Otherwise? Perhaps we're destined to go one at a time, perhaps all in one fell swoop. But why? Is it revenge, impure but simple, or does one of us know something he shouldn't, and we're all being picked off in case he ever opens his mouth? We were witness to some strange events, Oily."

"Witness to? Huh! We triggered most of 'em! But that's defeatist talk! I'm not going to succumb. *I* have a life to lose. I've got two boys at Eton, three businesses to run and Edith depending on me! But at least this meeting . . ." Oily put down his fork and grimaced, his plate only half-empty. "This meeting . . . encounter between us . . ." He floundered theatrically for a moment. "Not quite sure what you'd call an assault with a razor, followed by attempted poisoning! But at least it's cleared up one thing. It's not you, it's not me. One of our number you say is dead. That leaves three men."

"And what a trio! Not one of them at all likely." Dickie sighed. "Not one capable of murder. Killing, for God's sake— well, yes, we've seen enough of that. With rifle and bayonet. But murder? No. We all know the difference. Oily, what is it we're not seeing? Tell me in detail how you got that message today."

"By letter. Typed . . . No signature, of course. I kept my copy. Want to take a look?"

He passed an envelope across the table and commented as

Dickie glanced at the address and date stamp before he opened it up. "You can hardly be surprised you didn't get one. You're the only one of us not in plain sight. You have no forwarding address or even name. *A. Vagrant, Halfway down the Great North Road, England* doesn't hack it. Not sure I'd resort to the life of a wandering man even if it guaranteed my safety. I could never go on the run. Though heaven knows we all had good reason to bury ourselves in anonymity. Mud doesn't just stick, it swallows you and smothers you. I did consider changing my surname when I had sons to think about. It was lucky for us that back in Blighty, folk didn't give a shit. By the time we got out of there, the old queen and the last century were dead and buried. People were throwing off their mourning weeds, shortening their skirts, widening their trousers and going out to have a good time. No one wanted to look back to a distant war. There were excursions to take, trains and bikes to ride, seas to swim in, picnics to have." He gave Dickie a pitying smile and added, "Fortunes to be made. I did well in those Golden Years. I'm still doing well. And murky events that happened in the Transvaal I left back there in that benighted continent. We should never have been sent there anyway!"

"*A gentleman in khaki ordered south,*" murmured Dickie. "That's what you were, according to Kipling. Not many of us were gentlemen when we came back north."

"Oh, I don't know about *that*." Oily's voice was laced with sarcasm. "You did pretty well for yourself! Ordered east to the land of blazing sunsets, silks and perfumes, soft-footed khitmutgars at your elbow offering iced cocktails on the terrace . . . wasn't it?"

"India. Land of Regrets," Dickie spoke softly. "Not so much oriental romance—more a graveyard of exiles."

"I heard a different story. We ex-military types, we love a bit of gossip. I heard you'd fallen on your feet—nice cushy peacetime billet, hobnobbing with the gentry. Learning high and mighty colonial behaviour . . . What was it they told me— you'd been made aide-de-camp to some high-flying colonel, or was it a brigadier? In your progress up the ranks, you'd been offered not so much a leg up as a red carpet. Well?"

The needling was failing to have its desired effect. Dickie merely smiled and said calmly, "A colonel, then a brigadier. Remember, swift advancement comes at a price in battle zones, Oily. Dead men's shoes are never comfortable."

Oily was still having difficulty swallowing his resentment. He tried a different tack. "There must have been consolations for the battlefield derring-do? When you weren't hopping about the rocks, dodging the lead from Afridi *jezails*? What about the sprightly conversation over the mahjong tiles, holding the *mem-sahibs*' parasols and passing them a chilled sherbet along with a hot glance?"

He watched steadily until he saw the tightening of the jaw he'd tried to provoke and followed up with a further jibe. "Word is, you caused quite a fluttering in the *kala jugga*."

"I fear it was more of a clucking in the *moorghi-khana*, if you're searching for 'hen coop.' You need to have been there to understand Kipling."

"Funny, though—a man with your advantages . . ." Oily suppressed his thought, aware that in any difference of opinion between them, he'd always been outquoted, wrestled down or tripped up. "Still, I'd never have marked you for a bloke who'd just bunk off. It was never like you to take the cowardly way out. You always led from the front. In fact, I had you down as a bit of a berserker on the quiet. As earlier witnessed!" He rue-fully pointed to the wound on his neck. "Now," he went on briskly, "no clues as to the origin of this letter, if you can call it a letter, you see. Spicer's paper, number five Underwood machine—millions of them produced. Untraceable. I've had it professionally examined," he explained. "Fingerprints, the lot. Friends in the Met. If there is a clue we're left only with: the style. And even then, it might have been dictated to and edited by a professional typist for style and spelling in one of those rent-a-bureau places. They employ highly educated young ladies in those secretarial services establishments. I part own one myself. Don't suppose you have them in an academic backwater like this. They can probably all write their own letters."

"How very thorough of you, Oily! One might even say professional," Dickie purred, admiration a thin coating on suspicion. "Most would have just chucked it in the bin." He shook his head and read the note again. "No, what we're left with is content—a calculated display of very particular knowledge."

He murmured the text slowly. "'See justice done! If you want to know who snatched a fortune from under your noses, be in the market square in Cambridge at eleven P.M. on Saturday, the seventeenth of May. I will find you. Those crystals were not brown sugar!'"

"Ah. 'Noses,' you see. Plural. He's speaking to a group. To all of us. Inciting us to once again behave as a group. And we both heard with our own ears the original comment about the sugar! Six of us were present when it was made. Ghastly little Syd had decided we were looking at a pile of the best coffee sugar as purveyed by Fortnum & Mason of Piccadilly. Shiny, purple-brown lumps. He'd already licked his forefinger and was going to stick it in and have a taste. It would have killed him, you know! Painfully, over two days."

"And good riddance!" Oily snorted. "Greedy little blighter! Pity I stopped him."

"But, as you've noted, only one of the group of six men present at that time and place could possibly have written this. Why, after all these years? That's the puzzle! After twenty years!" he repeated. "Whose life has changed so drastically in that time, who is so discontented, so afraid, that he needs to slash about him with the sword of justice? This isn't an old comrades' reunion that's being planned; it's a scalpel-wielding on a swollen boil. Have you spoken to any of the others, Oily?"

"Yes. I could only contact two. Ralph and Herbert. Sydney couldn't come to the phone or write, his wife told me when I finally tracked him down. He's on his last legs in St. Thomas's hospital in London. They've given up on him and he's being moved out tomorrow into some nursing home where he can fade away peacefully."

"What's his problem?"

"She didn't say. She—her name's Grace—has one of those posho-plum-in-the-mouth voices ... Lord knows why she married Syd, who was as common as muck. Wasn't prepared to share much with a stranger on the phone. I had to get the information by devious means. It turns out that old Syd has succumbed to tuberculosis. The lady wasn't exaggerating the seriousness of his state—he's not expected to see the month out."

"I'll cross him off my list, then. I shan't be sending flowers. So—Ralph and Herbert? What a choice! What did they have to say for themselves?"

"I made time to go and meet both of them. Ralph hasn't changed. Still talks ten to the dozen. Weighs the odds and comes up trumps. You never did catch a glimpse of the card up his sleeve. He went back up north and got himself a job with a betting shop in Barnsley when he came out of the army. Did well. Prospered, let's not enquire how, and took over the business. Oh yes, our Ratty is a big noise in Barnsley."

"Poor Ratty! Poor Barnsley!"

"Still sharp, though! Always fought like a rat, and I mean that as a professional compliment. He's still ready to take a bite out of anybody he thinks might be up to a bit of no good. Not sure in a two-man fight whether I'd get the better of Ratty. But Herbert . . . hmm, Herbert's changed. Not the sharpest knife in the drawer, and I think we young officers decided that too quickly. He couldn't read or write when we first knew him, not because he wasn't all there, but because nobody'd ever bothered to teach him. The nearest board school was twenty miles away from his village, and, anyway, why would a ploughboy need to know his letters? We underestimated him."

"Not his strength and determination, we didn't!" Dickie was quick to disagree. "And he was always absolutely trustworthy. He had all the attack of a steamroller. On the slow side, but nothing stopped him."

"But would it take him twenty years to react in this way? Even with the brakes off? I hadn't realised you were such an admirer. Sounds to me like you must have written his references! He's got a doorman-security job with the Cavendish Bank in London. Still enjoying wearing a uniform, you see. Moved down to London after the war. Bought his old ma a house in Camden, and that's where he still lives. He and Ratty both received one of these letters as well. With assignations for ten P.M. And ten-thirty P.M."

"And you're booked for eleven P.M.?" Dickie gave a shout of laughter. "What the hell is this? The waiting room for Death? 'The Grim Reaper will see you now, sir.' Are you sure Syd's lost his marbles? It sounds like just the sort of batty *Boy's Own Paper* stuff he'd think was clever."

"*Once* thought clever! The kid was only seventeen when he joined our outfit. Storybooks were all the excitement he'd ever had in his life before that. It's why he joined up. Well, that and his two older brothers kicking him out of the nest. Hardly the right preparation for three bloody battles in as many days. He survived better than most of us. He'll have matured."

"Until this illness struck him down?"

"Yes. Totally out of it, according to the missis. For at least a month. These were posted last Tuesday. I noticed you looking at the post office stamp in the corner."

"Ten o'clock collection from Cambridge central. Hmm . . . I can see why you thought of me. And then, I hope, dismissed the thought. I'd have had the wit to ask a mate to post them in London."

Oily smiled and nodded. "When the three of us had compared notes and I'd explained a few things to Herbert, it was clear to everyone that we were being set up for something . . . unpleasant. No one's planning to shake our hand and pin a medal on us. The other two—and I agree with them—thought we were being lured here for purposes of elimination. Most probably by you. Sorry, Dickie, but Ratty had worked out the odds and you were a clear favourite. But I'm pleased to say all of us were determined to see it out. They're both here in town, and no, I'm not telling you where. You're still our top suspect. They each left a note at my hotel, clocking in as per my instructions. Silly panic, perhaps, but a bit sinister, don't you think? And why the hell fetch us to Cambridge? Why not some cesspit in the East End of London where crime goes not only unpunished, but undetected? I'd have picked Seven Dials."

"You're behind the times, Oily. The fuzz have sorted out Seven Dials. They've got some smart lads on the force these days. Can't say this sleepy academic backwater has the same reputation for crime solving. But, whatever else, our old army oppo seems to want us all in the same place at about the same time. Setting us up like a row of skittles. Everybody muster on the marketplace before midnight? Coo! Er! It sounds like a Boy Scouts–wide game devised by Baden-Powell. But I don't like it. Who the hell is this joker? Do you detect an element of madness here? Psychological pressure being exerted?"

"Of course I do! Madness! That's why everybody thought

of you first, Dickie! You were never the same after Pretoria, though you seem sane enough to me now."

"I'm in full possession of my faculties. I've tramped away my problems, ditched my religions and the few worldly goods I had, forgiven my enemies, rid myself—or thought I had—of the past. I'm a cleansed man! Of no possible interest to anyone. Not worth a bullet."

"I'm glad to hear it. But you'll have to be prepared to dirty yourself up a bit before we're out of this present bit of bother. We can't go on, Dickie, living under the threat of death by someone unknown for some unknown reason. I could have avoided Cambridge this weekend—just refused to play the game—but I'm not going to run from this for the rest of my life. I intend to face up to whoever this is!" The crisp soldier's voice returned, and his eyes narrowed. "I'm intending to flush him out and deal with him—permanently. I warn you now. I've made my plans. I shall chuck him in the Cam or dump him on the doorstep of the police. The Cambridge Constabulary will find themselves scratching their thick heads again and filing him alongside Ernest with an 'unsolved' sticker on his big toe."

"And what precautions have you taken for the evening, Oily? It doesn't take a genius to work out that if someone's gunning for us all, it's not in the market square that we're going to fall. Even General Sir Redvers Buller could have worked out that puzzler ... given half an hour, the very best military advice and a pencil to chew ... I doubt very much that your Edith, redoubtable lady though she be, would be capable of averting the full force of a professional assault—if that's what's planned."

"You don't know my Edith! Look here, how are *you* spending the evening? Why don't you join me and the wife? Pop round after dinner. Eight-ish? We could play a game of bridge in our room or something while we wait him out. It's just across the road from the police station, and I've alerted the hotel manager. He thinks I'm a rich eccentric and humours me, but that humouring extends to providing a guard in the corridor. Expensive, but probably worth it. Or we could go along together to the market at ten o'clock just for fun and sort this out ourselves once and for all. As of old!" Oily's eyes gleamed with challenge. "I'm still fit, and I see you haven't lost your survival skills. Under all that 'I'm just a poor old tramp' nonsense, there beats the heart of a man of war."

"Thanks for the consideration, Oily, but I've made my arrangements. I've accepted to eat dinner this evening as the guest of a bunch of academic tosspots in a college retreat."

"Eh? You? Why the hell?"

"Exactly what I asked my host." Dickie looked with speculation at his old comrade. "I think you must have seen him. The begowned two yards of pump water I was talking to after I duffed up the owner of Aunty's Tea Shop. You were watching through the window." He grinned. "He was so impressed by my style and bearing he asked me to have supper with his effete dining club."

"So that's what all that palaver was about! I did wonder if I ought to ride to your rescue. I thought you were in trouble and having to blarney your way out of it, as usual. But, Dick, I don't like the sound of that at all. What in hell do they want with *you*?" Oily said doubtfully. "Listen! Watch your back! That's not your world. They can be buggers, those academics! The ones smart enough to realise that Disraeli's no longer prime minister will be Pacifists or Marxists. Just for once, take my advice, man! Stand them up! You won't be comfortable in that sort of company."

Dickie smiled. "I rather think that may be the point of the exercise. I'm sure I'd have a pleasanter evening playing snakes and ladders with your Edith. But at least, I think, I can count on several hours of absolute safety tucked up somewhere in a college fastness."

"Which one?"

"Not exactly sure which one, but if I've guessed right, it's a harder place to penetrate than the Tower of London. If I can spin the entertainment out for an hour or two, I'll be all right. And if I survive death by spiced boar's testicles, I may stroll along to the market to hear the chimes of midnight sound an end to the evening's magic and see if I can't spot a villain. Or help sweep up the corpses."

Oily sighed. "So you're determined to go?" The familiar deflation of realising that his advice was—as it always had been in those army years—rejected, returned after a twenty-year absence to irritate him. "Well, sod you, Captain! I hope you have a lovely evening!"

"I'm sure I shall. Now, Lieutenant—apple pie, I believe. Yes, I rather think you must—the ladies don't approve of plates that are not licked clean. I shall have a goodly portion. Where I'm going tonight, I can't count on the food being at all edible."

Constable Jenkins tapped on the door and put his head round. "Prisoner's ready for you, Inspector. Particulars taken, such as they are. Personal items confiscated and logged. Belt and shoelaces removed. Shall I bring him up?"

"*Suspect*, Jenkins. Not prisoner yet. This is the nick, not the Scrubs," the inspector snapped. "He's under arrest on suspicion of murder, and he's going to help us with our enquiries. Someone else in the law and order business will have the pleasure of finding him guilty if I decide to charge him. At *that* point, he becomes the prisoner and goes up the road to the Castle Hill jail to await trial, judgement and sentencing, which will most probably be execution by hanging. Until then—technically—he's innocent. Innocent but under restraint. Got it?"

"Yes, sir. If you say so, sir," Jenkins muttered doubtfully. New to the job, the constable was still a bit uncertain in his dealings with his unpredictable boss, Chief Smarty Pants of the Criminal Investigation Department, who seemed to be making it up as he went along. And then he'd account for his eccentric methods as "The New Policing." Pat on the back one minute, boot up the bum the next; Jenkins had experienced both and understood the reason for neither. He was never sure how far he could venture an opinion. Sometimes it was encouraged. At the moment, the governor was smiling. Jenkins would chance his arm. "You've *seen* him, sir! The suspect? Bit on the mouthy side and slippery as they come, but . . . well . . . he's not exactly in his prime, is he? No danger to anyone. From a standing start, my granny could—"

"I have quite a few questions of a tedious nature to put to this gent. Our first attempt at conversation was interrupted. It may take some time, and I don't want him getting bored, excusing himself on a technicality, and legging it down the High Street before I've wrung the last drop out of him. Our guest is—as you've noted—slippery. The last time he did something naughty, he disappeared into the long grass for twenty years. Let's take no chances, shall we? Chop, chop!"

"MY DEAR DETECTIVE Inspector Redfyre! I've been patience on a monument throughout your preliminaries, but—really! That's an entirely redundant question you've just asked." The voice was out of keeping with the appearance—firm, even authoritative. Coming from the stage of the London Old Vic, every syllable would have been heard in the back row of the stalls, coming from the pulpit, every word would have been believed. "Shall we pass to the next one on your list? I'm sure you ought to be attempting to ascertain my whereabouts between the hours of midday and midnight on Saturday, the seventeenth of May. Last month, that is."

"Indulge me."

"Come now! You could be watching *Robin Hood* with Douglas Fairbanks in the matinée performance at the Alhambra as we speak if it's *thrills* you're seeking. What sort of response do you expect from a grizzled old soldier who's just been asked to drone on about a stale old war that no one remembers? We could repair to the pub down the road if it's company you yearn for and let a pint or two of bitter take the edge off the tales of derring-do. But if it's tedious and exact detail you require, officer, you must remove these handcuffs and provide me with a pencil and a large piece of paper, sketching quality, of course."

The suspect tugged at the single restraint chaining him to the special interviewee's chair, which in turn was bolted to the floor. It was clearly irritating him both psychologically and physically, the inspector noted with satisfaction.

"I'll change the subject when this one bores me."

"I gave up fighting a lifetime ago. My helmet is a hive for bees these days, I'm afraid. Abandoned, disused ... dangerous! More like a wasps' nest, perhaps. Wiser to leave it undisturbed. But as you seem determined to poke at it with a stick ..."

"On my head be it? Agreed. Off you go."

"Very well. It's twenty-five years since I took part in 'one of the longest and fiercest battles ever fought in the annals of war,'" he said in a mock-portentous tone, smiling as the inspector flicked away an imaginary bee from his ear. "Not *my* description! Oh no. That was our experience as thoughtfully put into words for us (and for posterity!) by our general, Lord Methuen. A good man, Methuen—brave and dogged. He meant well and was speaking in the flush of a third consecutive victory, you understand. Victories not due to inspired strategy, but the ferocity and determination of his troops, troops stiffened not a little by the presence of a brigade of Guards, a bristling pack of the Ninth Lancers and a naval squadron of English seaman gunners and marines. The best in the business with a cannon, full of skill and heart!"

For the first time during this interview, Redfyre sensed he had been treated to an honest comment devoid of sarcasm or scheming. That was surely a genuine glow of admiration in the old feller's eyes. But it swiftly faded.

"The old man was rallying us for the next onslaught. My own summary of the enterprise would be less gallant, more unprintably demotic. I would risk adding a charge of public profanity and antigovernment rhetoric to my charge sheet." He leaned across the desk to the farthest extent his shackle would permit and added with a bitter smile: "You might even accuse me of being an agitator!"

The dreaded word "agitator" was accompanied by a theatrical clattering of chains. The snort of irritation the inspector could not quite suppress did not go unnoticed.

"Just humour me, sir," Redfyre said evenly. "Swear as much as you like, but leave out the politics."

"I'm sorry, but I must again decline your invitation to reminisce. I'd be wasting your time. My South African experiences, fighting the enemies of the Great White Queen, can be of no conceivable interest to a ... *provincial* English constabulary." He left a brief pause to allow the insult to be registered. "We are separated from my youthful misfortunes by two continents, a waste of seas and a quarter of a century. To say nothing of the War to End War. I simply can see no connection."

The prisoner appeared to have found and touched a nerve in the phlegmatic officer. "Murder! That's the connection!" the inspector barked at him. "*Multiple* murders! It's hardly the Spion Kop for body count around here and may scarcely rate with an old warrior like you, but bodies carelessly left lying about on my patch will be accounted for and retribution exacted from the guilty!"

Then, more calmly: "And let's think of us as the *Cambridge CID*, shall we? You've met our Detective Superintendent Mac-Farlane and come out of that encounter with a bloody nose—figuratively speaking. The superintendent is nothing if not correct in his dealings with villains. You are aware of the quality of the policing you are attempting unsuccessfully to slur, so come off it! When recent deaths are calculated to have sprung from murky sources in the past, we have the habit— uncomfortable for some—of rooting around until we come up with what we're seeking. And, believe me, here in Cambridge, we have history by the bucketful to play with! Drawers and filing cabinets bursting with it! Bodies buried six deep! The whole damn place is built on bones."

The upwards twitch of the corners of the inspector's tight mouth was intended to be conciliatory. "Yes, we're busy blokes, but don't fret—you can leave any deriving of connections to us! Now then, you were about to tell me your whereabouts between the hours of midday and midnight on the twenty-eighth of November, 1899."

"Twenty-five years ago? Are you mad?"

The witness engaged with the cynical and remarkably rational gaze directed at him, then, resignedly, with a shrug of the shoulders, answered. Quietly. Reasonably. "I understand you were a soldier once upon a time? Before you took up policing? Then I invite you to imagine for yourself my state of mind and body on that date. Towards the end of a fifteen-hour battle— the third such in five days, starved, exhausted by a fifty-mile march, many officers shot dead and more than half of my company lying bleeding to death on a scorching plain behind me ... Are you still with me? Then add to that the bodily pain of a bullet wound to the arm, lungs full of putrid river water after a swim across a perilous river and the mental terror of being under unremitting fire from enemy snipers in the treetops on the opposite bank."

The languid delivery and the meaningful glance at the station wall clock that said, *Had enough yet? I could go on spinning this yarn for hours*, had their intended effect and needled the inquisitor into a flippant remark.

"What about the crocodiles? Surely they get a mention?"

"Not even a walk-on part for the crocs. Sorry. Those creatures tend to infest the Orange River to the south, not so much the Modder River. No, no. The Modder was for many years the scene of civilised regattas in the style of Henley—races rowed between willow-lined banks, all parasols and punts. A welcome, home-from-home entertainment for the British colonial settlers, don't you know. Crocodiles had long since been discouraged along that water course. Mustn't frighten the Memsahibs! It was very unsettling for us English lads—can you imagine? There we were, ready to go, bullets up the spout, bayonets fixed, the order to charge ringing in our ears and we were facing a four-mile riverfront. Only lacking an enemy. Where the hell were the Boers? Nowhere to be seen.

"We could make out a long line of rich green bordering the river. On the far side there were tall trees and, brightly white, shouldering through the greenery, stately buildings like those of an English spa town. We could clearly pick out the wedding-cake lines of the hotel and the grand bougainvillea-clad houses where the bigwig European businessmen of Kimberley liked to spend their weekends. And their ill-gotten profits. All that gold . . . all those De Beers diamonds, weighing them down. They got out pretty sharpish with their worldly goodies in their saddle-packs when the trouble started. They were back in London, Amsterdam, New York, shuffling their share certificates. Waiting for us to clean up their political mess and establish economic supremacy at the cost of our lives."

He caught the asperity in his tone and smiled. "But it all looked so familiar! I expected any minute to hear a tinkling laugh and 'Was that tonic or lime juice with your gin, Daphne?' ring out. Inspector, we might have been invading Henley-on-Thames! Raiding Royal Leamington Spa! It was unreal! Until the moment we caught sight of the Mauser rifles poking through the lace-curtained upper windows. And then the barrage started up."

"But you got across. Thanks to the purging of the crocodiles."

"The worst of the obstacles to crossing we had to contend with was the very large number of enemy corpses and dead horses swirling down from the carnage being inflicted on the Boer by the Argyll and Sutherland Highlanders holding our right wing, upstream of our position. There'd been heavy rain in the night, the current was fierce and the Scotsmen were ruthless killers. Or 'bonny fighters,' if you prefer."

"I do prefer." The rebuke was frosty.

The man smiled as he chalked up another point in the obscure game he was playing.

"You admired the capabilities of the enemy?" the inspector enquired carefully.

"Whoa there! Nothing treacherous in that, if treachery is what you're implying. And I wasn't the only man to notice. We were all impressed by their military prowess, including our commanders, who made many remarks to that effect in dispatches from the battle lines. No one had suspected that a group of Dutch settlers would be such a hard nut to crack. Ragged-looking scarecrows, not a uniform among them. The only flourish they allowed themselves was the occasional ostrich feather or a white cockade in their dusty old hats. The Boers of the Transvaal! Absolute sods when you got to know them at close quarters. Treacherous ticks! You wouldn't want to play them at cricket! But the best marksmen in the world— best horsemen, too, most probably. And equipped with the finest rifles: the Mauser 95, bought at great expense from Germany." He lightly caught the eye of the detective and added: "It struck some of us as odd, that. Dirt-poor farmers, scraping a living from an unproductive wilderness, yet armed with the latest imported machine guns, field artillery and rifles? Ordnance of European origin. French and German mostly. Far in advance of anything the British army could boast." He sighed. "The cream of Her Britannic Majesty's regiments was being shot to pieces by guerrilla gangs of rough-riding, sharpshooting farmers."

"But evidently, you made it over to the northern bank."

The old soldier nodded. "Some of us. Enough. We'd shot and bayonetted our way through the first line of Commandant Cronje's troops, dug in deep on the southern side. They were well prepared for us. Their barrels were level with our kneecaps as we came on, all unsuspecting, across the plain. They know how to keep quiet and hold their fire for the *moment critique*, the Boers. Cronje's clever idea, that—a double bank of defence, the first on the near side of the river. It took us all by surprise. They mowed us down like tall grass before a scythe. The old fox had placed his younger, weaker units down there in the trenches, saving his old beardies and his artillery for the more secure position on the northern bank.

"At great cost, we'd fought our way up close to the defence pits and were within yards of overrunning them when the Boers decided to call it a day. They never stood to the last man. They had an uncanny way of judging to perfection the moment the fight began to go against them and—without need of a bugle call—they all scarpered. Cronje's front line men had to take their chances and flee back across the river right under their own side's guns! That's Boer ruthlessness for you. Did he care? The old goat had a reputation for being unacquainted with 'the more chivalrous usages of war.' He wouldn't have hesitated to sacrifice his third-raters. They'd done the job they'd been set to do, after all.

"They'd brought us up short and given us a bloody nose, identified and shot a good number of our officers. Their hawks' eyes could pick out an officer's markings a mile away. And in *our* outfit, the officers put themselves in the front line. But I think the Boer were so confident of their marksmanship they knew that from up there in the treetops they could spot and spare their own fellows, even in the *sauve qui peut* that ensued. At one point, I found myself swimming alongside an escaping Boer lad not old enough to have a beard. At the same moment we stopped and trod water, just staring at each other, eye to eye. With his fair hair and eyes the colour of the North Sea, he could have been my little brother. I gave him a jokey salute, he winked at me and we swam on together. Matching stroke for stroke, inches apart. Each protecting the other from opposing fire, I suppose. Did it occur to us at the time? I'm sure it did. We went our separate ways when we grounded. Nothing in the rule book about that! 'Tactical use of enemy to facilitate preservation of self,' would you say? It seemed to work."

"One of your marines would have known what to do." The inspector's gritty response offered no absolution. "Were you still armed at this point?"

"I never let go of my Lee–Metford. I was staggering up the bank, gasping, vomiting river water, looking about me for my company, knowing I had at best ten seconds to live. The air around me was humming with bullets falling thick as hailstones on a pond, kicking up spurts of sand round my feet and all the way to the tree line, when I heard it."

"It?" So sudden and so deep was the man's descent into his past, the inspector felt almost embarrassed to interrupt his thoughts.

"The whistling! The Boers stopped shooting. God knows what the signal was—I never heard it—but like a well-rehearsed orchestra, they ceased fire all at once. There was an uncanny silence, bewildering, more threatening than the noise of battle had been. And then the whistling started. My knees buckled under me and I collapsed onto the sand."

CHAPTER 5

"Whistling? . . . Oi! Wakey wakey! You can't say something as far-fetched as that and then just doze off! Who or what was whistling? Human, monkey, freak wind or Wilfred the Whistling Coster Boy?"

The witness snapped back from the past and focused once more with irritation on the cynical face of the inspector. "Human, of course. But not the sort of frightful mouth music that rouses a heckle from the back rows of Wilton's Music Hall. This was whistling with a purpose, and it came from the tree-top perches of the Boers."

"Passing a message along the line to their mates? That's a new one! We could have used that in the trenches."

"No. It wasn't directed at their fellow soldiers." The man smiled. "It was meant for their horses."

"Eh?"

"Highly trained animals! Horses have a keen sense of hearing, and the Boer nags were taught more tricks than a circus pony from an early age. The men were—to put it mildly—fluid. As a blob of mercury is fluid when you try to touch it with a forefinger. I never saw them march anywhere. They arrived and left the battle on horseback. Alive, dead or dying. The previous week we'd been fighting our way towards Kimberley, encountering stiff resistance from their troops dug in on what they called 'kopjes.' A kopje is a steep, round-topped hill, and there was no

end of them sticking up out of the veldt, barring our way north
to Kimberley. Very simply, the Dutchmen arrived to ambush
us from the southern slopes of these hills. And they were certainly well concealed! I swear I was fighting the buggers for
days before I clapped eyes on one. Nothing visible but the dull
lead-coloured barrels of their rifles poking through the rocks.
And by the time you'd spotted that, the bullet that would hit
you between the eyes was on its way. Their positions were
impossible to catch sight of because they all used the new
smokeless powder. No expense on armament spared with that
lot. They'd arrive and abandon their horses, *untethered*, in the
shade on the far side. The horses waited. Never known to stray.
When the moment came for the Boers to do a bunk, they
simply stopped shooting and whistled for their horses. Yes,
whistled! And the animals came when summoned, racing up
to the northern foot of the kopje to their masters, who'd
scrambled down and were ready to take off.

"It was a while before I worked out what the significance of
the sound was. When first heard, it was eerie. Terrifying. But the
moment you understood—it became a wondrous sign of release.
They were off! Scarpering! My knees gave way and I sank onto
the sand in relief. Murmuring a prayer of thanks that I'd been
saved to live another day and do all this over again."

The inspector gave a tug to keep this man's head pointing
in the right direction. "So there you are, dripping wet on the
riverbank, not so much as an anthill for cover, but still armed,
certain death within a few paces and then—miraculously—the
sound that heralds your safety rings out." Then, military curiosity getting the better of him. "Did you take prisoners?"

"Ha! No. We collected a number of dead they hadn't managed to haul away, but that was it. We men weren't in the mood
by that time for taking prisoners. The previous two battles had
curdled our view of soldiering."

An expectant silence and a raised eyebrow greeted this comment.

The witness suppressed a sarcastic laugh. "My first sight of a Boer! And it wasn't a pretty one!" He leaned forward, fixing the inspector with a hypnotic grey eye. "It was at Belmont. Our first touch with the enemy. A smart young Guards officer advancing up the kopje on our right flank stumbled on a well-concealed shelter pit. A Boer, wounded in the chest, suddenly rose up from it. He struggled to his feet and mouthed something. A pitiful sight. He was clearly dying of thirst as well as his wound. The Guardsman whipped out his water bottle and stepped forward, holding it out to him. The desperado's response was to raise his rifle and shoot the officer's face off."

The inspector flinched, then pursed his lips. "That's war. These stories take hold of the common imagination and snowball out of proportion. Faults on both sides, no doubt."

Stung by the dismissive comment, the prisoner gave a withering response. "That's a very newfangled view of war, young man. War is as old as Satan. And it has only one rule. In the same battle, we were on the point of taking out a stoutly defended kopje when a man with comrades at his sides emerged from the rocks waving a white flag. We immediately ceased fire and our officer went forward to accept their surrender when— bugger me!—he threw down the flag and they all fired a volley straight at us. We captured the lot of them, including the flag-waver, and such was the humanity and discipline of my men, even he was spared the bayonet. And if you think that's just a snowballed story, you may check the facts in the *Morning Post*. Their correspondent was with us on the line. Edward Knight. He lost his right arm to a dumdum bullet in that encounter. Try explaining to a man with a throbbing stump that it's due to nothing more than the common imagination running riot, and anyway, he's probably done worse himself."

"Well, we have you inching forward rather than striding towards your objective—the relief of besieged, bombed, starving Kimberley. Were you able to reconnect with your platoon after your swim? Did you have further orders?"

"I found five of my original unit." With a thoughtful look, he added: "Not the ones I'd have liked to find still standing in some cases, but that's war, as you would say. The boldest and best go first. We managed to collect ourselves, stand to attention with our rifles to hand and even look as though we knew what we were doing when a senior officer came riding up with orders from Lord Methuen. They were about to clear the land between the river and Kimberley of enemy. Not an easy task; the place was still crawling with them. He eyed us up and came to a decision.

"He had a little job for us. It amounted to following the river westward until we arrived at the railway line running north towards Kimberley. It was vital that the line be secured. We were to be what I'd have judged a reconnaissance patrol-cum-outpost, though he called it a 'tactical sub-unit,' working the left flank of a four-mile-wide front. He showed us a hand-drawn map and pointed at the railway. 'We understand it hasn't been sabotaged by the Boer yet,' he explained, 'because they depend on it themselves for the running of heavy armament up to the siege site. We want it to remain untouched and will be sending in a company to guard and patrol it once we've got things straight here. Now, do you see this little box affair here? Where the railway line crosses the river? It's a shelter, guard station, horse-relay depot, that sort of thing. You must take it from whoever is in residence, should you find it occupied, and settle in there. Establish a forward base. You'll be relieved very shortly.' He gave us a confident smile as he said it. 'Draw your supplies,' he told us. 'For a week. Hard tack, tinned meat, compass, matches, whatever you need. Here's a chit.'

"He looked at the six of us, ragtag and bobtails, from the height of his horse, and something very like pity flitted for a moment across his noble features. He dismounted, put the map down on the sand in front of us and invited us to kneel with him while he poked at it with his swagger stick. 'Look here. If you take my advice, you'll travel by night. The Boer will pick you off in the daylight. By night, you'll stand a better chance. They'll be lighting fires, so you'll be able to spot them before they spot you. Cushion your boots with cloth if you're walking on a stony terrain and use the compass. If there's no moon to see it by, you'll have to strike a match. But for God's sake, not a Swan Vesta! They go up in a flare that'll alert every Boer between here and Kimberley. Here, take these.' He fished in his pocket and produced a slim package of American matches. 'These are more discreet,' he said, 'but hide the light behind a rock nevertheless.'

"He added a few words of jolly nonsense to cheer us up. Even handed us an early Christmas present, in case we were held up and unable to get back in time for the regimental celebrations. The general was planning—at last—to give the men a few days' rest. Coinciding with the holiday season and as a reward for a tough job dutifully done. He'd decided to let us stage some sporting events—"

"Sporting events? Are you telling me the men were doing the one-hundred-yard dash while Kimberley waited for your attention?" Redfyre asked in disbelief. "Fifty thousand townsfolk and troops trapped there, starving, being bombed by six-inch field guns every few seconds, women and children confined to the depths of the gold mines for safety days on end, and the Relief Force sits down and unwraps its Christmas presents!"

"I see you read the *Manchester Guardian* reports. I would paint quite a different picture. But ... 'Ours not to reason why, ours just to march and die!' In any case, the besieged of Kimberley were having a much easier time of it than the relieving army. They'd had supplies laid in with such forethought by Cecil Rhodes, who—what an irony!—found himself besieged in his own town. Others had fled the Transvaal while they could, clanking their jewellery, flashing their guilders and their pounds sterling and buying up first-class cabins on the ships back to Europe. Why was he still there? He wasn't saying. But he was keeping a close eye on his assets, that much was obvious. Every day a signal or an exhausted, often wounded, messenger got through from Cecil. Always the same message. More bellyaching about his relief. 'Methuen, where the hell are you? How much longer must I wait?' Every day his gold mines were out of action was a day's trading lost and a pain to him.

"They did still have their uses, though. Cecil made the grand gesture of opening the company mines for the use of women and children to hide in when the Boer cannons began to fire. The civilian death rate was minuscule—about twenty souls, they said, from start to finish. However, their military saviours—the British Army—were losing thousands every day. So we weren't too bothered on Cecil's account. By that time, a pontoon bridge had been established on the Modder and our tents and supplies were coming over freely. The Top Brass were established in the Grand Hotel that they'd cleared of Boer. Cronje had apparently been watching the fight from behind the French windows. He'd bunked off, leaving his meerschaum smoking in the ashtray.

"So my little band was preparing to go off into the wilderness while the rest of the regiment relaxed, with the promise of organised sports to pass the time. Besides a chance to shine in the running races, the football and the boxing, the men were being given a presentation tin of chocolates from Queen Victoria herself. They'd come out on the same troop carrier, thoughtfully labelled with the new year's date, 1900. Natty little things! We were glad to have them. You may have seen one? They are much collected, I understand. Red with a gold medallion of the queen's head. Inside, six bars of the best Fry's milk chocolate—"

"Bugger the chocolate!" Redfyre stirred impatiently. "A unit of six men? Even if you call them a tactical sub-unit, they're never going to be able to do work more suited to a platoon! And, for railway maintenance and doubtless telegraph repair work, you'd need a squad of engineers." A sympathetic shake of the head told the witness that the inspector, in spite of his youth, had his eye on the ball and was not to be distracted by a mention of Mr. Fry's best. "Six men being sent into uncertain terrain? With the vaguest of instructions? What half-wit gave that command? And what poor sod was put in charge of this suicide squad?"

"I was. Battlefield promotion, you could call it. Or a desperate decision taken in haste by an inexperienced and badly briefed officer?"

"What rank was conferred?"

"I was made captain. My old sergeant was made lieutenant. And we both regretted it as soon as our oh-so-helpful information officer told us we were being given the opportunity to take a day's course with the men on close combat techniques with the regimental experts before we set off into the unknown. 'Just a refresher, don't you know! Always worth having!'" His eyes narrowed. "Clown! But he wasn't wrong." His smile was angelic as he added, "I've always found 'three easy ways to incapacitate your enemy in twenty seconds' to be an invaluable skill. It's served me well, in and out of uniform."

"Only three?"

"It's enough for me."

The slow drawing of the chain through the manacle,

Redfyre interpreted as a subtle threat. It said clearly, *If only...*
He was glad he'd insisted on having the man wear a restraint,
even though he suspected he would never live it down in the
constabulary canteen.

The old soldier appeared unsurprised to be handed a sheet
of paper. "Ah! You'll be wanting a list of the weasels and wast-
rels I commanded, then? I thought that was where this was
leading. Here goes. Do you want me to list them in order of
rank or villainy?"

"Probably amounts to the same thing, but let's try rank, shall
we? Starting with yourself. Chief Weasel."

The man scribbled in silence for a few minutes, then passed
the sheet bearing six names back to the inspector.

Captain Richard Dunne (officer i/c patrol)
Lieutenant Abel Hardy (2 i/c)
Corporal Ralph Merriman
Corporal Ernest Jessup
Private Herbert Sexton
Private Sydney Fox

"You'll find they appear in order of experience, also. Worth
noting that, of the two privates, Private Sexton was several years
older than Private Fox. Herbert was a difficult man to promote."

Intrigued, the inspector followed up the odd remark. "Owing
to criminal tendencies? Lack of moral fibre?"

"No, no! Quite the reverse. One of the straightest and bravest men I ever had dealings with. Herbert was of limited
mental capacity, but bright enough to know it. He had no wish
for promotion. He adopted a paternal role towards Private Fox.
We all did. The kid was seventeen years old and just out of
training, having joined up the previous year. Young Sydney was
fresh-faced, naïf, youngest of three brothers and—I'd have

guessed—had been rather spoiled by his mother." He smiled. "I remember he was always hungry. On our march north we were short of supplies. Our daily ration of three hardtack biscuits and a can of bully beef had been reduced to one biscuit and half a can of beef. This was a nasty shock to all of us, but especially to young Syd, whose father owned a grocer's shop on some murky street corner in . . . Leeds, I think it was.

"Syd had clearly never gone short of rations before. He would gobble down his campaign biscuit for the day, then look about him in despair like an open-beaked chick on the nest. I used to break my hardtack in two when no one was looking and give him half, for which he was always tearfully grateful. Until I realised that young Sydney was creating occasions when he could be alone with each of us. A bit of quiet shadowing and I had it! The scheming little bugger was getting a half or a quarter of every man's biscuit! Not getting fat on it, by any means. With all the marching and fighting, not even Syd retained his puppy fat, but he was surviving well.

"When I was quite certain that the lad's behaviour was calculated, cunning and detrimental to the well-being and, yes, the discipline of the group, I had a word with the men. With each in turn. I told them to hold back. But Herbert Sexton wasn't listening. 'That poor little boy! He's nobbut a bairn! If we can't look after our own young 'uns, what are we then?'"

"Not a bad sentiment! I'm beginning to like Private Sexton," Redfyre said heartily, beginning to wonder quite where this road map was now leading him. Round the houses again, or off a cliff?

The prisoner's look, a blend of despair and pity for his naïveté, told him there would be no happy ending to this South African Christmas story.

CHAPTER 6

"So, reprovisioned, fortified by a refresher course in self-defence, out-of-date map in hand, the fearless six of the tactical sub-unit set off into the sunset to reoccupy and man the main artery of communication of the South African Empire?" Redfyre sighed. "Am I getting this right?"

The prisoner smiled. "Pretty much."

"Did they at least give you horses?"

"None available. We were generously given written leave to commandeer any strays we might find, British or Boer. But we did the first twenty miles on foot. By this time, we had learned to soft-foot it around the countryside, and we were glad of our khaki uniform, which was exactly the colour of the burned-out veldt, and glad of our light loads. Little food to spare, we were told to 'live off the land.' Antelope? Lizard? Ostrich? We found it easier to kill a Boer or two and steal their biltong. We found out later that the Boer had mostly decamped—a tactical retreat—upcountry into a more defensible position they'd been preparing for months, but their outposts were still about. Not that we'd ever sighted one of them—not even when they were in battle formation and firing at our lines! There were miles of trenches dug, barbed wire brought in by the ton. Another wheeze our armchair generals had failed to anticipate, another failing of our intelligence system." He groaned. "I think you know what was to follow, while we were enjoying our little jaunt into the backveldt."

"Magersfontein," Redfyre said quietly into the sudden silence. "The horrible business of Magersfontein."

"The tenth of December. The column they'd sent out to the east, four thousand Highlanders, Black Watch and Seaforths, drenched to the bone and lost in the darkness, were ambushed. Walked straight into it. They fell by the hundred. Densely packed as they were, one Mauser bullet could go through several men, and there were hundreds of Mausers firing down on them. Many poor sods fleeing the massacre were caught up on the wire fences the Boers had rigged up around their trap. They found them next morning, strung up like crows on the wire. Target practice for the sharpshooters."

"But these were Highlanders," Redfyre prompted him gently.

"The bravest of us. And the most tenacious. Ordered into an impossible situation. By dawn, they'd reformed their companies, hunkered down wherever they could find shelter from the firing and taken stock. Without their officers, they still made an advance. A group of clansmen on the right wing made off for the nearest Boer trenches and returned with prisoners and bloodied bayonets. The Guards and the Yorkshires were sent up to relieve them, and after a day's hard-fought engagement, they finally managed to extricate themselves and retreat back to base at the Modder River. We heard the din of the battle from our first bivouac camp, miles away by then.

"'Cor! D'you 'ear that, Captain?' young Fox said. 'That's the old man giving the buggers what-for! We should have been there! Shame we've missed it!' He was a bloodthirsty little tyke, so long as it was someone else's blood being spilled.

"To celebrate what we all wrongly assumed to be a British victory, Private Sexton scrabbled in his pack and brought out his Queen Victoria tin of chocolate. There were six bars in each tin. He passed them round and we had one each."

"What generosity! And what self-restraint! To have them still intact after—what was it?"

"Ten days. Considering the condition we were in, they were a lifesaver! Mine, eaten slowly at the rate of one a day, had kept me sane and ticking over! They meant so much to every man. More than cigarettes or money. Very few were traded. Fewer were stolen. And that's unusual for the riffraff army that we were."

Redfyre held back the compulsion to urge the man to get on with it. He sensed that the prisoner was not deliberately wasting his time. If he dwelt on the Victoria tins, he took them to be significant. The inspector knew well that, in a world of unimaginable pressure and hardship, men with few possessions would kill for a sixpence.

He stirred in his seat, then looked Redfyre in the eye. "I know what you're fishing for. You need to know which of us has been cutting a swathe through your peaceful town and why. We're all trained killers, but you need to know which of us was capable of murder. What you're interested in is the mental makeup of the men in my small unit, including myself." He smiled. "At that time, a subject of intense interest to me as well! Life and death were riding on the quality of the men I had been handed to lead. So if you're thinking chocolate consumption is any indicator of character—intriguing idea!—I'll declare: out of the six of us, four were normal guzzlers. Empty tins in packs by the time we started out. Ratty Merriman and Ernest Jessup had eaten theirs by the end of day one. Abel Hardy and I rationed ours a little better. It was the two privates who showed restraint. Herbert? No idea why. It could have been as simple as a concern not to open a Christmas present before Christmas Day. He came from a clean-living Methodist family, and apart from continually breaking the Sixth Commandment, he followed a stringent moral code. Sydney? Hard to say. He made a big stir about keeping his tin intact to take it home and present it to his mother. You got a lot of respect for expressing that sort of piety in the army at that time. We all supported him. Sydney's mum's tin was sacrosanct. Being less gullible—very well, being cynical—it was my thought that he was doing what some ghastly kids do—hanging on to his share until everyone had eaten theirs and then he'd produce it, eat it slowly and gloat. I still think I had it right. Still, we all were very grateful for Herbert's gesture. In a strange way, it bonded the company. For a while.

"Was it good? The chocolate." Redfyre asked. He knew the query would cause no offence. Tastes and smells—the pleasant ones—were precious to the fighting man, and sometimes these were the memories he carried with him the longest. And were the easiest to talk about. His own most personal letters to his aunt Hetty during the last war had been triggered by such moments—the scent of rabbit roasting over a campfire, the unexpected sight of a flower—a single snowdrop standing proudly in the middle of a sea of mud.

"It was very good! A bit deformed by the heat—the old lady hadn't factored meltability into her gift planning, and those days on the veldt were scorchers, but yes, incomparable! I still can't pass an advert for Fry's chocolate without salivating! . . . I say, Inspector, you look as though you could do with a cup of tea before we start on the truly heart-stopping moments I have lined up for you. After the high points of the thrill of bogus victory and the fleeting joy of chocolate, it all descends into blood, death and disaster. Fortify yourself!"

Redfyre walked to the door and had a word with Constable Jenkins, then went to the window and puffed nervously on a cigarette until the constable returned. He'd probably just put his job on the line. But it was worth a try, he reckoned. Time for a change of bowling to shake up that straight bat.

"Here you are, sir. You were right—there were some left."

"Any trouble with the super, Jenkins?"

"Naw, sir! I said as it were a requisition. He just grinned. And made a disobliging remark about your presumption, sir, though he used a term that would have had my granny reaching for the carbolic soap."

He put a tray down on the desk, carefully out of reach of the prisoner.

"Thank you, Jenkins. That will be all. I'll pour."

The prisoner was trying without much success not to laugh. Redfyre poured out two cups of strong brown canteen tea and put a plate of Peek Frean's chocolate digestive table biscuits in front of him. Some baker's brilliant notion of combining the buttery shortness of a biscuit with the nectar that was smooth chocolate.

"I shouldn't try dunking one of these in your tea," Redfyre advised. "It ruins both elements! These come to us courtesy of the superintendent. No Fry's chocolate available, but this is the next best thing. He keeps supplies in his locker. Even the strongest among us have our weaknesses."

They sipped and munched in companionable silence until the prisoner seemed not only ready, Redfyre slyly noted, but eager to continue his story.

"We stuck to the riverbank and kept our noses to the west. All we could do. We had a constant supply of disgusting cholera-ridden river water, but there were pure springs enough along the north bank to keep us going. We saw and tried to catch one or two masterless Boer horses, but they wouldn't let us anywhere near them. We can't have smelled right to their delicate nostrils. We tried the whistling trick to attract them, but they weren't deceived! We clearly weren't whistling the right tune. On the second day, we came across a spavined mule that had been cut loose by the Boers. After a bit of stomach-churning attention involving a penknife from Private Sexton—Herbert—who'd been a horse-handler back home, it recovered enough for us to recruit it to our cause and carry our baggage. And if the worst occurred, it would stew up and feed us for a few days."

"You must have been thankful for the qualities of Private Sexton?"

"Some of them," came the lugubrious answer.

"The cabin, when we came across it, was small, but from a distance, at least, seemed intact. The roof was sound, all the walls standing. These were of light stone dug out of the surrounding kopjies and blended with the surroundings. It had been difficult to spot, hidden away as it was on the shaded side of a spreading jackalberry tree. The river was a few yards to the south of it, and the railway line running north to Kimberley and south to Cape Town was right there where it was shown on the hand-drawn map we'd been given, two minutes' stroll from the cabin. We could see from a distance that it was, strategically, a good spot to occupy. Any trains running would slow to a crawl to get over the flimsy-looking metal strutted-erection that passed for a railway bridge over the Modder. It was the obvious place from which to plan a bit of sabotage or to leap aboard a carriage going in the direction of your choice or simply to keep an eye out for troop or civilian movements out of Kimberley or up to Kimberley. We had a pair of binoculars with us, and I gave the whole scene a careful raking before we decided what to do. I noticed that the telegraph wires that ran along with the railway had been shredded every hundred yards and were hanging in ragged swags from the posts that had not been blown in two. Culverts had been dynamited, rails were missing. No chance of communicating with the rest of the world, then.

"There was no sign of life, apart from the three horses and a pack mule that stood quietly whisking their tails, sharing the shade of the tree with the cabin. Two of the horses were small, wiry Boer nags; the other was a big rangy black. A good horse. As good as you'd find on an English hunting field."

"Three men inside?"

"Is what I reckoned. Well, two Boers and whoever had been riding the black. We took our time. Made our plans. Circled the cabin and kept our heads down. We'd gotten very good at moving stealthily. Men whose feet have tramped miles avoiding anthills, snakes, scorpions, decaying corpses and entrenched Boer and lived to tell the tale, have learned where to place those feet."

"The horses didn't detect you?"

"Of course they detected us!" He grinned. "But a carefully calculated—by us!—five minutes *after* they'd made a hulla-baloo when a pack of jackals decided to come into the reserve on the scrounge. We timed it well! An elderly Boer with a beard down to his chest and hair to his shoulders had come out shouting at them. He'd run off the jackals, quietened the horses and gone back inside to resume his quarrel with his mates. We'd heard raised voices, vicious voices, made out the occasional Boer word, even a laugh or two but the structure of the little building was pretty stout and not much of use had filtered through the walls. Chasing the jackals was probably the most exciting thing that had happened in the old feller's day. He must have been just picking up his argument when the horses caught a whiff of us. He came out again with an even shorter fuse, assuming the jackals had sneaked back, and gave the nags a telling off. They settled down. And we settled down and waited for teatime."

"Teatime?"

"Their teatime, not ours. In fact, they brewed up coffee for themselves. They always waited for the sun to lower before they got busy. We'd counted on them putting the kettle on and coming down to the river for a wash or a swim before dressing for dinner.

"The old feller came out first. He had a pee into the river, then started to take his shirt off. The moment it was up over his eyes, a khaki-camouflaged shape whipped out of the bush where he'd been going to hang it; thumbs found his neck and squeezed the life out of him in ten seconds. Our instructor would have been proud of the technique! The bloke never caught sight of his assailant: Lieutenant Abel Hardy at his most efficient. Abel pushed the body into the river and it swirled away.

"Five minutes later, a large, strong-looking Boer came out, towel round his neck, suspenders hanging over his hips. He called for his friend and, receiving no answer, strolled down to the river to see if he'd gone for a swim. He sank to his knees, rinsed his face and looked again. 'Piet! Where've you gone? Where's the coffee?' or some such. We'll never know. They were his last words. A naked man rose up from the reeds inches away in the river, grabbed him by his dangling suspenders, whipped them round his throat and pulled tight. When he'd finished gargling, his body joined the first, bobbing downstream with the strong current. Private Sexton doing his duty.

"At the same moment, Ratty and the Fox were under the tree securing the horses, making sure no one attempted to get away. I'd positioned Corporal Jessup fifty yards distant on a round-topped knoll with a rifle and a good view of both approaches to the cabin and orders to shoot dead on sight anyone who wasn't one of us."

"The third man?"

"I had no idea whether he was still in the cabin. My first thought was that the horse belonged to a messenger out from beleaguered Kimberley. A section of the Kimberley Light Horse had been caught up in the siege and were still quartered in the town. It wasn't a watertight situation. Troopers did occasionally get through with news and orders to get a move on. Ravings from Rhodes. As head of De Beers, he had a business to run. His gold mines and his diamond mines were inoperable when they were being fired at by the cannon the Boers had hauled up on the railroad. Long Tom! It had a range of four miles and had brought the city to a standstill."

"He had a point!" Redfyre said. "Wasn't that what the war was mostly about? Owning, controlling and making money out of the richest mineral finds since the gold rush? That's why you'd been shipped over there. To tell a race of Dutch farmers they did not have the rights or the expertise to operate the mines. That they should just get on peaceably with their farming and cattle raising and leave the engineering and mineral exploitation to those with the knowledge and resources to do it—the Uitlanders. The foreigners. The British, the Americans, the Canadians . . . but above all, Cecil Rhodes."

"A simple résumé, but it'll do. Though I wish the British who've loved their pastoral heroes since Cincinnatus hadn't stuck that label on the Boers! 'Plucky little countryfolk, defending their homeland in arms against our own mighty empire . . . We should teach them their place, but understand and be generous in victory!' Huh. I blame the foreign correspondents working for the press at home for encouraging that attitude. They were there for the story, the blood, the high drama. They were never there with their notebooks when we relieved farm after farm, settlement after settlement, town after town and set free the thousands of starving native Africans the bloody Boers kept as slaves."

"I believe most gentlemen of the press were even-handed, considering the intricacies. They reported from the battlefields but also from the field hospitals, both Boer and British. They told the unvarnished truth about Kimberley when they were at

last able to enter the city. Some had survived well, their complaints largely about the lack of choice on the lunch menu at
the Ritz; others had not. No African babies survived. You can't
feed babies on horsemeat, and Africans were at the end of the
queue for provisions. The misdeeds and inhumanity were not
glossed over. People back here at home were aware—and deeply
concerned."

The prisoner had heard all this before. His eyes narrowed
and he sighed with affected boredom. "There you go! Armchair
generals, armchair editors and now armchair policemen. The
people didn't know the half of it! Their views were formed by
heavily edited accounts from newspapers with axes to grind,
financial backers to keep sweet and papers to sell. Thank God
for people like Emily Hobhouse and Churchill's aunt Sarah,
who were on the spot, saw things they weren't supposed to see
and had the courage and tenacity to stand up and shout it from
the rooftops! The rooftops of Fleet Street! I salute those ladies!"
He collected himself. "I see. You've just winkled out another bit
of information about Richard Dunne. Socialist? Tick. Bleeding-
heart liberal? Tick. Suffragist? Tick. Activist? Tick—"

"Leader of men? Tick. Storyteller? Oh yes. I want to hear
how your merry band extricated itself from the problem of the
third man! You were telling me how it could happen that a rider
from Kimberley managed to get out of town and make it the
many miles down to your bend in the Old Muddy."

The captain grunted. "Storytelling? Well, at least it's not a
chargeable offence yet, as long as it's the truth, I suppose.
And—hear this, Inspector—I'm one for telling the truth."

"And I'm one for knowing it when I hear it," Redfyre said.

"I'd noticed. Many miles, you say? In truth, it was a mere
twenty. A half day's ride, though over difficult terrain. Anyone
attempting it would be hoping to spend the night under secure
cover. In a land crawling with Boer, wild animals and thugs like

me. The cabin was still in good condition because it was essential to many people on many sides of the conflict. It's a vast country, and the besieging forces around Kimberley were spread out over many miles. They had been much reduced by the calling up of troops to support the confrontation of the Ninth Regiment. Our lot."

He shrugged. "I guessed some unlucky messenger who thought he could outrun the Boer had been detained, captured . . . killed, most likely. If he was a member of the Kimberley Light Horse, he was an enemy of the Dutchmen. It seemed reasonable. Apart, that is, from the puzzle of the horse. The Light Horse used scrawny but deep-chested native-bred horses not dissimilar to the Boers' own mounts. Sure-footed, fast and made of whipcord. This black was a pedigree beauty. Wouldn't have survived a day as a dispatch nag. It was a rich lady's riding-out-on-a-Sunday-morning horse. So the rider was an unknown quantity. I took it on myself to deal with him, whoever he was.

"I gave the horse a closer inspection while I was waiting for Abel and Herbert to get themselves up from the river. It was restive. A lot of eye rolling and prancing about, and Ratty and Syd were finding it hard to control. Herbert took one look and murmured something soft to it. And it calmed down. Using sign language—he always had more words for the horses than humans—he drew my attention to the condition of the saddle which it was still bearing. I nodded to say I'd noticed. Someone had slashed it up with a sharp knife, poked out the padding, slit seams.

"Corporal Jessup was in position on the knoll. Ratty, the Fox and Herbert had dealt with the horses and were standing about, pistols at the ready. I signalled to them to hold back—I was going in with Lieutenant Hardy. We paused outside the door, listening and sniffing. Hearing nothing, smelling something foul.

"We went into a perfect routine for entering an enemy-held premises. In a second we were inside and covering every inch of the room with our pistols. After the brilliant sunlight, it was cripplingly dark and it was some time before we could make out what had been going on. The first thing that struck me was the stench. If you could blend fury, fear and pain into one hellish cocktail and release it into the atmosphere you'd have something approaching the stink.

"Along the two long walls were two unmade beds—lairs, more like—where the belongings of the two dead Boers were still scattered about. Beds? They were piles of brushwood tamped down and covered with sheep fleeces. Crawling with lice. Along the northern short wall was a built-in dresser stocked with pots and pans and—an odd nod to civilisation—a Delft-patterned tea set. Chipped and dirty. The second-best set, donated by some Dutch farmer's wife? In the centre of the room was a large table of scrubbed wood with a strange collection of objects laid out on it. At first glance, I wondered at the startling sight of a Bible sitting next to a bloodstained huntsman's knife. But my interest in the bad housekeeping faded when, through the shadows, I saw the livid gleam of a dead face. A young man tied to a chair. The eyes in his battered face were still open; he had died in agony. Naked to the waist, his chest was scarred and burned. We'd been on watch outside, overhearing not a quarrel between Boers, but an interrogation session. The two torturers had done their frightful work and left the man for dead, going to the river not to brew a reviving pot of coffee, but to wash the blood and vomit off their clothes and limbs.

"Abel tactfully closed the door behind us. 'No need for young Syd to see this,' he murmured.

"'No. Let's see if we can work out what was going on in here,' I told him. I advanced on the corpse to see if there were any clues to his identity.

"The eyes in the battered face followed my movement.

"After a second's paralysis, I was by his side, babbling reassurances. 'Captain Dunne, Her Britannic Majesty's Yorkshire Light Infantry, sir,' was the best I could come up with in my state of startled horror. "We're with the Relief Force. Hang on, we'll get you out of this. Water, Lieutenant! There's a jug on the table.'

"We poured the cool water over his head and eased some between his lips. He told me with his eyes he wanted to speak. As gently as I could, I poked the loose and broken teeth from his mouth, and he nodded his thanks."

The captain fell silent, and Redfyre left him by himself for as long as it took, adrift a quarter of a century in the past in that grim place. Finally, he said simply, "His last word on this earth was: 'boot.' Then his head drooped sideways and he died. Of his injuries, mainly loss of blood assisted by sustained shock to the system. Oh, how often I've wished he'd not had the strength to utter that! If he'd just kept his poor wounded mouth shut, none of this . . ."

He collected himself and pressed on. "By this time, our eyes had begun to work better, and Abel had found and lit an oil lamp. They'd left their tools of torment lying about. Two knives, a knuckleduster, ropes, cigarette ends . . . we scooped them up and stuffed them into a greasy pillowcase. The bloodstained Bible went in for good measure. It was printed in Afrikaans, and for strong reason the object drew my scorn and hatred. Next we took stock of the table and realised that amongst the clutter of dirty enamel mugs, plates full of chicken bones and a tray laid with coffee things, there were one or two very interesting items.

"Have you ever seen the glow of gold ingots by the light of an oil lamp?" he asked abruptly.

"Never even clapped eyes on a gold ingot, chum!" Redfyre said, surprised.

"You wouldn't forget. Gold needs a subtle light to bring out its nature. In sunshine it flares and flashes and dings the brain. That's why a woman or a man of taste will never wear gold until after twilight. There were six bars, less than the normal size. Heavy stuff, gold. These had been specially moulded, I'd say, to fit inside the saddle. No foundry marks or other official markings. Lined up like dominoes. Abel raised his eyebrows and gestured with his thumb at the door. I read his thoughts and nodded.

"He went over and gave a crisp message to Corporal Merriman. 'All's well. Danger over, Ratty. Get the Corporal down from that kopje. Then all of you—go and get buckets of water from the river, some brooms . . . whatever you can find. There's cleaning up to be done before we can bed down. Messy buggers, the Boers! Wait here until we tell you to come in.'

"He came back inside looking less dazed, back on track.

"'Did you make out: 'boot'? If he was speaking in English, I'm sure the poor bloke said: 'boot.' Abel, we'd better investigate. There may be a paper, a vital signal for the army tucked away in there. It's a favourite if obvious spot. We'll take a foot each. I'll handle the right one. Ready?'

"The riding boots were, you'd have said, almost new. And they were not produced in some backstreet saddlery in Cape Town! They were superbly crafted of the best leather and bearing the stamp of a London bootmaker. This would have been their first—and last—outing. It was Abel's strong, quick fingers that found it. The foppishly high heel of the left unscrewed, revealing a sizeable cavity. I thought wheezes like that had died out with Francis Walsingham and the Elizabethan spy rings! But in the Transvaal it was easy to slip back a century or two.

"Abel poked out a thin silk bag tied up tightly at the neck.

"'Hang on!' I told him, guessing what it contained. 'Best decant it carefully.' I went to the dresser and found a

Delft-patterned blue-and-white sugar basin. I dislodged a crust of dead flies and emptied the stained and caked sugar lurking in the bottom into a bucket. I gave the basin a wipe with the flap of my jacket, there being nothing cleaner in the room. Abel cut the fastening of the bag with his pocketknife and with a very steady hand poured the contents into the basin. You have never seen anything less impressive than the gunge that slithered out!

"Abel was certainly not impressed! 'What the hell's this?' he asked. 'Could it be opium? This is what it's supposed to look like in its raw state, isn't it? I'm not going to volunteer to try it!'

"'It looks to me more like a scoopful of muck from the veldt. A pile of dark, gingery earth interspersed with bits of what looks very like gravel.'

"'Bloody hell! No! Oh! Argh! This is someone's ashes! Have you ever seen ashes? I saw my aunty Mavis's when they scattered them on the rosebushes at the crematorium. They looked pretty much like this. Is someone smuggling Cecil the Almighty's ashes out of town for burial? Hadn't heard he was dead, had we?'

"'Not ashes. I know what this is! The crumbly bits of earth are just that! From a few miles north of here. But the larger crystal bits are what it's all about.' I poked at them with a pencil. 'Ranging from black in colour, through dark purple and reddish brown. Good Lord! Some of these are quite large. Abel, these are diamonds. Rough, untreated ones. Cleaned up and polished by a jeweller, they must be worth . . . Oh, I have no idea! A king's ransom? Whatever that's worth these days.'

"'No kings in these benighted parts to consult—or kidnap,' Abel muttered. 'But there are one or two demigods of business and industry who might pay for something nefarious on the quiet by transporting this stuff out of Kimberley. Payment? Bribe? Nest egg? Who's it meant for? Where's it going? You know, Dickie, it might have been better for us if they had been ashes.' Abel was always quick to see two moves ahead. He looked again at the corpse. 'I wonder if those turds found out who he was?'

"'I'd guess the rider gave away the gold as a sweetener, hoping they'd let him get away with the really important item he was smuggling in his haute couture boot. We're going to have to search his things for an identity. And then, at some time in the near future, we'll have to declare this lot and hand it in to the authorities. We wouldn't want to be hauled in for looting. A charge which any reasonably sharp-nosed army disciplinarian could make to stick, no bother.'

"We fell silent at this awful thought. And it was, believe me, a prospect to make the blood run cold. It was a new offence. Or rather a very old offence, restated by the army. Looting. Some young idiots had nicked a few bales of fabric and a couple of ducks for their supper—nothing special—when moving through a recently taken Boer town. Jacobsdal? The top brass had come down on them like a ton of bricks. The British army simply does not tolerate such conduct, we were all lined up and told. New regulations were published. Any individual arrested and found guilty of 'looting' was to be hanged immediately. Yes—hanged! And his battalion found guilty by association. While the looter swung from the nearest telegraph pole, his mates would be marched off south to base and spend the rest of the war in an army jail on punishment detail, their names forever sullied.

"Overstated and viciously cruel but effective. We didn't want to risk that.

"'What about the lads?' Abel wanted to know.

"'We prepare them for the worst. We give them the whole score,' I decided. 'I'm not wandering about the veldt until relieved with the weight of *this* round my neck. We come clean with them. We tell them that as soon as we get back to civilisation we declare these items. And to make sure no blame sticks to any man in this patrol, I'll write a letter to that effect and put it in my pack along with the stuff. Now we'll leave them laid out on the table so everyone can take note that nothing underhand's been done or is likely to be done. As far as they're concerned, the goods are in transit to Lord Methuen's Ninth Brigade and temporarily under the joint care and custody of this tactical sub-unit. We'll tidy up this poor young chap as best we may.' We cleaned up his face and put his shirt back on.

"Abel nodded agreement. Finally, 'Shall I get them in now?' he asked.

"Alarmed, intrigued and concerned, they filed in and we pulled up stools and chairs and sat down, all seven of us, including the dead gentleman, around the table.

"'Crikey! 'e's been in the wars! What the 'ell 'appened to 'im?' was Syd's sensitive comment.

"'Our dead friend here was so unfortunate as to run into a couple of murdering Boers. The pair you have met and dispatched. No idea who he is or what his business is, but he seems to have been a messenger of some sort out from Kimberley. My best guess would be that he was a De Beers operative. Look at the table. These are the goods he was carrying stashed away.'

"Ratty, eyeing the gold bars with relish, spoke out of turn. 'Cor! That'll be on its way down to Lord Methuen and the Ninth! It's our next year's wages we're looking at! That's ours, lads! Compliments of Cecil Rhodes!'

"But one of us didn't have eyes for the gleam of gold. To my horror, Syd grabbed the sugar basin. 'I know what this is!' he chortled. 'My mum took me up west to Fortnum's in Piccadilly for my twelfth birthday tea. This is sugar! But special coffee sugar! It's rock candy sugar crystals! She let me eat a whole basin-full and didn't make me have coffee with it.' Before we could say anything, he'd licked his finger and was sticking it into the pile of rough diamonds. Abel managed to get to his hand and smack it away from his mouth just in time.

"We explained the nature of his 'coffee crystals' and what the army's new rule on looting implied for us, should anyone decide to take things the wrong way and make an example of any poor innocent trooper. Death or imprisonment, in short. Everyone agreed that disclosure—and as soon as possible—was called for, and that in the meantime, it should stay where it was, safe on the table under everyone's gaze. We made practical plans for the concealment of it, should we be attacked. I wrote out the letter, we all signed it as witnesses and I put it underneath the sugar basin."

Catching Redfyre's exasperated sigh, the prisoner nodded and laughed. "I know! But there were no army regulations to cover these very particular circumstances! And, funnily enough, the table really was the safest place. Every man became its guardian dragon. Whenever anyone entered the room, he would automatically run a checking eye over the haul. We got so used to seeing the bars of gold, no one batted an eyelid when Abel reached out casually one morning and grabbed one to use as a paperweight to hold down his mother's recipe for beef stew while he chopped and scraped and filled a saucepan.

"And we got on with our duties. We cleaned and cooked and repaired, perversely taking satisfaction in having a roof of our own over our heads. We'd wake one another in the night to say: 'Cor! Hear that rain? Poor old Ratty, standing lookout in this! Hope he's found somewhere to shelter.' I ran a tight ship, and every man did his bit."

"Did you experience any military action?"

"We fired off quite a few rounds at the jackals. They came for the fruit. The tree wasn't called a jackalberry for nothing! Lemony-tasting and refreshing. We ate a lot of it."

"Your supplies were sufficient?"

"Course not! We scavenged for food like the jackals! The Boers had brought hardtack with them. Have you ever eaten biltong?" He pulled a face. "Hope you never have to. Plenty of game about, though. And we were good shots. Antelope tastes like venison, and Lieutenant Hardy was a dab hand with the roasting spit and the stewpot.

"But no enemy or friend hove into view. We exercised the horses, reconnoitred the area, watched the railway line, darned our socks and passed the time. Herbert put his skills to repairing the saddle of the black horse. An intricate piece of needlework, which he managed by equipping himself with shoe-mending materials nicked from the Boers' kitbags. There were several individual pouches contrived for the ingots within the saddle. 'Never know when you'll need to hide ten bars o' gold,' he said with a wink. 'That's been used afore, I reckon. A real bit o' craftsmanship that is!'

"Then, once he was satisfied with his repairs, he used the saddle and the horse for riding out on reconnaissance. He was the only one of us the black would tolerate near him." He smiled. "So poor old Herb found himself doing quite a mileage up and down alongside the railway track every day. With three horses and a mule in his charge, he had his work cut out."

Redfyre interrupted the domestic saga to ask what they had done with the body of the young rider. Had they established his identity, reported his death?

"We did," the prisoner replied. "Taped into his left armpit, he had a small light-case-cum-wallet. An *étui* is probably what he'd asked for at Asprey's when he kitted himself out in London. It was of the softest calfskin, but it can't have been comfortable even so in that hot, dry country. He was half French, half English, I was later to find out when I had time to do a little research. An employee, but also a relative of one of the Company's directors. I never did find out whether Louis Duvallon was out and about on the Company's business or making a well-funded break for freedom on his own account. I rather suspect the latter. It must have been excruciatingly tedious for a sophisticated chap like Louis to have been cut off from the world for six months with no sign of relief, bombed, shot at, starved by a rabble of discontented peasants. He can't have been enjoying Uncle Cecil's hospitality all that much, either."

"Can you be certain that he was a lone rider? Risky thing to do, wasn't it? Taking off through enemy territory like that all by oneself?"

"Yes. Indeed. That's what made me think he was engaged in clandestine, possibly criminal activity. But the suspicion was strong among us that he was not a single swallow. Just in case his friends turned up enquiring, I decided to keep his body available for a day or two before burial. There was a sort of outhouse on the cool southern side of the cabin. With a big stone slab for butchering and keeping bush meat, I assumed. We laid him out there in a rudimentary coffin we cobbled together from a pile of planks left over from the building."

"You buried him out on the Modder?"

"Eventually, yes. About a week after we arrived. The men were complaining about the smell. They had all been for stripping the corpse at once and heaving it into the river. Stupid, perhaps, but I felt I had a duty to do right by him. He'd looked me in the eye, after all, recognised me for what I was, an honest British soldier, and entrusted me with his fortune. Probably not his to bequeath, and certainly not mine to inherit, but it was a bond of sorts. Lacking volunteers, apart from a little grudging help from Syd, I cleaned and dressed the body myself in his own gear. Made it look decent. Then Ratty and Herbert between them dug a grave deep enough to make it jackal-proof, some distance away from the cabin. We all stood around, and I delivered the nearest I could manage to a Christian burial. We put a four-foot cross made of jackalberry boughs at the head of the grave with his initials carved on it. It was a big marker—a precaution, in case later anyone wanted to recover the body . . . Cecil Rhodes cast a long shadow in those parts. If he decided to make enquiries about the fate of his kinsman, it could have caused problems for us."

He lapsed into the deep silence Redfyre had learned to respect in the men he questioned. Then, haltingly, thoughts moving faster than his words: "Funny that!" he said. "It never struck me before—the day the company rode away from that foul place, I looked back. That cross had become part of the scenery. It wasn't there . . . It wasn't there," he murmured again. "I expect some lumbering animal had stopped to scratch its bum and knocked it over. Africa! What a country! It wears down, reclaims, silts up and covers over. And now no one will know he's there."

"No visitors apart from wandering wildebeest?"

"No. It was very strange. No one came near us. We could hear fighting going on to the east and Long Tom pounding down on Kimberley to the north, but we were in the calm eye of the storm. Nevertheless, we stayed uncomfortably tense and always on the alert for danger. It's easier to face an enemy when you can see his eyes. The worst is when you realise you've been looking into those eyes for months and he's sitting right in front of you."

"I'm sorry, you've lost me." Redfyre was startled. "Are you implying that one of you was a traitor?"

"In a way, we had our traitor. Not so much betraying his country as betraying his unit. In my book, that's as bad."

Redfyre nodded agreement.

"I woke up earlier than the others one bright morning on

tea-making jankers. It was day eight. The day after the funeral. I ran an eye over the table. Right number of gold bars. Diamond dross in the basin. Or was it? Something wasn't quite right. At that precise hour. the sun was slanting down through a high slit window and catching the rough stones. Where it should have been striking sparks of amber and red through the dust, there was barely a responding gleam. I gave it a closer look and ran a finger through it. It wasn't my imagination; the dust hadn't merely settled differently over the crystals. I stirred Abel awake and he came to have a look with me. 'Tip it out,' he advised.

"We poured it onto a clean tea cloth and examined it. The surrounding earth was the same. But the lumps were different. Abel fetched the magnifying glass he used for starting fires, peered and passed it to me. 'Some bugger's done a switch,' I concluded. 'These pieces are not crystalline. And they're all the same colour. Grey—dark to light. He's left one or two of the smaller diamonds on top for show.'

"'And I could take you straight to the very patch of river gravel, not fifty yards from here, that these ugly lumps came from,' Abel said. 'Who the hell? When?"

"'Remind me, Lieutenant . . . Did we have visitors yesterday between the hours of sun up and sun down? Did Lord Methuen pop in for tiffin? Did Her Majesty come to tea?'

"'Bloody didn't! And there was somebody here in this shack all day, coming and going, but always in pairs—as scheduled. None of us goes anywhere without his shadow around this place. I get sick to death of seeing your ugly mug every time I turn my head!'

"'It has to be one of us, Abel, doesn't it?'"

"'Or two of us.'"

CHAPTER 7

Outside the Wren Chapel, a dinner-jacketed Digby Gisbourne consulted his pocket watch. Two minutes before six. He resumed his pacing to and fro across the portico. He resented performing this menial welcoming duty, which could so easily and more properly have been done by the appropriate college servant, but of course, he hadn't dared make his views clear to the formidable Fanshawe. Too-big-for-his-boots Rendlesham had stepped in, frozen him and ticked him off for complaining when he'd raised the matter. Hadn't young Gisbourne understood that discretion—nay, secrecy even—was the quality to which their group owed its existence? And, as the youngest member, Gisbourne must expect to take on subaltern duties. It was no time at all since he was at Harrow—he could hardly have forgotten how these things work?

Digby scanned the busy street for likely candidates. Half the men passing were wearing day clothes—business suits and homburgs. Some were, like him, already in evening dress, prepared for one of the succession of end-of-term celebrations that seemed to start earlier and earlier these days. This would be the last of the year's Friends' dinners. He'd had a glimpse of the menu—impressed by the wine that Fanshawe was proposing, he was looking forward to it. He'd finished his academic year—a damned hard one, in fact—and was ready to indulge in a little relaxation, hilarity and good sport. It had been agreed that he should take the part of lead hound tonight. Perhaps he could teach the old fuddy-duddies a few new steps? He was on his mettle!

What had Rendlesham told him? "Watch out for an army greatcoat, an unkempt, tramp-like appearance and—mind what you say. You're not to frighten him off. It is vital that this one attend. He's very special, remember?" Digby shuddered. It didn't sound very promising. How did one greet a tramp in a friendly manner? His usual technique on encountering one such obstructing the pavement was to move him out of his way with the vigorous application of the point of one of his highly polished Oxfords. Digby presented an impressive figure with his wide shoulders and prematurely gnarled hands acquired from years of rowing. People of all ranks of society instinctively made way for him. The thought of communicating with a vagrant was giving him pause. A "Wotcher, mate!" and "'ello, me old mucker!" were the only verbal exchanges between down-and-outs he'd ever heard.

"I say! You must be he! My Hermes? Indeed, my Hermes Psychopompos?"

At the tap on the shoulder, Digby whirled around to face the stranger, whose silent approach he'd missed. The owner of the gravelly, educated voice. "Hermes who?" he heard himself blurting.

"Hermes Psychopompos. My divine guide to the Underworld. I believe that's where we're bound? May I present myself? For this evening, I'm Noël Coward. Not my choice of alter ego, but the whimsical jeu d'esprit of your man Rendlesham. I suspect he was not being altogether kind! May I present your card?"

In bafflement, Digby looked briefly at the card the tramp produced from the inside pocket of his greatcoat and waved it away, all his attention on the lean, handsome face sparkling with impish good humour. "Mr. Coward? Well, I'll be damned! You are a surprise! But, er—no, your suspicions are well founded. He wouldn't be. In fact, the words 'kind' and 'Rendlesham' in close proximity would curdle a sentence. But how do you do, sir? We're to perform introductions later, so for the moment, I'll be your soul-shifting Hermes. I'm rather charmed by the idea! I'll just say, I'm delighted that you could manage to get along at such short notice for our little soirée." And as the nearest cracked college bell started to bang out six: "Right on time! Well done! So, er . . . this way."

He was beginning to recover from his surprise and, heartened by the familiarity of the man's tone of voice, which much resembled that of his old housemaster, Digby felt confident enough to hazard a jest of his own. "But first—obol, sir?" He held out a hand, palm up, with a winsome smile. "I believe there is a fee for crossing the River Styx, though nothing more alarming than a raging gutter separates us from our dinner. The ditches are in full spring spate this evening, you'll find."

The man grinned and pressed a shining shilling coin into Digby's hand. "Sorry, no obol—a bob will have to do. It may prove well worth the charge—I understand that a dunking in the Sinister Stream bestows invulnerability. A quality I may find myself in need of before the evening's out."

"Oh, you require invulnerability, do you? That's extra. Messy business, dunking. And someone has to hold you up by the heel. You'd be looking at me a long time before you thought of Achilles's mother. Now, what was her name?"

"Thetis. I've always called her Thetis," the tramp returned the easy shot. His smile said that he'd understood the survival game was already under way, and the score was deuce on the warm-up alone.

"We'll cross here," Digby announced. "Follow me, and mind you don't get your feet wet." He leapt with the playful agility of a Greek shepherd boy across the frothing stream that bordered Trumpington Street.

Dickie gave a gracious nod of the head and murmured quietly, "And I'll be keeping my powder dry, too, young Hermes!"

THEY PASSED DOWN alleyways, through gardens fragrant with lilac and orange blossom, across shady courts, twisting and turning but always heading west towards the river. Dickie had a mental mapping system to rival that of a pigeon, but he doubted he would ever manage to find his way back out of this medieval maze without a guide. He knew every nook and cranny of the public space of the city, but the colleges were unknown and unfriendly territory. Disconcerting. Was he entering a trap or scuttling into a convenient hole for safety?

Dickie had learned always to be sure of a clear exit from any situation, but here there were no names, no directions, no numbers. If you had penetrated this far, it was assumed that you knew where you were, he guessed. From the clattering of copper pans and cutlery and the steam smelling strongly of frying onions issuing from an open window, he thought he'd located the kitchen, and heavenly voices raised in a snatch of "O Magnum Mysterium" gave away the position of the chapel. Ah well, if the worst occurred and he had to make a run for it, he could probably flee to the kitchen or the chapel and take his escape route from there.

Why the hell had Dickie gone along with this pretence, walked willingly into this situation? Pretended to believe the rubbish Oily had fed him? "All lambs to meet in the marketplace. Slaughter to commence at twenty-two hundred hours." What tosh! He ought to have made them come to him if they wanted him so badly. Lured *them* to the marketplace, at a time of his choosing. His own stamping ground. He could have fought back there, might even have engaged an ally to help him out. Solly was a useful pair of fists and always ready for a scrap. In any case, he hadn't been deceived by any of Oily's scaremongering. The thought that Ratty and Herbert would give up a day of their busy lives to answer that summons was ridiculous. He'd met Ratty again during his trip up north to Yorkshire. Quite a swell these days, old Ratty. They'd held a brief conversation. Two strangers who'd had the misfortune to share an uncomfortable experience, that's all they were. It had changed the shape of Dickie's life, ruined it, he sometimes said, but Ratty had brushed it all away. He really didn't seem to remember much of what had gone on. It was an irritating interlude for him, a hiccup in his career, and he wasn't overjoyed at being reminded of it. There was no way that Ratty would be exposing himself to danger in the middle of Cambridge.

And Herbert? It was unlikely that he would venture up to Cambridge, either, on only the strength of the anonymous letter. He was another who was doing a job he enjoyed and wanted nothing more to do with the past. He had never done anything out of respect for the group, Dickie had calculated early on. His loyalties had always lain firstly with any horse that may have appeared in his orbit and secondly to young Syd. If Oily was to be believed—and Dickie would check—Syd was *hors de combat*. Lying on his deathbed, face to the wall. No Syd, no group, would be Herbert's reaction.

Should Dickie have gone to the police with his suspicions? The thought of embarking on an explanation those muttonheads would be willing to listen to for more than a few seconds made him laugh. No, he was—as usual—on his own.

Still, cornered here in a college as he was, if the worst came to the worst and he *did* have to make a run for it, leaving bodies behind, he couldn't imagine who would step forward to challenge him here. There was no sign of bulldogs—those overstuffed bags of wind who paraded about, making life difficult for the students—inside the building. Genghis Khan could have ridden through with his slaughtering horde and the noise would have been ascribed to an outbreak of hijinks. In fact, the college premises appeared deserted. Everyone was dressing for dinner or doing a last bit of revision, he calculated, judging by the number of OAK UP signs he saw on doors.

They climbed a winding stone staircase up to the topmost floor, and here Gisbourne paused in front of a heavy door that had clearly stood there on the same hinges since the Middle Ages. He banged heartily three times, lifted the latch and pushed the door open.

Strangely, it was the cooking arrangements that Dickie took in first when he stepped into the room, so surprised was he to see them there, indoors, right alongside a large table laid for seven diners. It was a scene from any grand colonial picnic, and for a disturbing moment, Dickie was carried back to India. To service with a much-admired colonel. To a rare, peaceful summertime in Simla before the Great War. White dresses, tinkling laughter in the shade of the deodars and a phalanx of Indian servants cooking scented dishes on primus stoves. And a recently appointed, neat-waisted, suntanned young Captain Dunne fresh from his exploits in South Africa, dancing attendance on the Colonel and his family.

Scything their way though a ten-year-thick growth of suppression, a pair of mischievous eyes swept in and recaptured his memory. A soft, inviting voice. "It's a Persian dish. Do try some, Dick! I'd love to hear what you think of it." And emotion had taken him by the throat and squeezed out words and thought, as it always did in her presence. Gargles and grunts and mindless braying formulae were all she'd ever heard from him.

Dickie was aware that the same symptoms of speechless anxiety—down to the sweating palms—were unaccountably in possession of his body at this moment. Why the hell?

Here, a million miles away in Cambridge, a single chef in full white regalia was officiating at a range of cooking hobs, piling cooked food into chafing dishes. A piece of equipment driven by electricity, Dickie could only suppose, since there was no smell of primus oil evident, just the mouthwatering scent of slightly scorched meat—was that lamb?—with an undercurrent of butter, garlic and herbs. That *was* lamb! And there was the aromatic trigger for his unwelcome memory.

Shaken, but satisfied that he could at least account for his nervous spasm and therefore control it, Dickie achieved some professional calm by picking up his routine for survival. He swiftly assessed his surroundings. The lights of a range of tall windows, overlooking a courtyard of some kind, were conveniently open to air the room, but they stood many feet from the ground, and the drop below was long. The threat facing him would have to be of dire proportions before he exposed himself to such an exit three floors above ground level, where doubtless unyielding stone pavings would halt one's descent. He was no Douglas Fairbanks to leap out onto a hoped-for network of ivy and drainpipes. There lay certain death. A screen in Spanish leather to one side concealed a small door slightly ajar, he noted—leading off to a bedroom or study. A dead end. His sole escape route was through the door by which he'd entered.

This now closed with a velvet thud behind him.

The enemy had gathered some distance away to take his measure. In the background at the far end of the very large room stood a cluster of four dark figures formally clad in dinner jackets. At his entrance, they had all turned to look at him and had fallen silent. Digby went to join them. This was a calculatedly intimidating scene, Dickie thought, for any outsider lacking confidence. "The first one of these blighters

to raise a lorgnette to his eye the better to quiz me, gets that
eye poked out," he promised himself to ginger up his spirits.
But then, at his age, why risk it? Attack any of these gilded,
whey-faced effetes and he'd find himself hauled up before the
local magistrate, who might just happen to be the second
cousin of the master of the college, and he'd be condemned
to tramp the treadmill until he dropped dead. He almost
turned and made for the door while he still could. And probably not the first guest to do that, he thought, if he'd read their
game aright.

The tallest figure detached itself from the group and came
forward, hand outstretched. Dickie was almost relieved to
recognise Rupert Rendlesham.

"Noël! Is this you? Great Heavens! I believe it is! What a
difference a shave makes! I see you have chosen to live up to
the pseudonym I conferred on you and acquired a veneer of
brilliantined elegance to chime with the insouciance and the
ready wit. Gentlemen, may I present our guest who—for this
evening—is going by the name of Noël Coward? Though he
more regularly answers to 'Charlie Chaplin,' he tells me.
Loquacity and wit in one corner, mute buffoonery in the other?
I wonder what we may expect. Either way, we may be assured
of an entertaining evening. Perhaps we may encourage him to
embark on a debate with himself? Let me take your coat, Mr.
Coward, and I'll introduce you to the others. No footman
tonight—we're waiting on ourselves. You must forgive our
informality."

The greatcoat was whisked away to an antlered hat stand
by the door, and while pretending not to stare, Rupert was
covertly checking to see what his guest was wearing below the
all-encompassing garment. The secondhand dark grey serge
funeral suit that Dickie had bought from a pawn shop was
noted as incorrect, though acceptable, but Rendlesham tossed

his head like a startled horse at the sight of the red, green and silver–striped tie.

Oily had slipped it from his own neck without a second thought. "You can't go anywhere respectable without a tie, man! Here, take mine. I've got six more like it at the hotel. Edith buys them for me by the armful. She loves the colours, and stripes are all the go this season, she tells me. She bought a bundle yesterday over the counter at Ede & Ravenscroft and picked out this one for me to wear. Just cross your fingers it's not some college Tiddlywinks Club tie! That's just the sort of thing that gets them riled up, apparently! A non-tiddlywinker making free with the club tie! Gor blimey! It's another world! Unreal! These academic blokes are like orchids in a hothouse. They can only survive in a place like this, with their greedy roots sucking up expensive nutrients."

Dickie had agreed and accepted the tie.

Rendlesham was staring at his neckwear with a mixture of amusement and disbelief. He gulped. He fought off a fit of the giggles. He turned to share the joke with his companions. Snorts and gasps followed and then an inexplicable relaxing of tension amongst the dark-suited gents. Dickie guessed that whatever they were seeking from him as a dinner guest, he'd unwittingly provided.

The oldest man stepped forward. Time for introductions. Distinguished as their leader by his grey hair, which had the discreet gleam of polished pewter, and by his clear commanding voice, he introduced himself as Oliver Fanshawe. Fanshawe proceeded with slow solemnity to present him to the remaining three hosts. Hubert Sackville and Quintus Crewe, middle-aged, sharp of feature, cold of eye, were committed to memory. Dickie loathed them on sight but gave no sign of his antipathy. "And you have just met our most recent member: Digby Gisbourne. Like your good self, I understand, Digby is a native of our largest and what is considered by some to be our most splendid county, Yorkshire. By those who happen to be a connoisseur of cricket or puddings." He turned a thin, placatory smile on Digby, who frowned.

Ah! The first jibe, and it was a feeble one. A distancing shot that fell short of its target. Dickie had no sentimental feeling for his home county and no particular affinity with any other man who hailed from it.

"Indeed? And how about you, Mr. Gisbourne? Do you proudly claim your northern heritage? Are you one of those fellows who embellishes his conversation with sentimental phrases of a 'dark and tender and true is the North' variety?" Dickie asked pleasantly.

Digby Gisbourne took the remark in his stride. "Not at all. I was born in London, as a matter of fact, to a London mother of French Huguenot extraction. My father is, indeed, of Yorkshire stock—you are aware of the village of that name?—but I have spent little time north of the river Trent and feel no attachment to the place. Dark it is, I observe, but true and tender?" He shook his head. "Tennyson confuses his epithets, I fear . . . He should have used the words 'fierce and fickle' from the line above."

Fanshawe, restive, broke in. "Glad to hear it! There's none like a Yorkshireman for boring a party with his mawkish attachment to his roots . . . unless it be a Scotsman! Take care, Mr. Coward, that you don't provoke Rendlesham into waxing lyrical over Frinton-on-Sea, Essex, or Sackville into vowing his eternal fealty to Much Snoring, Norfolk. Society has pushed forward its horizons with the railway and the telephone. Matured. We are all citizens of the wide world these days. Though we are all—if only occasionally—tempted to regress into cosy *collegiate* loyalty by the wearing of a tie of doubtful taste and lurid colour. All of us here are members of this college.

St. Jude's," Fanshawe explained. And added slyly: "You, Mr. Coward"—a finger whisked out in the direction of Dickie's tie—"I note, are also a Cambridge, er . . . *man?*"

More titters. Comments were passed behind hands which flicked over mouths and back again with the speed of a camera shutter.

So! Hostility was at last unsheathed from the scabbard of courtesy. It slid out to the hiss of sneers, gleamed with the contempt of mocking stares. Dickie would have relished hitting them with a few such overwrought phrases, but he judged it too soon to be throwing down a challenge.

At last, he'd understood. Bloody Edith! was his first thought. And stupid old Oily! Between you, you've made me look a first-rate dunderhead! The sly insinuations were surely indicating that he was sporting the colours of one of the *women's* colleges. Hardly worn by the ladies since the Edwardian days of white blouses and cycling plus-fours, when it had been the fashion to copy men's clothing styles, ties on women's necks were a rare sight about town. He hadn't recognised it. But his hosts, obsessed as they were with college protocol, clearly had. There were two colleges exclusively for women: Newnham and Girton. Which one? Could he remember the colours? Not with certainty. He swiftly calculated the odds, consulted his gut instinct and made his decision.

He'd been wondering how to play this encounter. Quiet, unprovocative, subservient and annoyingly dull? Or—his preferred option—combative, using slay-and-spare-none verbal jousting? In a situation where he was outnumbered, outgunned and skirmishing on foreign territory, was that wise? No. It was asking for trouble. The only wise course open to him was to turn at once and make for the door and fresh air. But he'd learned a thing or two over the years from underdogs. Boer, Afridi tribesmen, Yorkshiremen. Clever sods, and they never backed down. They had the painful habit of jumping up and kicking you where it most hurt just when you thought you'd gotten the better of them. He'd stay and sing for his supper. And make this shower of shit join in the chorus.

He turned a beaming smile on Fanshawe. "*Man?* Did I catch the whiff of a question there? Well—manly enough to have survived three wars, is your answer. In very active service on three continents, serving three monarchs. But—too tedious at a dinner party to indulge in comparing medals, battle scars." After the slightest pause, he added, "Lives and reputations saved . . . I'm sure you agree. If *manliness* is a quality you insist on establishing in your guests before the aperitif is poured, may I suggest a simple way of checking my credentials? Select someone from your group—some Achilles, some Goliath—to escort me to the nearest tall tree—I believe I spotted a superb, smooth-boled chestnut down below in the court, and I'll piss higher up it than your champion. I'll even wager a quid on the outcome."

Dickie waited. He caught the look, half scandalised, half amused, saying, *There! Didn't I warn you?* that passed from Rendlesham to Fanshawe.

Digby Gisbourne filled the awkward pause by offering a tray of drinks to Dickie. "Will you have a glass of sherry, sir? Or would that have a debilitating effect on your urethra masculina? Spoil your aim, even? It's the finest from the college's Jerez bodega. Solera-aged in barrels a century old, I understand." He was stifling a giggle, and his left eye twitched in what might have been a wink.

"Hermes one minute, Ganymede the next, eh?" Dickie said jovially. "Watch it, young Digby! Remember the fate of an innocent shepherd boy snatched by Zeus to serve him his wine on Olympus! Have you checked the terms of your employment?" He shook his head and narrowed his eyes in warning.

"I'd read the small print if I were you. No sherry, thank you. I'll have a glass of Harrogate Spring Water, if you please. I see you have some." He took a glass and, smiling, held it up and affected to admire its purity against a candle flame. "Aged for a million years in the limestone rocks of God's own county."

He took a sip, then pointed to his tie. "It seems my tie is the focus of your attention. Deservedly so! It was carefully chosen. Gentlemen! Are you such prisoners of your ivory tower that you can be unaware? The town is celebrating the thirtieth anniversary this week of the founding of MFGCSS." He paused for a moment to gather the blank looks before continuing. "The Male Friends of Girton College Suffragist Society. As a mark of our respect and support, the men of Cambridge have undertaken to sport the college colours for a week. Why? You have answered your own question by simply asking it! So that men like yourselves would take notice of a gross injustice! Might perhaps consider doing likewise. Might calculate that, half a century on from the inauguration of the first women's college, the fact of being female deprives some of your brightest scholars of the degrees they have worked for and deserved." He paused for breath and was prepared to roll on in the same vein with some relish since he saw that each face—with the exception of young Digby—was frozen in disbelief and distaste. At last, someone interrupted him.

"Good Lord! Fetch him a soapbox! The fellow's preaching at us!" Quintus Crewe exclaimed, applying a monocle to his eye socket to emphasise his disbelief. "Is he confessing himself to be a foot soldier in the monstrous regiment of women?"

"Or a camp follower?" someone suggested peevishly.

"I'd have said, rather, a regimental pipe band, all raucous squeals and no sabres," sneered Hubert Sackville.

"Nothing like pinning your colours to the mast," Rendlesham offered.

"But you must be prepared to have them instantly shot to ribbons." Fanshawe wagged a warning finger.

Dickie thought he must be the first person to have mentioned the female cause—or possibly even the word "female"—within these walls. Judging by their startled reaction and the quips that followed thick and fast, he'd annoyed the hell out of them. He'd begun to understand how their game worked.

The hounds fell silent, eyeing him, assessing his lies and the confidence with which he'd reeled them off. Looking for his strengths? More likely homing in on the jugular, he decided.

As pack leader, Fanshawe broke the silence. He took a careful sip of his sherry to demonstrate a state of effortless superiority, then asked, "Did someone just sound *les trois coups*? Give a blast on the trumpet? I missed it." He directed a humourless smile at Dickie. "You have drawn our attention—what do you now propose? Is this the moment you produce your battered attaché case and try to sell each of us a souvenir Girton tie? A set of Trinity apostle spoons in white metal? A winsome teddy bear sporting a Jude's scarf?" He turned to the others, hands raised in appeal. "Rendlesham, you didn't warn us that you were offering us an itinerant haberdasher! A wandering huckster!"

"No salesman's pitch, I assure you!" Dickie said cheerfully. "The university outfitters carry stocks and can supply any gentleman wishing to display his support for the ladies. They open at nine. Mind you don't get trampled in the rush."

With understanding of the game they were playing had come a stomach-wrenching spasm of contempt, but also a measure of self-assurance. Several sharp barbs had been launched at his hide, but he had shrugged them off and lowered his horns. He knew what to do next. He'd snort a bit, paw the ground, choose from among them a target for his utter derision and charge. No need for a massacre. It would be enough to leave one ceremonial corpse behind in the sand as a warning to the others.

He began to relax. He even felt the stirrings of embarrassment that he'd sunk so far into idiocy as to prepare himself for an actual physical attempt on his life. What a chump! He loosened his grip on the knuckleduster he'd borrowed from Solly at the shelter and hoped the ugly metal contraption wasn't detectable in his jacket pocket. Overkill! The last time he'd used Solly's Sweetener in earnest, he'd nearly severed his own finger.

He glanced, still smiling, at the lineup of adversaries. A row of weeds! The worst he could suffer from this lot was a bruised ego. He'd settle for that. This was a deluded, self-congratulatory, twisted bunch of nincompoops, he reckoned, and he was looking forward now to giving them a comeuppance they would understand.

"Sadism"? Was that the word for their mental affliction?

Common enough behaviour, taking pleasure from inflicting pain on others. And as old as mankind. You had to wonder why it had had to wait until the present day to acquire a name for itself. The Marquis de Sade? One hundred years in the grave now, and good riddance! That aristocratic libertine had been a bursting boil on the face of humanity, Dickie thought, the one-man cesspit of the ancien régime. But he was a symptom of the disease, and no one man, however evil, deserved to have his name forever linked with such a condition. In his violent life, Dickie had seen many examples of cruelty, had even felt the hot surge towards it in himself, recognised it for what it was and controlled it.

But it seemed to be a mental condition readily inherited. Children, left unchecked, took delight in taunting and humiliating other weaker children. Some never responded to the civilising influences of kindly mothers and fathers, priests and schoolmasters. Some, indeed, were pushed deeper down into the pit by those very angels who were meant to inspire and correct them.

The row of weeds lined up against him deserved his pity, not his anger. For all their advantages of wealth and education, their veneer of civilisation, they were rotten at their core, and it was too late to save them. By the natural laws of survival of the species, they should be put down like rabid dogs. He'd shot down without compunction lines of men much less deserving of annihilation than this selection. Their supper parties, he calculated, were the mental equivalent of the snaring and torture of a defenceless kitten by a gang of little boys. They trawled the streets looking for someone who would provide them with good sport. A stranger who, with the lure of a place at their dinner table, would be a butt for their cruel jokes, their twisted wit. An hour's entertainment for them. A continuing shame for the victim.

Dickie knew what he had to do. He had to exact retribution. A retribution concerning which they would not be able to lodge a formal complaint to the university authorities or the police. In other words, no knuckle sandwiches on offer, no cracked shins or bloodied noses. Shame, but there were other, less dangerous victories to be won.

SATISFIED WITH HIS arrangements, the chef caught the eye of Fanshawe, bowed and excused himself, leaving the dinner party to "wait on itself."

Dickie cast an eye over the table, taking in its opulence. White linen, gleaming silver, hock standing in a chilling bucket, claret in its jug, brandy on the sideboard and a series of fragrant dishes lined up in battle order. None of which delights Dickie had any intention of tasting. Let these self-indulgent toads guzzle their way through the feast; he could never bring himself to "break bread" with such excuses for men. No one seemed eager to rush to table, and Dickie remembered that Rendlesham had told him: "Knives and forks at seven." Judging by the level of sherry in the glasses of his fellow diners, Dickie calculated they were counting on a further ten minutes' fluidity of formation. Testing their weapons. Encircling their prey. Digby Gisbourne helped himself to a second glass of sherry.

The bell had rung for round two, and Dickie decided to come out fighting. Against all the rules of chivalry, they had chosen the adversary, the place and the weapons. They could hardly complain if he used their choice of weapon against them.

When facing a group attack, always take out the leader first. He turned to Fanshawe with an affable smile. "The college of St. Jude ... With more than a score of colleges to choose from, I'm wondering what drew you to enlist with the patron saint of Hopelessness and Lost Causes?"

Bad move. Dickie cursed himself. This was clearly not the first time Fanshawe had addressed such a challenge, judging by the swiftness and length of his defensive response. Finding himself sucked into their repugnant game, Dickie was tempted to open his own score sheet. Quintus Crewe took up the bowling from the other end and suggested smoothly that an elderly itinerant gentleman ought, rather better than most, to understand the concept of hopelessness. Was Mr. Coward prepared to regale the company with stirring tales of his descent—or could it be ascent?—to his present position in life? A position that might be defined as a few square yards of a public space where pennies from the pockets of the generous rained down to support the indigent?

Ouch! Uncomfortably close to the jugular. Even young Digby flinched and looked concerned, he was pleased to notice.

Dickie stood tall and squared his shoulders, but before he could answer for himself, Digby Gisbourne had begun to speak, his tone emollient. "Dr. Crewe, you were perhaps not present when Rendlesham told us that our guest is an old soldier? That he served with distinction in the African war, last century? He could have chosen to appear at our table with a chest clanking with medals, outdoing any of us in a show of manly endeavour rewarded by a grateful country. We are all eager to hear, Mr. Coward, whether you would condescend to explain something of what transpired. These things are so quickly forgotten. We college types in our 'ivory tower,' as you call this splendid stone monument to learning, can list all the warriors and the skirmishes of classical times, from Agamemnon and the Trojan War to Mark Antony at Actium, but we have retained the vaguest knowledge of—what shall we say?—the Disaster at Koonspruit? The exploits of 'Bobs' of Kandahar?" His voice took on an artless innocence. "And I, for one, would love to know exactly how Baden-Powell of the Boy Scouts helped relieve the siege of Mafeking. How Captain Dunne of the King's Own Yorkshire Light Infantry, Captain Richard Dunne, thief and looter, escaped from the Pretoria jail, abandoning his deluded men to rot away in unjust incarceration?"

There it was! The challenge! The puff of smoke that betrayed the enemy's position. And it had come from the least likely quarter. There was no good reason that Digby Gisbourne should be in possession of his name and rank and history.

"You little rat!" Dickie said, but he said it only to himself.

So he had not been mistaken. He was, indeed, for all his fancy footwork, firmly fixed in someone's crosshairs. And had been for some time. Sufficient time to set up this farcical banqueting scene. His encounter with Rendlesham in the market square had not been by chance. He'd dismissed these men as eccentrics, sickening but harmless. But he'd deceived himself. Losing his sharp edge? The death of Richard Dunne, he judged, was firmly on the menu for at least one of these men tonight.

The bonne bouche, he calculated, rather than the aperitif. They would spin out his mental torment until boredom set in. And all thanks to wretched Oily's maneuvering. *We could make a stand in the marketplace . . . Well, come and play cards with me and Edith . . . You're mad to attempt it, but if you insist on going into that college, at least wear a tie.* He'd been given a choice, three choices, his decision delicately steered towards one. A choice of three killing grounds. Any one would have been acceptable to this adaptable, light-stepping killer.

But who would attempt the killing blow, and when? A gunshot would never be risked within a college building. For discretion, the blow would have to be delivered by hand. Up close. Eye to eye. None of these five clots was capable of that. He reckoned that, if he took them by surprise and knocked out the vigorous-looking Digby first, he could lay low the whole boiling in seconds, the ones that hadn't fled the scene screaming. So where was their weapon? *Who* was their weapon?

With a chill, he remembered the number of place settings. Seven. Where, then, was the seventh man? Surely it must be approaching seven o'clock by now? Seven guests for the seventh hour? That's what they were waiting for. His muscles tensed, his breathing quickened, his eyes flicked from side to side. A professional assessing the danger, realising from where it would come and preparing his muscles for the collision. Eager young Digby, in his inexperience, had given away the game too soon and had put him on his guard.

The deceptively innocent smile of polite enquiry on the face of this youngest weed was stirring a sickening memory. That expression of self-satisfaction—he'd seen it not long ago. In a newspaper? Dickie had a good memory for faces and names, and it had served him well in the past. His mind scurried this way and that, and suddenly he had it. In a library last year, reading the *Yorkshire Post*, he'd seen a photograph, an official record of a deeply boring and pompous assembly of local personages, fat old windbags, and he'd hardly glanced at it. One of the figures, the central one—philanthropist or lord mayor, something of the kind—had snagged his attention. On taking a second look at the bald, portly fellow, hung about with sashes and ceremonial chains, every inch the masonic manipulator Dickie despised, he'd dismissed his outlandish notion. The dignitary's name, when he checked, was at that time unknown to him: Gisbourne.

Dickie stared, assessed, added a few years to the cherubic countenance and subtracted a few curls from the shepherd-boy mop head, calculated, at last understood and hated. Every sinew in his body tightened. His breathing deepened. His greased fingers slipped into the knuckleduster in his pocket.

His voice was steady as he replied, beaming with good humour. "Ah, child! I fought side by side with men your age or younger. Boys whose voices had scarcely broken when they sang along with rest of us:

Such was the day for our regiment
Dread the revenge we will take.
Dearly we paid for the blunder—
A drawing-room general's mistake.

"We don't remember the names of the generals for good reason. But I will never forget the names of my fellow fighters ... Abel, Ralph, Ernest, Herbert and Sydney."

"Ah. I'm sorry, sir. What charmingly unpretentious names! They sound like the salt of the earth! All deceased, are they?" Digby enquired.

"No. The salt of the earth—or the common as muck, as I think you *wrongly* interpret that phrase—these men are not 'deceased,' nor do they 'pass over.' They *die.* As plainly as they

have lived. But the men I speak of are not all dead, I'm happy
to say. The Ernies, the Herberts and the Syds of the British
army don't die that easily, even when they're being used as cannon fodder. My men were what Wellington considered 'the
dregs' of the army, but they were tenacious of life. At the last
roll call, I discovered that they are, for the most part, very much
alive and kicking. And still killing."

He watched one face carefully as he spoke.

"But how dull this is!" he continued jovially. "Rendlesham,
I would have certainly turned down your invitation had I had
warning that I was expected to wallow in past military disasters.
If you suffer from such self-flagellating patriotic propensities—
may I suggest—to enter into the spirit of things—you clear the
tabletop after the second bottle of brandy and have some
illustrative equipment brought in? We could have a salt-cellar
sergeant or two, a pepper-pot private, a claret-jug general, a
front line of petits fours and a battery of brandy glasses bringing up the rear. I believe these are the items most frequently
put to use by fuddy-duddy old fire-eaters to illustrate their
unremarkable campaigns before they retire to the snooker room.
We could refight the Relief of Kimberley! We could follow on
with Ladysmith and Mafeking for the best of three Reliefs!"

Even his list of tedious dinner service items did not distract
Digby Gisbourne from his hunt for information. "Tell me, sir.
The young men who 'paid dearly for the blunder'—should the
world still fear 'the dread revenge they will take'?"

Dickie's eyes narrowed, and his voice lost its cheery enthusiasm. It took on the cold threat of a steel bayonet held within
lunging distance of a man's throat. "Oh yes, young Gisbourne.
It's not the *world*, however . . . not even the drawing-room
generals who should walk in fear . . . but if I were a certain
pepper-pot private, a certain conniving, murderous Judas, I'd
be shitting my britches. I'd be looking over my shoulder.

Constantly. Until the day I saw creeping up on me, my Nemesis in khaki."

THEY ALL WERE visibly startled by the rap on the door, though at least three of them were expecting it.

Dickie turned to look back over his shoulder but maintained his position, defensive and aggressive at the same time. Was he two steps away from his own easy exit, or a threatening obstacle to anyone trying to get away?

Fanshawe recovered quickly and called out a peremptory "Come in!"

The buttery boy put his head round. "Sorry to disturb you, sir. Here's your second guest. He's signed in."

He flung the door open to admit a dark-suited man.

Dickie was the first to find words. "Well, I never! Is this the moment to say: 'I get sick to death of seeing your ugly mug every time I turn my head'? I believe it is. Come in, man, and state your hellish business."

CHAPTER 8

Detective Inspector John Redfyre tucked his terrier under his right arm, struggling to keep the wriggling bundle of whipcord muscle in a half nelson. His door opened directly onto the cobbled lane leading down to the river, and even at this early hour on a Sunday morning, there was a good chance that there would be some energetic types out taking air. And anyone passing in front of Magnolia Cottage was fair game for a nasty nip from Snapper.

Jack Russells! Pathetically, Redfyre delivered the ultimatum every day—"One more ankle-chewing, one more escape, one more hysterical woof and you're out, mate! I'll replace you with a nice quiet Labrador." The threat fell on deaf ears, and the energetic little dog grinned back, secure in his master's love.

How do you explain to a dog bred on the desolate Yorkshire moors for the express purpose of chasing down and killing rats that he was now a city dog and should mind his manners? Particularly tricky when the city—*this* city—offered a seductive patchwork of wild green spaces. Grasses everywhere you looked, whether short-shaven lawns or unkempt wilderness lapping up against sober grey stone buildings. In just a few strides, Snapper's morning walk took him from neat civic pavement into the riotous water meadows of Coe Fen, where a herd of cows grazed, providing milk for the local dairy. It gave Redfyre a quiet satisfaction that the rich milk he stirred into his morning porridge had travelled less than a mile to reach his doorstep. The cows would suffer no disturbance from his dog.

He checked that the dog lead Snapper so despised was coiled in the deep pocket of his mackintosh, ready for an emergency. He believed that the terrier had at last got the message that he was allowed to walk and run and cavort freely, only on condition that he responded at once to a command to come to heel.

There was no one about. Redfyre breathed in the fresh Sunday morning air. He relished that blissful moment after the winds had blown away the night's stale air and before the maids of the town set about re-creating the sooty reek by lighting the kitchen fires. The sun was up and already gilding the creamy flowers of the magnolia in the graveyard opposite. The sight startled his senses awake and filled him with delight. Not English, the magnolia. Exotic. A recent import from China, or was it Japan? Out of place in a Saxon graveyard. But, by God! How could anyone not be stirred by the fleshy roundness of those blooms? As smooth as Aphrodite's thigh. As far as he knew, their quality had not yet been expressed on canvas. Unknown to the Dutch masters, overlooked by Manet and Fantin-Latour. Even Sargent had confined himself to lilies and roses.

In his abstraction, he had relaxed his grip on Snapper.

The dog hit the ground, all four paws scrabbling for takeoff. In a second he had shot through the narrow gap between bars in the iron fence and disappeared into the graveyard between Redfyre's house and the northern side of Jude's College.

"Snapper! Heel!"

The training had not taken, evidently. Redfyre watched in dismay as the tall, unkempt grasses stirred, marking the progress straight through to the centre of this dog's paradise. Rats, cats, the rotting remains of tramps' ancient fish-and-chip suppers, bones rising to the surface as the earth beneath the stones rose and fell with the seasons and the rainfall—there was enough here to keep Snapper busy all day.

And there was nothing for it but to plunge in after him.

As nimble as the dog and with the advantage of longer legs, Redfyre vaulted over the railings and began to track his way over the higgledy-piggledy tombstones, around unmarked mounds, watching out for broken beer bottles and other lethal traps as he went. As he drew nearer to the spot he'd marked as the place where Snapper had come to rest, he heard him call out. It was as plain as a human cry for help. A peremptory yap that Redfyre had heard often before. It invariably meant, *Where are you? Over here! Come see what I've found!*

He'd feared he would have to report the fresh digging up of a grave to the local vicar and offer his apologies with due restitution, but as he ducked around the low-lying branches of a concealing yew, he relaxed and smiled with relief at the comical and entirely harmless scene before him.

Snapper had found a friend.

The dog loved the gentlemen of the travelling brotherhood. The men of the road. Redfyre could never work out whether it was the dog who cast a spell on them or they who were able to magic the dog. It was undeniable that not a single tramp's hide had ever been punctured by Snapper's awful little teeth, and they never failed to make much of him. The surest way into the owner's pocket? It certainly worked. Not a week went by without a tap on the door, an ear-tugging and a few kind words for the dog, preliminaries to the handing over of whatever change Redfyre had in his pocket. Half a loaf or a cake from the table usually followed. He had never spotted a tramp's chalked sign near his door, but had no doubt that one of their secret signals was present and constantly renewed. He wondered which symbol expressed: "Nice dog lives here. Master, easy mark." In return, he had to admit that one or two of the knocks had alerted him to trouble in the neighbourhood of "Bum-bailiff coming on a bit strong with the little missis at number twenty," or "Old lag down the Anchor bragging about that robbery at the co-op . . . Just thought you'd like to know." He recognised that he had become the approachable face of local law and order, and was pleased enough to go along with that.

"Ah! There you are, you ghastly, disobedient little beast! Are you going to introduce me to your new friend? Perhaps he has room in his life for a Jack Russell who's about to be made homeless. You can wander off into the wide blue yonder together! And good riddance! Hullo there! Anyone at home?"

Redfyre had been talking deliberately loudly to alert the sleeping tramp to his presence. As he approached, he waited for the startled cursing to pour forth, but the man remained silent. Sleeping off a Saturday night drinking bout, he guessed. Quite a binge that must have been if he could remain oblivious of sharp spring sunshine slanting down onto his eyelids, the nerve-jangling yapping and the copper's bluff nonsense!

But, of course, no sentient being this side of the grave could have done that.

Suddenly alert, Redfyre paused in his advance to take in the scene. Snapper was now tugging at the sleeve of the man's overcoat. Redfyre recognised the uniform of the wanderer. A second- or thirdhand, worn-out, ex–army greatcoat. Warm, reasonably waterproof and a good stand-in for a sleeping blanket. The wearer of this useful garment was stretched out on top of a low-lying marble-topped grave with his head resting against the headstone. His feet, clad in heavily darned socks, offered themselves to the newly risen sun, heels together in a mocking V formation, one lividly white big toe sticking through to strike a discordant note of pathos. A pair of resoled brogue shoes had been lined up at the base of the stone with the care of a child going to bed. Or would that be a soldier's careful routine gesture? The man's face recalled that of a waxen effigy, time-darkened ivory, skin tight about the bones, the mouth slightly smiling. Though on approaching, Redfyre thought— perhaps a grimace? His hands must have been crossed over his chest until Snapper in his eagerness had leapt up and snatched one down to his level for an affectionate nuzzling.

Idiotically, Redfyre's first thought was, Lord! How do I tell the poor little animal his new friend is a goner?

"Come away, lad!" he said, scooping up the dog. "He can't hear you." He took out the lead and tethered him, grumbling, to the yew tree, then proceeded to investigate the tomb sleeper.

No pulse. Dead. Cold body. He judged the man to have been dead for some hours, perhaps even days. It was entirely possible for a bloke to have had a heart attack, realised that his moment had come and laid himself out to wait for death on an available and entirely appropriate piece of marble, Redfyre reasoned. His knowledge of the process of decomposition had been acquired over four years fighting in Flanders fields and was reliable, but he now entrusted such professional decisions to men in lab coats with thermometers and microscopes. He was most probably contemplating a death by natural causes that would lead to a five-minute enquiry by a bored coroner and a quiet shovelling away, unnamed, in a pauper's burial ground.

He sniffed the air above the body. A keen sense of smell was a trait the inspector shared with Bernard Spilsbury, the Home Office pathologist so revered by the CID. Not that it needed to be particularly keen to distinguish two sharp scents against the green background of mayblossom and sun-warmed grasses. Alcohol. Fruity alcohol rather than whisky or ale . . . brandy, perhaps? And, less pungent, the inevitable smell of rotting lilies, reeking of death.

There were no visible signs of violence. No blood, no torn clothing. Fights in defence of territory or simply drunken squabbles were the second-most-frequent cause of death, after disease, in the down-and-out fraternity. They left traces on the primary target—the face. Here was no broken nose, no black eye, no scratches or bruises. Redfyre turned his attention to the hands. He took hold of the right hand Snapper had been tugging at and inspected the knuckles. No signs of fighting. He checked the left. No broken bones or skin here, either. They were the hands of a hardworking man of middle years that he had expected, but oddly, they were clean, the nails freshly trimmed. The face had the austerity of one who was aware that death was close, but gave out the impression of peaceful acceptance. The eyes were fully closed. There was certainly no expression of horror—Redfyre had yet to encounter such in a corpse. He had begun to suspect that the dying eye roll of terror was no more than an invention of Victorian novelists. The face was well shaped—intelligent-looking, as far as one could judge. It would certainly not have appeared as an illustration in the pages of Cesare Lombroso's *L'uomo delinquente*. Anthropological criminology was not a theory Redfyre subscribed to. He had known too many villains with the features of the Angel Gabriel and one or two plug-uglies with hearts of gold and morals to match. Nevertheless, this was a face he would have been pleased to have engaged with, if only it could have sprung alive again.

The professional policeman surfaced, and Detective Inspector Redfyre of the Cambridge CID went about his business in a methodical way, scribbling on the pad he always kept in his trouser pocket, noting first of all precisely the condition of the scrubby grass surrounding the gravestone. He dropped to his knees and crawled about, much to the fury of Snapper, who was not invited to join in the game, inspecting bent stems and establishing the route the man had taken to arrive at the stone. With the sequence of light shower followed by flood of spring sunshine, you could almost hear the grass surging upwards, repairing itself, standing straight. By lunchtime, Redfyre reckoned, the track would no longer be discernible.

Scarcely believing what he was noting, he got to his feet and took his bearings. He sighted along the barely visible path of disturbed herbage and spoke to the corpse. "Now, what the hell were you doing coming straight out of the back of Jude's? The master's garden, no less! Leading to the master's lodge. Impressive friends you have! And which of them, I wonder, unlocked the door in the eight-foot-high wall so you could get through to die in here and ruin my Sunday?"

CHAPTER 9

"**W**ell, at least someone's happy," Dr. Beaufort commented. He nodded to the police photographer, who was hopping about the gravestones, eager, busy, in a world of his own. "It's not every day you boys get a whack at an outdoor scene in full spring sunshine with a subject that looks like a Plantagenet king laid out on his funeral bier. Who've we got? King Richard the Lionheart without his crown and longsword? Very photogenic . . . is that a word?"

"I know what you mean!" Redfyre agreed, responding to the doctor's flight of fancy. "My lads are more used to exposing their lenses to battered sides of meat on stormy nights down a dark alley . . . With this one, I looked for the embroidered cushion under the head, the pet whippet at his feet."

"I'll give your Man Ray over there a minute to indulge his artistic impulses before I swat him away," Beaufort said, eager to make a start.

The pathologist on duty was the one Redfyre would have requested if requesting had been possible. Dr. Beaufort was every detective's first choice. The doctor's bag remained unopened on the ground by his side, and Redfyre knew it would remain so until he had looked about him and absorbed the bigger picture. Then out would come the rubberised gloves, the tweezers and the sample bags. He could have sworn Beaufort had undergone police training, so attuned was he to their requirements. Redfyre smiled to himself. On the many occasions the venerable pathologist had worked with Redfyre's boss, Detective Superintendent MacFarlane, he would have been subjected to a regime of strict adherence to the Scotland Yard's Detective's Handbook.

Unhurried, the wise old eyes ranged around the graveyard, taking in the presence of tall, gangly Sergeant Thoday beating the bounds, returning to concentrate on the track through the grasses. "I say, Redfyre, have you noticed . . . ?"

"Yes, that was the first thing I asked the photographer to record. The sergeant is doing a preliminary sweep. We'll have the uniformed lads down on their knees later for a fingertip search, should it be necessary."

"You're hoping I'm going to take one look and say, 'Heart attack. Feel free to cart away and bury,' I suppose."

"Much depends on whether that gate is locked and where the key is. We can follow where it leads when we've had a closer look at the body. I hope you're in the mood to talk aloud, in words of no more than five syllables and, above all—indiscreetly— as you work?"

The doctor grinned. "You've never held me to what I say in the first flush of enthusiasm, so—yes. And my first indiscretion will be to say—are you sure, Inspector, that this is indeed a *corpse* we're about to check over? Do I need to remind you where we are? In the middle of university territory. You know what the young folk are like for practical jokes. When pissed out of their wits seeking a distraction from the stressful demands of examinations or just because it's a Saturday night, they often burst out into undergrad humour. The medics are the worst, with their access to body parts, real or faked. And they have a fertile imagination. Combined with a strong stomach and a head for heights, apparently. I've been called out to attend skeletons in indelicate poses on rooftops, severed heads—papier mâché, of course, and dripping gouts of tomato sauce—dangling from the chubby fingers of Henry VIII. This one looks particularly waxen to me from this distance. Someone made a clandestine visit to Madame Tussauds gallery and made off with one of her rogues? Ah! Your photographer's done with the camera. Shall we cease blethering and move into the presence?"

"Why do I feel as though we ought to be doffing our hats?" Redfyre murmured as they approached. "No idea who he is, but I can tell you this—he's no waxwork! He's real, all right, just lacking a pulse. Not exactly hiding, is he? I say—do you think that's part of it? Either he was some kind of a joker who thought he'd lay himself out with a last dashing gesture or—"

"Someone did it for him. Laid him out all neat and tidy, eyes closed, hands crossed over the breastbone. Regretful? 'Sorry about this, old chap. Least I can do . . .'"

"It did occur to me, though I can't see any sign of violence on the few bits of him that are visible. I haven't yet looked below the greatcoat. It covers him capaciously, from chin to calf. Could be anything under there from a pair of nail scissors to a harpoon."

They stared together in pity and curiosity at the body, automatically making a respectful sign of the cross.

"They say Death's a leveller," the doctor murmured, "but I don't know. It's hardly a scientific view, but it always seems to my jaundiced eye to accentuate differences. And sometimes it distorts. Subjects take on a deceptively saintly aspect—and the reverse. Looking at our bloke, I'd say 'saintly,' wouldn't you? He may have been an utter blackguard in life, of course. That's up to you to discover, my friend."

"Should we really go on calling him 'subject' and 'bloke'?" Redfyre said. "Seems a bit discourteous to me."

"Right. Look, it's the eighteenth of May today. St. Dunstan's Day, my diary told me when I opened it on receiving the phone call this morning. Let's call him after the good old Saxon saint, shall we? Dunstan?"

"Seems appropriate," Redfyre said, glancing wryly at the surroundings. "He rests surrounded by good old Saxon bones, after all."

After an inspection of the head and hands, the doctor declared his intention of removing the greatcoat, and they both set about undoing the strong horn buttons. "This was a splendid coat, two or three owners previously," Beaufort commented. "Great War: 'Officers for the use of,' I had one just like it. Not standard issue, sewn up in a hurry by the thousand, either. Specially tailored in London, I think we'll find, when we dig a bit deeper. Ah yes, here we are. Label intact. Jermyn Street. Do you want to note down the details? . . . Not that a London tailor will be able to help. The secondhand stall on the market may have more useful particulars to offer. Whichever—it's had careful owners, or lucky ones. No sign of damage—no bullet hole, no bayonet slash. Even the buttons are all intact and stoutly sewn on."

"No helpful regimental badge in the lapel?"

"No," Beaufort replied, smoothing down the front folds. "But look here. Two tiny holes. From a lapel tag? Right where you'd expect to find it. That could have come adrift when the body was moved—dragged along?"

"I'll tell the chaps to watch out. No marks of grass or damp stains down the front from pulling the body along. Perhaps they're on the back." Redfyre made a note.

The doctor silently assessed the condition of the limbs, and noting that they were in a sufficiently loose state, he began with Redfyre's help to peel the coat from the arms.

"You know, I think your guess at timing is a bit out, Inspector. Your Dunstan's been dead rather longer than you think. I'll let you know later when I've had him on my slab, but—first

estimate—not last night. The night before? Friday night? I'll
be able to get the night temperatures and a meteorological
report from the boffins and hear what they have to say. They've
solved more murders than we have, those chaps. Now, then . . .
take this, will you? You'll be wanting to look through the pockets."

Redfyre peered with interest at the body revealed. "Good
suit. Dark blue, loose weave, summer weight. Hardly worn. Sort
of thing you'd buy for a wedding or a funeral and put on once.
You can get them by the dozen on the racks in the secondhand
shops down Mill Road in April when the maids have finished
spring cleaning. Clean shirt. Tie slightly out of kilter owing to
the murdering hands, which made those weals on his throat,
would you say?" He paused for a moment, head cocked to one
side. "The tie, Inspector? You're a Cambridge man . . . Anything
strike you as odd?"

"Good Lord! It's a Girton College tie. I haven't seen one in
use for years. Another thing he picked up at the secondhand
stalls, I expect."

"I reckon. And one tie's as good as another when it comes
to a strangling. But it hasn't been used for that purpose. He's
been throttled by fingers on his throat. Elderly gent on a sparse
diet . . . It can't have taken much force to kill him. Sniff, Redfyre.
Notice anything?"

"Oh yes, I'd noticed. Spirit of some sort. Not whisky . . . that's
brandy, surely?"

"Yes. I think when we test those stains down the front of
his shirt, that's what we'll find." Beaufort took the man's right
hand and looked at the first two fingers. "Smoker, I see. Well,
at least the old bugger indulged in a few pleasurable activities
before he snuffed it."

He peered again at the neck. "Murder. We're definitely looking at a case of strangulation. Not a hanging, which could well

have been self-inflicted and tends to leave other traces, like a noose or other ligature, and a high point from which to dangle. I think we'll find our Dunstan was strangled to death, most likely by hand, possibly elsewhere, then laid out later in this place. No signs of a struggle hereabouts?"

Redfyre shook his head.

"Well, I think that's as far as I need go here." The doctor looked about anxiously. "And if we linger, we'll get caught up in the morning service. The organ's tuning up, and I noticed the vicar cycling up to the vestry door just now, corset creaking and moustache starched. I'll leave you to do the honours, if you don't mind, though the temptation to hang on and torment humourless old Reverend Turnbull with a few heavy jests about the carelessness of leaving bodies lying about in a graveyard is getting the better of me. I'll thumb a lift back to the morgue with the blokes in the meat wagon and get straight on with this. Ask your constable to nip off and tell them to give us ten minutes before bringing in their stretcher, will you, John?"

Watching Redfyre turning out the pockets of the greatcoat, he added, "Anything?"

"Hardly anything. Linen handkerchief. Bit of change—a few pennies. Ah, and a half crown."

Beaufort nodded, recognising the significance of the coin. "Which means we can't officially log him as 'destitute.' Fair enough! He has the price of a night's lodging on him. Show that to any copper challenging him and he couldn't be moved on for vagrancy. Accordingly, I shall enter him as 'identity not established, no known abode, occupation unknown' on my sheet."

"That would appear to be all in here. No fluff. And that's a bit odd. You wouldn't believe the contents of a tramp's pockets! But there always *are* contents. They carry their most vital possessions about with them, and the pocket fluff you can expect to be an inch deep and a rich mixture of tobacco crumbs, bread crumbs, birdseed, half-sucked Fisherman's Friend lozenges . . . Nothing like that here. Let's take a look at the other one . . . Ah! A bottle of brandy. Half-drunk. Good stuff, too!" He showed the label to the doctor. "A prewar cognac, bottled by and bearing the label of Jude's College cellars, no less." He raised a speculative eye to the ornate roofscape of the neighbouring college building just visible over the wall between the thickening green canopies of chestnut, beech and larch.

"Many of these old establishments have trading or family connections with southwest France," the doctor commented. "Bordeaux . . . Cognac . . . once an English province, Aquitaine. I've sampled many a liquid-gold memento of more spacious times at college dinners around the town. Look, I'll take that with me to the labs," he offered.

Both men handled the bottle with care, their hands sheathed in rubberised gloves.

"Um . . . birdseed, Redfyre? I'm sure you mentioned birdseed. Am I missing something?"

Redfyre smiled. "I'm not inventing! It's not unknown for vagrants to lure the town pigeons with a trail of seed, nab them, wring their necks and pop them into the pot they keep on boil down in the meadows. I sometimes take them an offering myself—a bag of pearl barley's always welcome, or a pound of marrow bones . . . a pheasant in the season."

"A sort of potluck supper?" The doctor found the idea entertaining. "Good lord! Well, power to their elbows! Too many of the blighters fouling up the pavements. Birds, I mean."

"Well, that would seem to be it," Redfyre said, turning the pocket inside out. "Our chap doesn't seem to have been a pigeon fancier. And there's no door key, no penknife, not even a pencil stub or a cigarette end. Again—no pocket fluff."

"Try the inside pocket," the doctor suggested. "My coat had

a discreet ticket pocket on the inside left, I remember. Just big enough for a love letter, a photograph, or . . . well, a ticket."

"Oh, that's interesting!" Redfyre took a white card from the ticket pocket and, holding it by the edges, showed it to Beaufort. 'Invitation to Dine,' does that say?"

"Someone dropped an *n* somewhere along the line," Beaufort remarked. "And—'invited to break bread with'? Who uses such precious prose these days?"

"The pretentious clots who think it's stylish to call their dining group the 'Amici Apicii.' Friends of Apicius. It *is* the Roman cook we're talking about, isn't it? The one who wrote a cookery book? With rather exotic recipes, rotting fish sauce and all?"

"I believe so, though you won't find it on your kitchen shelf. No one's yet thought to publish the text in English, though it's available in Latin. Or Middle German. The chap was no Mrs. Beeton! 'First, catch your hare and joint it . . . Five economical ways of cooking a turnip,' and all that . . . This old Latin was famous for expensive and exotic ingredients like suckling pig and nightingales' tongues. And his suppers consisted of several lavish courses."

The doctor frowned with the effort of struggling to dust off his classical schoolboy knowledge. He added thoughtfully: "These hosts, whoever they are, must be a very particular little appreciation society. Classicists and bons vivants. They shouldn't be too difficult to track down. Oh dear! Harmless entertainment if you can afford it, I suppose. But what's it doing in the pocket of a poor old tramp? He can hardly have been a dinner guest." He grunted. "Six years or so of a starvation diet, followed by a festive blowout . . . well, that could result in a collapse of the digestive system and seizure, leading to death. Is someone secretly carrying out a socio-culinary experiment?"

Redfyre pulled a rueful face. "This *is* Cambridge, as people are always reminding me. It's entirely possible, but we won't know until the learned paper's published. Perhaps if we're lucky, they'll pass it to you for expert review, but I wouldn't count on it. All we can do, Doc, is open him up and take a look at yesterday's menu. Vital information! It'll tell us whether he dined at the Hôtel Régence or Willie's Whelk Stall. Lord knows what you'll find; perhaps he washed it down with brandy! It was 'a surfeit of lampreys' that did it for King John when he sampled the culinary delights of Norfolk, and I don't suppose he was particularly malnourished to start with."

Even the experienced doctor blanched a little, Redfyre judged mischievously, at the thought of untangling an overrindulgence of young eels from a dead man's innards.

"No, indeed. Though it wasn't eels or songbirds' tongues that killed this chap, let's not forget, however intriguing the thought. It was a short, sharp throttling."

"**SERVES ME RIGHT** for asking!" Detective Superintendent MacFarlane rolled his eyes in exaggerated exasperation. "Have you quite done, Redfyre? When I trip across my inspector roaming the station on a Sunday morning and I enquire as to what the blazes he's doing here, that's just me being polite— I don't actually want him to tell me. I expect him to say, 'Just on my way out. Sorry to disturb you, sir.'"

He eyed his smiling, nonchalant inspector and added, "The good folk of the town are in church or chapel; the lowlifes are sleeping off Saturday night's junketing. Even criminals need a day of rest, and this is it. Bugger off home, Redfyre. I'm not in a mood to be treated to chapter and verse of your morning's adventures with a dead tramp in a graveyard."

"But we must consider the potential degrading of the crime scene, sir . . ."

"Who says it's a crime scene? You can't know yet. Oh, sit

down for a minute and listen." His attention drifted for a moment to a letter open on the top of a pile in his in-tray, and he said thoughtfully, "If you'd kept better control of your dog, our corpse would still be peacefully tucked up awaiting discovery next week by the Bat Botherers, or whatever those interfering old biddies are calling themselves these days." He shook with silent laughter. "I kid you not! They're booked in for an inspection of your St. Mary's Church and its graveyard." He looked briefly at the sheet. "Oh, look! It's scheduled for Monday teatime. That's tomorrow!" He savoured the imagined moment of discovery of the corpse by a group of very earnest and vocal city ladies. "Ho, ho! Can you hear the shrieks and screams? Can you imagine the flutterings and faintings?"

"A pipistrelle preservation team on manoeuvres?" Redfyre was charmed by the notion and exchanged a glance of boyish delight with his boss.

"Glad to hear you're an admirer," MacFarlane said cryptically. "Personally, I can't abide 'em! All nasty little claws, sharp teeth and dribble."

"And the bats they preserve are scarcely more attractive," Redfyre supplied dutifully.

"You're not wrong, sonny. And these pipi-what's-its, they've got leathery wings—fair makes you shudder! If they all caught the bat plague and died off tomorrow, really, who'd notice?"

Redfyre grinned. "It's because there are people like you about the place, sir, that we need people like the Bat Brigade. But I do know the group you mean. If I have it right, they are in some way involved with my Aunt Henrietta's feminist group. Secretive, amorphous and deadly. But I'd advise you not to underestimate them. In fact, I think you've got them quite wrong! Lady Laetitia and her handmaidens are a competent outfit. Had *they* stumbled upon the scene before Snapper, they would have proceeded from discovery of the body to solution of the case by teatime. They'd have had our man logged as an endangered species and the vicar arrested for keeping a disorderly graveyard."

"Don't! I've locked antlers with that lot before! Believe me—they've got antlers. Sharpened ones. Whenever they're out and about, accusations of bodily assault, trespass and foul language flow in and pile up on my desk. Accusations that are usually lodged against Lady L. herself. The ones that aren't are by the lady against me. Can't say I much mind being called 'an oafish police lout with violent proclivities,' but it's the paperwork! Weeks of paperwork follow on every sodding outing! The 'Fur, Fin and Feather Folk,' they call themselves officially." He allowed himself a moment to scorn the ear-catching alliteration, then, "Newly in association with the Royal Society for the Protection of Birds, I'm told. And now they're taking bloody bats under their wing—"

"Fur, Fin, Feather and Leather?" Redfyre could not resist.

A crafty expression flitted across MacFarlane's craggy features, and his eyes shifted again to his in-tray. "The vicar's notified me of the invasion, and he requires that we provide him with a protection squad. Ha! Some hopes! I was going to ask you, as a neighbour, to stroll across and smile a bit, keep an eye out and see that they do no damage to the fabric of the church. Or the fabric of the vicar." He sighed. "No green space or wild creature in Cambridge is safe from their ministrations. I blame Eleanor Roosevelt!"

Better not to press enquiries, Redfyre thought, and eager to cut off a diatribe about the "wimmin" of Cambridge and now apparently the "wimmin" of the USA, he remarked brightly, "But at least the body's not going anywhere, sir. He's in safe hands."

"Ah! They sent you Doc Beaufort?"

"They did. And lucky old us, that the good doctor is

conscientious enough to put down his prelunch sherry glass, pop his chop back onto the pantry shelf and pick up his scalpel, don't you agree, sir? He should have some results for us by tomorrow morning."

His shaft appeared to have hit home, since the superintendent glowered and said, "That's enough of your bloody cheek! I say again—it's a Sunday. I'm not supposed to be here. Nor are you. I just dropped in to get out from under the wife's feet. We've got roast beef, and her mother's helping in the kitchen. And if you detain me any longer with your exploits, I shan't get it rare."

"Sorry, sir! I'll think of you tucking into the pink sirloin and the horseradish in an hour's time when I'm down at the dissecting table, examining the contents of the murdered man's stomach," Redfyre replied with an easy smile. It was a lie. He was attempting—unsuccessfully—to prick the super's conscience. His arrangement to attend Beaufort's autopsy was for Monday morning. But he'd noted that his boss, despite the bluff and bluster, was intrigued. He'd expected to find him at the station. On a Sunday morning, his warm, wood-panelled office on the first floor of the ugly building in St. Andrew's Street regularly became MacFarlane's redoubt. A swift visit to the next-door off-licence to buy drinks for lunch had become a ritual. Redfyre let his gaze drift without emphasis over the array of bottles lined up on the superintendent's desk. He noted six half-pints of India pale ale to wash down the Sunday roast, along with two bottles of Mackeson's stout on the side in recognition of a mother-in-law visiting day.

MacFarlane sighed. "Go on, then! Help yourself to one of those glasses and pour yourself one of these, why don't you?" he invited his inspector. "No? Well, make it quick. So, the doc reckons it's a case of murder, does he? Strangulation? Funny, that ... Not many *blokes* get themselves strangled. Bashed over the head, shoved off a height, shot with grandpa's old rifle, lynched even. But a hands-on throttling ... nah! One chap with his hands around another chap's neck?" MacFarlane grimaced at the uncomfortable thought. "That's not natural!"

"In Cambridge perhaps, sir, but not unknown in a military situation. Trench raiding, overcoming a sentry, an occasion where silence is necessary or where no other weapon is ... er ... to hand. I believe it to be an aggressive combat technique now taught to His Majesty's troops as a matter of course. I rather think the handbooks refer to it as a 'self-defence skill.'"

MacFarlane grunted. "A gross euphemism, but none the less effective for that. Still, why would anyone waste their time and energy topping a down and out?"

"Down on his luck, certainly but I'm not sure about 'out.'"

"Ah yes, the half crown. Marks him as a professional destitute, at least. Knows the rules and plays by them. He's probably on record at the shelters. Follow that up tomorrow, will you, Redfyre? And a white linen hankie, you say? That's a novel touch, isn't it? Mucky red spotted square of cotton is what they usually carry about."

"May have been bought at a local store, sir. Something else I can ask Thoday to track down."

"But the brandy? Do you reckon he nicked it? There's only one place you can get this stuff, after all, and it's proudly displayed on the label. You can't get the likes of that over the counter at the Beer-Off shop."

"Perfectly possible. But only if he could get into the college in the first place, and we all know how hard that is to do. I doubt Houdini could manage it! They won't let the police in unless they're waving warrants and police-issue Brownings."

"And once inside, how in hell did he penetrate as far as the wine cellar? It's hardly the first room you wander into. And, for obvious reasons, college wine cellars are always under lock

and key and the key in the pocket of a gimlet-eyed male cus-
todian."

"Could he have swiped it from the drinks cabinet in the
master's lodge?"

"Even harder to access, I should imagine. Either way, we're
going to need to get hold of a plan of the college buildings."
MacFarlane frowned in dismay, anticipating the difficulty and
the tediousness of the task before them. "I say . . ."

Reading his thoughts and approving them, Redfyre was
already on his feet and reaching down two beer glasses from a
shelf. "Sure you can spare a couple?"

"The wife won't be counting. Hands off the stout, though.
That's for Hilda, my mother-in-law."

"*Two* stouts, sir?"

"That's what it usually takes."

"I thought you got on well with your mother-in-law?"

An unattractive expression of piety flitted across the superintendent's face as he said modestly: "In twenty years, she's
never heard a disobliging word from *me*. Because I've never yet
managed to interrupt her! Ply her with a couple of milk stouts,
though, and she'll collapse into her apple crumble and spend
the afternoon snoring on the sofa. Works a treat!"

MacFarlane took a deep swig of his beer and, fortified, said
carefully: "Bloody colleges! Unless you're perfectly sure of your
information and facts, don't think of going near them! You are
not to approach that college, Redfyre, until you have a full
report from Beaufort, have established an identity for this bloke
and get clearance from me. Understand?"

"Well, I wasn't thinking of ringing the front doorbell and
asking if they were missing a corpse! Wouldn't dream of storming the college authorities without backup and from a securely
defended position, sir."

"That's the ticket! Wish I could believe you. But on that

understanding, I say formally: you have the case and may call on Sergeant Thoday for assistance. Plus any uniform you need. That new lad—Constable Jenkins—seems handy, though he's got a bit of a mouth on him. You should get on well. And we've always got Dr. Beaufort in our corner . . . Be interesting to hear what our subject spews forth. Brandy, though . . .

"Oh my God! Brandy!" MacFarlane took another swig of his ale, his mind apparently somewhere in the past. A past he was revisiting, Redfyre judged, with a chill blend of horror and guilt.

"Inspector, there's more to this than meets the eye. Even a sharp eye like yours." He stirred in his seat, ill at ease, then, coming to a decision: "Look here—if you have a minute, you might try glancing through that black box file over there. Third shelf down." He pointed with his pencil.

Redfyre looked over his shoulder. "The one with the silver pull handle? It looks like a coffin, sir!"

"Yes, that's exactly what it is. A miniature coffin. A container for dead things . . . old bones, regrets, mistakes and memories. It predates you, Redfyre. Predates me! It goes back quite a few years, in fact. I inherited it from my predecessor, and I'm sad to say I've been obliged to add to it myself over the years."

He fell silent for a moment, then, responding to Redfyre's questioning eyebrow: "Dead cases. It represents—records, if you like—our failures. Unsolved crimes. Shamingly, you'll find about twenty of them. Thinning out latterly, I'm glad to say, as our techniques and training improve. Still, I'd rather nail it down and not have to add any more."

"But you think this present case is headed for the coffin box, I'm guessing?"

"It's got that feel about it. I can always tell. And this is the odd thing, Redfyre—and the reason I'm inviting you to make free with our darkest secrets—there's a precedent. Well, make that three or four precedents. Going back over six years or so, I'd say. If you sift through, you'll find a number of odd bods: some transients, all male, all unknowns and untraceable. Don't you worry your pretty little head, though: I'll mark your card and draw your attention to one or two that chime with this tramp killing of yours. All found dead on Cambridge streets. Their bodies deposited with no attempt to hide them."

"Not very compelling as evidence of a pattern, sir, surely? These things happen all the time. People succumb to war wounds, the Spanish 'flu, starvation, cold . . . Their bodies might well have been moved on to make them someone else's problem. I've known bartenders who were a whizz at discreetly spotting and removing the dead drunk—so why not the drunken dead? Are there any other features in common?"

MacFarlane wrenched his focus back from the past onto the keen, handsome face in front of him and prepared to watch it crumple. "One. They all seem to have belonged to the same dining club. A weekend feast, washed down with a claret and topped off with . . . a rare brandy. A condemned man's last supper? Who caught, tried and condemned him, Redfyre? And of what sin was he found guilty?"

CHAPTER 10

Did he really have time for this? Redfyre paused by the entrance to the church. On his way home to smarten up for his own lunch engagement, an inconvenient professional niggle had stayed him in his stride.

All was silent here. The morning worshippers had gone off to reward themselves for two hours' devotion with a roast and Yorkshire pudding and an afternoon's snooze to restore their strength for evensong. He rattled the side gate opposite his house in the lane and found it locked as usual. Someone had posted a handwritten notice asking the public to avoid the area, since demolition work was being undertaken in the churchyard and their safety could not be guaranteed. Any queries to be addressed to the vicar. The Reverend Turnbull had grudgingly appended his signature to this lie, bowing to the greater good and police pressure. Redfyre had personally advised the vicar that the body of a poor unfortunate had been found in the churchyard and asked him to tactfully ensure that parishioners and church employees were kept away from the scene until the police force had done its duty and tidied up.

Satisfied with the response to his requests, Redfyre could have walked on. But he gave in to an impulse and decided to climb over the iron grille and enter the crime scene for the second time that morning.

Although confident that the information he wanted would

be contained in Sergeant Thoday's meticulous report, he kicked himself for having failed at the time of discovery to inspect the wooden gate in the dividing wall between the college and the graveyard to ascertain whether the key had been left in the keyhole or had been removed. The omission was troubling him. He retraced his steps past the yew tree and the unoccupied tomb top and found the gate. The venerable old piece of oak had black iron fixtures and bindings, and the keyhole itself, vast in size, was also bound in black iron. Although clearly a Victorian Gothick flourish, it would not have disappointed as the door to an eleventh-century castle built by the Norman conqueror. Redfyre calculated that the key fitting such a piece of design must itself also be of some consequence. It was hardly the sort of implement you could pop into your back pocket and forget about or even dangle from a girdle. It was either still in the lock or hanging from a stout hook in some secure location.

He decided to put his eye to the keyhole. Would he be able to make out traces of a struggle or a continuation of the drag marks he'd found in whatever horticultural features were to be found beyond the boundary? A deep, damp flower bed would suit him very well. Redfyre had no firm hope, but since an immediate incursion into college territory had been banned by his boss, peering through the bloody keyhole was the best he could do.

No key obstructed his vision, and the hole gave him a surprisingly generous view of the neighbouring garden. Sadly but not unexpectedly, the telltale long grass that might have retained a trace ended on this side of the doorway and was replaced by a lawn, close-cropped and reticent as to recent activity. Beyond, he saw an arc of tall trees and bushes and could just make out the beginnings of a flower border. Here, an explosion of early peonies in various shades of pink made him smile. Exactly as he had expected. The lucky master had an enviable space for his private garden—south-facing and walled to the north. The very place to nurture your own English heaven.

As he peered, he was taken aback by a flash of colour passing across his field of vision. Lavender? Purple? He blinked and the figure—he was sure it had been a figure—passed back again with the same unnatural sideways motion. Stalking back and forth. At the same moment, he became aware of a musical sound. Singing? Well, why not? The city was full of glee clubs. Every college had one. He'd sung baritone himself with the King's Minstrels during his college years, and with the Clippers Barber Shop Quartet since he'd been back in Cambridge. He knew most of the other amateur groups and was aware that they were quite likely to pop up on the slightest pretext to serenade someone or other, and usually in eye-catching surroundings with a photographer present to record the spontaneous outpouring. There was St. Cecilia's feast day in November, St. Nicholas in December, the first day of May on Clare Bridge—why not the second Sunday of Easter term in the master's garden in full springtime fig? Intrigued, he put his ear to the keyhole. What he was hearing was not a Sunday hymn, nor yet the old English madrigal the setting would have prompted Redfyre to offer up in praise of Nature. He would have launched heartily into "Flora Gave Me Fairest Flowers" or "Banks of Green Willow." But this young-sounding solo female singer was looking to a more exotic climate for her inspiration.

He recognised the tune from the first six notes. It was very near the top of his own stack of gramophone records. It was the latest hit he'd bought, along with the sheet music, at Millers music shop in Sidney Street. He'd been entranced by the rhythms and had played it many times, singing along, learning the words. Puzzled, Redfyre wondered why a solitary young woman would be dancing the tango in a purple dress in a back garden, singing—and in Spanish, too—the sensuous words of "*Mi noche triste.*"

His ridiculous posture, louting about at a keyhole like a badly trained butler or a third-rate private eye, embarrassed him. This questionable behaviour, even if unobserved, was untenable. He shot upright in confusion, but his inquisitive nature, which he countenanced as "professional spirit of enquiry," won out over discretion. Looking about him, he spotted, lying on its side, a stout water butt he assumed had been overturned and emptied by his squad in the morning's meticulous search of the site for evidence. He dragged it over to the wall and climbed on top, remembering to clear his throat loudly in warning of his presence as he made the ascent.

Sticking his head and shoulders boldly over the rim of the wall he belted out his version of the song:

"*Percanta!*" he growled down to her, catching her attention with his gravelly baritone.

> *Que me amuraste*
> *En lo mejor de mi vida,*
> *Dejandome el alma herida*
> *Y espina en el corazon?*

He ended the verse with an accompanying flourish miming the pain of the alleged thorn in the region of his heart. He followed the pantomime with what he hoped was a disarming grin.

The purple vision swirled to a halt with a yip of astonishment. Instead of fleeing at once, as he feared she might, she held her ground. She adopted an aggressive posture. A cross face stared up at him in challenge. This was a girl who could deliver a thorn to the heart or a kick to the privates, he judged. If he'd been down there at her level, he would have checked her for concealed catapults or half bricks.

"Hey! Who do *you* think you're calling a whore?" she wanted to know.

His grin would appear to be losing its potency.

"Oh, I say, I do beg your pardon, Miss—er, I had no intention of—"

"Then why use that word to get my attention? *Percanta*—that's what you called me! It's Spanish. And it's not at all polite!"

"Oh, I don't know. Um, What about 'naughty minx,' then? Shall we settle for that? I don't happen to have a Spanish dictionary on me at the moment."

"You wouldn't find it there, anyway. I've looked. It's too rude for inclusion. I had to ask Carlos. He learned it in the *conventillos* of Buenos Aires, he says."

Redfyre decided not to interpret this as an invitation to wander off in dubious company on a word hunt down a South American backstreet and fell silent. They watched each other for a moment, ill at ease, seeking an acceptable means of disconnection from the situation and finding none, rather like a pair of terriers circling each other when token meaningless growling will go on until one backs off. Redfyre decided he was the clumsy oaf who had caused the offence and he would be the one to roll over in submission.

Before he could apologise, she decided to throw another log onto the fire of her glowing anger. "If you're not going to arrest me for disturbing the peace of the Sabbath, Mr. Copper, you can sling your hook and let me get on with my practice. Good Lord! Is there no corner of Cambridge where I can have a bit of privacy to polish my *corrida garabito*? Some of us have May balls coming up, you know, and a girl has to have something more adventurous than the waltz and the fox-trot in her repertoire these days. I'm paying a fortune for these tango lessons, and I'm not a natural dancer. I have to work hard and practice where I can. I thought I was quite safe here, halfway between

the dead"—she gestured in the direction of the graveyard—
"and the dying." Another flick of the hand towards the college
was accompanied by a derisory sniff.

Alarmed, Redfyre immediately asked, "Dying?"

"Oh, no need to sound the alarm! Put your bugle down and
stand at ease, copper. There's nothing to interest you here! I was
speaking figuratively. I meant in the sense of 'moribund.'
Elderly, stuck in their last-century ways. Some are over eighty,
some are just eighteen, but they're all stiff-collared stuffed
shirts. Nasty, hide-bound, misanthropic old fossils! Have they
engaged you to spy on me? You wouldn't believe how—"

"Hang on a minute!" He interrupted her outburst. The girl
was clearly deluded, if not completely loopy. "Copper, did you
say?" he asked. "But how on earth . . . ? You can't see my flat feet
from down there!"

"My bedroom window overlooks your front door." Another
vague wave in the direction of the upper storeys of the master's
lodge gave an explanation. "I see you coming and going with
your little white dog and your tall dark sergeant. The handsome
chap . . . looks like an advertisement for Dr. Benson's Beef-U-
Uppo pills. Before starting the treatment."

"Ah yes. His figure, indeed, lacks substance, but his moustache makes up for it. It is much admired about town. Name
of Thoday. The man, I mean . . ." he burbled.

"So glad you changed the colour of your front door," she said
inconsequentially. "Green is a much more suitable colour for
that house. The shiny black was too . . . citified. This isn't
Downing Street in London, though the troops of helmeted
bluebottles you attract to your doorstep give the impression of
Bow Street. All you lack is the blue light above the door."

Redfyre had heard enough.

This was an entirely predictable, overexcited reaction to
being discovered engaging in what she clearly judged to be a

dubious activity, he reasoned, but he decided to call a halt to her outpouring. Wiping the smile from his face and raising an eyebrow in an expression he hoped would give a stern dignity to his demeaning posture teetering atop a water butt, he cut short her stylistic evaluations. "I see my life is under the microscope, or should I say telescope?" he said, meaning it to cut. "Is this the moment when I ask *you*: Have they engaged you to spy on me? Well? Miss, er . . . ?"

"Oops!" Suddenly speechless, she smiled, recognising and acknowledging her mistake with a shrug. "Fair cop, Mr. Copper!"

"Ah! Then we are each confessing to episodes of Peeping Tommery?" he asked lightly. "Shall we find ourselves guilty and let us off with a caution?"

She smiled again and he realised he was speaking to a very pretty girl with an uncontrolled fuzz of light brown hair, large brown eyes and a trim figure. Not quite doolally perhaps, though he could not be certain about the concealed catapult.

"Very well. I agree. Off you go, then! I wouldn't want to keep you from your mystery solving." She turned on her heel, flashed a cheeky back *boleo* with her right leg and set off back across the lawn.

Now, who in hell was that? Redfyre asked himself as he scrambled down from his perch. Mystery solving? The wretched girl had just added another one to his list.

"AH! *THERE* YOU are, Johnny darling!"

Redfyre had dashed into his front room and grabbed the telephone receiver before it stopped ringing.

"And that's precisely where you should *not* be!" said his aunt Henrietta in reprimand. "You ought to be here in my drawing room, sipping your first sherry. You're expected for lunch here in Madingley. Had you forgotten? Your cousin Hugh arrived half an hour ago, and he's making himself useful. And very much at home ..."

Redfyre sank disconsolately into his chair, and starting with an anguished "Lord! Can it really be one o'clock already?" began to mumble his excuses. A short but punchy account of his action-packed morning followed.

Aunt Hetty was all understanding. "How exciting! I can't wait to hear about it. I shall go back into the drawing room and give out the reason for your delay at once. Discovering and ministering to a corpse in a graveyard, I shall say. That will entertain the girls! We have two female guests, new to the village—absolute corkers, both!—and they're dying to meet my dashing nephew. So, nephew, dash! It's ten minutes on your cycle. You'll be in time for the soup if I press everyone to have a second aperitif. Oh, and Johnny? Graveyards? Corpses? Be *very* sure to wash your hands, won't you?"

CHAPTER 11

GRANTCHESTER, SUNDAY, THE 18TH OF MAY, 1924

"**E**mma and Genevieve! Well, for once, Aunt, you did not exaggerate!" Redfyre said. "Top-notch young ladies, in their different ways. Sensible Emma or sparkling Genevieve? I think I can squeeze another cup out of this," he said, waving the coffeepot temptingly under her nose. Companionably, they finished off the last of the coffee, smiling to hear intermittent snores from Uncle Gerald's armchair and pleased to be able to speak frankly to each other in the peace of the drawing room.

"I thought you'd like them. They'll be a welcome addition to the village. Sociable, outspoken, active . . ."

"Potential recruits, are you thinking, for your illicit group of female desperadoes? Your hive of hexagons, buzzing with charming workers who tempt a man with honey and then sting him in the derrière? Your Third Way Forward Suffragists?"

"I can think of more attractive and more accurate ways of expressing it. But yes, why not? They will both have an entrée into university life once they're settled. They could be of use to us. I shall introduce them to Suzannah and Earwig, and they will judge general ability, identify particular skills and connections and advise as to deployment."

"Great Heavens! It's like taking a briefing from the head of MI5!" Redfyre smiled in a vain attempt to hide his irritation. "What are you, Aunt? Special advisor to *M*?"

"No, but she is pretty chummy with *K*!" The voice rumbled

up from the depths of Gerald's buttoned leather armchair. "Vernon Kell. Since last month, we should say Colonel Kell, don't you know. State security wallah. Runs the show. Very much in favour of the police—you ought to know that—and a fan of Sherlock Holmes. Hetty knows his wife . . . Constance, is it? Pretty little thing, she used to be. Has had a lot to put up with. All that China business . . . Puts a strain on a marriage, that sort of thing." He went back to his snoring.

"Ah," Redfyre said, subdued. "Another sheet in your CID file I have not been granted sight of, Aunt?"

He was teasing about the file. It did not exist, at least as far as he was aware. As he was the officer who had discovered the existence of his aunt's clandestine guerrilla women's group, he would surely have been asked to initiate such a document. And he would have been left chewing his pencil at the first line. For a start, he would never have been able to come up with a title for such an amorphous, anonymous gang of shape-shifters; it was hard to grasp the essence of a unit whose members had smartly chosen not to give themselves a name. And to go on, he could have written nothing intelligible about their activities and organisation. What were they? A secret suffragist society? Political pressure group? He knew what MacFarlane's comment would have been on viewing a draft of such a report: *A mob of underemployed, overprivileged trouble-seekers. Now the older ones have got the vote, they'll turn their attention to some other cause . . . banning things: beer, betting, dog-racing, St. Bruno's Rough Shag and anything else they think men are fond of.*

They never met as a group, and most of them had no idea of the identity of the others or the scope of the whole organisation. Hetty's husband, Gerald, had been an officer in the South African War over twenty years before, and perhaps his tales had inspired her in devising the tactics of the group. Like the much-feared yet admired Boer commando fighting units, they operated in small cells of about half a dozen, comrades who defended one another to the death and never left their wounded behind. And, in common with those leathery old Dutch farmers, Hetty's girls knew their terrain, appeared from nowhere, shot from the hip and disappeared into the bush. Redfyre would have been vastly entertained by the whole concept and cheered them on, had he not been chilled to the bone by their determination to achieve their aims by a ruthless cunning and disregard for their own safety.

Their campaign last Christmas had unintentionally triggered a series of disasters—three deaths, two attempted murders, and several ruined college reputations. And yet, as far as he could ascertain, the ladies were undeterred and unrepentant. They hadn't confided in him—he was a handy tool to be used when the occasion demanded it—but he had an uneasy feeling that they hadn't abandoned their schemes.

Hetty had drawn up a list of their aims and brazenly made him privy to it. He had noted and, in spite of the quibbles raised by his conscience, his sex and his profession, he had approved:

THE VOTE FOR ALL WOMEN AND MEN OVER TWENTY-ONE (IRRESPECTIVE OF PERSONAL CIRCUMSTANCES). WOMEN MEMBERS TO BE VOTED INTO SEATS IN PARLIAMENT IN GREATER NUMBERS (FOUR OUT OF A POSSIBLE FOUR HUNDRED SEATS IS REALLY NOT ON. AND THE PRESENT ACCEPTANCE THAT IT IS PERMISSIBLE FOR A WOMAN TO "KEEP WARM" THE SEAT OF HER SICK HUSBAND SHOULD BE OUTLAWED). THE ADMISSION OF TWO HUNDRED MORE FEMALE UNDERGRADUATES TO THE UNIVERSITY EACH YEAR. DEGREES TO BE AWARDED TO WOMEN WHO HAVE FOLLOWED THE COURSES, PASSED THE EXAMINATIONS AND EARNED THE QUALIFICATION.

This last to be retrospective. Hetty apparently still had her eyes on her own doctorate.

The other two national suffragist organisations had taken their eye off the ball during the war years, diverting their energy and skills into war work and encouraging men to join up and fight. They had called a truce from which, according to Hetty, they had failed to awaken. Even the firebrand Pankhursts had lost their impetus during the war years and declared at its conclusion that woman's influence was higher, her political rights more extended in England than in any other part of the world.

"Untrue! And a betrayal of the cause!" was Hetty's opinion on that. Years of progress seemed about to be lost unless her nameless ones could work their dangerous magic, which ran to blackmail, coercion, seduction and Lord knew what other forms of skulduggery.

"I'm sorry, Johnny," Hetty said quietly. "I see that my girls continue to be an annoyance to you. I'm afraid we involved you in matters you'd really rather not be concerned with last Christmas."

"Oh, I don't know, multiple murder is very much my concern. Corpses littering the streets of Cambridge will always be something of an annoyance. And you've apologised—quite unnecessarily, Hetty—about six times." He added with the mock severity of a nanny, "You know I don't accept apologies unless they come with the intention of never repeating the sin or the crime or the carelessness."

"Pompous prat!" said the armchair. "You should have taught the boy better manners, Hetty. What you're both missing is the real reason those two girls were putting on such a show. They were delighted to be here, without their parents. Note that! They had a good time just being themselves, I do believe. And in no small measure thanks to Johnny's bottomless fund of

funny—and risqué—stories. Those young ladies are both long-
ing for experience. In search of something, I'd judge," he
finished cryptically.

"I'd thought much the same myself," Redfyre said. "And I'll
tell you, whatever it is they're looking for, it's not me!"

Hetty sighed. "Sadly, you're right, Johnny. There you are—
good-looking, well-educated, decorated soldier with the gift of
the gab, and they are initially charmed, but then they learn that
you're a working man and poor as a church mouse. Nothing
wrong with that in today's world, but it's the *kind* of work you
do, John. 'My nephew's a policeman,' I say and watch the smile
fade from their lips, the light from their eyes. However point-
edly I put out the information that you are my heir and will
cut up for a fair amount of tin when I go, it's too late. The
damage is done." She sighed. "I don't observe the same adverse
reaction to your cousin Hugh. The mention of 'stocks and
shares' and 'the city' makes women of my generation fall back
a step and hastily change the subject, but these young things—
well, it seems to *arouse* their interest if anything. This pair
certainly put him to the question! In spite of . . ." She frowned
and hesitated.

"Hugh's appearance *is* a bit eccentric and his voice rather
loud," Redfyre admitted, saving her from a discourteous comment. "But—"

"Hugh has the looks and the voice of a bullfrog! Can't stand
the young tyke!" Gerald grumbled. "Banking! Huh! The chap
gambles with other people's money and calls it a profession."

"He's doing rather well, Uncle!" Redfyre objected. "I was
quite envious. I'm fond of cousin Hugh. I've always found him
dependable and—yes—clever. He's a good man to have in your
corner. Really, he's not as bad as he paints himself. And perhaps
the girls intuitively understood that."

"I'll tell you what the girls intuitively understood, my boy, and that's the implications of his gleaming new car parked in pride of place on my carriage sweep. Oh yes, I think those young ladies were aware of what he had to offer. I noticed that they accepted with alacrity when he asked them if he might drive them back to their homes. In his speed model, open-topped tourer Bentley. In British Racing Green. Wouldn't have minded a spin myself."

"A stinging reminder that all *I* have to offer in the way of transport is a ride in a borrowed police car. An old Riley with prisoner restraints in the back seats and general smell of Saturday night's vomit." Redfyre grinned. "Or, if she's a fresh air fiend, a precarious seat on the crossbar of my bike."

Hetty chuckled. "The girl who would rise to that challenge is the girl for you, Johnny! But Gerald's right. When it comes to choosing a life partner, most young women are impressed by a Bentley. It's only natural."

Gerald grunted. "More fool them! Tricky business, embarking on the marriage stakes. Not many make it to the last fence. Never mind looks and cash, young women ought to be hunting down a bloke who can make them laugh. We're a long time married. Ask your aunt! Without the stimulus of my daily quips, she'd have slipped her moorings years ago."

"True," Hetty agreed after some thought. "Though it was Gerald's detailed knowledge of Weatherbys Stud Book and his fabled collection of grape scissors that proved irresistible. Well, that's two more to cross off my list of possible girls about Cambridge."

Redfyre decided to head his aunt off the unwelcome subject of his continued failure to do his patriotic duty and marry one of the many women left bereft by the recent war. But he would use the bait of gossip to turn her head towards a more useful discussion.

"I met a strange girl today, Aunt. She's the reason I was late for lunch. I wondered if you might know anything of her. Her name would be a good place to start. I don't suppose your university acquaintances extend into the rather remote fastness of Jude's?"

"I knew the last master quite well," Hetty replied. "I have yet to meet the new one. Dr. Cornelius Wells. A classicist, I believe. Go on, though I can't imagine why you'd be talking about a female and Jude's in the same sentence."

"Sentence?" his uncle harrumphed. "Not even in the same paragraph! Not in the same tome! Fanatically against all things female. Including their own mothers, I shouldn't wonder. Perhaps especially their own mothers. Started off as a monkish establishment in the fourteenth century and has remained practically unchanged through dissolutions and purges into the twentieth. They've always had a reputation for remoteness and austerity, which they manage to offset by an extremely high academic standard. I'm amazed to hear my wife confess that she knew the last master." He peered over his pince-nez at Hetty, affecting the expression of a wronged husband making his dreaded discovery. "She leads a life quite her own, you know." The expression softened to one of surprise and pride. "Though I can't imagine why one of those marble saints at Jude's would have exchanged a word with my Hetty. Or where he would have stumbled across her. She's exaggerating again—"

"No. I said I *knew* him. I didn't say he liked me, Gerald. He didn't. And the feeling was mutual. He was the most appalling old stick insect! He certainly took his time departing this world. The line between indisposition and death was blurred by the passage of about twenty years."

"Many gentlemen turned their faces to the wall when Victoria snuffed it." Gerald nodded.

"Well, you're no use to me, Aunt. But it's clear that at least one barrier has fallen in that establishment. I met a girl who was, um, taking a stroll in the master's garden this morning."

"What on earth were *you* doing there?"

"I wasn't there. I was in the graveyard next door—the scene of the crime I told you about—looking over the wall and saw a strange girl dressed in purple, practising tango steps and singing to herself in Spanish. An exchange of views followed—I can scarcely call it a conversation. She said she was preparing for a May ball."

"Well, it wouldn't be the *Jude* college ball," Henrietta said knowledgeably. "I believe they're still arguing about the suitability of including the quadrille on the dance card. If the tango is on the menu, you'd be looking at one of the large, go-ahead colleges. I know that a number of King's men frequent the town's dancing clubs. They could have decided to inject a bit of life into the usual run of veletas and fox-trots and hire a tango band from London. Johnny, why don't you get hold of a ticket, ring up Earwig and invite her to go with you? She's a very skilled little dancer, you know. She goes to classes every Friday evening with Madame Dorine at the Palais de Danse round the back of the Corn Exchange."

"Good idea! Will you ring her, or shall I?" Redfyre asked, but his aunt was already scurrying to the telephone in the hall.

TEN MINUTES LATER, she was back, quivering with information.

"Yes. It's King's. And Earwig would love to keep you company if you can get your hands on a ticket. She reminds you it's Saturday week and tickets are most probably all sold. And she thinks she can identify your mysterious lady in purple! She guesses she could well be the most recent recruit to Madame Dorine's stable. Light brown hair—short and fluffy? Medium height? Slim on the whole, if a bit busty? Neat feet?"

"Possibly. I know twenty girls who'd answer that description."

"Now what else did Earwig say? Ah yes! It won't mean anything to you, Johnny, but she said the girl she's met is the spitting image of one of the fairies in *Flower Fairies of the Spring*—the children's book that came out last year—the Heartsease Fairy. Page ten."

"What on earth is 'Heartsease,' Aunt? And more pertinently, what on earth would Earwig be doing rootling about in a fairy book?"

"It's the country name for wild pansy. You must have seen them every springtime in the Grantchester meadows. When I was a small thing, the village children used to call it 'jump-up-and-kiss-me.' You know, the little violet-coloured, pointy-chinned flower faces that always look as though they're smiling up at you? Puckering up to give you a smacker?"

"We have the wrong girl, then." Redfyre scowled. The sharp tongue, bad temper and clenched right fist put him more in mind of that other purple flower of the English countryside—the thistle—and he said so.

"Not at all prickly! She's friendly when approached but reserved, according to Earwig. It must have been something you said, darling."

"I assume our friend Earwig lost no time in approaching?"

"Of course. She moved in. And when she found out who the girl was, she must have been pleased she'd made the effort to get alongside. This could be quite a coup! A happy find!"

"Well? Are you going to tell us she's a Pankhurst? Or a Fawcett?"

"Not quite that, I'm afraid, but intriguing all the same." Henrietta announced, smugly: "Your mysterious dancer would appear to be a Miss Rosamund Wells. Twenty-two years old, unattached as far as anyone knows. Family home in London.

Her mother having died last year, young Rosamund has gone to live with her father, Dr. Cornelius Wells, the newly appointed master of Jude's. In his newly acquired fiefdom, just over the wall from Johnny."

"God help the poor child!" said Gerald fervently. "To be installed in Jude's! A cruel and undeserved punishment for any female. I don't like to think of little Pansy-Face trapped behind that wall with two hundred reclusive, hair-shirted misanthropes! You must ride to her rescue, my boy!"

THE TELEPHONE CALL that greeted Redfyre on his return to Cambridge was from Dr. Beaufort.

"Glad to have got you at last, Inspector. Listen. We have an appointment with the marble slab tomorrow morning. I have to declare that I made a start on this right away—for various perfectly good scientific reasons, which I will explain when I see you. Could you make it earlier than we had suggested? Eight o'clock? I find I have two other cases queuing. No, nothing concerning you—there's a farmyard incident involving a pitchfork from over the Norfolk border and a domestic skull-splitting in the Mill Road MacFarlane hasn't bothered you with.

"But—your intriguing Dunstan chap continues to throw up the surprises. Contents of gut speak volumes and, Redfyre—they're not saying what we were expecting at all!"

CHAPTER 12

B y eight o'clock on a Monday morning, Addenbrooke's Hospital on Trumpington Street was well into the new day, alive with uniformed staff moving purposefully about. Redfyre found his own pace always quickened in emulation of their confidence when he entered the building. He took off his hat and, as he made his way down the corridor that led to the pathology laboratory, was warmed to note how many of the nursing staff recognised him and greeted him by his rank as they swished past in their starched headdresses, even offering him refreshment:

"Good morning, Sister."

"Good morning, Inspector."

"It's a fine May morning, Nurse!"

"Have you had breakfast, Inspector?"

"I've just sampled the Chelsea buns at Fitzbillies . . ."

"Then we can have nothing further to tempt you!"

He admired the smiling, efficient staff, working at the fore-front of medical research and care, and reflected that the whole machine was kept moving smoothly along on the rails by a woman: the matron. Redfyre had always entertained hopes that someone would have the wit to sack this valuable lady and reinstate her as Head of the Cambridgeshire Constabulary. Or Prime Minister.

Spearheading the pathology department, though he

modestly tried to give the impression that he was struggling against overwhelming scientific forces, was Dr. Beaufort. The two crime-fighting professionals liked and understood each other, recognising they shared not only the same qualities of intelligence and dedication, but the same flaws, which they found it wiser never to name, not even to each other.

Beaufort was already at work on the tramp's body when Redfyre arrived and he involved his colleague at once in his deliberations.

"It's the stomach contents that this case—rather precariously—rests on. Something of a surprise there, as I told you. But let's get quickly through the underpinnings, shall we?

"Identity: sorry, we're no further forward. Full examination of every item of clothing revealed nothing more than you got from your initial examination in the churchyard. No helpful name tapes, no tattoos, no identity tags. The suit underneath the worn old greatcoat was a good one, but again, the pockets had been cleared out. Nothing useful from the underwear: clean, ordinary Mr. Everyman stuff, the kind you'd buy at Eaden Lilley. No laundry marks, so presumably, these were washed wherever he called home. A tie—striped. You thought you recognised it as a Girton tie, I remember. Again, a tramp can come by these things as part of a charity handout bundle, or even off a washing line. It could be a Cambridge college tie—worn with cheeky sarcasm! Socks heavily darned. Shoes resoled and worn down. They've done quite a mileage. Full details noted down for you. And the items themselves bagged up for further inspection.

"General care of person: for a tramp, this is odd. Now, Inspector—you're going to have to do a bit of rethinking here. We deduced—on account of the invitation card in his pocket— that he was going out for dinner with these loonies who call themselves a dining club, and to that end, he might well have made an effort and had a bath and haircut and all the rest of it and—yes—he was freshly shaven, his hair freshly cut and he still smelled faintly of coal tar soap or the equivalent. His finger- and toenails were clean and trimmed. Now, I can accept that, in deference to the treat to come, he might have taken some trouble with his hygiene, but if this bloke was indeed a tramp, there'd be other clues to his condition. I mean the life of a tramp, with little access to running water and soap, if lived for any length of time, leads to bunions, blisters and callouses and the sort of ingrained dirt that a quick scrub behind the ears before dinner can't hide. On this chap, there was none of that. This is a gent who's been bathing regularly for years.

"General musculature: he's lithe and whippy, naturally a lean type. I wouldn't say undernourished, but there isn't an ounce of spare flesh on him. His teeth are in reasonable nick. I've done a dental plan of the mouth for you. A few fillings done some years ago, but when he flashed a smile at you, you wouldn't have looked the other way. In fact, in his prime, he must have been a good-looking fellow."

"His eyes? I never noted the colour," Redfyre said.

"Take a look now. Hard to say all this time after the event, but—dark grey? The sort that change with the light, but on the grey-blue spectrum. Definitely not brown. The hair—now pepper and salt, but must once in his youth have been a light brown. He could be Scandinavian or a bloke from Southend-on-Sea."

"Any wounds?"

"Oh yes. He's been in the wars, this chap! I mean—*actually* fighting in wars. Up close, front-line stuff. The Great War? He's about fifty, I'd say. So he could have taken part at the upper end of the recruitment age in the last one. It's just possible. A lot of keen blokes in their forties signed up, lying about their age. People turned a blind eye in the early days when the recruitment fever was raging. Nobody wanted to be handed a white feather of cowardice by some busybodying harridan on a street corner. 'Sir! Why are you walking the streets in civvies? Be a man and join up!' Even if you were merely being employed as a storekeeper back here in Blighty or over there in Northern France, shoeing horses miles behind the front where you could do no damage, it gave you the right to wear a uniform. And that's what most men of all ages yearned for: an outward sign of patriotic duty faithfully done."

"But he's been wounded, you say?"

"Yes. Here, you see. And here. Well healed. Old ones. But the sort you get in battle, not streetfighting down King Street on a Saturday night. Two bullet wounds, one in each arm. Flesh only penetrated, not bone. He was twice lucky. And this here's a graze in the flesh over the ribs that looks very like a glancing lunge from—of all things—a British bayonet or a blade with similar profile. Typical battle wound."

"God, you're right! Seen enough of those to confirm," Redfyre muttered. "Sharp cutting weapon, anyway. Couldn't be an assegai, could it? Too early? When were the Zulu wars?"

"1879. Too early for our chap. The first war against the Boers was sixteen years after that—1895. Hardly more than a skirmish, the throwing down of gauntlets. And the big one, the Second Anglo-Boer War, was in the final years of Victoria's reign. 1899 to 1902 or thereabouts. When did the old lady die? 1901, was it?"

"I believe it was. So, we're looking at a man who could have fought, certainly not against the Zulu, but against the Boer, either in the first or the second South African war. And/or played some part in the most recent Great War against the Germans."

"And there's always the Irish troubles. Rifles and sharp implements not unknown over the western sea . . . I reckon that narrows his identity down to about a million men." The doctor gave a hopeless shrug. "No trace of that regimental badge he might have been wearing? Did your blokes turn anything up? No? Pity. But there are pinholes on the left lapel. There was a badge of some sort at some time in there. Dislodged when the body was being dragged about? You're sure the men haven't found something in the grass? Perhaps over the fence, then. Old soldiers sometimes throw away their medals in a fit of belated regret, but they always hold on to the symbol of their regiment. Their soldierly family."

"Indeed. If they lose that sentimental tie, they are surely cut adrift."

With an apologetic smile, Redfyre fished in the pocket of his own tweed jacket and held out his hand, a small, shining object visible in his palm.

"Ah! Silver for an officer, wreath of laurel encircling a cross. The upper ends linked by a tablet saying 'Waterloo.' Now, there's a giveaway! Rifle Brigade," the doctor identified confidently. "Greenjackets. Sharpshooters. Among other things. Darlings of the Duke of Wellington in their heyday. A distinguished history." He gave Redfyre a keen look. "Am I to infer that you are one of those cases where a bloke's name influences his career or character?"

The inspector was puzzled for a moment, then, "Oh, I see! No, no! Never occurred to me. Being a country child, I was always good with a gun. I won the shooting cup at school. When the last lot broke out I had no family military tradition to follow, none of that 'I'll be following my father into the Guards,' stuff, so I went where my skills, if not my inclination, took me. The recruiting officers agreed, and I was accepted. Only four years of my life were spent in the army, but I understand the loyalty, the pride a soldier feels in his own regiment."

"And if you should be discovered dead in a back alley one

night without your ID in your pocket, your old regiment would be able to identify and claim you before even your mother was aware. But our search reveals nothing of the sort on this old bugger."

"Sadly, no. The regiments keep strict and full records. If we could place him with one of them, they'd tell us where and why he was discharged, good and bad conduct, and what he had for breakfast. And, Beaufort—speaking of food—you were going to tell me about his last supper?"

The doctor waved in the direction of a line of labelled specimen jars on the shelf of a cupboard. "All present and correct and ready for your inspection. No noxious substances, so you don't need a mask. He was quite definitely not fed any known poisons or drugs. Apart from the alcohol, which I'll come to . . ."

He pointed to the bottles and drew Redfyre's attention to the numbers on the front. "I thought I'd treat it like a menu and go through the courses in reverse order of discovery, if you see what I mean."

Redfyre peered at the bottles with distaste. "I can only count to three. Short menu? Hardly what we were expecting for a bloke who's just been invited to break bread with a coterie of epicures."

"Quite so. But there *were* eels! Now, how on earth could you have foreseen the eels?"

Redfyre gaped. "I didn't! I was making a silly joke, Beaufort. Displaying my very sketchy historical knowledge of food-induced deaths."

"Well, here they are. The first course. Not lampreys, I think, just common or garden eels out of the River Ouse a few miles north of here. They're in season at the moment. And these ones—a modest portion, by the way—are what a Cambridge man or a Londoner would call 'jellied.' In the Pie and Mash shops, they shuck their eels into rounds and boil them up in water and vinegar, flavour the stew with black pepper, nutmeg and lemon or herbs and let them cool. The eel is a gelatine-producing fish, according to an angling friend of mine, and what you get in your little round dish is usually four chubby pieces of eel in a shiny and nutritious jelly. Yum!" he added unconvincingly. "Kept the Victorian poor on their feet and working for decades."

"Right. And to follow that?"

"Jar number two. Common or garden apple pie. Mostly pastry, with a touch of blackberry jam for colour. Washed down with water. And that's it. A modest meal."

"Jar three seems to be almost empty."

"Yes it is. The last swab. And taken not from his gullet, but the inside of his mouth. Brandy. From the bottle we found with the body, I'm guessing. He didn't ingest any. Someone might have poured a shot into his mouth after death and splashed it about a bit, hoping the lumpen plod would assume he was a drunk."

"I'm afraid I did!"

"It's very easy to envisage a tramp who'd strayed into the college and helped himself to a bottle of booze. One of his fellow roughs challenging him for possession in the churchyard where he'd sloped off to down the brandy in peace and killing him in a drunken rage. A fight between down-and-outs, that's all. 'Nothing of interest to see here! Move along!' is what you're supposed to be saying, Inspector."

"Mm, I think you've solved the case, Doctor. MacFarlane may have been right again. Motive and commission of the crime understood, but neither party identifiable due to social circumstances. He had a feeling this case would be one for the 'coffin box.' Do you know?"

"Know of it? I'm a contributor! I believe quite a few of my

reports have ended up in that sinister little receptacle, one or two involving ingredients worthy of 'The Forme of Cury,' royal cookbook from the Middle Ages. I mean … Swan? Wild boar? Foie gras? Who on earth puts things like that on the table this century, and in Cambridge?"

"And kills the guest so soon after supper the ingredients are still identifiable in the laboratory? What *did* he say to annoy the chef?"

"Well, if you envisage a killer chef on the rampage, look no further than Bert the jellied eel maker and the pie man in Cambridge Market!"

"Do you have a time for the consumption of this meal?"

"Yes. From about teatime onwards on Friday, if my calculations about the time of death are correct. And the cause of death? I confirm our first estimates. Pressure on the carotid artery. Here and here. Do you see the bruising? Blood choke. The assailant knew exactly where to place his thumbs. It would have been over in seconds. No sign of resistance. And the attack came from in front. I'd say the victim knew his murderer and was not expecting trouble."

"Mm. Thank you. The pie stall is open for business every day but Sunday. It's certainly a possibility. I'll go and interview Bert about his jellied eels this afternoon, when MacFarlane's finished with me."

"Well, if you find yourself doing an exchange of recipes, ask Bert about the herb he favours. Every pie man has his favourite for eels, I'm told. Whoever cooked these loves his dill. Good choice, but unusual. Oh, and there was celery seed in there, too."

"WELL, WHAT DO you make of that!" MacFarlane slapped a large printout of a black-and-white photograph in front of his inspector. It was the item from the coffin box that he'd chosen to present first. Knowing that his boss was something of a showman at heart, Redfyre expected that he'd selected the most jaw-dropping of the pieces of evidence on the cold cases, and he leaned forward with anticipation of thrills or intrigue.

Finally, "Um," he said. "Er . . ."

"Ha! Speechless, are you? Not surprised! You're looking at the most worrying scene encountered in Cambridge crime fighting since the camera was invented."

"I'm afraid I'm not seeing what you're seeing, then, sir," Redfyre muttered. Feeling that something further was needed, he launched into a hesitant description of the subject, hoping that something pertinent would occur to him as he stumbled along. "It's a good shot of the Fitzwilliam Museum in Trumpington Street. Taken from across the street at an angle—which is the only way to encompass such a grand façade. Those bold columns, the giant portico, enormous tympanum laden with sculpture . . . I can't be sure whether it suggests a Roman or an Egyptian architectural influence. It certainly doesn't speak to me of Grecian grace . . ." This was offered uncertainly, and he waited for the shot that would sink him.

A sigh and a rolling of the eyes greeted his comments. "None of those, you chump! It's British! It's got the broad shoulders of a pugilist, the swagger of a bulldog. The architect was a pupil of Sir John Soane—George Basevi, the chap who gave us Belgrave Square and Ely prison. It's the architecture of empire! Everything the Victorians had to say about their country is there in stone. Look at the lions!"

"The lions? Ah yes, funny how such an exotic animal has been adopted by the British. *Gardant, passant* or like this pair, *couchant*, they're everywhere. Cuddly on the outside, but watch out for the teeth and claws. In fact, there are four of these beasts. I've long admired them. Two are on guard at the northern side and two snarling out towards the south. Only the southern pair visible here, of course. When I was a child, I was brought into town by a new nanny one morning and managed to escape her vigilance. By the time she caught up with me, I was halfway up the side of this one here, nearest the—"

"I said, *Look at the lions!*"

At last he saw it. "Oh! Sir, would you hand me your magnifying glass?"

Glass in hand, Redfyre passed it slowly over the lion he'd attempted to scale. "It appears to have grown an extra-shaggy mane . . . Oh, Good Lord!"

MacFarlane was all satisfied smiles. "Well, *you* didn't manage to get up there, but someone did. Back in 1919, three years before you arrived on the squad. That's not a thickening of the mane. It's a figure slumped over its neck. The lion has a rider! And the rider is a corpse! Some joker killed a man—knife stab to the heart—and parked him up there for all to see. And that must have taken a bit of effort and care in the dark, though if he was lurking about next morning watching for a reaction from the great British public, he must have been a bit disappointed! People bustle along here in their droves in the morning going about their business, and how many even noticed? If they did, they probably thought it was just another boring, juvenile joke by a bunch of drunken undergraduates. It wasn't spotted until a sharp-eyed nurse on her way into work saw that something was amiss and she approached, took a look, probably reached for his pulse and decided that this was a matter for the Cambridge CID. It still is."

"The placing looks very dramatic from the street," Redfyre commented. "What you can't see is that immediately behind there's a useful flight of stone steps between the lions. I managed to get up there using them on four-year-old legs. But hefting a lifeless body about—that would take some strength. Or backup."

The superintendent passed a second photograph to Redfyre. "A close-up of the unfortunate. I see the body has been secured in place by a rope fastening his hands together and passed around the lion's neck. Did the rope . . . ?"

"First thing they checked. It was the *only* clue, really—his clothes had been gone over and cleared of all evidence. The length of rope had been taken from a pile of rejected odds and ends round the back of the museum, where there was building work of some sort going on. Opportunistic? Or done by some perfectionist who's taken the trouble to do a reconnaissance of the site beforehand and nick a few feet of suitable cord. A planned killing? In fact, the victim was quickly identified. Well-known bloke about Cambridge, as it happens. Rather too well known! Quite a few people had a bone to pick with him, and the CID had a list as long as your arm of people who laughed and said good riddance when they heard the news of his demise. The knife used was the dead man's own. Fancy job with an ivory handle. Handle wiped clean, of course. Knife left in the wound. So again a dead end."

"Anyone I might know?"

"Shouldn't think so. He was one Ricardo de Angelis. 'Chiqui' to his friends and dancing partners."

"Heavens! A dancing instructor, are you saying?"

"Tango expert. From South America, he claimed. Worked in the Cambridge Academy of Terpsichore or some such. 'Madame Dorine's' to you and me. That's Dorine with an *I*, not *ee*. She really is French. Ricardo was very popular with the ladies who passed through his hands every week. Not so much with the men in the ladies' lives. Ooh dear! I was a DI in those days, and it was my case. I know who wanted him dead. Never able to prove it."

"Are you going to confide or leave me floundering?"

"One of his devoted and impressionable partners was Lady

Amelia Bullen, daughter of the Earl of Brancaster. An elopement with 'Chiqui' was planned shortly before someone decided
enough was enough and had the lad topped."

"*Had* him topped?"

"The father of the would-be bride had the strongest motive.
The Right Honourable Earl."

MacFarlane was the only man Redfyre knew who could
convey a capital letter in speech.

"I watched him drink a celebratory glass of champagne in
my presence when I went over to his family seat in the Godfor-
saken county of Norfolk to deliver the news. Gloating. Cackling.
Not a pretty sight. *He* knew that *I* knew he'd procured a murder,
and he didn't give a shit! Friends in high legal places, don't you
know. He was covered every which way. There was no possibility
that he could have attended to the matter personally—he's stuck
out there, miles from the nearest lemon and something of an
invalid these days." An expression of sly satisfaction betrayed
the superintendent's prejudice against all things aristocratic
and all things rustic. "Copped one up the Khyber, I believe.
Second Afghan bit of bother. Or would that be the third? All
the same, I suppose, being shot at from the rocks by vicious
tribal barmpots . . . And I took the precaution of putting one
of my good-looking detective constables into the kitchens for
a cup of tea and a slice of jam sponge while I was busy interviewing the master. The staff on these remote Norfolk estates
do love a good natter. And Constable Beck was all charm. He's
with the Met now and doing well. He got out of them the
information that the boss, the whole family and the staff were
tucked up in bed from an early hour on the night Chiqui
mounted his lion."

"But he had the cash and the clout to order up a killing by
other hands? And what other hands?"

MacFarlane considered this. "Clout, certainly. Not so sure

about the cash." He shrugged. "The going rate for a topping rises and falls faster than Mae West's bosom in midshimmy. Five years ago, we were just coming out of the war. There was a surplus of unemployed young men—trained killers, the lot of 'em, many with a souvenir German Luger hidden away in their kitbags being turned loose into the newly civilised world. Except that it wasn't. It was the same hard, grudging place it always had been. Some men—Londoners, mainly—hired out their skills. Surplus of gunmen, so lower fees charged. If he knew where to look, his lordship could have gotten a keen price. He'd have needed that. To my beady eye, the estate was looking as dilapidated as its owner. The housekeeper was moaning to DC Beck that they were understaffed. All the signs of an aristocratic family struggling with death duties and the other swingeing taxes the government put on them to help pay for the war. I'd say the earl couldn't afford the sum of money Chiqui usually demanded when he threatened elopement with some unfortunate girl."

"So this wasn't a one-off, doomed-from-the-outset affair?"

"Lord, no! Chiqui had form. A series of successful calculated extortion attempts. As long as he remained alive and fit to tango and the lady was still smitten, our Earl figured—quite rightly—that there must be the possibility of further demands or the ruining of the family name to consider. On the whole, a professional assassination was much cheaper and more certain of outcome for his lordship. He made sure that he and his household were well away from the scene and all accounted for at the moment the dirty deed was done."

"And that this information was duly passed on to your charming constable?"

"Constable Beck is bright as well as smarmy! He played along, don't worry! Certainly got more out of them than they got out of him."

Redfyre stirred uneasily. "But it's odd, sir. Your average professional killer doesn't go about laying his victims out in a very conspicuous position. He's in and out and back down his rat hole in the shortest possible time. He doesn't hang around rolling up his sleeves, flexing his muscles and hauling his handiwork into an eye-catching pose It's macabre!"

"Right! Cocking a snook, I'd call that. Taking the Mickey! And in Cambridge? Nah! Assassins operate in London. And their 'clients' tend to be foreign governments, business enterprises or criminal organisations clearing out spies, rivals, traitors . . . other professionals who understand the risks and play the game. They don't bother with a tuppenny-halfpenny dancing instructor, however annoying he was. And what sort of an assassin treats his target to a three-course dinner immediately before doing him in?"

He passed a sheet of paper with a short handwritten message to Redfyre.

"Finally! Here we have it. Contents of stomach: foie gras, turbot, beef Wellington. Three courses. No dessert, it would seem . . . probably watching his waistline. Plenty of wine and a large measure of brandy. Hmm . . . sir?"

"I know what you're going to ask. How in hell can they specify 'beef Wellington' rather than 'beef stew,' 'turbot' rather than 'cod'? Well, they can't, at least not definitively. That's the doc being helpfully imaginative. For our eyes only, this sheet. The page we actually filed is this one, listing the results item by item and in order of distance travelled down the tubes." He presented a further sheet bearing the heading of the Cambridge Medical Forensic Department. "Tedious but essential. A list compiled by a forensic scientist of the first order—Beaufort. He identified individual ingredients from the internal gloop and—bon viveur that he is—was able to reconstitute them into a credible menu. Beef in conjunction with the elements of pastry—flour and fat—amounts to beef pie, but when a soup-çon of black truffle is also present in the same stratum—well, that's your beef Wellington."

MacFarlane replaced the sheets and photographs in Chiqui's file and selected a second file.

"This one is less spectacular. But it's not so cold as the one you've just seen. Still on the books, in fact. I've parked these copies in here because I thought there might be a connection. The murder occurred just before your arrival on the force. I gave it to Inspector Beattie. Poor bloke—he had a lot of inter-ference from me, and even more annoyingly, the War Office. Or a section of it that's a little bit hush-hush. You'll see why. Again, we got a good shot of the crime scene before the press were aware and managed to clear up in double-quick time. You'll appreciate the need for that."

Redfyre looked carefully at the photographs, again admiring the clear eye and skill of the police photographer. He was look-ing at a very familiar Cambridge monument, and one much loved by him. A seven-foot-tall figure cast in bronze atop a plinth stood in the middle of the Hills Road at its junction with the short road that led to the railway station. The memo-rial to the men of Cambridgeshire who fell in the Great War.

Redfyre had seen many war memorials put up in the years after 1918 in France and England, and, unsurprisingly, they had all been sorrowful and restrained. Some were sculpted with such a depth of feeling and personal involvement that their beauty brought tears to the eyes of battle-hardened men. Nearly every family in the land had its known warrior, its own story of loss, injustice and sacrifice and their grief found expression in these respectful works of public art. But this one was the exception. Every time he passed the jaunty figure of the young soldier up high on his slab of Portland stone, Redfyre caught his eye and returned his triumphant smile. Sometimes he winked.

The private was striding out, bareheaded and rather dishev-elled, with the joyous freedom of natural movement that could only have been captured by a Canadian artist, Redfyre thought. Here was no stiff British solemnity, no elegant French cere-mony. The lad's helmet was in his left hand, held out in a gesture of offering to whoever was greeting him. It was deco-rated with a single rose and a garland of laurel leaves. Over his left shoulder, he carried his rifle from which swung a German helmet—the Tommy's favourite trophy of war—and a second victory wreath. The handsome lad was loping eagerly towards the town, flinging a last look back over one shoulder at the railway station where he had just left the crowded troop train bringing him back from France. Flinging off his old life and eagerly confronting the future. Job triumphantly done. It rep-resented, for Redfyre, hope, energy, and indomitable resilience.

"Taken some time after the third of July 1922 when the Duke of York unveiled it," Redfyre commented, unsettled by the silence and the knowing eyes scanning him for a reaction. "And judging by the presence of ceremonial poppy wreaths, this would have been on or near the eleventh of November, Armi-stice Day. Before my time, so it must have been the same year—1922. Wasn't there a bit of a problem with the ceremony? Troublemakers louting about with tomatoes and paint? An antiwar group? Communists?"

MacFarlane nodded. "They had a point to make. Usual boring, naïve rubbish from inexperienced young twerps. Away-from-home students, for the most part . . . They'd never try it on in their own homctowns. They were quickly seen off by a contingent of hot-tempered old survivors of earlier wars armed to the teeth with walking sticks and ear trumpets. A couple of our uniform boys judged their moment carefully, then strolled onstage and mopped up."

Redfyre pointed an unsteady finger at the base of the

memorial. "So *this* little tableau made its appearance some time during the dark hours of Saturday night and Sunday morning? If you'd missed it, it would have been found by ladies and gents heading for the Botanic Garden for their early Sunday constitutional, or worshippers on their way to the Catholic church a few yards away. You did well to clear up in the time."

"Yes. Not difficult. There was no blood spilled. It was just a matter of calling up an ambulance and stretcher from Addenbrooke's, which is all of a minute's drive away down the road. I think we weren't meant to notice it until much later."

"How did you hear of the incident?"

"We were alerted by one of our beat bobbies. The night shift. He was on his way back here to clock in and file his report, sun just up. A fine, clear morning. Good lad! He remembered that there'd been trouble here earlier in the day and made a detour to check that no one had sneaked back and done something silly. He walked straight past at first, did a double take and went back to have a closer look. He decided to stay on guard himself at the memorial to preserve the scene and managed to stop a passing messenger boy on a bike. Paid him sixpence to cycle to the station and raise the alarm. Another sharp lad. He bustled in and gave the constable's name and number first so we knew he wasn't having us on. And this is what greeted us when we arrived."

There was a second man in the photograph. He was not smiling, nor was he striding out towards a rosy future. He sat at the far end of the monument, facing the past, his back to the town, slumped against the plinth, head bowed over his chest.

"How did this one die?" Redfyre asked.

CHAPTER 13

"**B**roken skull. The Mourner at the Memorial died from the effects of a broken skull. Neat, quiet job. If you're a killer, it's a good technique to use against a target who is as strong as or stronger than yourself. What you do is tap your victim on the point of the jaw first to render him unconscious, then when he slumps to the ground, you sit on his chest, grab his head by the ears or the hair and bang it against a hard surface." MacFarlane illustrated the tapping, grabbing and banging sequence using his own meaty fists.

"Hard surfaces have accounted for more victims than knives or guns, I reckon. And there's always one to hand when you need it. Fireplaces and table legs being favourites, of course."

"Plenty of them around the area of a war memorial . . ." Redfyre suggested to move him on.

"Exactly. I set the lads to combing every inch of the pavings. Moving all those bloody wreaths about! Nothing untoward. But then, there wouldn't have been much of a sign. The subject had thick hair, and the skin of the scalp wasn't breached. Bruises and swelling had begun to gather, that's all."

"So he was killed elsewhere?"

"No. Right here on the spot! One sharp-eyed beat constable helping us out, thought of examining the plinth. He looked first all around the stonework at the height of a man's head, and there it was! On the western side, facing away from the road. Discreetly in shadow. The smear!"

"I thought you said there was no blood?"

"Brilliantine! He'd clearly been out on the town that night. Snappy dresser, our friend. Took good care of his appearance. Hair as thick as his, it needed a bit of restraint. There was a round patch—a stain on the stonework, and the gunk contained several hairs matching the hair of the dead man. He'd been lured round the back of the memorial and had his skull cracked, then was lowered and dragged the short distance round to the stern end."

Redfyre sighed. "And his last supper?"

A paper-clipped sheaf was put into the inspector's hand. "Read this in your own good time. You'll find the formula is becoming familiar. Wine and brandy again, following some fancy soup or other. My ma would have called it leek and potato, but I see the doctor has it down as vichyssoise. Then venison—appropriate for the time of year, November being well into game season, and after that, a blackberry tart and cheese."

"And his identity? Who was he, this man about Cambridge?"

"Again, all forms of identity were removed to slow us down. Odd, that! This killer apparently likes to suppress distinguishing facts about his victims. To allow himself the time to get away? But he goes to a lot of trouble to make sure their corpses are displayed, making them identifiable to anyone who knew them. There's no distortion or damage to any facial features. They all looked pretty enough for our photographer to take a portrait of them. We were getting the prints ready to take all round Cambridge to the hotels and restaurants seeking identification. They wouldn't have frightened the horses. But in the end, we didn't have to bother.

"We identified this one quite quickly. His wife came to the

desk at the station and reported him missing by lunchtime. Ernest Jessup. Working for a London firm of accountants. Big one. Ernest had brought his wife up with him on a remembrance weekend. A sort of keep-their-memories-bright reunion with old army pals. Cambridge this year because of the unveiling of the monument, which he'd duly attended that morning while his wife visited the shops. Mrs. Jessup was distraught, of course, and keen to be of assistance, but not very helpful. She didn't know her husband's army friends, wasn't interested in that part of his life at all. Couldn't consign the war and all who fought in it to the dust soon enough! She'd been lured to Cambridge with the promise of a trip to the theatre. She'd chosen a 'Music Box Revue' at the playhouse. It started at six. The husband left her half an hour later, sliding out, saying he felt a bit queasy. He'd come back before the end to walk her back to their hotel, he promised her.

"No surprises there—he'd done it before. He got bored and fidgety after five minutes. Claimed he couldn't stand confined spaces. But Mrs. J. claimed the only confined space that affected her husband was the one between his ears, though other parts of his anatomy came in for their share of criticism. Mrs. Jessup had remained at the show because she was having a good time and preferred to stay there on her own rather than have her gloomy husband ruin a perfectly good evening. Strapping lass, well able to take care of herself. Bit of a good-time girl before matrimony set in, I should judge. I gathered that all was not well in that ménage.

"Before you ask, Redfyre—yes, she did stay on for the whole performance. No chance she followed him out and did something lethal to him round the back of the war memorial." He paused for a moment, mouth twisting briefly in distaste. "Ahem! We know *that* because she ordered up two gin and tonics for the interval and the steward delivered them to her seat."

"The other seat remained unoccupied?"

"Oh yes. Right through from conjurer to audience sing-along finale, she was alone. The steward was quite certain on that point. He'd been keeping an eye out. Probably fancied his chances ... Anyhow, the husband didn't reappear. She stomped off back to the hotel for a gin-induced good night's slumber and came to report him to us as missing next morning. She identified him from one of the prints we'd had rushed through. Shrieks and screams!"

"Did she give anything away at all?"

"You've noticed people often say more than they realise in the stress of the moment? She did say something a bit odd. It sounded no more than the typical 'I told you so!' outburst you sometimes hear. But I followed it up.

"'I told him! I said time and time again, "Ernest, you're keeping bad company! You'll rue the day you took up with those scoundrels!"' she said.

"She regathered her wits about her, though, pulled herself together, shut her mouth and thought a bit before feeding me some cock-and-bull story about gambling debts he owed to a London mob. He'd come away to Cambridge thinking they were on his tail that weekend. She was lying. But I had no way of denying it at the time. Could just have been true. It only begins to look like a string of porkie-pies when taken in consideration with past—and future!—cases."

"Let's take stock, sir," Redfyre said hurriedly, watching his boss select two more files from the black box with enthusiasm. "We're looking at three unsolved cases so far: a Cambridge tramp, a London accountant and a South American tango teacher. A throttling, a skull-cracking and a stabbing. Who on earth would connect them? Apart from the oddity of the final meal, which I believe we can discount in view of the many hostelries in the city, there are two elements they have in common. One I don't yet understand the reason for—the bodies were flaunted, not hidden or disguised. Second, there's a military flavour to each. Working backwards, the tramp, Dunstan, we know to have been a soldier of some sort. The Londoner still maintained links with a group of old brothers-in-arms, according to his wife, and indeed, it was at a war memorial that the killer chose to place his victim. The tangoist—though not himself a warrior—we could argue was the victim of a military man. An officer who served in Afghanistan, I think you said?"

"Good man! You've been paying attention. Now take a gander at these two."

He slapped the two further files he'd selected in front of Redfyre. The inspector noted that they were of relatively recent date—opened and closed in the six months before he had joined the Cambridge force. MacFarlane went to the door to bellow for tea, leaving him to check the files for himself.

In the more recent of the two, dated June fifteenth, 1921, a distinguished figure, General Sanderson, had been discovered floating in solitary and perfectly dead state down the River Cam in a punt an hour after dawn, following the evening of the Trinity May Ball. He had been carried along by the current, lying apparently at ease on the cushions, eyes closed, hands tucked up casually beneath his head. The punt on its undirected course had been spotted by an early oarsman in a skiff who had stuck out an oar and manoeuvred it to the bank, where he'd engaged a student on a bike to summon help.

"Odd that it travelled so far downstream without getting stuck, sir?"

"I don't think it was ever expected to reach the North Sea. But its course was eased—the banks along that stretch are relatively frictionless. It's well kept, with all obstacles routinely removed and a strong current flowing. We even had punters come forward who remembered seeing the old bird, taking him to be asleep or drunk and giving his boat a helpful nudge off the bank back into the main stream.

MacFarlane's immaculate investigation involving measuring and timing the flow and linking it with the estimated time of death had borne little fruit. The ownership of the punt had been traced back to Clare College, where it had been reported missing when the two occupants, a Clare undergrad and his girl, had tied it to the bank whilst they went for a walk in the meadows bordering the stream at Coe Fen. The lad was adamant that he'd secured it firmly and thought it was taken deliberately. That stretch of river had been busier than Piccadilly Circus that night of the year, both on the water and the riverbanks, thick with raucous students trying to make it upstream to Grantchester for breakfast.

Passing by Redfyre's chair, MacFarlane commented, "Can you imagine the answers I got when I asked if they'd noticed anything unusual going on in the neighbourhood? Bloody smart alecks!"

Again, Redfyre found himself considering a military connection. "This general, sir, was he still active?"

"No. He retired straight after the war. He wasn't sacked—no one in the British army had the stomach for all that button cutting and epaulette chopping with all the real carnage still fresh. But he seems to have got up some people's noses, though no one would give the police any information. And their records are sealed to the bumbling plod."

"What was he doing in Cambridge? He's from Somerset."

"Came up with the lady wife to celebrate their oldest son's graduation, or end of his three-year stint, as doting parents do. Staying at the Garden House Hotel. Told Mrs. General that he was going out for a drink with some old college friends and she wasn't to wait up. That was the last she saw of him."

"He'd had a lot to drink, according to Beaufort, and a copious meal," Redfyre said, riffling through the sheets at speed.

"In view of the other cases, we followed this up. We wouldn't have bothered normally—people eat well when they're letting their hair down in Cambridge. But with the general, we checked every hostelry, restaurant, guesthouse and college kitchen in town. Not one had offered roast swan and all the regal trimmings. Not one! The nearest we could come to it was coq au vin."

"He died from a knock on the back of the head? Like Jessup?"

"Beaufort found splinters in the wound. Old wood, tarred with preservative. That cut down the search area. The general was bald, the wound unpleasant but clear. We found a match. On one of the planks shoring up the riverbank near the Anchor pub. Blood traces confirmed. The home office boys and the top brass, who were keen to keep a lid on it for their own undisclosed reasons, leapt on that. Clearly, the general had had a nasty accident while suffering the effects of overindulgence. 'Drinking too deep of the Old Falernian, eh, what!' was the conclusion of one old duffer—and he was the coroner! It was concluded that the chap had fallen, bashed his head and rolled right over the foot-high plank into a stolen punt that just happened to be drifting by. Huh!"

Redfyre retained the police scene of crime photograph and laid it out on the table in front of him. Then, sighing, he reached for the second file. "Who've we got here?"

"More 'Corpses About Cambridge,' I'm afraid. "January of that year. Fresh-fallen snow. It's the best documented scene of a killing in the annals of crime! There were present: more than twenty photographers, three reporters, two deans and one bishop. All on the spot at or near the time of death," he said with relish. "They all had plenty to say, and not one word was of any use. The buggers had seen nothing! And I believed them. Here—this official police photo says it all."

The church setting in the locating shots was easily identified. Redfyre found he was looking at a glamorous black-and-white photograph. A pair of cherry trees laden with snow on either side of a huge oak door and a majestic tower rising on the left of the image identified Great St. Mary's. The direction and depth of the shadows cast by the sun told him that it was taken in the early morning in the very centre of Cambridge. A further shot from the west where the tower gave straight onto the pavings below, opposite the Senate House, would have made a wonderful Christmas card, had its subject not been a corpse lying on its back on the snow-covered slabs at the base of the tower, arms spread like an angel's wings. A close-up of the neat, tidy body showed a face whose features were untouched by anything more than slight surprise at being caught out by death.

"And what was the cause of this? Did someone shout, 'Boo'?" Redfyre suggested cynically.

"It was swiftly concluded that this gent fell or threw himself from the top of the tower after dark the previous day. And don't forget, in the depths of January, dark starts at teatime."

"How is that possible? The tower isn't open for visitors in the winter months."

"Special opening on account of the snow. The photography clubs of Cambridge put pressure—and probably a fat fee—on the church authorities to have the tower opened up for them. They had a competition on at the time—'Landscapes of Academe,' or some such. It was well attended. What really gets these photo hounds excited is their slanting light. Like vampires, they're always to be found scurrying about at the crack of dawn and the last trump of day. There was a magnificent sunset that day, as well. That really got them going! I managed to get my hands on some of the resulting exhibits, just to see if someone had caught an image of a killer lurking. No use! But I had to admire the results."

"Well attended, you say?" Redfyre's suspicious tone echoed his policeman's concern for public safety. He knew the tower, though stout and impressive in its perpendicular style, provided limited skirmishing space for a group of visitors.

"Yup! Swarming with them!" the superintendent replied nonchalantly. "Overcrowding to a dangerous level occurred up there, and the parapet is quite low. With everyone peering through viewfinders, elbows out, jockeying for position. Some die-hard purists were even using cameras you need to envelop your head in a black shroud to use . . . I'm only surprised worse didn't occur. They're quite fanatical about their art, you know. Fiends! My first thought was that this could be a case of professional—or rather amateur—competitive spirit. A naughty push in the back to ruin a hated rival's focus . . . Everyone denied everything, of course."

Redfyre's finger traced the intact features on the close-up. "Who was he, this alleged faller-from-a-height?"

"An enthusiastic photographer. Local man. Registered member of the biggest club. The 'Fiat Lux', if you can believe it! Not much mourned, I think. He'd won the yearly prize the last three times, and people were getting a bit fed up with him. Rising politician. Tory. Hoping to stand for Cambridgeshire next time round. Independent means. Father was of the landed gentry and Royston Chilvers was his eldest son."

The calculatedly level tone of the superintendent's victim profile betrayed his dislike and prejudice, Redfyre thought. He replied with an attempt at humour: "That's at least five good reasons for bumping him off!"

"You're not kidding! I counted eight! By the time I'd investigated young Royston, I'd have given him a quick shove from a height myself!"

Redfyre tapped the photograph. "But he didn't fall, did he?" he suggested.

"No. Course not. That's no jumper. Not the bone damage you'd expect, not much bruising. He'd been placed. The forensic lads proved it by the depth and condition of the snow under and around the body. Pressure, displacement, ambient temperature, temperature of the overlying body, precipitation . . . those boys had a field day! The upshot was—you've likely guessed it!—he'd been bashed on the head at ground level, and his limbs arranged like a kid doing that arm-spreading malarkey. Trouble was, the press and the public took one look at the dramatic photos and decided he must have been pushed from the tower. Well, I mean! Bloke who should have been jousting in the mêlée at the top is found lying dead at the base? Join up the dots! What are towers for! That's what the human mind does. It looks for the obvious, the link between point A and point B. It's what's kept us surviving as a species for so long."

"It's only contrarians like us who pick at the scabs and say: 'Ah yes, but what if . . . ?'" Redfyre murmured.

"Exactly. And by the time we find out what if, it's too late. People have moved on to the next excitement. A correct version was put out in the press, but no one was listening! He'd gone down in local history as the Winter Icarus."

"Memorable!" Redfyre commented. "Do I detect the inventive powers of our local newshound?"

"You bet! And the notion of a fall was made indelible. The coroner hummed and hawed, and in deference to the lad's grieving family, put it down as another 'tripped and fell, banging his head,' sustained in the pursuit of an interesting photographic angle. You'll observe—because I'm sure we were meant to—that his camera has been carefully positioned on his chest with the safety strap still around his neck. And the lens was intact."

"A camera? Was there film in there?" Redfyre hunted eagerly through the file.

"Carrying the smirking image of the man about to attack him? No such luck! No film in there at all. It had been removed. Something else that stuck in the Coroner's throat . . . It was almost comical, hearing him trying to account for that."

"Last supper? Did you—"

"Possibly an exception to the pattern. Nothing remarkable. Lunch had been eaten on the day of death. Brown Windsor soup, turkey and a mince pie. That selection was available at Aunty's, the Dorothy and half a dozen city pubs."

Redfyre pulled the photographs of the general and Icarus towards him and studied them side by side. "There's something about the presentation . . . a similarity, a quality . . . not of the photographer, he's one of our lads, but the subject . . ."

Pointing first to the general: "Surely easier to drown him and just abandon the body, don't you think?" he asked. "Instead, someone lays him out, lounging on the cushions like a sunbather. I'm just surprised that the perpetrator didn't fit him out with a pair of fashionable sun goggles as worn at Antibes! This was well into daylight? Yes? Elderly gent, sun reflecting off his bald pate, reclining in evening dress for a solitary unpiloted cruise down the river? There must have been someone out there with a pocket Kodak tempted to snap him. Did you enquire? Oh, I say!"

Redfyre had suddenly become still as a pointing hound.

"Christ! I think you're onto something there!"

The two men looked at each other in dismay and puzzlement, each chasing an insubstantial and teasing thought.

"What the hell's going on?" MacFarlane wanted to know and then offered his own suggestion. "Some bugger is getting together a little collection? Holiday snaps? Souvenirs? The next offering in the Frith's series of *Beautiful Britain*? Is there in some drawer in town a private photo album that would make interesting viewing?"

"Nothing so whimsical, sir. No. I think we're dealing with a hardheaded killer who knows his business. And who possibly goes to the trouble of photographically recording his . . . accomplishments. A modern perversion? The deviance de nos jours? I don't think so. He could have been getting away with it for years. Cameras have been portable objects since before the war. They were carried into the trenches in kitbags. You can easily pop a Kodak into your pocket. We've got a series of murders— as I think you've realised—and it's on our patch. In our laps. And I don't think there'd be much help coming from the London Met, even if we asked very nicely. Do you have the resources to handle half a dozen, possibly more, cases, sir?"

MacFarlane groaned. "You know I haven't. If I manage to get out of bed in the morning, I've exhausted my resources. But there is a bright side to look on. Think on, lad! There may be six, there may be a dozen cases, but if it's a dreaded series we've got hold of, it's *one* killer we're looking for. That's the thing about a series. Solve one of them, and the rest come tumbling down like a stack of dominoes. You're right: we haven't the manpower to look at all these again. We'll have to leave them in the coffin box and hope that we can solve the latest one. And perhaps that will be the domino that brings down the rest."

Redfyre sighed. "May I make a suggestion? In the Jack the Ripper cases, the first and the last killings gave the most useful indications. Makes sense. The first time, any killer is less likely to know how to cover his tracks. He may have acted out of impulse with little planning. Made mistakes. In the last, he may have grown overconfident out of contempt for the police. Grown careless."

"It's the first pull of the trigger that gives the clearest insight into motive. It tells you about the killer's immediate location.

Murderers rarely operate far from home. They have a hunting
ground. It also identifies his choice of victim: prostitutes? Rich
and elderly? Italian tenors? His prey. So, let's say we were to
look at our own series, taking the whole range as background
and the first and the latest—as far as we know them to be—for
detailed investigation. Where the hell does that leave us? Cambridge is the hunting ground, all right. But the prey? An
Argentinian tango dancer and a vagrant? In whom would those
two arouse an impulse to murder?"

"Let's give it a go, sir. Firmly put all the other bodies in
between back in the box and thrash away at the first and last
until they give up their secrets. Do we have any other option?"

He knew what the response would be. The force, like all
other services and businesses in the country, was suffering from
the enormous losses of men to the war. And, unlike others, the
police force was not able—and on top of that, was unwilling—
to call on the thousands of spirited women eager to step in and
fill gaps as they had learned to do throughout the four years of
struggle. They were dangerously short of men of the right age
and experience.

"My remaining inspectors are up to their gum-boot tops in
country crime of one sort or another, from pig-rustling to
attempted witch-burning," MacFarlane said lugubriously.
"They're covering a bloody county, and now Norfolk's asked
for help with an outbreak of pitchforkings. You're my city boy,
Redfyre."

"Right-oh, sir. I'll pull in my focus and get straight on to it.
With the help of a sergeant and two constables, I should manage. We're making some headway already on the vagrant case.
If I can only worm my way into St. Jude's, I really think I may
make some progress."

"Redfyre! There's no warrant forthcoming. Don't look for
one. I want no trouble with the university authorities."

"I know the position, and I wouldn't even ask unless I had a concrete case. No. I shall seek help from quite a different quarter."

MacFarlane sighed. "Not another of your fairy godmothers? Last time one of those stuck her wand in, corpses rained down."

"Ah, but this one's a flower fairy godmother. And I have a very particular wish I intend to present to her."

CHAPTER 14

Sergeant Thoday arrived at the graveyard at three o'clock, keen to get on. He listened quietly, making notes as his boss refreshed his memory of the crime scene. No need for that. Two hours on his knees yesterday had fixed every unproductive blade of grass in his memory. Whoever had throttled the old soldier and laid him out with such care had, predictably, not neglected to clear away any trace of his own presence. Thoday was more interested in the new evidence thrown up by the pathologist. Now he was being allocated duties that included checking a bag of clothing and effects from the corpse of the tramp and tracking down their provenance. This was more the detective work he thirsted for!

"I need to know who he is, Sarge. Name and pack-drill by the end of the day. We won't get anywhere until we have an identity," Redfyre said. And when he was done at the morgue, the sergeant was told, he could well make further enquiries at the market and all the hostels and organisations that had contact with down-and-outs. "'That hairy vagrant who hangs around the market square' isn't good enough. We're not planting Dunstan in an unmarked grave.

"Oh, and when your feet are throbbing, Sarge, you can call in for a reviving cup of tea at Aunty's!" Redfyre suggested. "We've had reports of an altercation on the premises on the day in question—Friday. Someone from the café rang the station, alerting them to a fracas about to break out. Constable Thompson was at the desk, just clocking off, and he was dispatched and came running. Too late. By the time he arrived, a university official—a bulldog?—had already stopped the fight and cleared the ring, Thompson was told. Our birds had flown. The constable put in a report anyway. The super, it was, who picked it up and thought it might have some significance for our case. I agree. Check it out, if you will."

"You said 'birds,' sir?"

"Takes at least two to make a fracas. One of the combatants was reported to be a tramp. Well-known in these parts, I understand. Get the facts from Thompson—this is his patch. I'm interested in the identity of both blokes involved. And the self-appointed umpire—I want *his* name. Now, while you're busy doing that, I shall be in the marketplace sampling a jellied eel or two with Bert the pie man, and at teatime, I'm scheduled to squire a gaggle of lady bat-fanciers about the graveyard. Oh joy!"

Thoday was glad to be excused from the eels and the batty ladies. Redfyre was welcome to those. But he decided with silent truculence to turn the inspector's list of to-dos upside down. The clothes at the morgue weren't going anywhere. They'd keep. You couldn't say the same for witnesses. They upped sticks and disappeared or their memories failed. No! Attack the easily breached spot in any wall first, he reckoned. That was the best plan. Hang routine. Go for the obvious. And to Thoday, the obvious was Constable Thompson. It sounded as though he might have a few leads. This was his patrol patch, as the inspector had said. He'd know all the drifters on it by sight. With his elevation to the detective squad, local boy Thoday had become somewhat detached from the goings-on in the street. But he knew all the regulars. He'd expected to recognise the murder victim when he'd caught a glimpse of him on the slab from a distance. But, disappointingly, he hadn't. The coat was instantly recognisable. He was sure he'd seen it (or its twin) before. Always one or two of them parading about the place, even in high summer. The face had been harder to place. It had puzzled him. And then the obvious answer to his disquiet hit him: clean-shaven!

That was unusual. And possibly opened up another avenue of enquiry: How many barber shops were there in central Cambridge that would take on a shaggy tramp? He could think of a couple. Both run by men who enjoyed a good natter. Thoday grinned at the prospect. A few interested questions, and he'd have a name for Inspector Smarty Pants by the end of the day!

Thoday turned his long, eager lope in the direction of Parker's Piece. And soon picked out, on the fringes of the crowd sitting on the grass watching a cricket match, a reassuring presence sweating away the afternoon heat in navy uniform and helmet.

"Last Friday? Tramp? Yer, that were old Dickie!" Ben Thompson was perfectly certain, although he'd only caught a glimpse of him as he'd disappeared. "I'd know him anywhere! He's been missing for quite a while, of course. That being the nature of these gentlemen. Wandering. He's been away up north, word is, revisiting his roots. Some of them have roots, yer know. But there was no mistaking that beard and that thatch of hair and that swagger. Dickie has this special way of walking ... brazen as a bandmaster! Put 'im in front of a regiment and they'd march after 'im, all right."

Hole in one! Thoday kept the thought to himself and tried to stay calm. A firm, professional identification of an individual in prehaircut state was what he'd just been handed. The poor old sod had tidied himself up in preparation for whatever skulduggery had befallen him behind closed oak doors, if

Redfyre had read the tracks right. Well, now! With increased eagerness for the hunt, Thoday turned his attention back to the constable.

In between gasps and indrawn breaths responding to heroics on the cricket field, he ascertained that the incident was not as he had supposed—a disagreement between gentlemen of the road—but a scuffle involving Dickie and the owner of the tea shop. Unusually—Dickie being no trouble and never a lawbreaker—he'd gone for him. Thumped him in the bread basket and winded the old bugger! Been asking for it for years, mind, and no one blamed Dickie at all.

The self-appointed arbiter of the impromptu fisticuffs had been—no—not a bulldog, but a don. Tall, youngish, superior and wearing one o' them gowns. He hadn't stuck around to give his details. Never known to acknowledge, let alone help the police, those fellers. And Dickie himself had shown a clean pair of heels. He'd even abandoned a good sum of money, some of it in sixpences, on the pavement in his hurry. Thompson had picked up four shillings and five pence and handed that in at the front desk.

In response to Thoday's last-minute question of, "Anything else strike you as odd about the incident?" the constable considered, then slowly said, "Might be something. There was another bloke watching what was going on. Not connected with the skirmishing, but interested. More-than-usual interested. Everyone else in the audience had drifted off about his business when the excitement was over, but this bloke popped out of the shop and watched Dickie until he turned the corner. Then he went after him. Not rushing to catch him up. More sort of . . . trailing him. They might be able to tell you more in the café about *him*. They have some sharp girls on the till there. Better than Aunty deserves."

Three days had already elapsed since the ruckus in front of

Aunty's. Thoday decided that he would not leave his interview with the staff a moment longer and headed off to the market-place.

The girl in charge of operations at the tea shop (the man-ageress, she announced with pride) was, as promised by Thompson, "sharp." Not in manner, but in intelligence, Thoday judged. In her middle twenties, perhaps, she was confident and shrewd. And she fixed the sergeant's attention with a pair of merry brown eyes. She was intrigued and not a little amused by the drama she'd witnessed, and was very ready to talk to the sergeant about it.

She seated him at a discreet table and poured him a cup of tea. Alice, she said her name was, taking off her bcribboned cap and settling down at his table. Alice had seen the whole episode play itself out from beginning to end, and she was a good, suc-cinct reporter. She was aware of Dickie. He called in occasionally for a slice of fruit cake by the back door. Cake and a chat. He was a flirty old thing and must have been a bit of a heartbreaker in his youth, she thought. He could still make all the girls laugh. A real gentleman, and Alice could always tell. There were some you couldn't turn your back on without hav-ing your posterior pinched. But she had a way of dealing with that. Her knowing glance was a clear invitation to seek further and better particulars. He enquired. She told him. She smiled an indulgent smile when, in shocked tone, he warned her that she might well be risking an accusation of grievous bodily harm and should desist. She should be careful and ring him if she had a problem with any lusty tea-drinkers. He passed his card across, and she put it away in her pocket.

"It's the *other* feller you ought to be looking for," she said to him kindly. "Dickie was just being Dickie! You don't say any-thing disrespectful to him and get away with it, whoever you are. He's got a temper on him, but he's a bit of a slow burner.

If he attacks you, you've deserved it and then some!" She looked over her shoulder before continuing. "Aunty had it coming to him! Shhh, I never said that! He was smarming all over this customer in the straw boater. Flash the cash and you've got Aunty's attention! A visitor, not a regular. He was with a lady, his wife, and she was very well dressed with some good jewellery. Loaded, the pair of them! And very nice manners they had. Dickie came into the café—which he's never done before, so it must have been urgent. He was obviously keen to say something to Mr. Boater. But Aunty wasn't having it. A tramp in his select establishment? Never! Aunty said something like, 'Do excuse me while I eject this trash.' Charming! And then he tried to physically remove him. Once outside they could let rip, and they resorted to, er, language. Upshot was Dickie bashed him one in the stomach. Winded him. Aunty made us ring for an ambulance and had himself taken off to Addenbrooke's to make sure nothing had been punctured!" Alice had to break off to control her laughter. "He's been off sick since then." She chortled.

"Did the customer in the boater and Dickie ever get around to exchanging words?"

"No. Not as I saw. I don't think the customer wanted to acknowledge him. He seemed startled and embarrassed. Look, if we're going to go on talking about them, why don't we use the gentleman's correct name?"

"Good grief! You know it? But how . . ."

"It was quite entertaining how it happened. After Dickie had finished dancing about for the crowd and baiting the college bloke who stuck an oar in, he went off towards King Street. And that's where it all got a bit strange. There seemed to be something of a tiff breaking out between Mr. Boater and his wife . . . Edith, he called her. She'd ordered toasted tea cakes with her pot of Earl Grey, but he told her to put her coat on, they were leaving. 'Sod the tea cakes,' he said, just as the wait-ress walked up with them, hot from the grill! Bad timing."

"You're not kidding!" Thoday could conjure up with ease the buttery cinnamon- and sultana-scented treat and shared Edith's pain at the thought of it being whisked away from under her nose.

"Edith wasn't best pleased. And she told him so in no uncer-tain terms. She had a go at him for hauling her up to Cambridge 'just to cover for him,' she said, and added that she was going to the shops later, intending to spend a month's allowance in Joshua Taylor's and stuff him! And she was going to stay and finish her tea. 'Abe'—she called him 'Abe'—could go and chase after a filthy old tramp if he wanted more stimulating company than hers!"

"Ooh! Er . . . how did he react to that?"

"Backed off straightaway. Wanted to avoid a scene. Decided to go for the generous gesture. He called me over, tore a cheque out of his cheque book and said: 'Miss, my wife will treat her-self to a slap-up lunch, if that's what she wants. I'm signing this cheque, and you are to serve her whatever she asks for '"

"Hang on . . . I'm wondering why he didn't just slip her a ten-bob note and have done. Cash?"

"We get men like that. Businessmen, full of themselves, with records to keep and expenses to claim. He said to me: 'Please see that she is given a receipt, Nippy. I shall need it for the tax man.' Nippy! Where did he think he was? In a Joe Lyons? Then: 'Edith, my love. I'll get back as soon as I can.'"

"How romantic!" Thoday said unguardedly. "It's you, me and the taxman, Edith . . . But for now, for lunch, you're on your own." He shook his head in sadness for his sex. "Enough to put anyone off their food. Did she have much of an appetite, the lady?"

"I'll say! She went straight into the lunch menu! Brown

Windsor soup, steak and ale pie and mash with a bottle of claret
we fetched in for her from the Eagle, and she rounded it off with
peach pavlova and clotted cream. Coffee and chocolate mints
after. We don't take the cheques in to the bank for deposit until
Wednesdays. I've still got it in the till, if you'd like to see it."

She hurried back with the cheque. A Mr. Abel Hardy had
committed himself to paying an eye-watering twelve shillings
and sixpence from his account at a grand London bank.

Thoday turned the cheque over, hoping for and finding a
helpfully rubber-stamped address on the back. Not the smart
Hampstead residential address he'd anticipated, but even better,
perhaps—a business office in central London:

"ENQUIRIES AT," SUITE 1, BELVEDERE, THE STRAND,
LONDON.

Thoday took a deep breath and fought down an urge to give
the girl a congratulatory kiss. The male sex was already viewed
with scorn enough by this young woman. He scribbled down
the address in his notebook, along with the banking details. He
wondered what on earth had called a smart London business-
man, the director of "Enquiries At" (whatever that concern was)
to make a trip up to Cambridge with his wife in tow.

"That'll teach him to cancel the tea cakes!" he commented.

"Exactly what his missis said! I liked her! She winked at me
and left a large tip in cash under the saucer."

This was going well. Thoday gave Alice a beaming smile
and promised to come back for a leisurely cup of tea and tell
her what happened when he'd made further progress with the
case.

"Case?" Alice picked him up on this at once. "What case
would that be, then?"

Remembering the affection in her voice as she had spoken

of Dickie, Thoday was not prepared to spoil her afternoon, or his own chances, with this friendly girl by being the bearer of bad news. "Oh, a possible further, not-unconnected altercation at one of the colleges. It's all a bit delicate . . . You know what they're like, these academical types," was the slice of fudge he fed her.

Thoday snapped shut his notebook and raced off to his next—unscheduled—meeting. Edith Hardy. Was she still in Cambridge? Well-off tourists . . . it shouldn't be difficult to track down the lady and her husband. A phone call or two from headquarters to the usual hotels is all it would take. And last today, with just enough time to fit it in before the scheduled meeting at six o'clock back at the nick, a viewing of the tramp's—or, now that Thoday now felt secure enough to give him at least a Christian name, Dickie's—clothing and possessions.

AT THE OTHER side of the marketplace, Redfyre was also having some success with his investigation.

Bert the pie man was treating them both to a mug of tea and a dollop of culinary philosophy at the tea stall. They perched on a conveniently positioned stone boundary wall dividing the public space from the ecclesiastical and began "chewing the fat," as Bert called the exchange of information.

Oh yes, he'd been jellying his eels for years, and his father before him. The old man hadn't, however, been very adventurous. Bert couldn't blame him. Not much opportunity, really, in the olden days. Never much food to go around, and people weren't prepared to experiment with what they had. Now, today, well, every Tommy had had the pleasure of sampling French food. Horse meat, garlic, spaghetti . . . they had the lot. And the way those frogs fried their chips! That was something to write home to Mum about. But no one had yet bothered to ask him what herbs he'd put in his eels. He looked at Redfyre with curiosity.

"Go on, then," Bert challenged, pointing to the small white china dish of glutinous dark matter that Redfyre was holding in his hand. "Stick your beak in there and *you* tell *me* what I've put in it."

Redfyre smiled bravely, trying to banish from his memory the sight of the same substance bottled in one of Beaufort's jars, and stuck a fork in. He did not reply at once to the eager old eyes watching for a response. They would see through any insincere reaction.

"Mmm . . . good, cockle-strengthening stuff! The eely bit is perfectly cooked. Tender but resilient, and mildly fishy in flavour. I could easily mistake it for freshwater trout. The jelly, however, is the triumph! It caresses your teeth and glides down the gullet, exuding an aroma of herbs as it goes. Now what is that? Parsley, of course. And a touch of mint for freshness, but mainly . . . dill? . . . That's it! Dill."

Bert was pleased with the performance. And he didn't fail to notice that Redfyre was taking a further, more generous forkful of the dish. "It's dill, all right. I grow it myself in the back garden. But there's something else. Celery seed! Now, who'd ever think of putting a dried seed into a fish dish? But it works a treat. Folks don't know it's there, but they miss it all right when I run out."

Redfyre had his man.

He finished his plate and asked the question he'd warned Bert to expect. Last Friday, sometime after five o'clock—so he would have been a late customer—a man had eaten a portion of this very dish and had subsequently died. Of strangulation, Redfyre hurried to add, seeing Bert stiffen in concern. He assured the pie man that it had been the last thing the victim had enjoyed. Did Bert have any recollection of a man in an army greatcoat smacking his chops over a dish of eels at about that time?

Bert shook his head. "Naw! Sorry. Can't help."

After that facer, he went on to explain that he'd packed up early that day, straight after lunch. For the simple reason that he'd sold up. Had a good morning and midday session, and that was it. When the food's gone, you have to pack up and go, but plan to make more next week.

Redfyre was, for a moment, nonplussed.

"Tell you what, though! I can tell you where old Dickie got them eels!"

To Redfyre's surprise, he went on. "Sounds like Dickie you're describing. Vagrant, but Cambridge's own vagrant. Everybody knows Dickie. I ran out of eels because I'd had a prior order. I do out-catering as well as sell from the stall. You want to try the Salvation Army canteen down Mill Road. They ordered twenty jellied eel dinners for Friday night. The Friday before, it was tripe, stewed with onions. Cheap stuff, but healthy. And I always put a dash of cream in the sauce to make it special. No, last Friday the bulk of my eel delivery went off in two stewpots down the Mill Road."

Redfyre thanked Bert for his wisdom and his eels and vowed to return for more while the season lasted. He made off on the double for Mill Road. He just had time to squeeze in an interview before the bat ladies claimed his attention in the graveyard.

"SORRY, LOVE. WE'RE not open yet. You'll have to come back. There's no one here until five."

Redfyre grabbed the heavy tray of plates from the bustling lady's grasp and carried it through into the dining hall. She hadn't been impressed by his police warrant card, his authoritative manner had left her cold and his polite attempt to lighten her load was the last straw.

"'Ere! Are you deaf? Put that down! I said there's no one here."

He persisted. "Madam, you are here. I am here. A moment of your time and the answer to a question I'm about to ask will render inessential a visit to the police station to fill in forms."

Braving the sighs and snorts and glowers, he asked his question. "Last Friday supper. Here. Jellied eels on the menu. I need to know—who served them?"

"Nothing to do with me! Duties run Monday to Monday. So, last week, that would be Eliza. Eliza Campion."

He noted the name, pencil poised, and stared at her questioningly.

"You'll find her at home. That's number fifteen, Canary Row. The one with the window boxes. It's just off Covent Garden down the town end of the street. She won't want to see you at this hour. She'll be getting the tea on for her hubby. 'Ere—are you just for ornament, or are you going to make yourself useful? We *are* a charity, you know!"

Well, at least Canary Row was on his way back to base. "How many are we laying for? Twenty? Got it!" Redfyre deftly began to lay out the plates on the tables with a smile. He found the cutlery and placed a knife, fork and spoon by every plate. He remembered to drop a half crown into the box before he left.

Mrs. Eliza Campion swiftly answered the door of number fifteen when he banged on it. The doorway was the narrow entrance to a narrow, two-up, two-down house, and Mrs. Campion's two-across bosom spanned the space impressively, the flowery pinny straining across her front like a breastplate completing the defensive front line of pink and purple petunias in the window boxes alongside.

Taken aback momentarily by the flower-strewn parade of propriety, Redfyre raised his hat and readied himself to burble engagingly.

Before he could speak, she said automatically, "My husband is not at home. He does not receive casual callers." She prepared to close the door.

Foot-in-the-door time? Redfyre had never descended to intimidation. He took a step back and offered his card enticingly. "Mrs. Campion, I do not wish to speak to Jonas, but to your good self," he said cheerfully. "And, you'll find, I'm not at all casual."

"A police inspector? CID?" She handed back the card. "What's this all about?"

"May I come inside? Neighbours, you know! If yours are anything like mine, they have quick eyes and meddling tongues."

"Ah yes. Right-oh. I can spare a minute before Jonas gets back, I suppose."

She cleared the doorway, and he stepped into a gloomy entrance hall. Somewhere in the rear of the house, where life was lived, a kettle was bubbling its way up to a boil, and a quavering voice called out, "Eliza! Who's that at the door?"

"Nobody, Dad! Have you got your teeth in? Just chew on your rusk for a minute, will you?"

Redfyre was offered a chair at the table in the front parlour, a small room still crowded with Victorian furniture. There was even an aspidistra in a jardinière, its leaves dusted as meticulously as every other knick-knack. A print of the Fighting Temeraire hung on the wall, flanked by pictures of rosy-cheeked shepherdesses bringing in the flocks at eventide and milkmaids smiling happily under the weight of buckets suspended from shoulder yokes. Green velvet swags hung from a mantelshelf crowded with photographs of babies in bonnets and smooth-cheeked young men in pristine uniform about to go to war. The still air was cool but heavy with the scent of camphor and last year's rose petals in a dish of potpourri.

Mrs. Campion remained standing in the doorway, one ear

listening out for further disturbances from her father or the arrival of her husband. Redfyre plunged directly into his story, unconsciously taking his urgency from the lady.

"So, I'd be grateful if you could remember anything useful to us concerning a man who ate the jellied eels on Friday night when you were officiating at the shelter."

"I served twenty eel dinners! It's a popular option. But that'd be Noël Coward and Maurice Moneybags you're after," she said decisively. "Those two are the ones you'll be interested in."

"Why do you say that, Mrs. Campion?" Redfyre was intrigued.

She advanced into the room, closed the door and sat down opposite him on the chair he hurried to pull out for her.

"It's being said on the hush-hush that they're dead. My neighbour next door but one has a son who's best friends with a copper. He says there was murder done in the graveyard. Drunken fight between vagrants is the word. But you wouldn't come here asking me questions if it was just a scrap, would you? Are you here to tell me it was the eels that did for them? They both had the same things to eat. Eels and then apple pie. And Mr. Moneybags paid double for the privilege. He paid for them both, and then some. Seems a bit harsh to have paid to poison himself. And his mate." She added thoughtfully, "We've had no other complaints about the eels. In fact, Jonas had some. He's as fit as a flea."

"Don't be concerned, Mrs. Campion. The food was just splendid. Nothing to do with the matter at hand and, from personal experience of Bert's cooking, I can say I'm sure they enjoyed their meal very much."

Mollified, she began to unbend a little. "I had my eye on those two. Oh, not old Dickie! He's a regular and he's always an entertainment. Such lovely manners! Who'd have thought it! And his friend? Well, he was all that's proper, you'd say. Well off? Oh yes. I'd say rolling in it. Gold watch and cuff links. Stuffed wallet." She paused and gave Redfyre a shrewd look. "That's not to say as the man was ever in any danger from Dickie!" she said sharply. "Dickie would never stoop to robbery or any other unkindness. I've seen him give his last sixpence to someone who needed it more. But I did wonder what those two were doing together, and so deep in conversation. You'd have taken them for best friends or even brothers, they were nattering on so freely. They finished their meal and went off together, Dickie laughing and booking a place for next Friday. He looked different. Cheerful. It's surprising what a haircut can do for a man. And he'd gotten rid of that awful beard. He's not so old, you know, under that thatch. And a fine figure of a man when he stands up straight." She turned a reproachful look on Redfyre. "I *do* hope as how nothing dreadful has happened to him."

The lady was scathing when he asked if she had any idea what his surname might be.

"Certainly not! He's probably not even 'Dickie.' These are men who are on the run from someone or other, or something—sometimes just from themselves. More than a few have been in prison. They don't want their identities known for any number of good reasons, police harassment being one of them. Why do you think we accept all this 'Buster Keaton' and 'Kaiser Bill' rubbish? We're not a branch of law enforcement, you know. We just feed the starving and clothe the needy, whoever they are, wherever they come from. And we ask no questions. Except for, 'Do you want vinegar on that?'"

The handsome young inspector took her by surprise by sticking to his word and leaving briskly. "Mrs. Campion, you're an angel!" he announced, getting to his feet and picking up his hat. "Jonas is a lucky man. I'd better be off before he catches us together!" When at last she began to crack and giggle, he added in a more serious tone, "Your information has been of immense value. Thank you. And, er, I'll keep you informed about the fate of your Dickie."

"MADAM! WAIT!" THODAY yelled.

He pounded up the pavement in front of the entrance to the Regency Hotel as the taxi driver opened the door to help Mrs. Hardy inside with her luggage. The smart lady who turned upon hearing him looked as though she were off to Scotland to spend the season on the golf course or stalking some poor creature with a view to shooting it for the pot. She was wearing travelling clothes with brogues and a businesslike cloche hat with a jaunty grouse feather on the side. She certainly had no wish to be detained, and raised her head with the forcibly snooty stare of a woman whose hat was pulled stylishly down over her eyes. Those eyes were green and unwelcoming.

"Yes? Are you speaking to me, young man? Did I forget something?"

"Mrs. Edith Hardy? In that case, yes, madam, I think you've forgotten *Mr.* Hardy." Thoday had checked inside the taxi and, as the manager had warned him, it certainly looked as though she was about to leave by herself.

She glared at him. "If only! Sonny, I've been trying for years! Who the heck are you? Does he owe you money?"

Thoday showed his warrant and introduced himself. "A minute of your time, if you please? It's urgent. A local man has been found dead, and we believe your husband may have information as to his identity."

"Can't help you. Sorry. But if the deceased is a Cambridge man, why would you expect Abel to mark your card? We're Londoners."

With a charming smile but deadly intent, Thoday snatched the travelling case from her grasp and put it under his arm in a marked manner. He felt himself a figure of fun, standing there on the pavement with a lady's dainty piece of Vuitton luggage, leather label dangling, held hostage under his armpit.

"Look here! I'm catching the five o'clock train to London, and the CID aren't going to stop me without an arrest warrant. Got one? No? Right then, hop in, you can talk to me as we go."

Thoday relaxed and calmly stowed the case away inside the taxi while the driver secured the larger cases at the rear. He held out a gallant hand and helped her to climb in, then duly hopped in after her. It was a five-minute drive to the station, and the road was reasonably clear. He'd have to work fast. Luckily, she seemed direct in her responses.

No, she had no idea where Abel Hardy was. Did she, then, wish to report her husband as a missing person?

"Missing? Never! He's not even a *person*! More of a shadow."

And no, she wasn't worried. He was always doing this. Business trips. Hard worker. Successful. Mean as cat's meat with the cash, but you can't have everything. He took her out and about sometimes when he went somewhere interesting, just to keep her entertained. Sometimes for show, because he wanted her to play the little wifey for clients. Not often—she wasn't very good at that. Never liked the clients much. Or their wives. Bath had been nice, and Bournemouth. Cambridge, not bad. She'd enjoyed the punt on the river.

"And how about the lunch at Aunty's café on Friday?" Thoday asked.

She grinned. "Excellent! Worth every one of his pennies! That's when he nipped off. I knew he was coming up here on a job. He did warn me, so I suppose I can't complain. He was tracking somebody. Did you know he was a detective?" she added with pride. "Not like you, a state functionary. He's more your Sherlock Holmes. Private. It's one of his businesses. He specialises in finding people, for personal as well as legal reasons. At least, that's how he got started. After the war, a lot of people had gone astray one way or another and needed to be caught up with." She gave a mischievous smile. "Of course, some didn't want to be found! That made the job harder and the fees bigger—in line with the effort expended. And the effort, I noticed, with Abel, was in direct proportion to the size of the client's bank account. I help him with his books, so I know his secrets. Most of them. He's got a staff of five working for him now, but he still likes to keep his hand in. You've no idea the number of people who need help with their problems on the quiet. He does divorce cases as well, if you're ever interested. He's very good at it. Catching the wrong people together at the wrong time. On camera, if you take my meaning. He's been in and out of more bedrooms than Casanova."

Thoday looked about him with a stagy show of alarm. "I'll be sure to keep my name out of Mr. Hardy's books!" He'd decided that the way to loosen Edith's tongue was through humour and fellow feeling, and he added incautiously. "And my ugly mug away from his lens! Can you be sure he wasn't lurking behind the laurels with his little Kodak vest-pocket camera just now, snapping us eloping together in a taxi?"

She gurgled attractively. "No, I can't! I often wonder if he's set *me* up for an indiscreet shot! Who'd be married to a professional divorce arranger? It's like living on the slopes of a volcano." She turned an admiring gaze on the tall, smiling sergeant. "Though I must say, if I were being entrapped myself, I'd be rather pleased to be snapped next to a good-looking young chap with a dangerous moustache." She placed a gloved hand gently on his knee and leaned so close the straw fabric of her hat grazed his cheek and the scent of her exotic perfume tickled his nose. It wasn't the eau de cologne or Yardley's "Lavender" that his sisters favoured, and he found it unsettling. Disturbing also was the change in the tone of her voice as she

murmured, "Now, if I were to choose this moment to say something incriminating and foolish in the hearing of our
cabby—something like, 'Darling, did you remember to tell them
to put the champagne on ice at our hotel in Brighton?'—he
would track us both down in no time. A quick but unpleasant
court appearance, a write-up in the *Times*, and that's the end
of your career. For the rest of your existence, Sergeant Thoday,
you'd be branded a cad and a professional gigolo. What's my
silence worth to you?"

Edith enjoyed the sergeant's fleeting look of horror before
digging him in the ribs with a peal of laughter. "It's all right! It's
only me, Edith! Dutiful wife on her way home to the familial
London hearth. Still, I have learned some surprising skills from
that arsehole. And the best one? If I decided to disappear, I could.
And he'd never find me. I'm probably the only person in the
world who could say that. I have the skills and the means."

Thoday shuddered. He didn't doubt it. He had the uncomfortable feeling of one who had just offered a Friskies doggy
treat to a wolf. He swallowed and pressed on. "His other businesses, Mrs. Hardy?"

"The others are property—buying and selling manufactur-
ing premises, mostly. What with the war damage, there's been
a lot of cash churning about in London. And if money's on the
move, Abel usually manages to direct some of it his way. And
there's the secretarial services chain he's just started. So many
well-educated girls in the world looking for an opportunity to
work! The unlucky ones run into Abel. He's an excellent talent-
spotter and ungenerous paymaster. Not so good at names. He
wanted to call the business 'Friday's Girl.' I made him change
it to 'Adsum!' Seeing as all the bosses who want to snare these
young ladies for their employ are public school educated, I
thought they'd respond to a snappy Latin word for 'Here I am!
Present!' A familiar word they've used all their formative years."

"Yes, it sounds like someone reporting for duty," Thoday said doubtfully. "And Man Friday . . . from *Robinson Crusoe*, I suppose? Changing it to Girl Friday . . . Friday's Girl . . . and we all know what *her* attributes are, according to the rhyme . . ."

"Yup! 'Friday's child is loving and giving.' And I see you agree—we want none of that on office premises!"

"Any more businesses we can rename?"

"No. That's all he's *told* me about."

"And the gentleman he went off in pursuit of?"

"Eh? How do you know that? Is this why you're searching for Abel? Well, he was no gentleman. A tramp. He was trying to get at Abel. Came into the tea shop, bold as brass, calling his name. Funny, that—he shouted 'Lieutenant Hardy' at him to get his attention. Lieutenant? Abe always told me he was a captain . . . so perhaps it was someone who knew him from way back? I guessed he must have been an old army contact, fallen on hard times. Hoping for a handout. Anyway, Abe wasn't best pleased to see him and didn't interfere when the fat old feller tried to chuck him out. But he was interested, all right—he went straight off after him. But in a detective sort of way, like . . ."

"Trailing him?"

"That's right. And that was the last I saw of him this time round. Worried? No! He's always doing it. He knows I'll just get on and fend for myself . . . I find things to do, but with the boys away at school, I'm not so busy as I was. Well, here we are, Sergeant. Anything else?"

"One last thing," Thoday asked on the off-chance, scarcely expecting an answer, "Did you happen to notice a gowned university man the tramp was talking to outside the tea shop?"

"Oh yes," replied the detective's wife. "Six foot two inches tall, dark hair, midthirties, shifty-looking cove. St. Jude's College."

Thoday began to burble. "But how . . . ?"

"He was wearing a college scarf. In May? Bit odd, I thought. Perhaps he was flaunting his credentials? Wanted to be noticed? Anyway, it was blue and green with a silver stripe. I had a lesson in college colours at Ede and Ravenscroft. Such charming gentlemen they have in there. Is *that* the man you're interested in? The reason for all this palaver? I thought we'd get there. Well, good luck with that one! He's not someone *I'd* like to tangle with, not without a blackjack in my hand."

At his request, she gave him her telephone number and he gave her his card, asking that she should contact him to let him know of Abel's safe arrival back home.

Thoday looked at his watch and decided to stay in the taxi, watching as she skipped in through the crowd towards the ticket office, followed by her porter and her luggage. Why had Edith Hardy fed him such an overflowing portion of codswallop? Did he really look that stupid? Perhaps it was the moustache that gave him an unserious air.

Confident that she was not doubling back, he turned to the cabby and redirected him back in to town. "Addenbrooke's Hospital, please," he said. There was just time for a quick survey of the tramp's effects. Shouldn't take long, he reasoned. Tramps travelled light.

Minutes later, he was at the morgue, being welcomed by an assistant. Dr. Beaufort wasn't available, but he'd left all the effects at Thoday's disposal, and the corpse itself was still in the cold room, should the sergeant need to inspect it, or indeed have someone identify it. "Oh, and the doc said to tell you to give the label a whirl . . ."

Thoday emptied the bags out onto the bench provided and sorted them into piles. Very little here. Every garment had a pathologist's label pinned on it with an identifying number and the occasional comment in Beaufort's writing. Some of these were perceptive to the point of pernickety, Thoday judged. Look at this one here. *Sock found on left foot: hole in toe. Favours left foot? Not so with shoes. Right foot shows heavier wear. Worth checking?* Thoday sighed. So he'd forgotten to trim his left toenail. That, or the socks—or could it be the shoes?—were secondhand. And that went for every other bit of clothing. The greatcoat and the suit were both good quality. Bought at a market stall? Donated by some generous and well-off person to one of the many charities for the homeless in town? No way of knowing. This was hopeless.

He reached for the greatcoat. This was the most significant item, he felt. Everyone he'd interviewed had referred to "Dickie" as wearing a greatcoat like this. He looked at the label. Label? There was one sewn firmly into the inner right-hand side of the garment. It had been specially tailored in Jermyn Street, London, by "Somerton & Snape," who had thoughtfully added a serial number. 204. Customer number? Garment number? Small business, probably—all the top tailors he knew were located in Savile Row—and the number was a low one. Worth trying, he thought. Show your bosses you've covered all bases.

He was allowed to use the telephone to contact the tailoring firm in London. An assistant told him he was very happy to oblige and was quite confident that he could retrieve the information requested if the officer would care to ring back in ten minutes.

Thoday gave it twelve and rang back. "Ah yes, Sergeant. We have identified the coat. It was tailored for an officer involved in the recent unpleasantness in France. In fact, it was the second such garment he commissioned from us—in 1916—the first one having been unfortunately—er, rendered beyond repair by enemy action. It was made for a Major Richard Dunne of the King's Own Yorkshire Light Infantry. We do not hold a current private address for the gentleman as, like most military men, he is—was—stationed abroad for much of his time. We have always communicated with him at the HQ of his regiment in Pontefract, Yorkshire."

Thoday broke off with effusive thanks, unable quite to hide his excitement even on the telephone. Could it really be this smooth, this easy?

He brought his notebook up to date and went back to stare again at the worldly goods of Major Richard (Dickie?) Dunne.

He turned his attention before leaving with his prize information to the region of the feet, which had raised a question in Dr. Beaufort's mind. He thought back to his own appearance at the strange scene in the graveyard. He hadn't managed to get a very close look at the corpse, what with Redfyre and the pathologist hogging the space, but he had noted, and been rather taken aback by, the state of the feet. He remembered the pathetic V shape they'd made, with one white big toe exposed for all to see. And below, neatly lined up, the stout walking shoes.

Why the hell? Thoday found himself asking. The bloke had been strangled. Everyone was sure of that much. So some bugger had killed him, laid him out on a tombstone—oh, very entertaining, that!—and calmly taken off his shoes before pushing off. It made no sense. Thoday thought some more. It had to make sense. Killers were not raving lunatics as a rule. They thought about what they were doing, unless it was a spur-of-the-moment rush of blood to the head, in which case they usually confessed straightaway. This was not one of those cases.

No. Someone quite deliberately, and with much malice aforethought, had decided to kill off Major Richard Dunne, KOYLI. He'd done for old Dickie in a neat military way and left the body lying to attention. Was this a misplaced gesture of respect for an old soldier—an old comrade, possibly—on the killer's part? Or was it a derisive two-fingered salute to the forces of law and order?

The feet? The shoes? There was a message there for him, if he could just—

Gradually, a dark thought began to form, a burgeoning thundercloud. Thoday attempted to reason it away. It grew larger and more ominous. It was staring him in the face. Glowering at him.

He scooped up both socks and both shoes in his hands and went to find the morgue assistant.

"I say! You offered to let me take a gander at the corpse again? That would be okay? Fine! I wonder, could you also help me with a little experiment?"

H e heard them from afar. Trilling laughter and shouted
commands. Even the swiftly stifled shriek of someone
falling out of a tree perhaps.

"So sorry I'm late, vicar!" Redfyre excused himself as he
stood for a moment shoulder to shoulder with the clergyman
at the gate, watching in dismay as half a dozen ladies crashed
about the place, making it their own. "I say, have I missed the
party?"

"I'll introduce you to their commander," whispered Reverend
Turnbull. "This is just the forward reconnaissance unit. You *are*
going to stay, aren't you?"

"I'll show my face. Perhaps steady the ladder while they
climb. I'd be better prepared if you told me what they're trying
to achieve."

"The Lord knows," Turnbull said, casting a reproving eye
up to heaven. "It's to do with bats. They're concerned for them.
For their survival as a species, I mean. I honestly don't think
they have much regard for your individual little furry pip-
squeaker. The ladies are conducting a location study to establish
existing and evaluate future habitation requirements of the
order Chiroptera," he recited. "We—that is to say, mankind—
are destroying their habitat, apparently. We're building over
their territory, displacing God's creatures to house people: farm
workers and the like, who, it's found, have been living in

squalor unrelieved since the Middle Ages. Men who risked their lives in battle against the Hun to ensure our safety are now thought worthy by a guilt-stricken government of a decent roof over their heads and running water in their houses. Old barns and suchlike agricultural buildings where the bats nest . . . I say, do they nest?"

"I believe they roost, vicar."

"Thank you . . . are being torn down and swept from the face of the earth. We are witnessing, indeed are responsible for, the disappearance from our countryside of the cosy, unhygienic, flea-infested, dung-filled niches these wretched creatures have heretofore, by the grace of God, inhabited."

"Amen," said Redfyre incautiously. He suspected that the vicar had not sufficiently worked on his thesis and hoped it would be a little more polished and more carefully slanted when it was presented as his thought for the day on Sunday. "I'm no fan of mankind, either, Reverend. Or the bats," he added hurriedly, hoping he'd covered all bases and catered for all shades of opinion. "But I can't say I've seen many signs of them flying about the graveyard. Perhaps, like police inspectors, they keep unsociable hours? Now, the magpies! I wouldn't mind at all losing a few of those infernal birds! The graveyard's infested with them. Noisy blighters! At least the bats are silent. Tell me, vicar—do you have bats in your, er, roof space?"

"Bat droppings have been found on the rear pews on the southern side of the church. It's thought they are nesting in the rafters, finding access through a hole in the roof, which the ladies are, as we speak, attempting to locate."

"Sounds expensive," Redfyre said, believing he'd guessed the true reason for the vicar's long face. "Roofs, holes in . . . that costs money these days. If you can even find the blokes to do it, that is."

"No. You misunderstand. They are hoping to find the hole

so that they may *enlarge* it and facilitate ingress for the pipistrelles. The congregation, Lady Laetitia tells me (and she is a member, so feels free to speak for them), will expect it. As Christians, we must all shuffle over a bit and concede some space to Brother Bat."

"Umph! Well, the congregation had better expect to parade on Sundays with umbrellas raised," Redfyre grunted. "And wait till they get a whiff of the droppings. It's not a good preparation for the Sunday roast. Mark my words—there'll be a backlash. But in any case, I shouldn't worry too much. Looking at this scene of activity—Great Heavens! Can that be a punt pole they're poking out the trefoils with?—what they are actually doing is not encouraging, but *discouraging* the bats. The creatures are not tolerant of disturbance. Wherever they are poked at and annoyed by these fur, fin and feather enthusiasts, they will pick up sticks and move. In my book, the FFFs present a much bigger challenge to the pipistrelles than the new agriculture. Devastation and depopulation follow in the ladies' wake. But they don't know it. They bang the drum and redouble their efforts."

Redfyre cut short his sentiments. Surely that had been MacFarlane speaking?

"You may express your views to Lady Laetitia, then, for here she comes. You've been spotted, Redfyre ... Ah, my dear lady, may I present to you our friend, neighbour and guardian angel, Detective Inspector John Redfyre."

She ignored the vicar and seized Redfyre's right hand in both of hers in an overfriendly manner. "Hardly any need for an introduction, I think. I know you from Sunday services, Redfyre. You have a lovely baritone. I'm Laetitia Lowestoft. Your aunt Henrietta is a great friend of mine. She often speaks of you. At last our paths cross!"

Laetitia was known to him by sight. "Once seen, never

forgotten. Sadly," the super had sighed. She was slender and tall, standing eye to eye with Redfyre, and though well into her thirties, a strikingly good-looking woman. Unfashionably long, glossy dark hair had been persuaded to coil and twine around her head, endowing her with the authority of a Greek goddess whose sphere of influence was of the mind rather than of the flesh. Her white linen blouse was immaculate, her jewellery restricted to no more than one military sweetheart pin, carefully positioned just above her actual heart. He allowed his eye to skip fleetingly over the pin, having polite regard to its placing on a charmingly uncorseted bosom, just long enough for him to identify its regimental source. He recognised the silver eight-pointed star with its central red cross as the emblem of the Coldstream Guards. A "lady" by rank, in her own right by birth, she was unmarried. The badge, worn with pride almost ten years after the war, told her tragic story to the world.

The classical beauty above the waist was at odds with the tweed knickerbocker trousers, socks and mountaineering boots below. She had dressed for the north side of the Eiger rather than a gentle English churchyard, Redfyre thought. She caught his eye on her feet and responded archly, "Climbing is a skill one has to acquire in pursuit of winged creatures, Inspector, be they bats or golden eagles."

Redfyre was certain she was quite up to pursuing both.

He was politely offering his services wherever she thought it best to deploy them when the shout went up. A small girl in tennis skirt and plimsolls was teetering on a stepladder placed on uneven ground under a large tree whose spreading branches gave evidence of some nesting creature or other. The shout turned into a squeal of joy.

"Madeleine! What have you found?" someone called up to her.

"Magpie's nest! You never know what you're going to find

in the hope chest of one of those thieving birds! Naughty, naughty bird! They'll go for anything shiny! And this is freshly polished. It's not been up here for long, I'd say. Someone will be missing this! Laetitia will be able to identify it. Laetitia! Come and catch."

Laetitia obliged, hurrying over with Redfyre. She caught the tiny object with ease and turned it this way and that. Her manners obliged her to pretend to consult with Redfyre, ex-soldier that she knew him to be, although he was quite certain that she had known at once what it was.

"Someone is, indeed, missing this!" He held out a hand quivering with eagerness to take it from her.

"A lapel badge, silver, belongs to an officer, would you say?" She handed him a cue along with the badge.

"It's a rose. The white rose of York, surmounted by a crown and cradled by a French hunting horn—*un cor*. It's the insignia of the King's Own Yorkshire Light Infantry. The KOYLIs to the rescue. *Cede nullis!* That's their motto, ladies. Yield to no one! Good advice." He raised his head, laughed up at the finder and, in his excitement, blew her a kiss. "Madeleine!" he shouted, "the Cambridge CID loves you! You've shortened our workload by a fortnight!"

He slid the badge into his pocket, then, turning from the astonished girl, "Lady Laetitia," he said, "something's come up—or down. I must make some telephone calls. Good luck with the bats! Will you excuse me if I shoot off?" He reached for her hand, aware that he was behaving rather badly and, having no time to explain, was expressing his feelings through an unexpected and probably unwanted handshake.

Mystified, she returned his hearty squeeze. "Well, I'm not sure I *will* excuse you! I was just beginning to enjoy your company." And surprisingly: "*Dieu! Que le son du cor est triste au fond des bois!* Though not so *triste* for some, perhaps, I see from the gleam in your eye. More—enlivening? I shall want to hear the end of this *partie de chasse*, Redfyre."

THEY MET, AS arranged, towards the end of the day, gathering with notebooks around the table in MacFarlane's office.

The superintendent, perspiring and red in face, was slurping his way through a pint of India pale ale when they entered.

"Just back from lending a hand—more like a well-directed boot—up in Norfolk," he informed them. "Anybody complaining about his lot as a city copper gets sent straight up there to measure and note the span—that's the distance between the tines, for those of you of a nonbucolic persuasion—of fifty pitchforks, widely dispersed over a hundred-square-mile area, and match one of the buggers to the puncture marks in the back of a sixty-year-old farmer who's gotten up the noses of a whole village for donkeys' years."

"What fun you have, sir, when you take a day off," Redfyre said, smiling. "Sergeant Thoday and I have had that rare thing, an excellent day here. He's interviewed two pretty ladies, and I have investigated two of the more disgusting creatures in God's bestiary. What was Noah thinking when he let them aboard? Bats and eels! We have come up with the answers to many questions in the case of the graveyard tramp. We've had a minute or two to compare and consolidate notes but have much more to say."

Redfyre and Thoday produced their notebooks, pencils at the ready, eager to share their information.

"May I just say, before the sergeant gives his account," Redfyre said, "that I have asked for a phone call to be directed up here to your desk outlet, sir? It will be from the records office of the King's Own Yorkshire Light Infantry. We communicated with them about an hour ago. They were most helpful and told me they would have information for me before the end of the day. Hoping for six P.M. We have two links, sir. Thoday has tracked down the greatcoat owner, and then there's this, retrieved from the graveyard . . ." He placed the lapel badge on the desk in front of MacFarlane. "Swept off the greatcoat in question in the course of the dubious nocturnal activities. Rescued from a magpie's horde, courtesy of Lady Laetitia and the Bat Brigade. I told you they'd solve it!

"He would appear to be a Major Richard Dunne—in 1916, at any rate, on the evidence of his Jermyn Street tailor, as Thoday will tell you and we're awaiting confirmation and information from his regiment. And the sergeant has gone yet further. He has a possible identity for the man Dunne met in Aunty's tea shop, the man Dunne was trying to establish contact with. The man's wife, who was also present at the altercation, declares him to be Lieutenant—or perhaps Captain—Abel Hardy. It seems likely that the two were in the same regiment."

"Right then, lads, off you go. Tell me all!"

MacFarlane listened with attention to all they had to say, shooting the occasional pointed question to one or the other, filling in, seeing connections, planning ahead. A day in the fresh air of Norfolk seemed to have sharpened his wits, Redfyre thought.

"Rank of major, are we thinking? Humph! Demobbed, we assume. Bit old for the army. Shall we say 'retired'? And taken to the roads. Wouldn't be the first time. And the higher they are, the harder they fall. Probably done something he doesn't want his family to know about. Some awfulness he wants to atone for? A mental breakdown is probably what we'll find is behind all this. They've got a word for it nowadays, which we can quote in evidence in the reports. No one's going to argue with 'battle-induced neurasthenia,' because no one knows what the hell it is. These days it can't be shell shock, nervous breakdown, or even memory loss that afflicts a man. It has to be something with a Greek root: dementia praecox, psychosis, amnesia. Something along those lines, and the higher your rank, the more difficult it is to pronounce your condition."

The superintendent showed particular interest in the ex-army man Dunne had been trailing. "This mysterious overdressed bird? Straw boater and a college tie, claiming to be a detective? Don't much like the sound of him! Though his wife sounds quite a strider. And he's disappeared, according to his missis? Ho, ho! Have you tried ringing up that business address you got off the back of the cheque, Thoday? 'Enquiries At'! The Strand! . . . The Director is unavailable, eh? Not surprised to hear it. He's gone to earth. With or without his wife's knowledge and collusion. I think your suspicions concerning the lady are probably merited, Thoday. Next time Edith's up for interview, I'll take her on. See how she fancies a trip to Brighton with *me*! Give it another go tomorrow morning. We may have to send in the local London coppers to make enquiries on our behalf. That'll be the city police. Sharp lads—they'll stand no nonsense. My money's on this Abel Hardy. Takes a day trip up to Cambridge, tops his old army mate, buggers off. And are you saying you passed him in front of KOYLI?"

"Yes, sir. And I asked for any other close associates they had on record to be presented for our consideration."

"Good lad!"

"I spelled out that it has to do with a case of multiple murders in civvy street by a man or men with a military background. That got their interest! You could hear the closing of ranks down two hundred miles of telephone wire. Form testudo! Defences— hup! Clash! Clatter!" Redfyre's lively version of a Roman centurion's barked command had Thoday unconsciously straightening his back, but MacFarlane was not impressed.

"Not funny, Redfyre!" he objected.

The inspector had forgotten for the moment that the super-intendent's intense patriotism and his thus-far-undisclosed military experience, though comfortably in the background as a rule, occasionally surfaced, and when they did, they trumped every other consideration. Rough and unemotional as millstone grit he might well appear on the surface, but Redfyre never had any doubt that, if worse came to worst and the enemy was inside the palace, they'd find that the last door's last defence would be MacFarlane's own arm slotted through the bolt ring.

"Sorry, sir! I meant no respect to a venerable regiment. But every section of the British army has had trouble over the last few years with renegade elements. No one's surprised—battle-hardened trained killers, experts in arms, some of them insane, suddenly released back into a society that's moved on and has changed its values . . . well, it's to be expected. Will we ever forget that scandal in the Guards? They'll want no publicity of that nature! If they have any potential assassins on their books, they'll chuck them at us like a hot potato and let the civilian forces of law and order deal with it."

"All the same, Redfyre, when Yorkshire calls, I think it's only courteous if a Yorkshireman answers them. I'll take the phone call."

"Yes, sir. Thank you, sir." Redfyre found that he meant it.

AT 6 P.M., with military precision, the phone rang.

"General Whitcliffe?" The super appeared startled, but recovered quickly. "How do you do, sir? Yes, you are through to the Cambridge CID. Superintendent MacFarlane here. Ex-KOYLI, sir, rank of major on demob . . . You are? You did? Very kind of you to say so, General."

MacFarlane's eyebrows danced a jig, signalling surprise and delight, across the desk. "You have the information? Excellent! I will take notes as we go and look forward to receiving the written copy in tomorrow's post . . . Good of you, sir! Now, before we proceed, may I say I am not alone in the office. I have before me two of my best chaps, who are on the case and looking forward to hearing what you have to say. With your leave, I will include them in the conversation."

The exchange lasted ten minutes. It seemed interminable to one trying to interpret the shifting creases that passed for expression on MacFarlane's weathered features, and Redfyre was glad of the occasional repetition for their benefit of a vital word. ". . . tactical unit . . . distinguished conduct . . . medals all round . . . looting . . . hard labour . . . war psychosis . . ." The pencil flashed as he wrote down salient points. Redfyre noted that he covered three pages of his notebook. And finally, "*Cede nullis!* Yes, indeed, sir! Bad apple! We'll 'ave 'im, sir!"

MacFarlane put down the telephone and his pencil and stared silently at the wall, his furrowed brow giving the lie to the cheery confidence of his leave-taking.

"WELL, THAT WAS a bit of luck! Your query, Redfyre, got through to regimental HQ at a moment when the top brass were gathering for their end-of-year meeting. In the omnium gatherum hour before anyone had thought to pour out the sherry. Someone called out a name and good old General Whitcliffe took an interest. 'Leave it to me, I know the characters concerned,' he told them, and buzzed off with a couple of clerks to raise the dust of decades in the file room. And he *did* know. He was always a hands-on, leave-it-to-me type. And he was there, in South Africa, at the same time as our blokes. He was ordered south with Lord Roberts to clear up the mess after

Magersfontein and rode into Kimberley knee to knee with him.
Well, well!" he said again, annoyingly.

Unable to stay silent another moment, Redfyre asked quietly,
"Are we looking for heroes or villains, sir? The words we caught
were rather contradictory. And puzzling."

"They're sending a written report. I want you both to read
it carefully the minute it arrives. It's coming down the Great
North Road in the saddlebag of a motorcycle dispatch rider.
That's the importance they're attaching to the case. But for the
moment, enough to say—both heroes and villains. The regiment is still interested in a small unit of six men who managed
to get their names recorded for various reasons in the Boer War.
We're looking at a mixed bag of mixed-up individuals. Don't
trust any of them if you come face-to-face with them."

"Them, sir? I thought we had dealings with two men, the
tramp Dickie and now Abel Hardy, his possible killer. Exactly
how many men are still involved in this case?"

"Six, when it all kicked off. Though some may be dead. I
want them all gone over, every detail. Past and present. I'll
decide if they have a future! That coffin file case of the corpse
at the war memorial? Jessup? Anybody check his regiment?
KOYLI! They've got him recorded as dead. He could be number one. With Dunne and Hardy either perished or on the
loose, we're reduced to three to interview. They're dropping like
flies. I want the remaining trio found and interrogated, whatever their state of health or wealth. Write these names down:
Herbert Sexton, Ralph Merriman, Sydney Fox—and you can
add that madam Abel Hardy was or is married to, Edith. Go
down to London and fetch her up here, Thoday. We'll have a
little chat. And, if all else fails, what about, as a wild card—find
out if Sydney Fox's mother is still alive. He was the youngest ..."
He consulted his notes. "Seventeen at the time. She may be still
with us. How old would she be? Um, er—in her seventies,

would you say? Not impossible. Young Sydney may have confided something in his old ma."

He marshalled his thoughts, drew his notebook closed again
and began.

"Don't want to bore you with stuff you're already familiar
with . . . Look, how much do you fellows know about that
ghastly business in South Africa?"

Redfyre answered first. "My uncle saw action there, sir. I've
helped him—or hindered him—many times as a youngster to
refight some of those battles. Magersfontein, Modder River,
Bloemfontein, Spion Kop . . ."

Thoday smiled, bemused and out of his depth. Too young
for even the Great War, to him the Boer War was very ancient
history. "I was a Boy Scout, sir," he offered. "I dutifully read our
founder Baden-Powell's accounts of his exploits in Mafeking.
And I've always enjoyed *The Boy's Own Paper* adventure stories.
But that's it."

MacFarlane grunted. "Our two blokes, the tramp Richard
Dunne and the man he tried to contact, Abel Hardy, in fact knew
each other well. Their army records chime with each other step
for step for many months in South Africa. Dunne was captain
to Hardy's lieutenant. Both men were promoted virtually on the
battlefield as the Boer, crafty sods, learned very early on how to
pick out and shoot dead the enemy officer rank. Records say both
men were deserving of the ranks they held. Outstanding courage,
leadership qualities and initiative shown by both.

"Following on the battle of the Modder River, they were
sent off with a small company of men—a total of six—as a
penetrative unit with reconnaissance and stealth attack potential to take control of and survey damage to the railway line
north to Kimberley in the middle of Boer-held terrain. 'Hold
position until relieved' was the instruction. In other words, a
suicide squad."

"Poor souls," Redfyre murmured.

"They survived. I can't say 'against all expectations' because there were, you can bet, no expectations at all. No, the men survived thanks, I'm judging, to the extraordinary leadership and boldness of our tramp, Dickie Dunne. After relief by engineering elements of the Ninth—about a month later—he marched them back into base, now under the command of Lord Roberts—with my General Whitcliffe at his side. So I had an eyewitness account just now of the unit's procession into camp with their well-gotten gains!"

"Sorry, sir—gains?"

"The buggers! They'd somehow killed off the Boers who were holed up in the place they were to occupy and relieved them of a cargo of gold ingots they'd intercepted. Gold on its way down to—we presume—Cape Town and shipment on to Blighty. They handed the whole lot over to Bobs—Lord Roberts, freshly in charge of the British forces. Along with the horse that had been carrying them. Plus a lot of valuable survey information, which helped get the rail and wireless communications going again in double-quick time. It was quite a feat for a bunch of raw recruits with a fortnight's fighting under their belts. The general was impressed and took an interest in their future careers. Luckily for them, as it transpired. Whitcliffe is a doughty advocate. A man you'd want in your corner. The six were all decorated, given a special medal for constancy or initiative or something. The Queen's Own Award for Duty Done."

"Gold? Kimberley? Smuggling? Why does that make my whiskers twitch?" Redfyre said.

"Because you've been reading *The Boy's Own Paper*, too?" suggested Thoday. "The latest adventure, 'To Kimberley with Captain "Duty" Dunne?'"

"Mmm . . . well, no work of fiction ever had a conclusion as

painful as the one that overtook our boys. That early chapter
of derring-do ended all too soon for them. In crime, betrayal,
disgrace and imprisonment. A four-year sentence of hard labour
breaking rocks and laying track under a blistering South African sun." MacFarlane sighed. "And when I tell you the end of
the tale, you'll wonder, as I do, why on earth the six men who
all survived and made it back eventually into good old civvy
street, lived on peaceably for another twenty years, each thriving in his own way, many miles apart, before suddenly
rediscovering one another and fighting like ferrets in a sack.
Why? What was the trigger? What really happened to them
all in South Africa? We've got the KOYLI dates and listings
coming down to us. We'll know what medals they won, the
dates of their trial, imprisonment and release, but we won't
know their story. If we can't shake the truth out of the survivors,
we shall have to get hold of their nearest and dearest and"—he
paused and considered—"ask them to confide. Find that trigger,
the change in circumstances. A sudden revelation and we've
got the motive for two, possibly three murders. And I don't
intend to stand by and arrest the last man standing!"

CHAPTER 16

The documents sent down from Yorkshire were pounced on next morning, examined, exclaimed over, absorbed and mined for information. Actions were planned, tasks divided and handed out by MacFarlane.

"From London to Leeds," he said with grim satisfaction. "We're spreading our net wide, but needs must! No one's wriggling out of this through inattention. There, that's you lads fixed up for the next three days. And you can thank your lucky stars and your self-sacrificing governor that you haven't been handed the mucky end of the stick. Never send a man where you wouldn't go yourself. I hope you're marking and learning. One of us has to do it—go to Yorkshire. To interview an old lady who is most likely gaga." He sighed a sigh of martyrdom. "I'm assigning this task to myself. I'm bound for Leeds tomorrow morning. No, no need to be concerned for me—the local lads are sending a squad car to pick me up from the nearest railway station, and I'm spending the night with an old mate. I shall be back by Friday afternoon. During my absence, Redfyre, you've got the ship."

Redfyre and Thoday were ready for a breath of fresh air. Leaving the superintendent to work through a list of phone calls, they walked together to the morgue, where Redfyre checked on Thoday's extraordinary theory concerning the feet of the dead man. He stood, boots in one hand, staring at the well-tended feet of the corpse.

"By God, you're right, Sarge! Placing the boots so carefully—jokingly, almost—it wasn't the killer 'avin' a larf at our expense. He had to do it because their feet were different sizes. This poor chap isn't our hero Captain Richard Dunne, everyone's favourite tramp, at all. It's someone else. Someone he's met down in the graveyard or over the wall in Jude's College grounds and decided to kill. Using the approved and taught commando silent killing technique. He decides to cover up the murder—for as long as he can, to allow himself chance to get away—by swapping clothes and identity with his own. He doesn't mind 'dying.' If we fall for the story he's built up for us, the blundering cops will take one look and say, 'Dead vagrant. Drunk as a skunk. Another one.' Without further enquiry, the corpse will be noted and dated by the coroner and shovelled into a pauper's grave without a name. If it should be identified as 'Old Dickie,' well, that's no problem. As a tramp, he's ditched his identity years ago. He'll just change his name again. Either way, he's away free as a bird and no one's looking for him."

Back to practicalities, Thoday speculated: "So he left him wearing undergarments and suit that were unidentifiable and difficult to change in the dark on a corpse, then put his great-coat on top. With everything taken from the pockets."

"Except for the half crown, Sarge. He knew the police couldn't just have him shovelled away as a vagrant if he had the price of a night's lodging on him. Them's the rules! He knows what we know of legal etiquette and left it there deliberately, I'd say. Why else pass up half a crown? It's a goodly sum for a vagrant. No—Dickie Dunne wanted the body identified as Richard Dunne of Cambridge, logged and buried under that name.

"Then there's the dining club invitation card. I wonder if he overlooked that or left it in the inside ticket pocket because he wanted some sharp chaps to find it and investigate? I'm seeing a pattern. But the really tricky part was the socks and shoes. He couldn't expect to pass off as a man of the roads a corpse with manicured, bunion-free feet with—let's guess—fine wool socks and Trickers handmade half brogues that fitted beautifully. Shoes bearing the maker's individual last number, which would establish with one phone call the customer's name. Off come socks and shoes and he replaces them with his own disreputable ones. Except that he puts the worn right sock on the left foot. And—more important—he can't put the shoes on because they won't fit!"

"The assistant and I struggled. Couldn't be done, sir."

"Do we have any information on the height or size of feet of our second gentleman of interest? Mr. Abel Hardy?"

"Fits the bill, sir. Listed in the notes and service records that came down from Yorkshire. Hardy is tall—six one with size-ten shoes. Dunne smaller—five eleven with size nines."

"So he leaves the smaller shoes—the size-nine brogues—neatly by the tombstone in a soldierly way. Meanwhile he pulls onto his own feet the socks and the larger shoes of the man he's just killed. No problems there for a tramp. They prefer a roomy shoe, padding them out with wool and even newspaper. And, tracks covered, or at least, blurred, off he marches into the night in his shiny new city shoes."

"We'll be needing a positive ID of our corpse, sir. Teeth? There's a record of dentistry carried out in Doc Beaufort's notes. There's always fingerprints, but dental records are faster."

"Good thought! Do that first, Sarge. Find out who Hardy's dentist is and check with him. If we get a match, that will be the moment for you to haul in Mrs. Hardy."

Two impossible tasks! Remembering what Edith Hardy had said about her ability to disappear, Thoday responded with less-than-eager agreement.

"TEETH FIRST, THEN Edith," Thoday reminded himself. Back at the nick, armed with the doctor's diagram of the corpse's teeth, he settled himself at the telephone and worked out his plan of attack. How do you locate a possible victim's possible dentist, with, possibly, a practice in London? He looked again at the plan of the teeth. Several gold fillings— that was the most distinctive feature. A rich man, his dentistry wasn't going to be done by a suburban bloke who'd fire in cheap fillings from a distance; a hardworking man, he wasn't going to travel far from his office to get a toothache treated. Thoday calculated that his appointments would be made for him by a secretary from his office phone. He wouldn't have entrusted care and concern for his teeth to Edith. He thought for a moment then decided that low cunning was his best bet.

He lifted the earpiece and asked the operator to connect him with Enquiries At in the Strand. A cool female voice answered.

Thoday remembered that Hardy's discreet and well-trained office staff had given the police the cold shoulder when they had first contacted them. If Edith's account was true and this was indeed a detective agency her husband was running, then discretion would certainly be a priority. As a police sergeant, he would always be given a frosty reception at Enquiries At.

He introduced himself: "Hello. Regency Hotel, Cambridge here, and this is the manager speaking: Mr. George Smithson." He explained that her employer, a guest at present staying with them, had been laid low by a problem with a wisdom tooth . . . impacted, most likely . . . much pain was being suffered along with the not-unexpected fever. An excellent local dentist was being called in to deal with it, of course . . . *Mrs.* Hardy had left the day before and was unavailable for consultation . . . would Miss . . . er . . . Chapel kindly supply the name and number of Mr. Hardy's own dentist, whose number he was too confused and feverish to remember, in case the local chap needed to confer with him and check on Mr. Hardy's dental history? "You know what these dentists are like!" he added confidentially. "Worse than doctors when it comes to territory and discretion. Best to get it right!"

Miss Chapel was all concern. Oh dear! That had flared up again, had it? Of course she could help. The information was right at her fingertips in the Kardex file. A moment later Thoday was in possession of Hardy's dentist's name, Harley Street address and telephone number.

"Mr. Sharpe? Cambridge CID here. I have a question regarding one of your patients, Mr. Abel Hardy . . . Now, if I read off to you the contents of his mouth, perhaps you could confirm that they do correspond to your patient's record? . . . That's it! Right down to the gold fillings and single porcelain jacket crown." Thoday tried not to sound too triumphant. He expressed his warm thanks to Mr. Sharpe and somehow managed to dodge the dentist's concerned question about the state of health of his well-heeled client.

So the chap on the slab was confirmed: Dunstan was Mr. Abel Hardy. And his friend and suspected killer, Dickie Dunne, was out there dancing in the breeze, showing a clean pair of calloused heels. Thoday left a note of that important piece of news for the boss before he set off in pursuit of Mrs. Hardy.

He was off to the railway station, but he didn't think he would be dashing off to London. Not if he'd read Edith and her dangling luggage label right. Just to be sure, he rang again the number she'd given him. The same carefully enunciating maid answered, "Sorry, sir, the mistress is not available at the moment. She has gone to Cambridge with Mr. Hardy." *Gotcha, Edith!* he thought and grabbed his trilby hat.

Midday was a slack hour at the station. Neither of the two porters prowling about in action was the one he was looking for, so he went to the small, tobacco-smoke-filled room at the end of the platform where he thought he might find them with their mugs of tea in hand. The four men of assorted ages assembled in the snug were sullen and suspicious, but willing to hear him out when he showed his credentials.

"Four minutes before the London train gets in and we get to work, so off you go, then, Sergeant," the eldest told him firmly.

He introduced himself and asked pleasantly if he might know their names.

Jim and Fred Pearson, Enoch Smith and Christopher Sands declared themselves in age order.

"Thank you, gentlemen. It's actually Fred I need to speak with. I recognise you from yesterday afternoon. About four-fifty," he added.

"Thought it might be me you were after," the young man replied cheerfully. "I remember the moustache. Done a runner, has she?"

"Could you just confirm which platform you carried the lady's luggage to, Fred?"

"Course! Number six, Peterborough train. And it's all change at Peterborough for stations north." He added slyly, "Still, that's the lady's own business, ain't it? Why should I give her away just cos you ask nicely? You might be 'er 'usband for all I know."

"I assure you, young man, that there is a very good reason. But I respect your concern for the female sex. She's not married to me, or anyone, I think, at the moment. And she may be in danger," he added, lying to grease the wheels. Well, not entirely a lie, since MacFarlane had her in his sights. "I'm investigating a serious case, and I just need you to confirm something I already know. So you're giving nothing away. The lady has nothing to fear from me."

The hoot of an approaching train had every man including

Fred on his feet, tapping out pipes and downing tea mugs. As he dashed for the door, Thoday grabbed him by the arm and yelled over the noisy free-for-all: "Woodleigh Spa, Lincolnshire? That's what it said on her luggage labels, isn't it?"

The porter rolled his eyes suggestively. "Yer! That'd be it! Lucky for some, eh?" and raced for the approaching train.

Oh, Edith, Thoday thought, shaking his head. When I report this to MacFarlane, he's going to have to ask you to leave your green haven in the English countryside, the golf, the swimming pool, the Kinema in the Dell, the cocktails at six and the unquestioned if questionable goings-on with—I'm guessing—a gentleman who is definitely not your husband. And exchange that blissful setting for an interrogation cell in his nick.

MACFARLANE'S CHORTLE WAS as bone-chilling as a knock on the door from the Spanish Inquisition.

Thoday felt sorry for poor Edith. Her barely disguised excitement, her French perfume, her coquettish manner were all, in retrospect, due to anticipation of an amorous interlude in a notoriously louche pleasure ground, deep in the middle of the English countryside. Brighton? She'd planted the notion of a flight south in his head, and any other bloke without detective training would have missed that luggage label. She'd turned left instead of right at the railway station and gone north. Thoday had done his job, though with some regrets, and could now in all conscience chuck Edith into MacFarlane's lap.

The super signalled for him to stay in his place as he reached for his telephone. Thoday's reward, apparently, for his quick unmasking was to be allowed to hear the clanking of her chains being applied as MacFarlane pursued his quarry up to Lincolnshire.

"You were thinking, Sarge, do they have the telephone up

there in the hotel at Woodleigh Spa? They certainly do! It's in constant use! And always manned by the most discreet, plum-in-mouth desk staff. There is no way through their armour of reticence for the casual enquirer. I have established my own system of blasting through it."

"But why, sir, would you—"

"Missing persons, Thoday. You'd be surprised how often they fetch up in Lincolnshire!"

He turned his attention to the telephone. "Hello? Ah yes? Cambridge CID here, Superintendent MacFarlane. And your name is? Right, then, Benson. You have a guest at present, a Mrs. Edith Hardy, who is spending time with you. She checked in last evening. Come off it, Sonny! Now listen! I'm giving you a choice. Get her off the golf course, out of bed, prise her fingers off her gin and French—do whatever you need to do to deliver the message I'm about to dictate. The alternative—ask your manager. He knows the routine from experience. If I have to come for her myself, I shall arrive with a squad of policemen in an hour and a half. They will be resplendent in uniform and have big feet and loud voices. They will conduct a disruptive search of your most intimate recesses, Benson. While *I* am looking through the books . . . The message? 'Edith, get yourself back to Cambridge police station at once. There's a train at six-thirty, and an officer will meet you and escort you here. We have very serious news for you involving your husband.' That's all. Oh, just one other minor item—Mrs. Hardy's companion? Benson, don't be boring! At the moment I'm mildly amused, but if I have to galvanise my squad and come up there and turn over every stone . . . Indeed? Thank you for your cooperation, Benson. I'll stand the men down."

"The train, sir? This officer . . . ?"

MacFarlane beamed. "Mind doing a bit of overtime, Tho-day? I rather thought you'd earned the job. She'll be glad to see a familiar face when she arrives. Take her straight to the morgue, will you, Sarge? You know the drill. That should sober her up a bit."

THODAY HAD BEEN allowed to use the station Riley to pick up Edith. To his relief, she was actually on the train. She recognised him, but was anxious and silent when he greeted her. She grew even more anxious when he told her they were to call in at the hospital morgue before going on to the police station in St. Andrew's Street.

The corpse who had been Dunstan, the tall, elegant man with the manicured feet, was lying ready for inspection when they were shown through into the morgue. An assistant turned back the sheet over the head and presented the face for inspection.

Edith, pale but controlled, approached and looked intently at the waxen face. No shouts, protests or even tears. "Where's he gone?" she whispered to herself.

Thoday remembered his drill. "Mrs. Hardy, do you know the identity of the deceased?"

"Yes. That used to be my husband. Mr. Abel Hardy. What happened to him?"

"Thank you, madam. Will you step this way and sign a form to confirm identity, and then I'll drive you to police headquarters, where Superintendent MacFarlane is waiting to answer your question and ask some of his own."

"KILLED BY A military man, I'd say, Edith. The old blood choke method." MacFarlane demonstrated. "He won't have suffered for longer than a few seconds. It was a very professional assassination."

"'arf a mo', Super!" Edith said surprisingly. "I've been thinking about this. Abe may have been pushing fifty, but he kept himself in good shape. And he was quick on his pins. Had to be in his line of work ... detecting, I mean. The types he had to work with! It would have taken some strength as well as knowledge of a stranglehold to get the better of him. Who was he with when it happened?"

"You tell me, Mrs. Hardy. We're thinking death occurred on Friday evening. Sometime after six o'clock, judging by his last meal."

"His last meal? What would that have been?" Edith was puzzled. "He didn't eat it with me! I had to dine all by myself at the hotel. Not nice! Everybody stares! I was there—in the hotel dining room—from seven to eight. I expect that's what you want to know. I have no idea who killed Abel."

"It was jellied eels. His last meal."

"Don't be daft!" The green eyes scoffed at him. "There's no way Abel would eat jellied eels!"

"You seem less surprised that he got himself killed, however?"

"I'm not surprised. Been expecting it for years. Went with the job, didn't it? The types he mixed with! He was a detective, like you, except that my husband didn't sit behind a desk all day putting the frighteners on innocent ladies. Like I told your man Thoday, he often wandered off. I did sometimes think he might never be coming home again except in a box."

"When were you married?"

"Seven years ago. Look, are they going to let his body come home? I ought to get back and make some arrangements. He's got no family, but he's got businesses and a staff to think about. They'll have to be told." Pale with alarm, she shot to her feet, smoothed down her linen skirt and tugged up her gloves.

"Sit down, Mrs. Hardy. This is a serious business. Murder has been done, possibly several murders, and you're going to help me clear them up. The faster you tell me everything you know that's relevant, the better it will be for you. As it stands at the moment, you were here with him, accompanying him on one of his ventures. A partner in crime is what a jury is going to think. Who could have known that the would-be killer was destined to become the has-been killed? You would, Mrs. Hardy. The accessory before and after, possibly during the event. And all the damp lace hankies in the world won't deceive a Cambridge judge and jury, smart fellows that they are. Besides, when they enter, er ... Philip—your office manager?— into the equation, who can predict how stony their attitude will be? This is a moral, Nonconformist part of the world, Edith. In this county, we have no Woodleigh Spas, no Brighton. They would not be understood or tolerated."

She was a smart woman. She made her calculations and caved in, but MacFarlane remained vigilant.

"Abel was a soldier for most of his life. He retired after the war in South Africa—invalided out, wounded, he told me, with a bit of money saved and a pension of sorts. He put his money into one scheme after another, but they didn't work out. In 1918 or thereabouts, when it was clear we were winning the war against the Germans and the men would be coming back home any minute, he had an idea—another idea! For a business. Starting out in a small way. Small indeed! Just Abel and his secretary. That was me! He was getting on a bit—forty-three?—and I was much younger, twenty-five. We started the agency from his mother's front parlour. He had just enough savings to buy a typewriter and telephone and place an advertisement on the front page of the *Times*."

"What did the advert say?" MacFarlane asked.

"*Military Gentlemen desirous of reconnecting with old colleagues are invited to make use of our discreet and swift location services. Enquiries at ...*" she recited. "And he gave the phone number." She smiled. "That wretched phone never stopped ringing! So

many callers asked the same thing—'Am I through to Enquiries At?' The newspaper typesetters had spelled 'at' with a
capital 'A.' People seemed happy to use it. It just stuck.

"Just after the Kaiser's war, it was. You know the chaos. Army
units split up. Families, too. Men missing in the thousands. So
easy to lose track of loved ones." Her expression hardened. "Or
hated ones."

"Bit off more than you could chew, did you?"

"We got all sorts. Abe was very good at making connections.
He greased a few palms, got to know the right people—clerks
and record keepers and suchlike in the regiments. He could
always be bothered, Abel. Fell into a conversation as though
he'd only just spoken to you the week before. People liked him.
Told him their stories. The enquiries came in, and it paid well.
He took on another girl to do the typing and I helped him with
the tracking down.

"And that's when it got interesting! Some people didn't want
to be found. Were being tracked for sinister reasons, you can
imagine. Unpaid debts, treachery, 'that watch I lent him,' 'that
sergeant who had it off with my wife while I was in Mesopo-
tamia.' It took some skill, but Abe caught on that he could
charge a fee of those who didn't want to be found, just to keep
his mouth shut."

"Ouch!" said MacFarlane. "Asking for trouble, playing one
side against the other."

"He was very good at it. He got caught once when the two
sides compared notes and decided he needed to be taught a
lesson. Lost a front tooth in that little spat. Still, he was always
a good fighter in a dirty sort of way. Hard to lay a glove on Abe!

"Then, one day, something peculiar happened. Abe was
contacted by a very senior army officer who interviewed him
from his leather armchair in a club in St. James's. He wanted a
man found—a fellow officer—and Abe got the feeling that it

was for no good intent. The client clearly hated the bloke he was hunting for. Well, Abe located the bloke and reported back. The gent was delighted and paid up on the spot. With a bonus. Then he asked if Abe's services extended that little bit further. Experienced military man that he was—oh yes, he'd taken the trouble to enquire into Abe's records, which were impressive and 'shall we say—a bit mixed,' he suggested delicately. Could Abe see his way to being of further assistance?

"Abe didn't twig at first! Didn't catch on, he swears he didn't, but a week later, I caught him chortling at something in the *Times*. The bloke he'd run to earth had fallen off the top deck of a number fifty-two bus. The bit at the back. The fall alone might not have killed him, but the bus following on a few yards behind certainly did. Nasty! I couldn't think why Abe was laughing. Ironic? Two days later, a messenger arrived at the office with a small parcel. When I opened it, out popped twenty lovely, brand-new five-pound notes and a typed note with them: *Many thanks for discreet services rendered*, it said."

"A hundred quid? Bloo . . . Well, I never!" said MacFarlane in astonishment. He kept Edith fixed with his dark, double-barrelled stare, his fingers were leading a life of their own, scribbling a short note to himself. "Have you a date for what we might call this 'first contract'?"

"Um . . . In 1919. It was the week before my birthday. So it would have been coming up to the seventh of April." She fingered a row of pearls at her throat. "Abe peeled off one of the fivers and told me to get myself something nice."

MacFarlane's fingers registered another thought.

Her expression hardened. "Thinking you're in the wrong job, Sunshine? You could be right. There's a vacancy now. Interested? That's when it all started up. The phone calls! 'A friend of mine assures me that—in complete confidentiality, of course—proof of the undertaking will, naturally, be required.'"

"Proof?" MacFarlane leapt to his feet in his agitation. "What sort of proof did they expect of cold-blooded murder? A foreskin, a right ear, a head on a plate?"

"Nothing of the sort, Superintendent! Abe was never less than civilised. And by this time he was a dab hand with a pocket Kodak. He'd been involved with lots of domestic cases . . . you know, marital." Edith's chin went up defiantly. "The arrangement was that cash came in, half on requisition and the other half on completion. When the job was done, Abe would take a shot of the corpse—always identifiable and in a recognisable situation chosen by the client—as proof and put it in the post. They could never be traced back to him because he did all his own developing. He held on to the negatives in case he ever had trouble with a client not playing the game."

Trying for a calm he didn't feel, MacFarlane asked, "And does he still have these gems on file somewhere?"

"Yes. You're bound to find them when you raid the premises, so I'll earn a Brownie point and tell you—red metal file cabinet, northeast corner of the stockroom next to the bottom drawer. The key's on Abe's keyring. Did you find it?"

"I'm sorry, no. It isn't listed with Mr. Hardy's effects. Taken from the scene by his murderer, we must assume. Now, Edith, regarding his attacker." MacFarlane's tone became less stiff, more confidential. He put down his pencil to indicate, with misleading intent, that her following statements would be off the record. "Think on, lass! I'm fancying his old army superior officer, Captain Richard Dunne—Dickie—for this one. Would that sound reasonable to you?"

To his surprise, she burst out laughing. "Dickie Dunne? Kill one of his own men? Not likely! Look here, Superintendent. I've never met Dickie Dunne, but I've heard all about him." She rolled her eyes. "Too much about him! Abe was very uncertain when it came to the Captain. Loved him and hated him. Dickie was always his superior—man as well as officer—and that stuck in Abe's craw. I really think Abe's desperate attempts to make something of his life—preferably a large pile of money—were driven by rivalry. He always wanted to brag to Dickie that he'd made a better go of it in real life outside the army. It was his only chance to outrank him. But there was something more than just the jealousy . . ."

Her voice trailed away as she collated her memories and feelings. MacFarlane didn't prompt her, realising that she was using him as a sane and sensible sounding board.

"There was something in their experience that had marked Abe. Like a mental scar. Something he kept quiet about—something he held Dickie responsible for. I can't be certain, but I do know that he never let him go. He kept tabs on him, you know. Watched his progress through India and his further exploits in the recent war. When the day came that he discovered the Captain had taken to the roads and abandoned career and life, he rejoiced. Drank a whole bottle of Islay malt. Oh, Abe might well have killed Dickie Dunne, yes, but the man Abe described to me and logged over the years would never have killed one of his own men. He saved all their necks, you know. In Pretoria. *Do* you know?"

MacFarlane grunted, not wishing to stop her flow. "Carry on."

"The top brass were determined to set an example. The British were within sight of winning out in the province. Parading through townships, victorious. The men were seeing civilisation again with High Streets and shops full of things they couldn't afford to buy. They had to get the military out of the country with a good clean record so the politicians would have a clear field, Abe said. Both sides had dirty secrets they wanted to draw a veil over—like the concentration camps, the treatment of the native Africans—do you remember that in the papers? Well, there was something that it was in their power to do. To show how upright the British Army was. Looting, because it affected the general civilian population, was taken as a cardinal sin, and swingeing punishment was handed out for it. Men were hanged, Superintendent, most of them innocent."

"I have the details of the men's arrest and trial from KOYLI headquarters," MacFarlane said.

"Huh! What that won't tell you is that they were innocent. Betrayed. In fact, 'fitted up,' to use Abe's words. Some arsehole—also Abe's vocabulary—had gone to the bother of nicking some trinkets, shiny stuff from a shop worth about tuppence ha'penny, and putting it away in the men's lockers in barracks. Only the six in Abe's old platoon. And whoever it was had informed the police section of the army. Anonymously? Or had a deal been done? Abe has always thought the latter. But Captain Dunne accepted responsibility for the whole shebang and answered up for them in court. There was quite a hoo-ha, and with some big guns on his side, Dunne got off with his life and his men with him. They were all out in a year."

"And you're thinking ... ?"

"He saved his men from an unjust and terrible fate. A man like that would never throttle another soldier under his command. Not even a rogue like Abe, who certainly had it coming."

MacFarlane stirred uneasily in his chair. Her reasoning was faulty and showed how little she understood of the fighting man, but he was beginning to warm to Edith. Time to put her on ice and follow up some other leads he'd noted down. He told her she was being released into the care of the Regency Hotel for the next two days, and then, if all was well, she might make arrangements to transport the corpse home. After she'd finished explaining exactly who Philip Drew was and how he came to be caddying for her at Woodleigh Spa.

The moment she had left, MacFarlane reached for his telephone.

"Put me through to Scotland Yard, please, extension two-oh-seven? Jimmy! Mackie here. Could you check something for me in records? 1919, first week of April. A man died falling from the top deck of a number fifty-two bus. All I have is the initial news report, which is a bit thin. I can hold the line . . . Any witness statements? Could you read out the relevant bits? Relevant to my suspicious mind. Aha! 'The victim was observed to be in an altercation—even struggling as physical contact was actually made—with another man . . . Tall, slim, raincoat, fedora pulled over face . . .' No one ever arrested. Jimmy, mate, I owe you one! Would the murderer's identity repay the favour?"

Poor old Edith! MacFarlane wondered what vocabulary Abe would have called on to express duplicity and underhanded misrepresentation. A direct *Hey, old girl, I've just had a spiffing offer! All I have to do is kill a man and get away with it and a hundred pounds will be my reward. What do you say? Beginnings of a tidy little business?* Nothing doing! But if the dirty deed had been done "accidentally" and the old girl had had a chance to riffle her fingers through those irresistible crisp napkin-sized fivers . . . MacFarlane decided the word he was looking for was unprintable, but "con trick" and "quackery" came fairly close. And, if Edith could be taken in by her own husband, how much more likely was it that she was wrong about Dickie Dunne, whom she'd never even met?

CHAPTER 17

Redfyre and Thoday spent Wednesday morning alerting railway, bus and even motorcar services in the city that a man of no fixed abode answering to the name of Richard Dunne was being urgently sought by the Cambridge CID. This man would be required, on apprehension, to help the police with their enquiries regarding a recent crime in the city. Anyone spotting him was asked to telephone the police or report to any constable.

"Bit late, sir, don't you think?" Thoday asked. "I mean, smart chap like him, he'll be miles away by now."

"We have to do it by the book, Sarge. Though I agree our Dickie bird has most probably flown. It doesn't feel quite right to me, though. There's something we haven't spotted yet. Little things for me just don't add up, and it's making me a bit fractious."

"The most obvious being what on earth were, not one, but two old KOYLIs doing having a barney in the graveyard? Old enemies—old friends, sometimes—will have a fight over booze, women, even sleeping space. I've never heard of anyone putting out an expensive contract with a London hit man to rub out a harmless vagrant," Thoday agreed.

"That's the thing, Thoday. And I'm not at all certain the murder was done where we found the body. My mind keeps going back to the door in the wall between Jude's College and the cemetery. Why is the key missing? Where was it on Friday night? Where is it now, and are there prints on it? Did our Dickie actually turn up for his epicurean last supper? Have you thought, Sarge, that he may be dead himself? We could stumble on his body any moment—but only if our feet are in the right place. And why did our so careful murderer leave behind a clunking great clue?"

"Clue, sir?"

"This one," he said. "I've been carrying it around with me." He took the small white invitation card from his wallet and showed it to Thoday. "I shan't settle until I've tracked them down. These Friends of Apicius who invite people inside to dine and die. Let's go where Dickie's been leading us and take another look at the crime scene, shall we?"

THEY GLOWERED UP at the college windows, looking for an indication of life being lived, and saw none.

"There's a connection, Thoday. Over there. And I shall have to gain entry to investigate it. I'm sure it's in that place that our chap encountered the pair of thumbs that choked off his life."

"You'll never get inside a college without a search warrant, sir." Thoday, a born and bred Cambridgeman, shook his head knowingly.

Redfyre smiled. "I'm not envisaging mounting a frontal attack, going in with a warning blast on the trumpet and a rattle on the snare drum. But a sneaky rogue might creep about and find a sally port left open. Might even find a *dea ex machina* who'll ease his path." He looked up, located the window he thought the girl Rosamund had indicated was her own room and lined it up with his own upper floor front. Worth a try? His smile widened. "How's your lettering, Sarge? Mine's terrible, and I need some help with a notice. Let's step over to my house. Mind the dog."

Minutes later, to his mystification, Thoday was at the kitchen table, glass of lemonade at his elbow, copying out a brief message on a large sheet of drawing paper. "There you are, sir. Best copperplate!" He read out his work:

PERCANTA!
4:30

"Is this a tip, sir? Should I call in at the bookie's and put a bob on Percanta in the four-thirty race?"

"No horses involved, sadly. But I am risking all I've got on a certain little filly."

FEELING UNCOMFORTABLE AND anxious, Redfyre tapped on the locked door between the graveyard and the master's garden at half past four.

A shadow passed over the keyhole, and the remembered voice said softly, "I've got the key. Do you promise to misbehave yourself if I let you in?"

The large door swung open on silent hinges and he stepped through into enemy territory.

"I can spare you a few minutes. I'm free until five. Clever of you to choose this time of day. It's the quiet time between morning work and evening entertaining. Rosamund Wells—I prefer 'Rosa.' How do you do, John? Yes, I know who you are, John Redfyre. I've heard all about you from Earwig."

"Indeed! Then I'm only surprised you let me in," he said, and hoped his smile was not as ingratiating as his comment.

"After six weeks of living in this institution, I'd admit Vlad the Impaler for a little distraction! The key took some finding. It wasn't where it should have been. Look, there's a hook for it halfway down the wall, right beside the door. But I thought that if someone had locked it from the wrong side—that is, your graveyard side—they might just have chucked it back over the wall. Someone had. It was right over there, in the middle of the lawn." Detecting a groan swiftly stifled, she added quickly, "Calm down! I picked it up in my hanky. Not that you'd get any prints from it—the surface is too rough. Are you going to tell me what on earth was going on over there on Friday night? I've heard rumours, some of them quite mad and rather frightening. I live here, you know. I'd like to know why the police are suddenly interested in Daddy's back garden."

Redfyre told her as much as he thought she ought to know, sparing her the details. But she seemed to be ahead of him in her speculations.

"Poor old chap! How grim to die like that—alone—and with no one knowing who you are! Who on earth would bother to kill an old tramp? Why here? And all that business with the key . . . It's clear from the little you're telling me that someone from here, the college side, accompanied him or dragged his body through and put it on a tombstone. Yes? But the killer didn't come back the same way—he could have just locked up after himself and replaced the key. He must have made off through the churchyard and on to Trumpington Street. Didn't want to be seen on college premises? Or just not the master's lodge and garden part of the college?"

Redfyre looked down at the thoughtful face, which, though concerned, had a thread of excitement in the widening eyes. Her delicately pointed chin was raised in question, her mouth rather redder than it should naturally have been, and he guessed at a little lip rouge daringly applied. Today's dress was blue linen with a white collar. What had Hetty told him was the country name for heartsease? "Jump-up-and-kiss-me." Well, the children of Grantchester were to be commended on their poetic insight, he thought. A moment's glance at that face and any man would have gone weak at the knees and breathed those very words.

But Rosa wasn't offering an invitation to dalliance. As he stared and buckled, she was taking charge of the situation. Was this what Theseus had felt as the bossy Medea handed him the end of a ball of thread, a sword and a pep talk? *The labyrinth is that way, and the minotaur you're looking for is at the end of it, chewing on the bones of his last victim. Good luck! You'll find me here when you emerge.*

"Are you listening?" she asked suspiciously. "I was saying— why not do this the proper way and enter by the front door? My father's the master, after all. I'm inviting you as my guest to join us for tea at five o'clock. Present yourself at the entrance and address the porter. Give me a few minutes' start to alert him. Off you go. I'll lock up here."

TAKING HIS TIME, Redfyre strolled out through the church-yard and onto Trumpington Street and down to the entrance to St. Jude's. His long strides were carrying him too fast towards his destination, he reckoned. "A few minutes," she'd said. Why hadn't he asked for more specific timing? He decided to waste some time dallying in the rose borders that lined the cobbled path down to the front door. Well worth anyone's attention, they were well tended, thriving in their sunny position and already budding. Thanks to his aunt Hetty's enthusiasm for the flower—a delight that she spread to anyone within earshot in the summer months—he managed to identify several of the species. He found one, a dark red beauty, at that moment of perfection when the bud was bursting into a rounded flower head. He plucked it and threaded it into his buttonhole.

Forbidding, cold, grandiose, were his first impressions of the building. The porter in his antechamber was en suite with the architecture. But he was efficient. Although he could only have been in receipt of instructions for a minute or two, he was very collected and greeted the guest by his title. "Detective Inspector Redfyre? You are expected, sir. The master will see you directly. He is at present finishing business in his office and will escort you down to take tea with him in his parlour on completion. Percy will accompany you. Percy! Master's office, if you please."

He clicked his fingers and a young buttery boy stepped forward, briefly touching his own forehead with two fingers. And they set off into the labyrinth.

REDFYRE WAS LEFT by his guide at the door of a first-floor room. He knocked and entered upon hearing a shout to come in.

The first thing he noticed was that the large, airy room occupied a corner of the building and commanded a wide view of proceedings below in the front court. The master, now turning from the window to greet him, had probably been watching him make his way down the path, including his deviation through the rose planting. Oh Lord! He'd seen him help himself to that particularly luscious red bud and stick it in his buttonhole.

The master was as imposing as the room, which could have been designed with him in mind. His height was all the more impressive for being swathed from shoulder to ankle in a voluminous black robe. With memories of sadistic cane-swishing, black-gowned brutes still haunting him from his school years, Redfyre found himself for a sickening moment on the back foot, dry mouthed and speechless. The figure raised bushy eyebrows to signify that he had noted Redfyre's presence, but raised the palm of his right hand in a gesture that clearly said, *Hold on! I'm in the middle of something important, and you are an interruption in my day.*

"Now what was I saying? Ah yes—petty larceny about the college will not be tolerated. When discovered, it will be dealt with in a consistent manner. Any culprit making off with college property will be asked to leave and not return. Consider yourself, accordingly, dismissed from service with St. Jude's, and understand that no character references will be forthcoming, should you seek employment elsewhere. Yours, etc. That will be all for today, Miss Wells. Teatime calls, I believe."

Redfyre turned to look at the silent figure seated at a desk bearing a shining black-and-gold typewriter. Rosamund, whom he had seen just minutes ago, had been taking dictation in shorthand. Now she closed her notebook and put down her pencil, smiling back at . . . her father? Her boss?

"Outbreak of silver-stealing in the pantry," the master said by way of explanation. "The culprit was satisfactorily tracked down and has now been dismissed. The villain seems to have been working his way through the colleges, but his career of crime stops here."

Redfyre interpreted this piece of staged flummery as an assertion of power. *We have our own methods and resources and never need to call on institutions like the local police force* was the implication. How was he supposed to react to the man? With a demeaning *Do let me know how I may help you in a professional capacity, Master*? A forelock-tugging, deferential yes-sir-no-sir subservience was clearly expected. But eye-to-eye good manners and respect where earned came more naturally to Redfyre.

He nodded at Rosamund, who seemed to be mischievously enjoying the encounter she had set up, and decided for the second time that this girl was worth watching. As also, it now appeared, was her father. "Miss Wells? So good to see you again! I thought our paths might cross, so I brought up a small gift. Stolen from your own garden, I'm afraid. I must hope that your father isn't minded to arrest me for it and suppress a character reference. A rose for a Rose. A red rosebud." With a gallant gesture, he snatched the rose from his lapel and handed it to her. "This one is a very old French variety, I believe. Its name is 'Dark Secret.' Do you see, it starts out almost purple, the colour of venous blood on its way to the heart, then, the heart having worked its life-giving magic, it bursts out into the bright red of arterial blood. And its perfume is intoxicating."

Rosamund gulped and murmured something unintelligible. She politely sniffed the rose, then took it to a vase of sweet peas standing on the mantelpiece and pushed it into the water with them.

Redfyre turned to the master, and hurriedly Rosamund remembered her duties. "Father, may I present John Redfyre, who is our neighbour over the north wall and an inspector with the Cambridge police force? John, this is my father, Dr. Cornelius Wells."

Dr. Wells moved forward, hand outstretched, and the two men muttered polite formulae, eyeing each other with interest.

On closer inspection, it seemed to Redfyre that the gown disguised rather than exaggerated the man's athletic build. He had the strong shoulders of an oarsman and the sure-footed gait of a fencer. His features were more difficult to determine, covered as they were with outbreaks of facial hair. The dark eyebrows were a luxuriant windbreak for the bright eyes now scanning him from head to foot, the well-trimmed short beard slightly peppered with grey offering the only evidence of advancing age. The voice was also youthful. Firm and clear, it had none of the querulous academic affectation Redfyre had dreaded.

"Let me get something straight, Redfyre. I want to know to what exactly I owe the pleasure of your company this afternoon. Are you here to complain about the noise, prune the roses or ask for my daughter's hand in marriage?"

This was more like it! Brusquerie with a touch of humour—exactly what Redfyre appreciated.

"None of the above, sir, you'll be relieved to hear. Your students are ideal neighbours—silent and invisible, your gardens are tended to perfection and Miss Wells has sensibly rejected my advances. We shall be free to exchange views and information on a subject of equal and vital interest to the college and the Cambridge CID."

"Then may I suggest we repair to my domestic quarters and embark on the discussion over a cup of tea and a scone or two? If rumour has it right, my back lawn would appear to be the centre of your current enquiries. I shall be entertained to watch the law on its knees seeking clues to . . . to what? I can't wait to find out! Follow me."

THEY SETTLED TO their very English overtures over their very English tea in the master's drawing room, where tall windows stood open onto the expanse of lush lawn that separated the college land from the Anglo-Saxon graveyard. The usual conversational pawns were deployed.

"Heavenly, isn't it?" The master picked up and echoed his guest's thoughts. "Do you see that old mulberry tree over there? They say that it was planted by the poet John Milton himself."

"Like the one at Christ's?"

"Same vintage. King James was very keen on establishing the silk trade, and to that end purchased a job lot of mulberry plants in 1608 and sold them off all over East Anglia at six bob a hundred."

"Mmm . . . The poet Milton, if we're to judge by the folklore, would have been more of a gardener than a poet. His trees are here, there and everywhere. My aunt in Madingley lays claim to one. Every town a recipient of a tree and planted by his very own hand. Quite an achievement for someone who was no more than a babe in arms at that time," Redfyre ventured.

"And in later years, a man much more of a disposition to have dug them up rather than cared for them."

"So we're to understand, if last year's biography of the great man has it right. Did you . . . ?"

"I did. Much enjoyed!"

They exchanged knowing grins, each pleased with his showing in horticulture, classic verse and local history. Rosa rolled her eyes and yawned rudely.

"Pour your friend another cup, Rosa, love. And he looks like a man who can manage a second scone, topped off as it is with clotted cream and early strawberries from the home farm."

"Farm, sir?" Redfyre looked about him in surprise.

"The college is rich in land in various parts of the county, Redfyre. We own a particularly productive farm up near Huntingdon. I think it came to us by way of the deathbed will of some Cromwell or other. They produce much fine fruit and bring on their strawberries in glasshouses. Though I must ask you again—are you perfectly sure my daughter turned you down? This is quite a spread she's laid on in double-quick time, and I don't think she had me in mind! A slice of leftover Victoria sponge is what I usually have on a Wednesday."

He directed a good-humoured gaze at his daughter, who reddened perceptibly and replied at once.

"It was meant as an apology, Father. I was rude to the inspector the first time we met, and I hope that he will accept an offering of early strawberries as a show of contrition."

"For a man who spent four summers in the wastes of Flanders dreaming of little else not so long ago, strawberries will cancel out any debt, real or imagined."

The master laughed. "In Scapa Flow, it was jam roly-poly with custard I used to dream of."

"You're a military man, sir?"

"The Royal Navy. Not in an active way in the last lot, you understand. Advisory. Signals Intelligence."

Into Redfyre's puzzled silence he added lightly, "I'm not one of your lifetime academics. I'd rather *live* the life of Odysseus than study it."

"An unusual candidate for the mastership of a college?"

"Oh yes. The previous master was pretty ineffectual. He was sick for his latter years and, this being the sort of establishment where you die in harness, the college decayed along with him. Rudderless, no compass and no following wind. A bad situation. There was no obvious successor—four candidates who all loathed one another—so someone thought of making a bridging appointment, bringing in a piece of grit, a breath of fresh air, to wake the place from its medieval torpor."

"I understand." Redfyre spoke uncertainly. He did not really understand, his mind racing to fill in gaps and tie up ends. The whole story of this appointment smacked of manipulation from a higher source. The Admiralty? SigInt? Room 40? This self-styled "piece of grit," this disarming pudding fancier, might well be a formidable character. Rosa's father was beginning to look very like one of the stout supports of the English establishment. Could he be persuaded, tricked or charmed into telling a policeman what had gone so wrong in one of the country's oldest and most prestigious colleges that a tricky, fire-eating commando force of one had to be smuggled aboard to sort out the problem?

"Of course, I was an undergraduate here myself once upon a time and I took a degree in the classics, so I had a slim but essential qualification for the post," Wells was explaining. "The surprising thing, Redfyre, is that I've grown to quite enjoy what I'm doing. Hard at first to armour oneself against all that 'But, sir, you may not! Tradition allows ... The previous master would

never . . .' nonsense, but I'm making headway. My regret is that
my daughter is sacrificing a year—it may, despite my best
efforts, amount to more than a year—of her young life here at
my side. I know she misses her London life."

Redfyre was touched to see Miss Wells nip around the table
and kiss the top of her father's head.

"Who else would employ me, Pa?" she asked him. "At least
I'm finding a practical use for my qualifications."

Her father answered Redfyre's enquiring look. "Clever girl,
Rosa—"

"Oh no!" she interrupted, "Pa! Please don't give John a false
impression! I'm no Philippa Fawcett to outshine the male top-
wrangler in finals! Never think it!"

"Perhaps not," her father resumed, "but too sharp and active
to spend her days darning socks and doing good works. She
has successfully completed a course at the Lilian Carstairs college here in Cambridge. She's a shorthand typist and a secretary.
They're not the same thing, she tells me, and she is both. She
can do shorthand, as you saw for yourself, type at a rate of knots,
organise an office—organise *me*. I couldn't manage without her.
And, Redfyre, it's a portable skill. Rosa could walk into any
office and take it over. As long as we men are too lazy to learn
the skills for ourselves, she could have access to the highest and
most powerful departments in the land," he concluded with
paternal pride and—Redfyre thought—a dollop of ulterior
motive. The man seemed to think like a spy. "Trouble is, here,
surrounded as she is by pasty-faced scholars, day in, day out,
life's a bit dull for a girl."

"I had understood that you were planning to go to the Trinity May Ball, Miss Wells, to relieve the tedium?"

"Oh yes. But not with some dashing Trinity sportsman! One
of our own men has acquired tickets and has invited me to
accompany him. One of the young readers. Digby Gisbourne

is rather sweet, but I don't think he's capable of doing a very energetic quickstep, let alone a tango."

"What a coincidence! I shall be there, too. With a friend of yours—Earwig Stretton. I'm sure Earwig will insist that we swap partners when they strike up a tango, and I will happily step my way through it with you."

"There you go, Rosa, my love! That's a very decent offer! But just be sure not to annoy young Gisbourne. He won't think much of seeing a chap with the inspector's dashing good looks cutting in on his partner for the evening." The master turned to Redfyre and confided, "Gisbourne is the son of one of our most generous benefactors, you understand."

Redfyre shook his head in unaffected puzzlement. "Gisbourne? Should I know the name?"

"He's not a Cambridge man, though when he sets up shop—and you may take me literally!—in town next year, he will be! He's the son and heir of Gisbourne the Family Grocer. Young Digby is going to be a very wealthy man. In these straightened times the college has been lucky indeed to have him."

"Oh, it's no penance, really, spending an evening with Digby," Rosa hurried to say. "He may not be much of a dancer, but he's very lively and entertaining. He's easy and a good talker."

"He'll need those virtues in the career he's chosen for himself," her father commented. "He's one of those chaps who know from an early age what they want to do with their lives. Gisbourne has his eye set on the highest office in the land. He fully intends to be prime minister one day. Makes no secret of his ambition! Now, I ask myself—is that honesty, disarming in its naïveté? Or honesty, alarming in its directness? He's starting off by oiling up to the local dignitaries and party leaders here in the county with a view to being appointed Tory candidate for Cambridgeshire in the next elections in two years' time.

A much-sought-after position, apparently. A man to keep an eye on."

Did Redfyre imagine the amused look that slid between father and daughter at the comment?

"But that's enough of college gossip! Now, tell me about the murder that occurred on my back lawn last Friday night, and how we may help you shake out a few clues. My gardener is due to give the grass a short back and sides tomorrow morning, but I can hold him back if you wish."

Realising that the interest was genuine, Redfyre decided to break his rule of never involving a nonprofessional in his enquiries wherever possible and invited father and daughter to accompany him on a reconstruction of the crime as it might have occurred. A sweep of the lawn and a thorough inspection of the flower beds producing nothing of interest, they unlocked the gate and went through into the churchyard, taking in the bier that had held the body and spending a minute of silent contemplation by its side.

Rosamund appeared moved, and in an effort to better understand the circumstances, asked a few simple questions of Redfyre. "At which end was his head? . . . You say his boots were . . . here? At the foot? Why? If he took them off himself, he must have been attacked while he was lying stretched out trying to get to sleep? The boots tell you that he was not killed on our back lawn. I'm rather glad of that! Or else that he was throttled to death and then his murderer went to the trouble of removing his victim's footwear and placing it tidily by his side?"

"But such a natural gesture!" Dr. Wells commented. "Exactly what an old soldier—or an old sailor—would do. Done just the same myself for years . . . Had you thought, Redfyre, that if he didn't just stroll in on his own two feet and place himself on the stone, ready for death, it would have been quite a task for anyone to heave and drag his body all the way across my back lawn, through the locked gate—showing intimate knowledge of the college grounds—then undertake an ad hoc valeting service on the corpse and its clothing?"

"I certainly had," Redfyre managed to say before the master in his enthusiasm rushed on.

"And the clothing ... you say he was wearing an army great-coat? Well, anyone can acquire one secondhand these days. Anything useful in the pockets? Like a receipt for a meal at the Savoy or a ticket stub for the Palladium?"

Was the shove in the right direction fortuitous or calculated? Redfyre wondered.

"As a matter of fact, we were lucky enough to find one item. Overlooked by whoever cleaned out the coat. In an inside ticket pocket ...."

Redfyre took out his notecase and produced the Invitation to Dine card from the Amici Apicii, watching the master's face carefully.

Cornelius Wells took it with a wondering look, read the script on the front and then turned it over to check, as Redfyre had done, for pencilled messages or reminders on the back.

The inspector had expected a stone-faced, professional response, but was rewarded with a series of changing expressions that flitted in apparent spontaneity across the unguarded features. Astonishment, disbelief, anger, satisfaction and resolve—Redfyre identified all these emotions.

Finally, "Let's go and sit down in my drawing room again and consider this," Wells said. "I have something to tell you in return, Inspector. High time to show you my pitiful hand of cards, I think. Rosa, come. You must hear this, too. I'm afraid, in my overconfidence, I may have exposed you to something very dark and distasteful."

"Dining clubs are a fairly normal feature of college life, surely, sir?" Redfyre's tone was one of mild inquiry. "I was a member myself of such a one when I was up. Two, in fact! The 'Convivium' and the 'Goblin Men.' The first was expensive and pretentious, the second I hardly remember. For good reason—it had rather more to do with quaffin' than gobblin'."

Cornelius Wells nodded in agreement. "We've all done it. So you can imagine, I was astonished and—if I'm honest—a wee bit insulted when I was approached in the matter of the Jude's mastership. 'As temporary and as brief a tenure as you wish,' I was assured at a very private meeting in London."

Redfyre interrupted him. "Private, sir? How high did this go?"

"High enough to make my head spin! There were the college people you would expect . . ."

"The chancellor?"

"And the all-important vice-chancellor. Also the sitting member of Parliament for Cambridge and a shady-looking chap with a Ronald Colman moustache. Hear-all-say-nothing type, if you know what I mean. Intelligence outfit written all over him. A few men were hovering about with fountain pens and notebooks at the ready."

"To investigate a dining club?" Redfyre was baffled. "This speaks of a concern deeper than that springing from a collegiate matter. What sort of shenanigans could have so disturbed them? Political? Criminal? Why didn't they just come to us in the CID?"

Wells pulled a comically pitying face. "This country's dirty secrets are kept within ivy-covered walls by choice. 'No need for police boots tramping through peaceful courtyards,' I was told. Though your name had come up at an earlier stage." He smiled. "As a safe pair of hands. A receptive ear. Your skills are highly valued in the . . . um, inner circles, or perhaps I should say rather, 'opinion-forming cabals' of Cambridge society." He looked questioningly at Redfyre, but encountering an expression of puzzlement, he moved on. "In any case, the appointments panel concluded with a reassurance: 'We're reasonably certain that no crime has been committed, after all.'"

The two men shared a knowing glance. Reasonably certain? They both knew how to interpret that. These people were damned sure it had happened and were determined to hush it up.

"This heavyweight committee added lightly: 'It will take you no time at all to flush out this menace.' When I questioned the use of a strong term like 'menace' in relation to the student habit of harmless overindulgence in food and wine after the privations experienced at their boarding schools, heads were shaken and a tutting chorus tap-danced around the table."

"They made it clear that you 'didn't know the half of it'?"

"Exactly! I was made aware that this bastion of propriety, this pinnacle of academic excellence—my own alma mater, for God's sake!—was decaying from the inside, of a condition that was set out to me as a cross between dry rot and the Black Death!"

Redfyre sympathised. He would have reacted in exactly the same way to the committee's suggestion—with amusement and disbelief. He would have told them in clear terms what to do with their proposal. But, like the master, he was alarmed by the subsequent events and discoveries and in no mood for false bravado. Hindsight had shone its light into a very dark corner.

"So the upshot was that, though grumbling a protest, I agreed to take on the mastership for a term with the brief of digging about in the sewers of college life, uncovering any unpleasantness hidden away there, and after the requisite exorcism, presumably reburying the thing." With a rueful shrug of his shoulders, he confessed: "In fact, I quite looked forward to playing the new broom. Making some changes in staff, checking out the financial health, quelling the internecine fighting that had been damaging the college for decades." He sighed and admitted that a single term was a ludicrous suggestion. He was now approaching the end of his first year and nowhere near achieving his aims.

"The dining club, surprisingly, proved to be the least intractable of my problems. This trumpeted oh-so-secret society that was rumoured to be gnawing away at the very foundations of the college's morality was no Hellfire Club. And was anything but secret! Indeed, the members themselves were the only people in college or town who were under the illusion that their doings were a secret. I was given no help with establishing the identities of the membership initially. Everyone discreetly denied any knowledge. So I attacked on another, less well-armoured front. The kitchens! These diners provided dinners, somewhere here in the college. And they damn well didn't cook the food themselves!"

Redfyre smiled and nodded in approval.

"Interestingly, our college kitchen knew all about 'the goings-on,' yet denied any involvement. They huffed and puffed their disapproval. 'That bunch o' loonies!' were a law unto themselves. They operated in secrecy, and no more than once a term at irregular times somewhere up in the Cromwell wing.

At the other end of the college premises. The chefs they used, men imported from the town's best restaurants and occasionally up from London by train, operated within the confines of the top residential floor. A grand set of rooms up there—one of the best in college—is occupied by a long-established member of Jude's. The mad diners were only a bother when they ran out of implements or ingredients and sent a runner down to the main kitchen for a slab of butter or a cream whisk. Was the master, my head of the pantry wanted to know, aware of the risk of fire in Cromwell? Since the college had been electrified, newfangled stoves of some description had been put to use on the club dinner nights. That couldn't be legal, could it?

"The man's objections were valid, and I told him so. Enquiries, I said, would be made at once. And they were."

"But no immediate action to close them down?" Redfyre said carefully.

"Oh no! I wanted to catch them at it! Breaking a few regulations, even boring ones like the fire rules, would be the very best method of putting a stop to activities. No one argues with the fire regs! If I were to pull out their plugs on the grounds of—what? The running of a drinking club in the style of the ancient Athenian 'andron'? By the world's authority on ancient Greeks? The suborning of the young men of Jude's, perhaps? The unlicensed entertainment of assorted people of the town? I'd have been laughed out of college, Redfyre.

"I held off and pursued my enquiries. I have to admit I was disturbed by what I initially found. And, with my daughter's help, I was to discover much worse. Have you any idea what these men are up to? No? I think I have an inkling, though I may just have glimpsed the tip of the iceberg. I don't know whether to give a world-weary laugh or howl with despair for mankind. You shall judge! And, I hope, advise.

"Look—this club, the Amici Apicii? Huh! The worthy

Apicius should sue! It's surely defamatory to be claimed as a friend by these rogues. There's a shifting and changing membership of between six and ten, as far as I can work out. Who knows? Perhaps they're aiming for the classical nine guests for the ninth hour, but the best they can do is six for six? However, they have a central core: this classical scholar Fanshawe. He's a world authority on Alexander of Macedon: his hero, whom he in no way, thank God, resembles! He's also one of the two frontrunners for the position of master of the college when I hand over the reins. He can't wait! Wherever I turn, he's there! Ingratiating himself, trying to impress. I shall be very careful not to accept any dinner invitations from him. Fanshawe has many well-respected books and papers to his name. He's well established in academic circles. But I sense that he's . . . flawed. There's a hairline crack in his bell, if you know what I mean."

"Is he influential, sir? Is he listened to?"

"Oh yes! He's an attraction for younger men of all ranks and years in the college, it seems, on account of his character and tastes. He exudes sophistication. He's well travelled, a connoisseur of wine and food. More sinisterly, in my patriotic book, he does himself no credit when he sets himself up as a challenger to the views of the older generation, who chose to send the young men to war in their millions."

"'Pacifism'—the word that seems to have dropped out of your vocabulary, sir," Redfyre said with mock reproof, "is an easy doctrine to tout at the moment. And selective pacifism, even more alluring."

Wells grunted his agreement, looked with sharp assessment at the inspector from behind his eyebrows and ventured further: "I have caught him out using in front of students that fallacious phrase: 'Lions led by donkeys.' Wormed his way out of it, of course, by quoting Plutarch at me. Claims that he in turn was quoting a Macedonian general and the animals in question were lions and deer. Correct, of course, but not so catchy as the one currently in vogue. And Fanshawe is very much a man seduced by a turn of phrase. He's a neat hand at phrase-turning himself. And they stick in student's heads. The thicker heads. No—Fanshawe's a dangerous scoundrel in my book."

After a moment's silence he added grimly, "Redfyre, I have built a picture of what goes on at these bacchanalian routs, and—"

He caught Redfyre's anxious look in Rosa's direction and hurried to say, "Oh, it's all right! Stand at ease, Inspector! It doesn't disturb Rosa to hear this. She's a London girl, you know. *Bloomsbury,*" he confided as indisputable proof of her worldliness. "No, it's not sexual licence they indulge in. I should more properly have compared his social occasions to an ancient Greek gentlemen's drinking party—a symposium as described by Socrates or Xenophon. But without the acrobatic and obliging young lady flute-players. And certainly without the suggestions of orgiastic goings-on that have recently scandalised us in certain publications seeking to reinterpret the classical texts. No, it's torture that excites them. Mental torment of a selected victim in the pursuit of some gratification my own mind thankfully cannot grasp."

"Father is trying to avoid mentioning the name of the Frenchman de Sade," Rosa said primly. "But I expect he's wasting his time trying to spare the blushes of a police inspector. Can we just agree that these fellows are twisted, inhuman creatures? What they do when the urge to inflict pain on a fellow man comes upon them is trawl the streets of Cambridge looking for a suitable victim. He must be of low intellect, eccentric, negligible on the social scale—any or all of these. With charm and grace, they engage his attention and invite him to dinner. What an honour! Once there, they ply him with the good food and wine they all enjoy and tear him to shreds.

No, not physically—at least, that's what we first thought—but mentally. They have a game, scoring points like runs at cricket for each telling quip they make. They encourage the victim to talk, express opinions, then make fun of him, and when they've had enough, they turn him loose back on the streets. We had a very derogatory Anglo-Saxon term for that sort of nonsense at my Academy for Young Ladies in Kent! I bet Freud has a Greek-based word for their mental condition."

"Several," Redfyre said gloomily. "In the force, we come into contact with more psychopathic types than you'd believe. Nothing surprises me. Though I remind myself that, to the Greeks, 'psyche' was 'the soul.' A disease of the soul rather than of the mind, I often think, and therefore incurable by human agency. The mind is receptive to improvement, education, enlargement, but who can influence or even locate the soul? That's what every day finds me struggling to comprehend."

"It was the understanding of their game that led to an entirely practical thought in my Freud-free sailor's mind, Redfyre," the master chipped in. "A simple man's reaction against all this 'try to understand their thought processes' guff." His glance slid unemphatically over his daughter's head. "Who did the washing up? Hey? What? Sure as eggs they didn't soil their hands! I had the bedder for the Cromwell wing brought to me. Mrs. Hemple was a fount of information once she got going. A cup of tea and half a dozen custard cream biscuits loosened her stays and her tongue. On these 'dinner nights,' she'd been requested to do extra hours and been paid double her usual rates. She and her daughter were paid to turn up at ten and tidy up. They hauled the dirty dishes away in a basket, replacing them in the pantry next morning. With careful questioning, she became quite chatty. She had arrived early one evening with Ruby to find a stranger, the guest for the evening, on his way out. The ladies thought at first there was a fight going on. 'Some

Spanish bloke,' as Mrs. Hemple called him, was being escorted from Fanshawe's rooms by two men in dinner jackets. Not so much escorting as 'strong-arming' was her impression. The foreign gentleman was loud, singing and shouting both. He seemed angry. He shook off the two Jude men, fell down a few stairs, picked himself up, yelled at them in Spanish and shot off. The Jude men, seeing Mrs. Hemple standing there open-mouthed with her mop and bucket, told her to go away and report back in an hour.

"And, this is where it gets interesting, Redfyre—the Jude men followed him down the staircase and out of the building. Like sheepdogs? It's a tricky place to find your way about. Cromwell wing is a bit of an outlier. If you turn left instead of right as you're rushing out, you find yourself engaged in a cov-ered way that takes you through to my own territory. To the master's lodge and garden and eventually on to the back door of the graveyard. They wouldn't want a drunken, angry Spaniard plunging about the place looking for the exit. But how far did they escort him?

"It was Mrs. Hemple's parting shot that blew the lid off the jam jar. 'Could it have been the same man, Master?' she won-dered. The same as the body found on the lion at the museum? It had been in all the papers. Only they said that chap had been an Argentinian. Was that the same as Spanish? Poor gentleman had been found stabbed to death with his own dagger, and set to ride one of the lions like at a Wild West rodeo.

"I froze at that. But I found the words to get Mrs. Hemple to repeat what she'd said. The body had been discovered on the morning after the dinner party here in Jude's, where an angry Spanish speaker had been followed from the college by two of our dons. Rosa researched the facts in the press . . ."

"And we found that all Mrs. Hemple had to report was accurate. Mr. Ricardo de Angelis, dance instructor at an academy of terpsichore in town, had indeed been stabbed to death. No one was arrested for the crime," Rosa said.

"Could that be the reason you signed on at the tango school when you arrived in town, Miss Wells? Playing the detective?"

"She doesn't 'play detective,' Redfyre!" The master was quick with his reprimand. "She finds things out efficiently—faster, apparently, than the men we pay to be detectives! Things that perhaps your force ought to have established for itself some time ago. I'm here doing a job I don't want to do because your lot have not done their job adequately."

Before he could apologise, Rosa stepped in, eager, he thought, to short-circuit an awkward exchange. "Yes, John, you're right. It *was* the reason for joining, but I stayed for the dancing! Why don't you come to a session this Friday? The day after tomorrow. You could warm up before the May ball. There will be people there that you know. It's to be a special event. The last meeting of the year. Madame Dorine always takes the class outdoors and they waltz, tango and fox-trot their way down King's Parade! She's allowed to put a small band on the lawn by the college gates. People wander out of the bars and alehouses with their glasses in hand and join in the fun. It's by way of being a recruitment display and everyone is in their best bib and tucker and dancing their socks off. Do say you'll come!"

This was the last thing Redfyre wanted to do on his Friday evening. He needed to work overtime on his notes, but above all, he did not want to expose himself to the public gaze while posturing his way incompetently through a tango. He looked regretfully into her wide blue eyes and murmured, "I shall be delighted, Miss Wells. Shall I pick you up or meet you there? Ah, you'll be escorted by Digby Gisbourne, of course."

The master harrumphed and turned Redfyre's attention

back to his earlier question. "So, to this proliferation of corpses, the dance school would appear to have made its contribution. Can you reassure me, Redfyre, that it is a safe environment for my daughter? I think, Inspector, you may have fuller and more reliable records than we have here in college. Rumours? We have those in plenty. That's different. I can give you any number of the ones that were whispered in my ear, if you want to hear them. The theme is consistent. Men—noncollege men have died not far from here following at least one of these Jude's blowouts. May I return the question? How many, to your knowledge?"

"We have an assortment of between six and eight unsolved cases—some of which may be discounted on further inspection, but I will give you details. Finances being restricted, staffing at a low ebb, I find myself reduced to examining closely only two of them. The possible first, the tango man, and this latest, the tramp in the graveyard. I should perhaps add that there are other features in common. A military thread, for instance, will keep gleaming through."

Was it wise to be confiding this information to Cornelius Wells? Redfyre felt that the master and his daughter probably had more information to impart and would respond in kind when he divulged a little of his own to them.

"Military? You'd be looking a long time at this shower before you saw any sign of a military connection," muttered Wells.

"The nearest Digby Gisbourne has ever come to things military, I should imagine," Rosa said, "is prancing his way through a set of the Lancers!"

"Well, what about that! My dear, that card slipped out of your sleeve, and the inspector, I see, is about to pounce on it."

Redfyre was smiling at Rosa's confusion. "Ah! Another bit of sleuthing? This Gisbourne the Grocer fellow—could it be that you're getting close to him for reasons other than cheerful accompaniment, Miss Wells? Do you view him as a member of our dining club, or as a potential victim?"

"We've got him pencilled in as a member of the group, Redfyre. No more than that. The youngest member. The rest are all dons, so he stands out as a rather unusual choice. I expect because of the clout his father wields. And by clout, I mean cash, of course. Someone pays the wine bills, after all. Who knows how the minds of these men work and what their domestic arrangements are? If it's further names you're looking for, I'll tell you what we have. All supposition, rumour and blind guesswork, you understand."

He listed the remaining suspects he knew of: a Rupert Rendlesham, effete wine-bibber and all-round clever scallywag; Hubert Sackville and Quintus Crewe ditto. None had yet gone down. All three were still in their positions at the college.

"But look here! Why don't we stop faffing about and ask the chap Fanshawe a few direct questions? If he's at home, that is. He seems to be keeping his head below the parapet. I had a call from the senate house just before you arrived. He was supposed to be at a ceremony on their lawn this afternoon, handing out certificates of some kind, but he didn't turn up. I told them I'd look into it."

"Always ready for a bit of lion-bearding," Redfyre said cheerfully. "Coming, Miss Wells?"

THE DOOR TO the set of rooms on the top floor of Cromwell wing was a formidable obstacle. Of thick wooden planks itself, it bore a further layer of defence drawing—pinned to it. OAK UP, it said firmly on the back of an envelope. In a Cambridge college, this signified that the traditional medieval oak screen barring entry (long vanished now) was erected. *Keep out!* it warned. Its authority was never breached.

Dr. Wells and Redfyre automatically backed off on seeing

it and looked at each other, puzzled and wrong-footed, neither man wishing to break with centuries-old custom.

Rosa was unimpressed. "Such nonsense!" she said and tore the notice down. "Father, you must do something about this silly tradition. Even the bedders obey it. Look—one of them's abandoned her bucket and mop still full of soapy water in the alcove over there, rather than carry it all the way downstairs again to the sluice room. Oak-ups are bad for housekeeping! And judging by the smell creeping out from under the door, the poor lady's going to have her work cut out when she finally gains entrance."

As one, the two men stepped in front of Rosa and began to mutter suggestions that she should at this point leave matters to them.

Pale faced, she seemed to understand. "No, Pa. No, John," she said calmly. "Three is a more useful number. You may need a runner. Do what you have to do. I promise I won't faint or squeal."

The two men eyed up the solid door and then looked at each other.

"I'm a CID inspector," Redfyre said firmly. "I can break into any premises I suspect of harbouring a crime without a warrant."

"And I'm the master of this college," said Cornelius Wells. "Short of necks, perhaps, I can break anything I like under this roof. Your shoulder or mine? Both together?"

With a tut of irritation, Rosa nipped in front of them. "No keyhole, so no one's locked it from the outside. I don't think any of these old rooms have so much as a bolt on the inside. Let's try this first!" she said and lifted the catch.

The door began to swing sweetly open on oiled hinges.

The stink of rotting flesh, elevated to a peak of sensory experience by a high note of eastern spices, had both men coughing and gagging. Even Rosa, determined to impress them with her coolness, fished about in her pocket and produced a lavender-scented handkerchief to press to her nose. They stood in the doorway, ears straining, listening for a sound, anything other than the filthy noise of bluebottle flies, thick and busy at the open chafing dishes lined up along the table.

"The flies!" Rosa objected. "Are they getting in through the windows? The curtains are drawn, but someone's left the windows behind them wide open! Shall I shut them or leave them?"

"Leave!" both men called together. "And draw back the curtains so we can see what we're doing, would you?" Wells added.

"The table's laid for seven. A strange number," Redfyre commented. "But no guest even sat down. Plates and cutlery are unused. The food has been carefully presented, but not a spoonful has been toothed! The claret's uncorked but untouched. It's the Mary Celeste all over again! Where are the diners?"

He approached the dishes and angrily swatted at the flies. They counterattacked, loudly expressing outrage at the disturbance. In an effort to remember his professional status, Redfyre peered more closely at the dish of lamb standing in pride of place. "Ah! Where are we? Wednesday afternoon . . . Yes, I'd reckon this muck's at least four days old. This is Friday night's supper. I wonder what put them off their food."

Rosa had been prowling about the room so as to avoid a confrontation with the grubs. "Well, they got started, at any rate. They had a glass of sherry each," she said, counting with a finger. "No. Four had a sherry. One had a glass of . . . just spa water, I think. There's no sixth or seventh glass." And, in a tight voice: "Inspector, do you think you ought to take a look next door? Behind the screen over there, you'll find Fanshawe's study-cum-bedroom, I expect."

A nod from Wells sent him on his way. Trying not to appear dramatic, he slipped on the pair of rubberised gloves he always kept in his jacket pocket to avoid leaving fingerprints, rounded the Spanish screen and disappeared.

After what seemed an endless time to his companions, he reappeared. "Nothing of note. Bed's not been slept in."

Wells ground his teeth in disappointment. "I must say—I thought you'd find old Fanshawe gutted and butterflied on the bed."

"No such luck."

Rosa had continued to perambulate about the room, scowling with concentration.

"Pa!" she exclaimed. "Friday evening. We were outside on the lawn having a glass of champagne with Fanny and Louis and his brothers, do you remember?" She turned to Redfyre and added, "That's the Robertsons, old family friends from London. We were laughing and talking and not paying attention to anything around us—you must have noticed how secluded it is down there. Louis suddenly broke off in the middle of a sentence. He has sharper ears than a horse. "What's that?" he said. The rest of us had heard nothing. "Breaking glass and a shout. Over there." He pointed towards the college.

"And Pa reminded him where he was. In a college full of undergraduates celebrating the end of their year. Louis laughed and went on with his story."

"What time was this?" Redfyre asked.

"We never uncork champagne before six, and we were a long way down the first and hadn't started on the second," Rosa said. "So it would have been between six-thirty and seven when we went inside to have the dinner the cook had left out for us. The Robertsons don't much care to dine in hall."

"There's no sign of broken glass in here," Wells murmured.

Rosa had gone to the central window of the three, pointing

out black scuffmarks below the sill. "That's shoe polish!" She leaned out. "Oh my! Come and look," she said, and in a steady voice: "There's broken glass out there in the court. Broken body, too."

Redfyre was with her in a stride, pulling her away from the sill. He leaned over, the master alongside, and they took in the details, muttering to each other.

"That's Fanshawe! I'd know that silver thatch anywhere," Wells said. "Dead, of course." For a moment, his deliberate calm cracked as he appealed to Redfyre. "What the hell, Redfyre? Why Fanshawe?"

The inspector kept his response low and professional. "We'll assume, unless the pathologist has other ideas, that if that is indeed Fanshawe, he met his end on Friday evening, falling headfirst onto a very resilient stone paving. A flower bed, he might just have survived . . . And there's the glass. The remains of a sherry glass, is it? Look, still clutched in his right hand. And there's the sherry bottle—just beyond his head, that spreading dark brown stain."

"John, shall I go and call for the police? More police, I mean?" Rosa asked.

He answered, "Please do that, Miss Wells. Though I'm the officer in charge . . . Superintendent MacFarlane is away in the wilds of Yorkshire." He looked at his wristwatch. "Nearly seven. Probably sinking into his first scotch or tucking into his beef and puddings. I'm what we have left in Cambridge, I'm afraid." His voice firming: "Tell the officer at the desk I need Sergeant Thoday and two constables as a matter of urgency. And an ambulance. I'm at a crime scene at Jude's. I'll be needing the pathologist, as well—Dr. Beaufort is already on the case. And I believe it's connected."

Rosa gasped, repeated the names Thoday and Beaufort and ran to the door.

The detective in Redfyre was intellectually intrigued by the situation the prisoner had just thrown at him over the desk: an enclosed scene of a crime quickly discovered. All the possible suspects were present in the same small room, as were all potential witnesses. Guilty and innocent alike had been subject, without possible objection or quibble, to the questioning of their commanding officer, and the nonguilty had every personal interest in discovering the culprit and bringing him to justice. Counsels, judge, jury, even a choice of executioner—all were immediately available and under orders. Had the captain handled the investigation correctly? Given the eventual outwash with its flotsam of dead bodies, ruined careers and recrimination, Redfyre feared that something had gone wrong. Tremendously wrong.

"You're right. It should have been a dead cert!" The prisoner once again read his mind and responded to his thoughts. "And one day, if our relationship—such as it is—isn't cut off too abruptly, Redfyre"—with a quick gesture, he indicated hanging— "I should like to ask how on earth you, a professional, would have proceeded."

The moment he'd been working towards had arrived, and Redfyre seized it. He returned the prisoner's challenging stare. "Why wait?" he suggested cheerily. "Looked at clinically, what we have here is a textbook crime scene. Do you agree? May I suggest that we try to put aside any distracting emotions and ancient loyalties to find a solution to your problem? It's high time someone spoke the name of the guilty party. The man whose original crime has wreaked such havoc with your life and that of others and placed you right there, sitting opposite me in manacles—I think I know his name."

He left a pause for this news to impress and continued thoughtfully: "It seems impertinent of me to sit here all these miles and all these years distant from the action and say to the chief protagonist, 'I know what happened. I know your secret,' but *I* have access to information of a special nature. Records, sealed even to the participants, are opened to a policeman who knows how to play his cards right. And I haven't hesitated to rig the deck to get to the bottom of this festering sore. Some sources, like the King's Own Yorkshires, were pleased to share with us the details of one or two of their heroes and villains without any strong-arming."

"I'm thankful to hear that at last someone in authority has been seriously looking into the case. It took a few corpses to claim your attention, but I do believe we may have gotten there." The tone was almost teasing.

Redfyre responded with an equivalent lightening of mood. "You've no idea what I've suffered in the pursuit of the truth! I've skirmished with the master of a college, danced a fandango in the High Street, battled with a squad of pipistrelle protection ladies . . . I've even toothed a jellied eel."

"And they say a policeman's lot is not a happy one."

"People are always telling me, 'Ah yes! But this is Cambridge.' Sometimes, fancy footwork is of more use than a truncheon and a helmet, and I've put on a display of my most impressive *boleo*s to crack this case. We each have our special advantages, Captain Dunne. Between us, we should at last begin to make some progress, solve a few mysteries. What do you say?"

He waited for the grin and nod of assent. "Now, your original request when you came in this morning, if I remember, was for a sketch pad? Prescient of you!" He took a pad from a drawer and found a pot of pencils. At the invitation to sketch in the environs of the cabin, including stabling arrangements, latrines, the railway line, the river, points of the compass and estimated off-plan positions of Kimberley and the army HQ, the captain obliged with speed and neatness. He drew his last line, put down his pencil, turned the map towards his interrogator and gave Redfyre a challenging but not unfriendly look.

Suddenly, it appeared to the inspector that he was the one under scrutiny, his skill being put to the test. Well, so be it. The accused opposite him was a prisoner playing for his freedom, possibly his life. The poor bugger could have no way of knowing how much of his military career had been the subject of an enquiry in depth, but also at speed, by the Cambridge CID. Redfyre had cards left in his hand, and would hold them in reserve for as long as he needed. His adversary was a man he could respect and, yes, even like, as many others had. But Redfyre was not about to be affected by the dramatic story his investigations had produced.

False accusations of theft and looting had been levelled against the captain and his men towards the end of the war, resulting not in the hanging of one guilty party, since the captain had accepted responsibility on their behalf. There was no way even the rigid and pitiless military court could stomach the execution of a much-decorated war hero. And the outcry against such a punishment would have echoed loudly in the English press back home in London. It was considered wiser to sentence all six men to four years' hard labour in the army jail. Even if they survived the four years, their names would be forgotten. But the captain had made friends in the regiment and impressed senior officers by his bravery and general soldierly behaviour. What's more, inconveniently for the prosecution, he was the man who had brought back the "Kimberley Deposit," as the gold shipment had been called. It would have been the work of a moment for the captain to sign the official form, which was hurriedly put together and presented to him, a document exonerating him from all charges, and he could have been set free. But he had followed his principles and remained loyal to his men, fighting in their corner to the last and going down with them.

Even though, as perhaps only Redfyre understood, he had disliked and mistrusted each and every one of them. Cynically, Redfyre wondered if the captain's motivation had been to take a swing at the higher ranks he so despised in the only way open to him. A waste of a good man's time and reputation if so, Refyre reckoned. Those men were impervious to shame.

THE CASE HAD become a cause célèbre in the army, dividing the old-fashioned flog-'em-and-hang-'em top brass from the younger, lower-ranking officers who had learned much and fast about modern warfare in the burning crucible of South Africa. Captain Dunne was a hero to many. To the few who held the reins of power, he was a challenging, self-righteous thorn in the flesh, best silenced and held incommunicado in some remote place.

As the war rolled to its close, the question of what to do with the contents of the prisons was mooted. Without a roll on the drums, since the much more important matter of the civilian concentration camps that had been established on both sides of the conflict was wringing everyone's withers and claiming the headlines. But the army prisoners could hardly be abandoned in such a far-off place. Who would supervise them? They were military personnel, after all, whatever their crimes, and could not be abandoned to civilian jurisdiction. Their fit

of pique and exercise of power largely forgotten, the old mar-
tinets had died off, retired or turned their attention to mischief
elsewhere, and the decision to free the men with a general
amnesty—very quietly given—was considered on the whole to
be the least complicated thing to do.

Captain Dunne was rescued from enforced work on the
railway by secondment to a mounted infantry unit about to sail
to India to fight on the North West Frontier. They were short
of experienced men up there on the fringes of Empire. They'd
had plenty of recruits from young bloods like Churchill who'd
woken up and realised that this guerrilla war in the tribal lands
on the borders of Afghanistan was the sole conflict where a
true blood-spilling fight was being conducted, and if they
weren't quick, they'd have missed the action. But there was a
dearth of seasoned officers of middle rank. A Colonel Harris
had, according to Redfyre's informant in the regiment, decided
Dunne was exactly the type of man he was looking for. He had
gone personally to the jail and delivered an ultimatum to the
prisoner: "Your choice, Dunne. Break stones for rail ballast until
someone blows the whistle, which may take a year or two, or
leave tomorrow with your rank of captain intact to pursue your
army career. Soldiering on the North West Frontier. So: a slow
death or a fast one?"

Dunne had chosen to die quickly and gloriously. In the
company of the smart young Indian Army officers and their
stylish and well-educated seniors, he had flourished. Displaying
a courage that amounted to recklessness, he had impressed and
won more medals—and, it was rumoured, hearts. A good con-
versationalist and an entertaining storyteller, he had been
welcomed at the social gatherings of Delhi and Peshawar and
Simla. That was as far as Redfyre's informant could track the
subject. Or anyone. For some reason, the army career had been
abandoned. Captain Dunne had vanished from the records.

There had been the inevitable speculation in gossip-ridden India. That he'd "gone native, loincloth—the lot!" That he'd "found religion. Gone off to Tibet to practise Buddhism." No, none of those. "*Cherchez la femme* . . . Eh? What?"

If Redfyre wanted to know more, it would have to be elicited by careful questioning from the man himself sitting opposite, smiling gently, reading his mind.

UNCONSCIOUSLY, BOTH MEN leaned forward over the table at the same moment, eager to get on, the map between them. Any observer would have recognised two commanders planning a military operation.

"Let's clear away the undergrowth," Redfyre said briskly. "You can be absolutely certain that no one other than your company of six came near the cabin and its environs at the time of the crime or the twenty-four hours before?"

"Certain."

"So if you're telling the truth, the diamonds were taken out of the basin at some time before breakfast on the eighth day— the Wednesday. The day after the funeral."

"That's so. It could have happened on the Tuesday, but I was there on the spot directing things every minute. I would have noticed any funny business. My best guess is that the stones disappeared when Lieutenant Hardy and I were absent on the railway line. It makes sense."

"You've told me you normally worked together in pairs—a rough precaution, I'm assuming, against a quick pocketing of a slab of gold or an interesting lump from the sugar basin?"

"That's true."

"Useless!" Redfyre commented. "Well-intentioned, perhaps, but I shall rule it out as a consideration in the little enquiry we're about to pull off. It doesn't work. One of each pair goes to the latrines, for a bath in the river, tracks down an antelope and gets lost for half an hour . . . knows the truth and is loyal to his other half or is in it together with him. People alibiing each other is a continual hazard. I discount such stories. No, any alibiing your men came up with should be regarded as not to be trusted without further evidence. Still there is one advantage to this pairing system of yours—it reduces the activities of the company to three instead of six. Let's go through the day's activities between breakfast and breakfast for each pair, starting with yourself and Lieutenant Abel Hardy."

"Nickname 'Oily,'" the captain supplied.

"Why Oily?"

"Oh, you know the army, everyone has to have a nickname."

"Ah yes."

"The men catch on to quirks of character with alarming speed. The lieutenant did have a certain, um, emollience of manner. To begin with. In the nicest way—if two men were scrapping, he would intervene. Pour oil on troubled waters? I think the men had in mind the useful qualities of an oil can on engine parts rather than personal charm."

"A fixer?"

"A bit harsh, but yes. He also was capable of seeing things through. An ideal lieutenant, in fact. We had the same kind of grammar school background and Christian upbringing. Much in common."

"So you trusted him?"

"As much as I trusted any of my men, or even myself. Which is to say, hardly at all. Let's say, rather, I understood him."

"Tell me how you spent your day."

"Reconnaissance. We took the Boer mounts after our communal breakfast. We went north up the railway line, scouting for sign. Passing riders, game . . . We rode for five miles. It took us some time because we were also logging on a chart the extent of the depredations to rail infrastructure and communications.

We thought it would be of some use to the engineers if they ever came near the place. And it kept us busy. In fact, it was of use, I believe. On our return, we handed it over and the rail, and the telegraph system was repaired in seven days before the march into Kimberley. The engineers were the most efficient of our forces, since no officer knew enough about engineering to put his oar in and ruin their plans."

"All was well back home at Lemon Tree Lodge when you returned?"

"Just fine. Completely normal. The lads had put yesterday's stew on to reheat, and we had supper at the table. We bunked down for the night. It was Syd and Herbert on outpost duty that night, and off they went. The other four kipped down inside the hut. We had erected a bivouac tent just by the back door for the outpost lookouts, and when they were relieved at crack of dawn, they went and put their heads down there. They were allowed to sleep in until midday. I don't think the stones disappeared during the night. Some of us were light sleepers— goes with the job. We'd have woken up if someone had been creeping about sieving the contents of the sugar bowl. I think the dirty deed was done before suppertime."

"What steps did you take to retrieve the stolen diamonds?"

"Swift, stringent, ruthless. Without fear, favour or regard for rank."

"The only way," Redfyre commented.

"I sent them all into the outhouse, watching each other, and there they stayed until called in for their individual interviews. In alphabetical order.

"I made it an impersonal process. I told them each exactly what had happened and made no bones about the consequences for every man in the unit if the stones were not recovered. Then I ordered a strip and I searched each man. Thoroughly. I searched his clothes, every seam. Each man presented his kitbag, and I searched that, too. Wallets, chocolate tins, sewing cases, envelopes, the lot. Nothing. Every man was as clean as a whistle. When I'd put the fear of God into them, I told them that war does strange things to a man's mentality. I understood that. If whoever had taken the diamonds came clean and discreetly handed me the loot within the next twenty-four hours, I would take no further action."

"And yourself, Captain?"

He'd anticipated Redfyre's question and smiled. "I subjected myself to the same routine. I chose Private Sexton to conduct the search of my person and effects. Choosing Hardy, the only other officer, would have been the correct procedure, but might have been misconstrued by the men.

"Next up was a search in possible hiding places. The cabin was sparsely furnished, and it didn't take me long. No result. I had the lieutenant perform the same duty and he, too, came up empty-handed.

"We were left with the possibility of a hiding place outdoors. In a wide, unbordered landscape that stretched in every direction from Boer to Boer! None of the men would have been so unwise as to go far alone in that place. I wouldn't have done it myself. So we were left with the immediate vicinity. Not so easy. Between the river and the Kop lookout station, we were faced with a square mile of rock-strewn, channelled, porous ground where a thousand hidey-holes for a small number of diamonds were to hand.

"They all had convincing alibis for the previous day. Each swore that his pair had been in his sight all day when outside except when visiting the latrines . . . Yes, I checked the latrines! I was never convinced that the great outdoors, the unforgiving veldt would have been chosen as the deposition spot. They all hated and feared it. Scuttled in and out, looking over their shoulders whenever they had to leave the cabin. And for good reason. Anything buried would have to be put in at a good depth, even something small, or it would be dug up by some inquisitive snout. Herds of wild creatures ran right over the terrain, stirring up the dry as dust soil. Hard to remember exactly where you'd left a few ounces of diamonds in that wilderness. I wouldn't have chosen it, and I didn't think any of the men would have, either."

"The Kop? The stables?"

"Both. No result. I even checked the horses' hooves and the freshly reconstructed pouches in the Frenchman's saddle. Clean. You know, Redfyre, I still think about that wretched cabin! I know in my bones those stones were there, close by. I'd been outwitted by one of my own men. One of the number had had the nerve, the selfishness and greed to take them and the cunning to conceal them. Somehow one of us got out of that situation with the stones and profited from them at a later time. Is still profiting from them after all these years! It rankles, Redfyre. Like a festering arrowhead in a wound. I left it behind when I went to India, tramped it away for years after that. But it's there, still buried, polluting my blood."

The handsome face was looking every moment increasingly like the noble but strained image of a medieval saint. Redfyre rang for Jenkins.

"We've got ourselves a two-pot problem here," he said. "Jenkins, bring us a second round of this excellent tea, will you? No thanks, we're fine for chocolate biscuits. Have another, Captain?"

And then the uncomfortable theory struck him. He wriggled in his seat, trying to get his thoughts in an order he could present to the prisoner.

"Chocolate! Can we go over the kitbag inspection again? Can you bear it? Tell me again about the status of each man's Christmas present."

"Ah! Yes. Indeed! By this time five of us had eaten the entire contents of their tins. Each man had preserved the tin and put it to good use—keeping letters, sewing needles, the little pay we had. Which was never interfered with, I have to say. Everyone knew exactly how much the others had. Pay was sacrosanct." He paused for a moment, lost in the past. "Only Sydney, I think I told you, had his preserved tin intact. For his adored mother. I had a premonition about Syd's tin. It wasn't in his kitbag when Oily and I were searching the cabin.

"Oily went to the outhouse where they were all waiting and asked him where it was. He took it out of his pocket eventually when Oily barked at him. He must have left it in the outhouse in the care of one of the other blokes when he was called in to be searched and retrieved it later. The others shrank away, staring, hostile. Oily was suddenly afraid that a situation he couldn't handle was developing. Two against four, officers against the ranks. Sensibly, he ordered everyone back into the cabin and told me what the problem was. The rest stood around the walls, silent and mystified while I sat with Syd at the table. I made him put his tin on the table between us and asked him to open it.

"The kid said 'No! I won't!' and burst into tears. I offered him one last chance before taking it from him. He still defended it, shouting that we knew it was for his old ma. Had we no shame? He'd always made a big fuss about keeping it intact, and even sneered at those of us he'd seen taking a bite or two of our bars. Though he'd very readily accepted a share of Herbert's six bars when we'd celebrated. I had to inspect it. Feeling a crass heel, I seized the tin and prised off the lid. I realised it was coming off with surprising ease. I wasn't the first to lift that lid!

"Inside were two bars of Fry's chocolate remaining. Two! He'd been deceiving us about his single-mindedness and good intentions regarding his mother. He was acutely embarrassed at being caught out in front of his friends!"

"Um . . ." Redfyre started hesitantly. "Hard to put yourself in such a tricky situation from this distance, but, er, had I been there, I'd have jolly well given the two remaining bars a thorough going-over. Height of the summer season. By day at least those bars must have been in what my chemistry master would have called a 'malleable and ductile state.' Eh?"

"You're right! It occurred to me that they might have picked up a crunchy filling, moulded in during their melted state. I took a knife and cut one in two. Lengthways. It was certainly squidgy, but it was entirely made of chocolate. No filling. The second one also. You can imagine the self-righteous fuss Syd made! I'd ruined his mother's present. No, he didn't want to eat it now that I'd gone and spoiled it. The others could have it. He owed them, anyway. He flounced and pouted; his tears dripped. He showed every sign of hating me and encouraged the others to do the same in his snide way. And it worked. They did begin to mistrust me from that moment. Quite simply, Syd, in the face of the worst his officer could do, had proven himself innocent of a dire crime. Their further thought was that perhaps *that* officer had something to hide under a trumped-up accusation. After all, I had previous form for doing down Syd! Who had declared that his biscuit-scrounging proclivities should be discouraged? I often caught him looking at me sideways with the dying trace of a knowing sneer on his face."

"How did you resolve the problem of accounting for the, er, treasure trove when you made it back to the regiment?"

"It was Ratty who made the sound suggestion! He always went straight to the point. We all sat down and began to plan how best to avoid any charge of looting. Ratty got fed up with all the ratiocination! He said, 'For Gawd's sake! Just declare the gold! They'll be thrilled to get their hands on it! Ten secret pockets, ten bars to fill them. Nobody's going to turn round and say, *And what else do you have to declare?* Come out with some half-baked story about what may—or may not—have been a handful of uncut diamonds that we carelessly allowed to go missing, and the odds are they're going to get suspicious. We'd all be questioned and tormented until we cracked and spilled the beans, and then we'd be shot at dawn for treachery.'

"He was right, of course, and that's exactly what we did. We wrote off the diamonds and declared the gold."

"When did you last clap eyes on Sydney Fox?"

"At the trial in Pretoria. Where we suffered the faked accusation of looting and the hiding of stolen goods in my locker and those of all the other five who'd been in that reconnaissance unit. A scurrilous affair from start to finish. I know who finished it—their sententious, pious judging faces, mostly dead by now, are always with me. But who started it? Which ill-wisher, which Judas, planted the stolen goods on the six of us and the information with the top brass? We all had our own theory. And the time to think about it. The whole lot of us went down for four years. But you know this. You've checked my records?"

Redfyre nodded. "Your old regiment were very helpful. And concerned. Like family, you may try to escape them, feel embarrassed for them, but they don't forget you. You may remember a General Whitcliffe? He remembers you, Dunne. With, I'd say, respect and affection."

Dunne fell silent for a moment and decided not to comment. The Book of Commendation was closed to him, apparently forever. "We were sent to different prison squads—quite deliberately, I'd guess, to prevent recrimination and revenge killings breaking out, and we didn't see one another again during our time in South Africa. It was rumoured that Syd had gotten himself let off in some sort of deal by threatening to go to the press with his story. I can't say I blame him.

The newshounds would have leapt on it. There were packs of them still on the spot, digging up any filth they could: Youngster risking his life on Her Majesty's service, led astray at worst, innocently involved at best by his older comrades . . . it certainly had *Daily Herald* appeal. I suppose someone saw sense in the end, because Syd hopped off back to Blighty to help out his father in the shop. His two older brothers who should have inherited had died, and the now-experienced soldier and man of the world was recalled to be the sole stay and support of his old pa. So, word is that Syd slipped on his apron and spent the rest of his days slicing bacon and being polite to housewives. It's still there, the corner shop. I went to visit one day and got slung out by a smart young lass for scrounging. I just hope Syd managed to keep his sticky little fingers off the chocolate. History hasn't recorded what his old ma thought of her empty tin.

"The trial and the scandal could have ruined us, but the timing and the distance killed off opprobrium. I told you, no one was interested in that distant war. We'd relieved Mafeking, hadn't we? The mineral wealth was flowing again, and we were at peace. Celebrate. Move on. Meantime, I acquired a veneer of sophistication with some wonderful officers in India. Abel Hardy came home and thrived. He has quite a business empire in London. Make what you like of that! Herbert Sexton left his village and bought a house for his mother in London. He has a job that he loves because it enables him to wear a uniform. Security, I'd guess, is all he was ever seeking. Astute, undervalued old Ratty Merriman owns a betting business up in the north, and Corporal Ernest Jessup, before his untimely death here in Cambridge, was doing what he loved—he'd become an accountant and was doing well for himself with a big London firm. So a year's stone-breaking doesn't seem to have held anybody back in the long run. They put it behind them."

"And you?"

"I never could. There were other matters more important than a few gems that broke my heart and my spirit, but—God!—it's the thought that they may still be there out in the veldt that rankles. That and the need to know which one of us it was who could do that to his fellows drives me crazy."

Redfyre sighed. "Tell me how you got the gold bars back safely to base."

"We used the original pouches sewn into the saddle of the black horse. We didn't want any marauding Boers to intercept them, and we weren't handing them over to anyone of lower rank than a major accompanied by at least four witnesses! In fact, two days after we were relieved by the engineers unit, we set off back east and found the Ninth again. Under new management. Aiming high, I rather peremptorily demanded an audience with Lord Roberts himself, and to our surprise, he granted it."

A look of pure affection passed briefly over the strained features.

"This was 'Bobs of Kandahar'?"

"Right! Field Marshal Earl Roberts, VC. Hero of the wars in Afghanistan. At that time, in retirement in his home in Ireland. While we were away in the wilderness, the army had suffered some terrible defeats. The high command couldn't cope. Someone had the bright idea of shaking the mothballs out of the uniform of our greatest living hero, and he was ordered south to sort it all out. He arrived in the Transvaal just before Christmas. He was sixty-eight at the time, but still a fire-eater and a good tactician. The troops adored him."

"I remember Kipling's verse!" Redfyre announced, and the captain smiled to see the sudden transformation from worldwise copper to eager schoolboy as he prepared himself for recitation.

There's a little red-faced man,
  Which is Bobs,
Rides the tallest 'orse 'e can—
  Our Bobs!
If it bucks or kicks or rears,
'e can sit for twenty years
With a smile round both 'is ears—
  Can't yer, Bobs?

"That's a very unconvincing attempt at a demotic accent!" Dunne commented, and in a supple switch of tone, added a couple of lines in the true voice of a soldier of the line:

Oh, 'e's little but 'e's wise
'e's a terror for 'is size
An 'e does not advertise—
  Do yer, Bobs?

"Fan of the music hall, Kipling! And none like him for giving a voice—however rough—to the common soldier. And he didn't exaggerate the military acumen of Lord Roberts. He is—was—'Our Bobs,' who led us into Kimberley in double-quick time, riding the very tallest horse the army could provide. Very soon after that, he'd gotten Piet Cronjé in the bag—and his missis!"

"And you met him? You spoke to the great man?" Redfyre was aware that he sounded awestruck, but didn't much care.

"He listened to what we had to say and bustled out himself to the horse lines to take a look at the black. Kipling gets it right, you know—he was a true horseman! And Kipling was in South Africa at the time, reporting the news. I like to think that the very horse he saw him prancing around on was *our* horse! I think Bobs was more taken with the animal than the contents of the saddlebags! I saw him riding it often after that introduction. He was intrigued by the pouches and had the saddle taken away to the army saddlery in Cape Town—for copying, I expect. Well, it was a good effective design that deserved to be reused."

The prisoner looked questioningly at Redfyre, who had suddenly frozen, still and focused. "What?"

"Say that again, will you?" Redfyre told him.

But the captain didn't need to. The chain rattled noisily, underlining his anger and despair as he raised both fists to pound the sides of his head in frustration.

Redfyre moved the tea tray aside and pulled the map back into position between them. "Now, you had mentioned that anything to be secreted for later retrieval in this landscape should be buried deep and the spot clearly marked? Take a pencil and add the burial site, would you? The place where you laid Louis Duvallon to rest in a wooden coffin. In a deep hole dug by corporals Merriman and Jessup."

Captain Dunne responded at once with a large black cross in indelible pencil. They looked at each other.

"X marks the spot, I think," Redfyre suggested.

"Or did," said Dunne thoughtfully.

"You remarked that on the day you rode away, you didn't see it? The wooden marker?"

"It had been removed, hadn't it? Deliberately. Someone standing around the grave at the funeral ceremony had had plenty of time to learn the coordinates by eye. Had lined it up, triangulated it, I'd guess, with the Kop and the cabin and the river. Oh, there were plenty of points you could use for reference later."

"But meantime, the thief would much rather no one else was aware of Louis's last resting place, if that rich earth 'a richer dust concealed.' Someone might think of digging up the body and taking it back to Kimberley. Couldn't risk that, so, as one of the last things he did—in the night perhaps—who was on duty for that last patrol?—he knocked down the marker of a cross and pulled it away from the site of the grave. Dismantled, it was reduced to two meaningless bits of firewood. In one season of dust storms, bush fires, animal interference, without that cross, all trace would have vanished. There'd be only one man who could and would ever think of finding it again."

"A man who had patience. Was prepared to wait. Had the wit to work out that nobody was going to get out of there carrying a bag of diamonds in his pack or up his jacksy." Dunne spoke almost in admiration. "All that searching and we were never going to find them on him! He had them in his hand for less than five minutes!"

The memories of events never considered as relevant came flooding back and began to pour from him. "It was the day of the funeral. The grave was dug, I was preparing the body in the outhouse and he was helping me . . . I thought he'd volunteered to do that unpleasant job to avoid the manual labour of the grave-digging . . . I nipped out for a few minutes to check the depth of the hole and order Ratty to go down another foot . . . When my back was turned, he must have nipped back into the cabin, scooped the bigger lumps out of the bowl, replacing them with river gravel, artistically scattered a few flakes of diamond over the top and slid them straight back into the silk bag they came in. The bag! We didn't realise it was missing. I would have assumed, even if I'd bothered to wonder, that it had been chucked out with all the other Boer detritus when we cleaned up the cabin. Perhaps he'd always had the idea of reusing it! And had hidden it away in preparation for this moment? Then, as you caught me saying, Redfyre, a good, effective design deserves to be reused! He went back to the body, unscrewed the heel of the Frenchman's boot, reinserted the package, reassembled it and hauled it neatly back onto the corpse. Then stood back and admired his handiwork." With a wry smile, he added: "I even complimented him on his dedication. The state the body was in . . . Well, it was not a pleasant task, you can imagine. Although, by that time, for us, one rotting corpse among thousands was hardly remarkable." And, slowly, "We were all experts in dealing out and dealing with death."

"Are you thinking it was this same shit who brought about the false charges in Pretoria? So that, with you lot out of the way and himself having cut a deal and being on the loose, he could, once demobbed and out of uniform, make his way back to Lemon Tree Lodge and retrieve his plunder at his leisure? Either then or even years later. It was perfectly safe where it was."

"Yes. All that. I have to believe no one else was involved. Suspicion has always curdled our dealings with each other. I almost cut Oily's throat the other day . . . and all the time it was ghastly little baby-faced Syd."

Memory stirring, he added, "But, Redfyre, Sydney Fox—he's at death's door! At a hospital in London. Tuberculosis, and he's been out of action for some time, according to Oily, who always finds out these things. He can't have been rampaging around Cambridge, frightening the shit out of all of us this last bit. And why start with innocent old Ernest Jessup, twenty years later? What did he do to attract murderous attention all of a sudden? That list of corpses around Cambridge you say you have—old Syd can't be responsible. Can he?"

"Possibly not. Though his partner in crime may have interesting things to tell us!" Redfyre said grimly.

CHAPTER 20

U p in the wilds of Yorkshire: "Drop me here, Constable," MacFarlane said. He'd decided to get out and walk the length of the gravelled drive so that old Mrs. Fox, Syd's mam, could get a good view of him. He'd noticed the net curtains at the front bay window had twitched as the police car approached.

He saluted the driver, screwed his bowler more tightly onto his head—always a good breeze blowing in Yorkshire— buttoned up his khaki cashmere overcoat, squared his meaty shoulders and began to crunch his way rhythmically down the drive. He knew from hand-to-hand experience the devastating effect a cohort of KOYLIs could have. Even a solitary figure of MacFarlane's size and bearing gave pause for thought.

Had he overworked his preparation to interview the aged, reclusive mother of a man himself at death's door, a man who featured on his interview list concerning crimes committed in distant Cambridge? Crimes originating in a murky scene acted out a quarter of a century ago in a far-off continent? The link was tenuous. He would be required—all too literally—to account for this trip. In cash terms to his superiors, and much more trickily, in terms of motive, to the watcher within.

Yes, he had probably oversteered, he admitted. Turning up on her doorstep, dressed like a posh thug from the intelligence service, slim briefcase tucked under the arm in unconscious replacement for a swagger stick. Still, some ladies actually liked the look, he'd heard. And you should never underestimate the opposition. Tough breed, Yorkshire widows! You had to prepare for the worst and hope to emerge from any encounter without acquiring a crack on the jaw or a conjugal knot around the neck. How old had Redfyre reckoned this one was? Seventy-four? He should be all right.

He crunched on, his step unfaltering. But he recollected the advice given him just now by his young police driver on the long drive up from the railway station. When invited to mark Mac-Farlane's card, he'd replied eagerly enough and with Yorkshire brevity and pungency.

Yes, he knew the old girl. Old Ma Fox. By reputation, of course, like everyone up here, but he'd actually met her. Twice. Burglaries reported. He'd attended the scene and taken her statement.

"Was she lucid?" MacFarlane thought he'd do well to establish this.

"Was she lucid!" the constable spluttered. "Sir! She grabbed the pencil from my hand and the notebook and corrected my notes! Frothing on about apostrophes and punctuation. Said she was going to insist on having from the governor a written explanation for the low standard of literacy in the West Riding Police Force. And it'd better be in good English!"

"Ouch!" MacFarlane's sympathy was not feigned.

"Oh, she's got all her marbles, if that's what you're asking. Cunning old crow! We knew the amateur jokers who'd done both jobs—course we did—but we were so riled by the time she'd done with us, we were ready to shake their hands and let them off with a caution. Just kids, they were! But they got five years hard in the reformatory." He added bitterly: "She made sure of that. Up here, it's who you know . . ."

Anyway, it wasn't wise to argue with money in these parts, he'd advised. And that old girl seemed to have it by the bucketload. Her husband, old Freddy Fox—'Purveyor Of Fine Foods to Fine People,' he'd sneered—had landed some juicy contracts for supplying all the army depots in the north during the war years. "You can imagine what the average mud-and-bloodstained trench rat made of that slogan when he prised the lid off his tin of stringy horse meat stew." The business had gone from strength to strength. Rumour was, they were planning to move into the richer grazing grounds in the south of England next. "Under new management," he'd added in portentous tone.

A nervous maid responded to his knock on the door. She solemnly looked at his CID identity card, comparing the affably smiling features before her with the grim professional photograph pasted onto the card and decided that he'd do.

"The mistress will see you now in the parlour, Superintendent. Will you step this way?" And with a swish of the ribbons on her long-out-of-fashion evening-uniform headdress, she set off down the hall of Rosemount, Briary Lane, in the village of Wilby near Leeds, halfway between the golf course and the reservoir.

Her mistress, who had been seated in an armchair within curtain-twitching reach of the window overlooking the front garden, now arose and came unsteadily to meet him. Largely, he thought cynically, to demonstrate how feeble and thoroughly unprotected she was. Her black silk skirt and white blouse of Edwardian cut emphasised her vulnerable state. He took the thin, cold fingers she offered him by way of handshake, trying not to crush them in his bear's paw, and murmured the usual polite formulae for greeting a respectable old dame who has, to her great personal inconvenience, allowed a policeman to intrude upon her calm existence.

"Now then, Beattie," he said with a growl of brusque friendliness, "this won't take long if you answer up straight and true.

My car's parked round the corner, so as not to give your neighbours anything to gossip about. I have good manners, you see,
for a policeman. I can be in it and back on my way to the Leeds
nick in ten—"

"Inspector!" she interrupted him in a firm, angry voice, stripping him of two ranks in one word. "My name is Beata, not
Beattie! And to gentlemen of the police force, I am Mrs. Fox."

"Thank you for enlightening me. I'm Hesketh Frogmore
MacFarlane. Mackie to my friends. Superintendent to you,
Missis. Shall we proceed?"

She narrowed her eyes and nodded. "If we must. But
first . . ." She tugged on a bell pull, and when the maid entered
with a bob, called briefly for "the tray, Maisie. The drinks tray."

Turning again to MacFarlane: "Six o'clock is not a social
hour in this village, Superintendent. You have missed the tea I
had thought of offering you when you made your initial
approach and suggested five o'clock. Cook had prepared a very
good barm cake. Pity."

The tray must have been waiting on the hall table, since it
was brought in at once.

"What may I offer you? We have sherry, scotch, spa water,
lemonade or my bilberry cordial diluted with tonic water."

MacFarlane's eyes ran longingly over the Red Label Johnnie
Walker before he remembered his early start and exhausting
journey and the convivial evening he was looking forward to
with his old army mates, and his eyes flicked back to the
intriguingly purple-red brew in a ship's decanter.

"Would that be bilberries from the moors?" he asked.

"I picked them myself, not a quarter of a mile away. It's last
year's harvest, of course, and at its best full flavour now. I find
that half Barbados and half white sugar give the best colour. I
put some down every year as I have done since I was a girl."

"Then that's what I will have, thank you."

Jones obliged, tinkling glasses and squirting tonic. Without being asked, she served her mistress a large, rich sherry.

MacFarlane sipped and appreciated. He waited until Mrs. Fox had taken two good sips of her sherry and then embarked on his interview.

"Tell me about your son, Mrs. Fox. Your son, Sydney."

"Syd's dying. Haven't you heard? You've come the wrong way. You should have gone south to London. The hospice annex of St. Thomas's Hospital. He turned his face to the wall two weeks ago. I'm expecting the bad news any moment." And, suspiciously, "Are you the bearer of that bad news? Are you sure that's not why you're here? No? Well, my Syd's a good son. He's leaving me well provided for. I went down to see him—oh, a month ago to say goodbye, and he informed me of his testamentary dispositions. I am to keep this house and have a good pension for life." She sighed. "Such as it will be for a widow who's about to lose her one remaining son."

"And he served in South Africa, I understand. Did he tell you about his time down there?"

"He wrote me a letter every week. The post was better in those days before the war, even the post coming from South Africa."

"Do you still have his letters?" MacFarlane tried to keep an eager edge from his tone.

"No. That was one of his last requests. He told me to burn all his correspondence and the family photographs."

"What! Bit odd, that. Did you, Mrs. Fox?"

"Half and half. I burned the letters but kept the photos. Not his right to say, I thought. There were more people in those pictures than Sydney. They were family studies. His father and two older brothers as well, and I wasn't going to erase them from my life on a whim from Syd." She took another fortifying sip of sherry.

"Quite right. I've been trying to get hold of a picture of Sydney in his prime. Would you mind?"

"Only if you're prepared to come clean and tell me why you want to know what Syd looks like."

A few moments later and the maid was returning with the family album. She pulled out a small table and sited the ornate leather-backed book on it by her mistress's armchair. MacFarlane pulled up a chair opposite and settled in for a surprisingly comfortable chat with the old lady. He'd done this dozens of times with his elderly aunts, and he knew which remarks produced a response.

"So tell me, Beattie—which of these handsome lads is the eldest?"

"That's Joel."

"And this is?"

"Henry . . ."

The story, mostly a sad one, unrolled.

"Then this little bubble-haired scallywag must be—Sydney."

"His looks didn't last," said the doting mother. "His hair turned from blond to brown and lost its curl. He ended up quite ordinary-looking. He's bald now; he had quite a corporation before the disease took hold of him. He took to hiding it under sashes and gold chains when his waistcoats gave up the struggle."

MacFarlane looked into the dark eyes, hard as obsidian. Strewth! She must have been a bugger to please, he thought.

"But he always had a sharp brain, our Syd. He went off a-soldiering because there was nothing else for him to do except for helping in the shop. We just had the one then. No way Syd was going to dirty his hands serving the community. And with two older brothers ahead of him, he was never going to inherit the business. Though he had a way with Joel and Henry. Could twist them round his little finger from an early age. They were devoted to their little brother. They would never have seen him go short."

"Was he prepared for South Africa? That dreadful business?"

"Who was? Of course, he hadn't expected a posting any farther away than Hull! He'd never have joined up. But there he was. Stuck with it. He made the best of it, though, and came away back home with a tidy sum he'd saved. "There's nothing to spend your pay on, out there, Ma," he told me. He invested it in the business. Had to, really, Joel and Henry being dead. They died together in that snow of the winter of 1901. A crash in the Hawksnest Pass, making the Christmas delivery in the truck."

"Did he make any lasting friends in the army?"

"He didn't much like the men in his unit. You can't pick and choose in the army, but he was billeted with some real stinkers. He especially disliked his officer . . . a captain, I think. Dunne, his name was. He had it in for our Syd. Everyone noticed. Never missed a chance to do him in. But there was one who came to visit every year. A really good friend to Syd. Saved his life several times, Syd would say. 'Uncle Herbert,' we all called him."

"What was that, Beattie? Why 'uncle'?"

"Oh, that was what Syd's *son* called him. Turn a page or two . . . here we are. There's Syd posing at the front door, just back from the wars. Very brown, three inches taller and a lot thinner than when he'd left. They starved our poor boys! They were down to one biscuit a day sometimes. And here's the girl he left behind. Grace."

"Pretty girl!"

"Far too good for him. Her family came from down south. They'd been silk workers immigrating from France. Not much cash to start with, but lots of business sense. And fancy ways. I never knew what she saw in Syd. Anyway, Grace waited for him, and they were wed as soon as he came back. And that's when it started."

"What started, Beattie?"

"The boom, they called it. Syd said Grace had brought a bit of a dowry with her in a continental way, and he had his army savings. He took over. He bought up the rival shop in the village. Next year he bought three more out of the profits, and it snowballed. Everything he and Grace touched did well. Well enough to send their son to one of those private schools. I came out against sending a seven-year-old kiddie off to a school in the south. With his rough Yorkshire ways, he'd get a right kicking, I said. They just laughed. Of course, they were right. They'd employed a nanny for the little one right from the start. A London nanny who spoke proper. And his uncle Herbert had been giving him training in shooting and self-defence every summer holiday for years. Said he was preparing him for entry to Sandhurst military college.

"But in the end it didn't take. Waste of time! My grandson was much more interested in pursuing a university career. He's been reading history at Cambridge . . ." Beattie's frilled bosom swelled with grandmotherly pride, and her string of Whitby jet mourning beads stirred into a pattering applause. "He graduated last summer. And now he's working for his doctorate, and eventually he'll enter Parliament. Killing things and people was never going to be Digby's way in life."

MacFarlane bit back a facetious riposte to that rosy view of national politics.

She turned over a page or two and pointed. "There they are! Uncle Herbert and Digby and some creature they'd just stalked and shot up on the moors. And here's my lovely grandson as he really is: wearing his gown and mortarboard on the front lawn of his new college four years ago."

"Oh, I know that ivy-shrouded doorway. That would be—?"

"St. Jude's Cambridge. Ah, is that the connection? Is that why you're here? Has something happened in Cambridge?"

MacFarlane was flummoxed. He had no idea himself why he was up here, wandering down Briary Lane with Mrs. Fox and her family album. He had no wish to alarm her with garbled stories about bodies littering Cambridge and all occasioned by a contact with Jude's. Witnesses always liked to be proved right. They loved to say, *I told you so!* He'd press that button.

"Beata, you've guessed my secret. Got me bang to rights! Yes. It's all to do with Cambridge. Cambridge politics, to be exact. The state the country's in . . ." He shook his head, despondent. "The powers that be can't be too careful. His grandmother isn't the only one to spot young Digby's potential, and enquiries have to be made. In the most discreet way, of course! We are not a police state. But we are conscious of the growing danger of a certain revolutionary presence jostling for position with the *pots de chambre*."

"Reds under the beds, do you mean? Up here in Yorkshire? Never! Where do you think you are? We've got a golf club opposite!"

"Um, er . . . indeed. The prophylactic powers of the golf course are underestimated, I've always thought." He hurried on. "But the force does keep records, and in the case of an aspiring politician, especially one from the north—that dark, mysterious place!—questions are asked of us. If we don't know the answers, we have to ask someone who does know. And what better authority than a granny? I wonder, may I take away with me—for instant return, of course—these two photographs from your collection? This one and that one. There, that should set a few inquisitive minds at rest."

Seeing him get to his feet, Beattie rang for the maid.

"Oh, before I go—can you just confirm the year your son Sydney decided to change his surname by deed poll to . . . er, what was it?" He pretended to refer to his notes. "Here we are: Gisbourne?"

"1903. Just before his son was born. He thought it was a smarter name for the child and for the grocery chain he was planning. He'd just bought out a store called Gisbourne the Grocer, and he thought he'd help himself to the name as well. The old Gisbourne had just died, so he wasn't using it anymore. And it had Yorkshire connections, Sydney said. You know, Robin Hood and all that. There was a Sir Guy of Gisbourne fencing with Douglas Fairbanks in a film last year. My cousin took me to see it at the Palace Picture House in Leeds."

"Now I remember! Cracking film! You're right, Beattie! Guy of Gisbourne—the hired killer out to get our Robin, wasn't he? Well, well! Let's keep it in the county, shall we?"

The old lady came along with the maid to see him to the door. As he was handed his hat, MacFarlane looked at the strange pair, women from a past century playing out well-rehearsed parts. He had the unsettling feeling that, once the door had closed behind him, they would fade away and dissolve, leaving no more than a trace of mothballs in the air. He read a mute and hopeless defiance in their eyes. They knew all but could determine nothing. A woman who had lost her husband and two sons, was about to lose a third and—possibly worst of all—was about to lose her much-loved grandson to . . . what? To the sophistication of the south, to the rarefied uplands of academia, to the bear pit of politics, or to the remorseless attentions of Superintendent MacFarlane, CID?

They must not see the pity in his eyes, he thought. He could at least spare these proud women that insult. He took his hat and with an ancient flourish swept it across his front and bowed. Without irony. They bobbed their heads in response. He straightened up, winked and said cheerfully, "*Cede nullis*, eh, ladies? A Yorkshire motto, and a good one. Embroider that and hang it over your beds. And thank you so much for the bilberry cordial! An excellent vintage!"

A hangover and a late night were not the best preparation for interviewing a man who made his living from book-making; MacFarlane knew that. And warning enough perhaps that the man's nickname, according to the notes sent down, was "Ratty." MacFarlane would read nothing into that until he'd met the man. He rather approved of rats. Survivors, they were. Intelligent scavengers and good parents. He'd studied their habits in the trenches and knew why they held such hor-ror for most. But "bookmaking"? The profession—and that was a flattering term, rarely attached to the world of gam-bling—was thriving again now that the men were back home. Ratty Merriman was involved with what was technically an illegal activity, something the Betting Act of 1906 had done little to eliminate or even restrain. It was increasingly popular, and it was tolerated by the police—when necessary. MacFarlane knew that bribery was rife in most of the county forces, and so long as their activities were performed with some discretion, the bookies could thumb their noses cheerfully at the law.

"Mm, Park Parade. This is the place. I wonder which one of these emporia is acting as the front for the ponies?" he muttered to himself as they drew up outside a recently built row of shops.

"The one at the end on the left. Ease of access or egress." The driver grinned. "Basilio, the barber of Milan. You can get a haircut and lose your shirt at the same time."

As MacFarlane laughed and asked his police driver to wait, a commissionaire strode down from the row of shops that appeared to be his patch and approached the car. He was wearing a military-style greatcoat festooned with gold cord, and he addressed the superintendent with smiling aggression.

"Oy, you! Mister! Round the back, if you wouldn't mind! Bad for business, police cars. And this heap's got 'rozzer' written all over it."

MacFarlane was all amazement. "Naw! I'll tell you what's bad for business . . . a bag of wind got up in a pantomime uniform. A toy soldier who goes about annoying the customers." A left fist shot out with the speed and directness of a jackhammer, smashing into the doorman's solar plexus. MacFarlane ignored the spluttering and the wheezing and turned to his driver. "Did you see that, Sarge? Clumsy oaf fell right onto my fist! Must be drunk! Stay where you are and fetch me if he stops breathing. I may be some time."

A whistle, a beckoning finger and a cheerful guffaw greeted him as he approached and sized up the barbering salon. "We've all wanted to do that, Mister! Or should I say, Superintendent? Ralph Merriman at your service. And watch yourself with me! I've got army training, too! Come on through. Rita—that's my wife—has got the kettle on."

In the office behind the salon, Ratty found him a chair, cleared his desk and got down to business at once. "I should have come to you. Made contact. Years ago. But with old mates, it's not easy to know the right things to do. Anyway, Ernest dying like that . . . He was murdered, you know. To shut him up. I think Ernie'd gone too far and threatened to go to the police. He was talking about it. Or he may have been trying to blackmail someone. I'm talking about Ernest Jessup, ex-Corporal Jessup. We were close in the South African business. Kept in contact after we got back to Blighty. He was doing well for himself. The last time I saw him, which was in London, he told me he'd gotten a promotion at the firm—he was an accountant in civvy street—and had been given a really top-notch client to work on. With assistance, of course—it was a sort of training spell for Ernest. He was out to make an impression, you can imagine, and he was always careful anyway. He saw something he didn't much care for in the new account. Things didn't add up."

"And you can't be doing with that in accountancy," offered MacFarlane.

"It seemed like such a mad idea, he thought he must be mistaken, so he said nothing to his tutor, but on the quiet he made enquiries with the Inland Revenue, the Property Registration Records, Somerset House, and other bodies and made a very strong case of . . . not sure what to call it."

"Try 'fraud,' 'embezzlement,' 'theft' . . ."

"Naw! None of those. Big sums of money coming into an account without any explanation. No bequests, no wins on the stock market, no loans. Just cash out of the air. In large sums over the years."

"I can't think of a word for that, either. There's no such thing as regular windfalls, and good luck doesn't cover it. The horses?"

"Not in these amounts."

"Am I going to be allowed to hear the name of this Midas with the golden touch?" MacFarlane asked.

Ratty breathed deeply. He'd shot off at a fair lick on hearing the starting pistol, but he seemed about to refuse at the first fence.

"Before you commit yourself, Ratty, let me tell you that I know all about the unit and Pretoria," he lied. He didn't really know the half of it. "I even know the name you've got on the tip of your tongue. For Ernest's sake, you should confirm."

He fished in his pocket and produced a photograph. A

solitary figure, head bowed as though in mourning, was sitting on the steps of the war memorial, surrounded by wreaths.

"He was just there with the British Legion, paying his respects to the fallen. Someone bashed Ernie's head in, Ratty, and dumped his body there. You could be next."

Ratty looked with undisguised sorrow at the lonely body of his friend, and his mouth tightened. "Those bloody diamonds! They were bad luck! I knew they were trouble, but who'd have thought they'd follow us home?"

"Diamonds, Corporal Merriman? Er, would you like to turn back a page and give me a chance to catch up?"

MACFARLANE TOOK NO notes. He merely nodded his head sadly as Ratty finally came up with the name. It took far less effort for him, on shaking hands in farewell with Mac-Farlane, to look furtively from side to side then breathe, "Flapdoodle."

"What was that, Ratty?"

"Flapdoodle. The three-thirty on Saturday. York Races. You'll get good odds. Just place your bet somewhere other than Barnsley, eh? I don't want to attract the attention of the law."

MacFarlane grinned in appreciation. "Will do! And thanks!"

"And . . ." The cheeky grin faded from Ratty's face, and MacFarlane saw the drawn, determined features of the young corporal appear for a moment. "When you get your hands on the treacherous, murdering shit . . . Well, you're a soldier. You'll know where to put them! Squeeze hard. For Ernie!"

"I will at that, lad! And when I've done with 'is balls, I'll 'ave 'im by the neck!" MacFarlane vowed.

CHAPTER 22

"Great Heavens, sir! You're back early." Redfyre jumped back in surprise as he entered MacFarlane's office with a pile of papers for his records.

"No, just earlier than you were expecting, it seems. I came back yesterday more dead than alive—the trains are a bugger! Then I snatched a few hours' sleep and came in at six to dig through this pile of awfulness you've left for me. I can hardly begin to digest what I have, and I see you're about to add to it. Sit down man, and, give me my bearings. Start with this cove, Fanshawe, now gracing the marble slab in the Trumpington morgue. Did he fall, or was he pushed? I see you won't commit yourself."

"Not until I have Doc Beaufort's report, which is expected this afternoon."

"You're kidding. You know as well as I do that the doc talks as he works, unlike some, and he'll have given you chapter and verse. But anyway, before we plunge in . . . Yes, thanks for asking, Inspector, I had a very successful time gathering poisoned fruit in the north."

He passed two pages of notes over the desk. "For entry in the file. Stick them where you think fit. Both interviewees came up, one consciously, one unconsciously, with the same name. Now Fanshawe. Pity he'll never be able to spell out that name for us. I wonder if he was looking at the same murdering features when he experienced his defenestration."

"I was just bringing the police photographs of the body and locating shots of the scene, sir." Redfyre passed them over.

"And you say it was you who discovered the body? Looking down from this here window?" MacFarlane pointed with his pencil to the distance shot. "Mm, as I recall, my last words to you were, 'No way you'll get a warrant to enter St. Jude's.' And there you were, hours later, up in the highest interior recesses of the college."

Redfyre decided on jovial insouciance for his response. "No storming necessary, sir! I was invited to tea with the master and his daughter, Miss Wells, in their drawing room. A room that interestingly overlooks the graveyard, where our tramp who has proven to be not a tramp met his end."

"The master, eh?"

"Good man! He was most helpful. He'd make a good investigator. And thanks to his position, he had the means to organise the scene of crime swiftly and to everyone's satisfaction."

"I bet! Principally *his*. Everything hushed up and shovelled out through the back gate, I expect. In earlier days, Fanshawe would have ended up in the Cam. He'd be halfway to King's Lynn by now and no bother to us.

"And this is the corpse? A Friend of Apicius, are you saying?" He studied the close-up of the broken body with its thatch of silver hair. "Hard to make out where the blood puddle ends and the sherry puddle begins. Drinker, was he?"

"I'd say, certainly one of the Friends. An epicure, but not known to be a drinker to excess. Dr. Beaufort's preliminary assessment is that he had in fact drunk only half a glass of sherry on this occasion. He had fallen, holding, or had thrown down after him as a distraction, a bottle of sherry the contents of which the doctor calculates—in difficult circumstances—correspond with four or five servings having been already dispensed. That would be half a bottle of that size."

"Any idea who his drinking companions were?"

"Some. The table was laid on Friday evening for seven people, sir, so there's a hefty clue. Here's a photograph of it. Miss Wells counted four used sherry glasses and one that had contained nothing but water. Fanshawe was clutching a glass when he fell."

"The seventh man?"

Redfyre shrugged. "A bloke who signed himself in the visitors' book under a jokey pseudonym. Hardy?"

"We know he was about the place at the crucial time. He left his body behind in evidence. You can't be clearer than that."

"I've made off with the college refectory signing-in book, sir. Here, take a look."

MacFarlane took the book he was handed and studied the page for Friday the sixteenth. "The meal started at what hour?"

"Seven o'clock on a Friday."

"The dons—they have to sign a book like the students? Don't they object?"

"No idea, sir. It's only on weekends, apparently, and particular to Jude's. It helps the chefs keep a tab on numbers and cuts down on waste. Even the colleges have to watch their budgets these days.

"The first three—no, four—signatures are H. Sackville, Quintus Crewe, Digby Gisbourne and R. Rendlesham. Hmm ..." He pointed to the page. "You did notice the placing of these?"

"I did! And the ink. Amateurs! Still, given the circumstances, they may have been a little bit unsettled. Not their usual sharp selves. I've asked the science department to enlarge and evaluate."

"These are, at least, their bona fide signatures?"

"They are, sir. I've had them all in for questioning and made them show me. I've interviewed the serving staff and other diners who claim to have observed all four of them, sitting together near the door. The four have clear and accurate memories of the menu. D. Gisbourne was voluble in his condemnation of the quality of the rice pudding. Skin too thick, apparently. They all tell the same tale. Their story is that during the aperitif upstairs in Fanshawe's rooms, before they had a chance even to seat themselves, a quarrel of a nasty nature broke out between the two townies who'd been invited. Fanshawe was mortified by the unsavoury display and pettishly called off the banquet. Dismissed the four of them to the dining hall. They claimed not to be best pleased to end their day with shepherd's pie."

"And Fanshawe remained behind up on the third floor with the two warring guests? They ask us to believe this codswallop?"

"I've listened and noted, sir," Redfyre said wearily. "I made a public performance of taking their fingerprints. Mostly to annoy them, but also to compare with those on the glasses upstairs in the Cromwell wing, where the incident occurred, and as a precaution in case of flight. They're all poised to go down very soon."

"Exactly! Redfyre, I don't want that Gisbourne fellow going any farther than the Parade—"

"It's all right, sir. He has been duly warned. And Miss Wells, who has access to college records, is compiling for me a list of home addresses and close family contacts."

"Did she think of doing that for the victim? I take it his family has been informed?"

"It wasn't easy. Fanshawe was one of those chaps whose whole meaningful life is—was passed in college. He had to clear out of his rooms during the vacation at some point, if only to fumigate and redecorate, but he went kicking and screaming and hanging on to the door handle. His nearest and dearest is a sister in Norfolk. So he doesn't have to travel far from his books. He stays with her in the holidays. He has a small cottage on the estate, apparently."

"Right-oh. Now tell me, Redfyre, why the hell it took four days before anyone noticed the body. Did no one come looking for him? Did no one clap eyes on the corpse?"

"Someone had taken the precaution, on leaving, of putting the OAK UP sign on the door. So of course, no one tried to enter, although the door was unlocked."

MacFarlane drew in a breath with irritation. "Well, of course!"

"And if you'll look again at the wider shot of the courtyard, you'll see that the centre of the court is full of exotic shrubs—there's a particularly good magnolia. He landed on a strip of paving—a water channel, I'd say—but his body, lying flat as it was, was not noticeable from the far side. I had to lean right out to catch a glimpse of it myself."

"Guests? Did you have the sense to—"

"I did. I signed for it in triplicate for the porter, sir. Here it is. Two guests, indeed, for that evening. That nice young Mr. Gisbourne brought in the first: a certain Noël Coward, at six-oh-two, and then later, at six-fifty, we have a gentleman who appeared by himself but with prior instructions from Fanshawe to be admitted. Known in the portering trade as a PG, persona grata. Let 'im up, no questions asked! This was a certain Count Draco of Draconia, apparently. The porter maintained his sangfroid. He 'gets all sorts at this time of year,' he tells me. 'But the ones in capes are usually quite harmless.'"

"So Fanshawe marooned himself up there in his ivory tower with Dickie and Abel for company? A pair of hardened veterans, one of them a hired killer. You're in your right mind, Redfyre—would *you* have done that?"

"Lord, no! Well, not unless I was the one who'd hired the killer in the first place, sir. And I wanted to be quite sure I was getting my money's worth. Unless I'd lured my victim or victims up, then arranged for the fox to be let loose in the hen coop." He grimaced.

"And at the end of the day, who've we got left standing? A cast of dodgy characters. Out of the trio in the room of doom: Fanshawe's dead, Abel Hardy's dead, Dickie Dunne's done a runner. I think my arithmetic can handle those numbers. Our course is clear, wouldn't you say, Inspector? Get that bloody Dickie Dunne here as fast as you can. Countrywide appeal. Can you get an artist's sketch done? We have no photographs . . ."

Redfyre made a note.

"But I'll tell you, Redfyre, there's another villain left standing who by rights shouldn't be! The man who's behind all this bother. His eye strayed to the coffin box back on its shelf. "I'm going to have a rubber stamp made and take out all those case files and stamp them 'solved,' and I'll write the name of the bugger responsible on each of them."

Redfyre got to his feet, retrieved the coffin box and placed it on the worktable once more. "I'll leave that there until the day we can screw the lid down and bury it," he said.

"Why us, Redfyre? Eh? Going right back to that Chiqui bloke—what's the Cambridge connection? I can see that the dirty deeds we've got in here could all have been done by Abel Hardy: 'By special appointment, hired killer to the military.' Up from London on a day-return jolly."

"They've got his dabs all over them. But what's the pot of jam that drew him to our peaceable neck of the woods? And who's behind him, paying for death?"

"Oh, *him*? I found him up in Yorkshire, Redfyre, the skulking rat responsible for all this mayhem. You know me—I'm not a man to suffer 'hunches' gladly. Hunches are an excuse for sloppy method, but by Gow, I'm glad I followed one of my own and went up there! It didn't take me long. The answer's not hidden!

It's writ large in every town. Brazen as you please. Advertising itself."

He reached under his desk and produced a large carrier bag. "I brought the station a present back from the wilds."

"Oh, sir, thank you from all of us," Redfyre said uncertainly, receiving the bag. "Oh, I say! How generous!" he murmured as he unwrapped a large tin of biscuits. "Assorted Yorkshires. Shortbreads, chocolate fancies, gingersnaps ... As the label says, there's something in here for every taste. I claim the nut cluster!" And, meeting MacFarlane's impatient stare, "I had noticed, sir. The name on the tin. A 'household name' in the north and soon, I hear . . ."

"To be under new ownership."

"About to expand into the south."

"They're growing like Russian Vine, Redfyre. I went looking for the roots. And like poor, daft Ernest Jessup, I tripped over something in the undergrowth no one was meant to find. Look—here're my notes. I'll give you a minute to read them and see if you don't agree."

He watched as Redfyre read, shook his head, then, coming to the end, nodded sadly. "You'd worked it all out, hadn't you?" MacFarlane commented.

"I couldn't believe it. Didn't want to. Wrote it off as a hunch, sir. I had him right in my hands yesterday." He smiled. "But he's going nowhere. Can't afford to go underground. He'll keep until all our evidence is in."

"Can we afford to just give him free rein running loose about Cambridge, knowing what his game is?" MacFarlane was showing an unaccustomed uncertainty.

"I think so. He's exposed. In fact, his game's over. His tool, his murderer for hire, is lying chilled in a drawer in the safekeeping of Doc Beaufort. Likewise, his Machiavellian go-between, ringmaster Fanshawe. Dickie Dunne, I'd say, was a victim on his list who proved too quick and clever for him, but he's been smart enough to remove himself from the scene anyway, like an eel in the sand. I'm surprised you didn't trip over him in Yorkshire."

"So we're saying he's achieved his aims. Worked his way through his list. A list that corresponds to the one General Whitcliffe sent us. Dunne, Hardy, Jessup . . . all witnesses to his shameful crimes in the past, whatever they were. Let's just settle for theft involving diamonds, according to Ratty, treachery and false allegations . . . calumny, that's a good one . . . yet, Merriman and Sexton remain unscathed. Why?"

"Ran out of time?"

"Ratty knows—Ernie Jessup confided in him. I warned him to keep a sharp eye out. Unnecessary, perhaps. That chap's got the sharpest pair of eyes I've ever seen, and then he's got Rita guarding his stumps." He rolled an expressive eye. "Sexton? Photographic evidence, which I'm about to show you, would indicate that he's an ally and no danger at all. No, barring police interference, the future of this amateur lies in his own soft hands."

"All the same. In my book, sir, he's poison. Bad stock, like your Russian Vine. Hacked back for the moment, but still deeply rooted. And in our patch. I'll be watching him until you feel strong enough to seek that arrest warrant."

IN WHATEVER COMPANY Earwig Stretton found herself, she became the lightning conductor. Redfyre smiled and waved at his old friend across the crowded King's Parade. His thought was not a flattering one. Earwig herself would have used a phrase like "life and soul" or "catalyst" to describe the effect she had on a crowd, but Redfyre knew that she drew trouble down towards her and anyone who happened to be taking shelter from the storm in her environs. When he saw

Earwig loom over the horizon, he put on his tin helmet and prepared for the flash bangs to go off. He gave her another wave, which clearly indicated, *I'm here and happy, and I know what I'm doing. Carry on—you don't need me.*

With Madame Dorine's dance demonstration about to take off, Earwig was passing on last-minute instructions to the band assembled on the green by King's College gates. It was a rather large band, he noted, tough and professional-looking. Not one of them had cooed to a relative or friend in the crowd. "I recruited the ensemble in London," Earwig had said. The saxophonists in particular, with their patent-leather hair slicked down about their gaunt faces, could have featured on any constabulary wanted list. But they were paying close attention to Earwig. Or were they simply ogling her? She was worth a second and third look in her fringed, low-cut yellow silk dress. He noted that this group was equipped with supplementary instruments not often seen in refined Cambridge musical circles: guitars, tambourines, rather a lot of drums and surely more trumpets than were needed.

Satisfied with the band's response, she fought her way over the road to grab him and kiss him on both cheeks. "So glad you could make it, John! How lucky we are with the weather! A perfect spring day. King's chestnut has put out its blossoms to greet us. And you, too, darling, you've made an effort! That suit's perfect. And the shoes! Black and white, eh? Very daring!"

"My two-tone wing-tip Oxfords? You approve? They're all the go at the Palais de Dance. I chose not to wear my chocolate and cream with the nonslip soles because I hardly think we need worry about losing our footing on this surface," he said, knowing that she never picked up on his irony.

"They're not so good for a waltz, but just fine for the tango," she said seriously.

"I was going to make exactly that remark about the band.

Where did you find those villains? There are two sax players in the second row that we've had on our books for years. Bigamy on the left and burglary on the right."

"Don't be silly, John! They're lambs! Cecil and Georgio, if those are the two you're referring to, are members of the London Symphony Orchestra. They're moonlighting. And Lazlo and Igor on the front row are at present appearing with Ramon and his Romantics at the Savoy."

"What about the bruiser with the squeezebox on the right? The one in a fedora and leather trousers."

"Felipe is the world's best on the bandoneon. He's played all over Europe with Carlos Gardel. But here's Madame Dorine, dying to meet you. She's been trying to catch my eye for five minutes."

Redfyre smiled. "She caught *my* eye ten minutes ago!" he said, meaning it to be annoying.

Earwig performed the introductions and promptly disappeared, leaving Redfyre lost for words in front of a beautiful Frenchwoman in possibly her early thirties. Her bobbed, glossy dark hair, hooded brown eyes, wide red lips and daring décolletage were intimidating. Like a Long Tom field gun, you could admire its lines in profile at a mile's distance, but at close range with its barrel pointing straight at you, there was no choice. You chucked away your musket and ran.

"Take no notice of Earwig, *madam*," he found himself muttering treacherously in self-defence. "All her geese are swans. I've never had a lesson in my life, and the only practice I've had was in Parisian dance halls on leave from my unit. I'm afraid I'm more skilled at killing people than dancing with them."

"Then the tango is your dance, Monsieur Redfyre! That is its dark secret. It is a dance of barely disguised violence and hatred. The girl spurns, even kicks out at the man, and he despises her. He lusts after her, which is explicit in a properly danced tango, but ultimately, he throws her away like a soiled glove. Perhaps later . . . ?"

With superb stagecraft, she turned from him and began to make her way over to the band just as a kettle drum gave out three peremptory raps and a saxophone snarled a pay-attention flourish. The crowd fell silent and cleared the roadway. They'd done this before and knew what to expect. Madame Dorine spoke in a clear voice in perfect English with the merest trace of a French accent. It hardly mattered what she was saying; the crowd was entranced. People began to emerge from the ale-houses and cafés along the parade, and a noisy party from the Eagle had daringly brought their drinks out with them.

Redfyre gathered that she was promising a demonstration tango to kick off with, a dance with her partner, Alexis. Alexis stalked forward, lean, dark, tightly trousered, menacingly unsmiling, and bowed deeply to applause and good-natured wolf whistles from the crowd. After that, the dancers of her school would perform a waltz, a fox-trot and thirdly, a tango. Finally, the audience was invited to take part in a general excuse-me and choose a partner from among the dancers of the school, who would teach them the essential steps.

The band blared out, taking Redfyre by surprise. They were excellent. They made his heart beat faster and his blood pump in rhythm. His feet, in their appalling shoes, would not keep still. Someone had chosen 'La cumparsita' for the opening dance, a tune known to everyone. Dorine and the smouldering Alexis threw themselves from the first beat into the jerky, stalking rhythms, the saxophones restrained but carrying the swirling tune up above the dark bass notes like a wreath of nose-tickling smoke. Alexis's long, dark limbs entwined with unbelievable speed and sinuosity with the slender ones of Dorine, clad in red chiffon. They were male and female, fluttering flame and carbon-black embers. They were love and loathing. Indivisible, but eternally in conflict.

Too soon for Redfyre, the dance swirled to a conclusion. With a move that owed more to the techniques of jujitsu than the dance floor, Dorine thrust out an elegant leg and threw Alexis, in choreographed unbalance, over her hip. With both arms raised triumphantly in the air, she fixed him to the ground with his throat under her high red heel. The applause for the demonstration was thunderous. An odd moment for Redfyre's thoughts to turn to his aunt Hetty, but he wished, as he gave a piercing whistle of approval, that she'd been by his side to see this. She would have been scandalised, horrified by the louche spectacle, and laughing her socks off as she told him so.

At last, he spotted them. Rosamund Wells was wearing the lavender-coloured dress he'd seen her in when he'd climbed up on the water butt in the churchyard. She'd enlivened it with a diamanté bandeau, secured a green-and-purple peacock's feather over her right ear and a long rope of pearls dangled over her slim bosom.

Redfyre's heart thumped, and his muscles tensed on seeing that her hand was clutched firmly in that of a multiple murderer. If MacFarlane had it right.

Digby Gisbourne was not at his dying father, Syd's, bedside. Nor was he dutifully writing letters of condolence to the family of his mentor, Oliver Fanshawe. No. He was here, ungrieving, unashamed, making flirtatious conversation with Pansy-Face, as uncle Gerald had called her, and waiting in the lineup of dancers about to entertain the crowd with their prowess in the waltz, fox-trot and tango. In view of the whole of Cambridge. Despite himself, Redfyre found himself admiring the man's spirit and insouciance. His bloody cheek!

The inspector was more concerned to note that Digby's eyes never strayed far from the upturned, animated face of

Rosamund. He'd seen men paying court to suitable but unloved ladies before and was shocked to realise that in the scene being played out, young Digby would appear not to conform to that stereotype in the slightest. He was chattering away in a completely natural manner, bending his ear down to her level to hear her responses and laughing heartily. Uncle Gerald's dryly flippant comment came back to him: "Choose a woman who can make you laugh, Johnny—that's life's secret."

The villain Gisbourne seemed to have hit the jackpot. Rosa would make a wonderful wife for a rising—or risen—Tory politician. Hostess, aide-de-camp, confidante. But, even leaving aside the murdering nature of the man, how did Gisbourne measure up? Rich, ambitious, philanthropic, conversable . . . good-looking if you didn't mind that lofty, captain-of-the-first-eleven look, he supposed. Redfyre sighed.

With a surprising change in tempo and tone, but with no less enthusiasm, the band swung into "The Vienna Woods," and a troupe of a dozen couples forming a double line drifted, swooning faces and twinkling feet into the dance, circling, interlacing, forming and re-forming figures. How in hell they managed that on a road surface Redfyre was at a loss to imagine, but he was resolving, like many in the crowd, to sign up for classes as soon as he could arrange it.

Naughty Rosa had been less than truthful about Digby's prowess on the dance floor, he decided. The chap was no Alexis, but he moved with skill and seemed to be greatly enjoying himself. But Redfyre decided to mark him out of ten only when he'd seen his tango.

He reckoned Digby scored well on his fox-trot. The couples floated around, swaying and gliding effortlessly to a sweet jazz tune Redfyre thought he recognised: "Whispering." Then, in contrast, came the part that everyone had been looking forward to—the class demonstration of the tango. After a solo on the bandoneon so thrilling and musical Redfyre swore he'd never listen to an accordion again, they plunged into the dance he'd seen Rosa rehearsing. To his irritation, he noticed Gisbourne was throatily singing the words into her ear in the smoochy parts. To his further irritation, he had to mark him seven out of ten for the full performance.

As soon as the dance ended and the free-for-all broke out, Rosa was faced with a line of eager young blades who fancied their chances of being taught a move or two by the prettiest girl present. All blocking his way.

Chewing over his disappointment, he found himself being tapped on the shoulder. He spun round to find Dorine laughing at him. "May I have this dance?" she asked. "You see, I have chosen my pupil. I'm out to recruit you!"

Redfyre swallowed to see that people were making way for them with speculative glances as she steered him onto the road. He decided that the only thing to do was adopt his routine for facing enemy fire. Straighten your spine, square your shoulders and freeze your face. Perfect preparation, he thought, for the challenges of the tango.

Dorine was a delight. Medea one moment, sylph the next, her touch, varying between whiplash and feather stroke, guided him through it. He even began to enjoy the dance and actually caught himself growling in her ear once. Remembering her short way with Alexis, who had ended his dance spiked on his back in the dust, he didn't try it a second time. In an abandoned moment, he discovered that if he swung her sideways and upwards, she seized the chance of showing off some very intriguing scissor kicks. He had strong arms, and lifting her slim frame was no effort. He did it again. The manoeuvre also had the advantage of drawing attention away from his feet, which were often uncertain about direction, and length of step.

He stiffened for a moment as Digby Gisbourne stalked by

with a pretty girl barging deliberately into his shoulder. Dorine pulled Redfyre close and whispered in his ear, "He dances the tango like a Cossack. You dance it like a Frenchman." He thought he would never hear anything more flattering said of him and finished the dance cock-a-hoop, with the crowd-pleasing Gallic flourish of a hand-kissing for Dorine.

The excuse-me ended too soon for the crowd, leaving them shouting for more. This was not unexpected as Earwig, who seemed to have appointed herself *commère* for the occasion, jumped up onto the wall in front of the grinning band and announced that they would now have an encore.

Dorine leaned to him and whispered a suggestion Redfyre was delighted to take up.

A minute later, he was raising his glass of lemonade to hers in the select bar of the Eagle. "*Santé*, Dorine! A huge success! We've earned this. But won't you—"

"All's well! Earwig can manage. And this won't take long. I wanted to speak to you as a policeman. About Ricardo de Angelis. Chiqui. Five years ago. He was stabbed to death. No one was ever arrested for the murder. I've always wondered …"

But never quite managed to come to the station and make an appointment, Redfyre thought suspiciously. *Why this moment?* Aloud, he enquired, "Did you know him well?"

"I was his professional dancing partner in those days. I took over the school later from the owners when they retired. I identified his body. He had no family in the country, no close friends. I'm the only one who would think to ask about him."

"But not the only girl who might think about him," he suggested, and aiming for an impression of efficiency, hauled a name up from the black box file. "One of your pupils, a Miss Amelia Bullen, I believe, was amorously involved with him?"

"Nuts about him! Completely barmy!"

"Do you remember what happened to her?"

"She'd been working here in Cambridge in a bookshop. To get away from a lonely life in the family home in Norfolk. An uncle of hers found her the position. After Chiqui was done to death, her parents insisted that she return home. That's where she still is, I assume. Under lock and key, I shouldn't wonder. I send her Christmas cards, but she never replies. We all know her ghastly old father was behind it. But you didn't wait to hear my question. Are the police ever going to come up with the name of the man who actually stabbed him? I don't like to think he's at large out there in the town, perhaps serving me my half pound of cheddar, sitting next to me on the bus, signing on for dancing lessons—"

He cut her short. Tense and eager to be off, he said more than he ought. "Don't worry, Dorine! Buy your cheese and take the bus with confidence! The most sinister face you'll have to confront next dancing term will be mine! The knife man is dead. He can do no more damage. But tell me, this uncle of Amelia's—do you know his name?"

She shook her head. "I don't think I ever knew it. Sorry."

As he shouldered his way through the crowd, a quick backward glance revealed the always disquieting sight of Earwig arm in arm with—should he be surprised?—his aunt Henrietta. Now, where had Hetty sprung from, and why had she not greeted him? Oh Lord! Had she seen him tangoing? Good manners stayed his step. He ought to go over and speak to her.

At that moment, the two women were approached by a third, and three heads began to nod and bob in eager exchange. Madame Dorine seemed to have things of import to convey. Ears burning, Redfyre groaned and hurried on.

B ack at the station, he dashed into MacFarlane's office. "Quick, sir! I want you to take a look with me at the Chiqui file again. I've just been interviewing the person who identified the body, and—"

"Dressed like that! Have you been auditioning for the front line of the City Slickers Shoeshine Band? There's the box. Help yourself."

"The address of Amelia's Bullen's parents, the Earl and Countess of Brancaster . . ." He riffled quickly through. "Here it is. Melton Hall, near Kettlestone. Now, did Miss Wells manage to present the promised list of addresses and contacts for the dining group? She did? Good girl!"

MacFarlane was already tearing open the envelope that had been put in his in-tray.

A stubby finger ran down the neatly typed list, stopped, stabbed at a name and he chortled. "Gotcha! Here's a match! Melton Hall!"

He handed the list to Redfyre, who took up the tale. "This is where he spends his vacations. The home address he's given is actually the home of his sister, the lady of the manor. Oliver Fanshawe! He's the uncle of the girl Chiqui was involved with. That's the military thread connecting him with the killings. Well, not so much a thread . . . more like the first small stone that starts an avalanche. The retired general—old Brancaster—learned of

Abel's special services by the military grapevine, confided between armchairs in one of their clubs when the port was flowing. 'I say, old chap, if you have a problem that needs to be solved irrevocably and discreetly, I can give you a number to ring . . .' Uncle Oliver listens sympathetically to his sister's story of attempted blackmail—perhaps he is genuinely fond of the niece he tries to help—and is persuaded by his brother-in-law to arrange for Chiqui's last tango to happen in Cambridge, giving his family a safe alibi of fifty miles or so. It must have added another stimulating dimension to Fanshawe's intellectual torment soirées to know that their victim was leaving the party, going on somewhere to keep a further date with death."

"Heathens! They probably noted down the poor fool's last words. Wouldn't surprise me. At least he had a good meal . . . beef Wellington, wasn't it? Apart from the pudding, according to the doc. He must have flounced out before the pudding."

"And encountered his nemesis lying in wait below in the street, delivered into his hands, drunk, incapable and quarrelsome, by a couple of the Amici," Redfyre said. "Information from Dr. Wells. He says two men helped him down the stairs and off the premises. Hardy! An easy job for a man of his experience. Just lend a steadying arm to a drunk and offer to escort him home . . . you're going his way, after all."

"Unless," MacFarlane interrupted, "Hardy was already there? A guest himself at the dinner table? No need to be kept waiting down below, stropping his knife on the sole of his shoe or picking his nose. And it would give him all the time he needed to size up the victim. To assess his strength and locate his weapon, if any."

"Good thought! Hardy would quickly notice that Chiqui carried a knife in his belt. The work of a moment to wait until you reach the Fitzwilliam then nick his knife, plunge it into exactly the right spot, as he'd been trained, wipe the handle and string the body up in the place you'd chosen. Wait until daylight—which would be early in, what was it? June? And nip back with your pocket Kodak. The resulting shot would swiftly make its way by post to the general, releasing the second half of the payment. The body remains unremarked until an inquisitive nurse on her way to work decides there's a pulse that ought to be taken."

"And when Ernest Jessup makes a nuisance of himself, the Fox-Gisbournes scratch their heads and say, 'What was that number again? Let's leave this to able Abel, shall we?'" MacFarlane speculated. "He became the useful tool, the recourse for the elimination of the rest of the group. Dickie was on the list, all right. Ratty would have followed."

"Hardy didn't flinch at the notion of killing his old mates." Redfyre's voice was not questioning; it was pronouncing judgement. A heavy judgement.

"Contracted killers don't suffer from soft hearts, nostalgia or loyalty, lad."

"No. I do rather wonder why he's getting special attention from us, sir? Clearly a villain. Numberless crimes to his account. But all we have is his corpse. We can't even hang him once, let alone a dozen times for his misdeeds."

"You can only be a victim once, and it's in this capacity that he's of interest to me. Someone had his hands round his neck and squeezed. He may have deserved it, but I want to know whose hands they were and to be able to prove it. A confession will do."

"All the same—an utter scoundrel and doubly shameful behaviour towards men he'd fought alongside! I'd say he got off lightly." Redfyre's voice was tight with indignation.

"And all to preserve the secret of whatever wickedness or shame Sydney Fox had been mired in during his posting in South Africa. His presumably ill-gotten cash was spent on acquiring further wealth, but also to launch his one and only precious son Digby onto an unsuspecting world. Politics! Every aspect of the lad's life would be put under the microscope, and he'd be constantly in the public eye. He stood no chance—he'd be ruined if ever the story got out."

"We only have Ratty's word on that, sir. And when you spoke in Yorkshire, he didn't claim to know the whole story. It must have been bad, wouldn't you say, to have reverberations on another generation twenty-five years later?"

"Dickie Dunne will know."

"And where the hell is he?" Redfyre asked, shrugging hopelessly.

"No sightings yet?"

"None, sir. The constables have done a good job checking on all his known haunts in town. There was a lot of, 'Why don't you talk to Mrs. Jones at number seventy? Well, you could try . . .' They were sent spinning off on wild-goose chases. The captain had hidey-holes, doss houses and prime cribs all over the place. And the PCs were very impressed by the loyalty everyone showed. No one's come near to giving him away."

For the first time, MacFarlane was able to eye the black box without frustration. "Well, while we're waiting for the postmortem on Fanshawe, I can start exhuming these one by one and adding a footnote." He gave a hideous grin. "Tying a label to the toes. Always a pleasure, that! I'll go ahead. You, Redfyre, may worm your way back into that college. We aren't done with them yet. Someone knows who tipped Fanshawe through the window and poured a libation over him. And that Cornelius Wells . . . something not quite right there. He's another one who makes my whiskers twitch. Is he protecting Digby Gisbourne and thereby the college's interests? You'll get no funding out of a hanged man. This daughter, Rosamund Wells, sounds like a load of trouble to me, but you never know your luck. Sometimes the clever Dicks and Doras trip up in their own nets. See if you can get close, Redfyre. Without rocking the boat.

"Oh, and send young Thoday down to London, will you? With backup. I've just arranged for a squad of city police to join the party. They'll handle the financial crime aspect of this better than we can—the city's right in the middle of their patch, and they're used to sharp practice by plausible persons. They'll have some pretty blunt questions to put to Enquiries At, and rather blunt methods of extracting answers. Including a touch of dynamite, if necessary. One of their lads is an ex-peterman. No safe defies his delicate touch for long."

REDFYRE OFFERED TO pick up the pathologist's report himself from Trumpington Street when the phone call came through that it was ready. He had other business round the back of the morgue.

Dr. Beaufort was brisk, as usual. "This is a trifle rushed, Redfyre. But given the college context with potential witnesses packing their trunks and disappearing for nigh on three months, I thought speed might be of the essence. I, too, am bound for Dover and the ferry to the Aegean Isles very soon.

"In fact, it was quite straightforward. He died falling from a height. Damage done listed in the report, all consistent. No sneaky little pinpricks in the armpits or dagger-shaped punctures. He fell and died of the fall."

"Any signs that he might have been helped on his way down?"

"One only. Fingernails. All intact, by the way, so he wasn't involved in a fight. I tweezered out a couple of tiny threads of fabric. He could have picked them up brushing against someone in a corridor, slapping someone on the back, it's that insubstantial. Very dark blue. Navy, really. Gents' suiting, not evening dress. Over to you. I think you know where to look. But I'd advise you to hurry—they're having an end-of-term clear-out in the morgue, too."

"Had he been drinking?"

"No. A half glass of sherry. Nothing to turn the head, though his body was soaked in the stuff and the empty bottle broken by the side of the body. Sorry I can't be of more help. But Redfyre, experience tells me that barring a surprise confession, you'll never get this past the Prosecution Service—rightly so, in my opinion—as anything chargeable. They'll see it as nothing more sinister than suicide at the worst, accidental overbalancing at best. So there you have it: unexplained accidental death, because no one wants to hear of a suicide. Especially not the colleges."

Report in hand, Redfyre made his way to the offices at the rear of the morgue and engaged the attention of a young man on portering duty. He asked what the situation was regarding the effects of one of the corpses: Vagrant Unknown/Richard Dunne. On learning that the "combustibles" were about to be sent down to the hospital furnace, he ordered a halt and requested the bag of possessions to be brought back up to him for a last-minute examination. A two-bob piece changed hands, and in surprisingly short time, Redfyre found himself handling a familiar greatcoat now smelling eye-wateringly of Lysol.

He took it out and placed it, folded, on the bench, then ran an enquiring hand over the fabric of the suit below. And snagged one of his own fingernails. It was as he remembered. Loose-weave, summer-weight tweed. Dark blue.

A WEEK LATER, all the notes had been typed up—evidence, such as it was, collated. MacFarlane had filled out an arrest warrant. They just needed the right man to wave it at. But no one was giving away Dickie Dunne's whereabouts. His Cambridge friends and protectors maintained a mystified silence. Negative reports came back from areas all over the country he was known to have frequented. "He could be working his passage back to India, for all we know," MacFarlane grumbled to Redfyre. "Croaked on some exposed northern moor. We'll never hear about it. I'm going to shove the Fanshawe file, slim as it is, into the coffin box. When the chief suspect's a corpse and the Prosecutor is narrowing his eyes and shaking his head, I'm not exactly encouraged to keep the case open on my desk. It would be interesting to find out for certain whose fingers squeezed Abel Hardy in too tight an embrace, but not knowing isn't going to keep me from my sleep. In fact, I'm relieved that the garbage is off our streets for good."

He sighed and came to a decision. "In they go, both of them. Hardy and Fanshawe! *Requiescant in pace*, the shits!"

CHAPTER 24

R edfyre was trotting to keep up with his dog on his usual route through the meadow on Coe Fen. The day had been warm, and the night air was bringing a welcome freshness that descended, trapping the almond scent of the May blossom in a low-floating layer where it blended in an enchanting cocktail with the green river smells. It was one of those magical twilights that faded slowly into a pale grey night, which lasted no time at all before the horizon brightened again. If a Viking longship had ventured upriver and moored in front of him, he'd have leapt aboard, grabbed an oar and gone off adventuring. With his sharp grey eyes and his dark blond hair, he would have surely been accepted by the crew as a long-lost brother.

He shook the illusion away and grinned. Midsummer madness, he told himself. The town was in the grip of it: Strawberry Fair, maypole dancing on Jesus Green, Shakespeare in the master's rose garden. The summer party mood of the town seemed to have spread to the riverbank, and behind him, he heard lively shouts of puntsmen pulling in to their berths at the Anchor pub just downstream, while in front, the boozy, raucous laughter of the usual crowd of vagrants clinking bottles around a campfire.

Was it the smell of something delicious roasting on a sharpened willow stick that had attracted Snapper? He realised that the crowd had gone abruptly silent at the very moment the little dog took off at a ninety-degree angle from his route and charged, unseen, through the tall-growing Queen Anne's lace towards the encampment.

"Here we go again!" Redfyre sighed and set off in pursuit. Nearing the bonfire, he saw silhouetted against it a crowd of about twenty ragged men. Silent, on their guard. Redfyre checked them for horned helmets and broadswords before walking up more circumspectly. When he was within hailing distance he called out in his usual bluff, officer's voice: "Hello there! Please don't, for God's sake, feed my dog a sausage! He's just had his dinner!"

"You're too late, Redfyre! He's already wolfed one down. How about you? Fancy a Newmarket banger? They're good," a gruff but friendly voice answered.

A tall shape broke from the herd and stepped forward. He was holding a fawning Snapper in his arms. The dog seemed enthralled by the close contact with the old and doubtless strongly scented fisherman's smock tied up with string about the middle regions of his new friend—or kidnapper?

"By Gum, lad, you've taken your time! I was going to have to come into the nick under my own steam tomorrow morning and surrender!"

The vagrant company moved, muttering like a Greek chorus, closing ranks in a protective shield around the man in their midst. One word from him, and Redfyre—though probably not Snapper, he thought—would end up in the River Cam within seconds.

Only one thing for it. Shoulders back, head up, he scanned the group and quickened his pace towards them, like one going to meet his friends. "Well, well! Is this the moment I say, 'Major Dunne, I presume?'" He stretched out a hand. "John Redfyre, Cambridge CID. Pleased to meet you at last. Any friend of my dog is a friend of mine," he added. And many in the crowd knew he meant it.

Hesitant, the men looked to Dickie Dunne for a signal. He tucked Snapper under his left arm, put out his right and shook Redfyre's hand. The company of tramps sighed in relief at the ancient exchange of peace signals and began to move about again. One of them, whom he recognised, appeared at his elbow with a sausage on a slice of bread. "Here you are, Inspector. I've put some mustard on that."

It was indeed delicious. He washed it down with a bottle of ginger beer, conscious the whole time of Dickie Dunne's eyes on him as he chirrupped on engagingly about the excellent weather and the quality of Mr. Musk of Newmarket's pork sausages. His talk disguised the weight of MacFarlane's expectation—command, in fact—that hung heavily on him: "As soon as apprehended, read the villain the riot act and wheel him in sharpish!"

"Major Dunne!" he said, "If you would care to call in at HQ tomorrow, since you seem to be free, you'll find me at my desk from eight o'clock onwards. Time for a parley, I'm thinking."

"I'll be there, Inspector. Oh, don't forget your dog. Little beauty! And a good ratter, like his master. He's down here a lot. Makes himself at home. Till tomorrow, then!"

HE STRODE IN at exactly eight o'clock the next morning as invited and was shown to the inspector's office.

Redfyre looked with keen interest at the man who had eluded them, the man so many witnesses about the town had hurried to describe and defend. His barber had talked in distracting detail about his haircut, even particularising the side of the parting and the length to the tenth of an inch. No change there, but the clean-shaven features after three weeks on the lam had acquired the slightly raffish nobility of a Sir Walter Raleigh. He only lacked the earring.

"Major," Redfyre said, using his correct rank with military punctiliousness. "Thank you for coming in to help us with our enquiries. We're investigating the death of an academic, a Dr. Fanshawe, the unfortunate event occurring in the course of a dinner party in the gentleman's own rooms at St. Jude's College, held on Friday the sixteenth of May, three weeks ago. We understand that you were present as a guest at that event. Will you confirm that?"

The piratical image intensified as he grinned sardonically back at the inspector, clearly critical of the policeman's stiff official tone.

"Yup! I was there, all right," he said. "Damned strangest party of my life! As bad as Belshazzar's feast. Worse, in fact—we didn't get as far as tasting the food, and there were no skimpily clad girls present. Not even a corseted master's wife. We'd been lured to"—he lowered his voice and hissed dramatically—"a *symposium*. In the classical style, if you understand what I'm saying. Disturbing, what! Others felt the same."

He left a pause for Redfyre to absorb his meaning, then went on lightly. "It was so boring, one of the guests was moved to chuck the host through the window! Hardy? Was that his name? A dark-haired bloke. Lost his rag when Fanshawe murmured something in his ear, picked him up and pushed him out through the open window. Couldn't have that! Jolly bad show, I thought, and ran over to intervene. The soldier's way." He stuck out two large, calloused hands and demonstrated. "He struggled, I feared for my life—the chap was clearly doolally—and I oversteered. When you get around to charging me, if you can ever fight your way through the circumlocutions, I shall say, 'I confess to the manslaughter of Abel Hardy.'"

He held out his hands again, but this time symbolically, for the handcuffs.

MacFarlane chose this bad moment to burst into Redfyre's office.

"You got him! Might have waited for me to have a go at him first . . . Oy, Jenkins! Get in here and put this fellow in cuffs—the ones with the extending chain—and take him down to the cooler to think about his sins over the weekend."

"Sir!" Redfyre leapt to his feet. "Major Dunne has come in of his own accord to give a statement. I have not arrested him for any crime."

"What are you waiting for? Giving him a chance to disappear for another twenty years? We're not having that! Jenkins!"

Dickie Dunne watched the exchange with a detached amusement, smiled and said a polite thank-you as Jenkins applied the cuffs and led him away. At the door, he turned back and said affably to Redfyre, "We'll speak later, perhaps? I'm sure there's more you'd like to know."

"Sir, sir! There's a gentleman below at reception who needs a word. Urgently."

"Thank you, Jenkins. Does he have a name, this gentleman?" Redfyre was writing up notes on his lengthy weekend interview with Dickie Dunne. The South African story, which he was making every effort to tell succinctly, kept wriggling away from him in a lively way. He did not wish to be interrupted.

"I expect so, sir, but he's not giving it. Or 'vouchsafing it to all and sundry,' according to him."

"Who's the 'all and sundry' down there, this bright A.M.?"

"We've got two stolen wallets, three tarts, a lost dog and the char lady, sir."

"Did he 'vouchsafe' his business, at least?"

"Only when he got fed up with me. Lost his rag, banged on the counter, and shouted, 'Is this the way the Cambridge police normally handle confessions to murder? *Multiple* murders? If I'm not sitting in front of the inspector within thirty seconds, I shall decide better of it, walk away and take my confession elsewhere.'"

"Ouch! I bet that cleared the waiting room! What bad manners. Better get your skates on, Jenkins, and ask him to come in. Er... not wielding a blood-dripping axe or anything, is he?"

"None of that, sir!" And, suspiciously, "Though it didn't help that the shopping bag he's carrying with him says 'Baxter the

Family Butcher' on it." Jenkins rolled his eyes in exasperation. "Joker! But there's no accounting for what he might have got in there. Four pork chops? His laundry? The head of John the Baptist? I'll take a look before I show him in. He's well dressed and full of himself. But he strikes me as the sort who could turn nasty. Do you want me to hang about, sir? Apply the cuffs to this one as well? We've got a spare set."

"Won't be necessary, Jenkins. I think I know who it is. And yes, I think you're right! He's playing with us! Just flash the bugger a knowing smile and escort him up."

"AH! GOOD MORNING, Mr. Gisbourne. We last bumped into each other on the dance floor, so to speak? Tangoing to the Latin sounds of Felipe and his bandoneon band. Have you come forward to confess to dislocating my right shoulder in the encounter? No need! Not even my pride was hurt."

"Stop arsing about, Redfyre! Rosa warned me you were a smart aleck, so just drop the act, will you? I'm here to sort out several crimes about Cambridge for you. Crimes committed over, um . . . let's say the last five years. I'm sure you keep good records. You'll know the finer details. Just write out a formal statement, will you, and I'll sign it."

"Of course. We won't turn down such a generous offer, but I would first like you to answer a few vital questions of the who, when and why nature. I think we know most of the answers, but let's introduce a little method, if not quite the proper procedures, shall we? As the first of the killings we're both interested in occurred five years ago—that offence also a result of tango-induced emotions, when you were a lad of sixteen, busy on the playing fields of Eton?—I am prepared to discount any confession of yours to that crime."

He reached into a file box, extracted a single sheet and passed it over the desk. "Now, Mr. Gisbourne, you have there a selection of six related cases we have on our books, all requiring closure. Look on this as a menu for your perusal. I'm striking out the first one, a Mr. Ricardo de Angelis, as being only indirectly connected with the Gisbourne family."

Digby took it and stared, aghast. "Six, you say? Six?"

"Unless you want to add to that number?"

"No, no! Certainly not!"

"Perhaps it would help if you concentrated on the last one on the list. The very recent strangling of an old soldier called Abel Hardy on college premises, more precisely in the rooms of a colleague of yours, the gentleman who features in the victim list at number five. (Dr. Fanshawe having been only minutes before thrown from his window to his death in the court below.) You were a witness to both deaths, and have already given us your, shall we say, preliminary and incomplete statement. Following which, you disappeared. But better late than infinitely on the loose, I suppose. Pick up where you left off. And went to ground for"—he glanced at the wall calendar—"well, nigh a fortnight. Why don't you take up the tale from the moment the party started?"

"I'll take it from the moment the seventh guest entered, if you don't mind. I can't say I was keeping count of who was drinking what. Except that Captain Dunne, Knight Templar that he is, was drinking pure spring water. He turned round and greeted the last guest as though he'd been expecting him."

"Oh, he had. Counting on his arrival, I'd say. He was preparing to kill him."

"It happened so quickly. I suppose that's what they all say . . . We hadn't even sat down to dinner. Still, with two old ex-soldiers facing up to each other with murder in mind and twenty years of gathered venom bursting out, who would wonder at the speed? Those men were trained to deliver the first blow and make it a cruncher. I know that much." He suppressed a shudder.

Redfyre looked with more care at the figure in front of him.

This was the same man, handsome, broad-shouldered, who had cut a dashing figure on the dance floor, but he seemed much reduced now. The effects of a bad conscience, perhaps? Unusual for a murderer of this scale to have a conscience. Redfyre frowned, his mind darting back and forth.

"Fanshawe saw the danger and dismissed the other guests?"

"Yes. He dropped a hint to Rendlesham. 'Go down to the refectory, the three of you,' he said. 'Digby will come down and join you in a minute. Be sure you leave a space for him.'"

"So the first two signed in fountain pen, blue-black ink, and passed the pen to Rendlesham, who then—quite literally—left a space and signed on line four. When you came down—and you're going to tell me how much later—you filled in the gap. But in your haste and confusion, understandable after experiencing two killings within seconds of each other, you used your black ink, italic-nibbed pen. The trailing loops of the letters *y* and *g* on Digby run over the following scrawl by Rendlesham." He tapped the file on his desk. "Excellent forensic methods we use these days. Photographic evidence, particularly when enlarged, impresses a jury."

"Stop showing off! I've no idea how long I was trapped up there with three—three!—cold-blooded killers. As I was trying to tell you, they erupted into silent but deadly action. It was over in seconds. And I can tell you, it's nothing like the choreographed fencing bouts you see on the silver screen: a twenty-minute reel of nimble footwork, snarling insults and swinging about on drapery! Oh no. Nobody wastes time shouting, 'Have at you, sirrah!' Hardy didn't so much make an entrance as an incursion! He ignored the captain's jeering and rushed with no warning straight across the room at Fanshawe. Fanshawe! Why him? At that moment, I had no idea what his crimes had been. I just thought he was a sadistic turd, and I was about to resign from his dining club. Couldn't see why it had such glamour and status attached to it. I was going to tell the new master—Dr. Wells—at the end of term.

Seemed the most tactful timing. I wasn't certain how much longer the college could depend on enjoying his mastership.

"But here he was—Fanshawe—being manhandled in front of the open window by a man with a very bad reputation. He wasn't expecting the attack. He tried to fend him off with his hand and scrabbled about with his feet, but it was useless. He shrieked once as he disappeared over the sill, and we all heard the thump as his body hit the paving stones below. Hardy strolled to the drinks tray and picked up the bottle of sherry. He poured the rest of the wine out of the window, looked at us and intoned in mock priestly speech, 'Let us remember the fallen,' and then threw the empty bottle after it on top of the body. Then he turned to deal with me. I knew I was next."

The young man's voice began to fail as he recalled the horror and the fear. "What sort of man does that? Kills his fellow and mocks him with a libation poured down on him as he's taking his last breath?"

"A soldier. I've seen worse," Redfyre said quietly. "Tell me about the other soldier present. Did Captain Dunne react?"

"Of course. Like lightning. But he'd taken up—I'd guess—a strategic position by the door. I was nearer, standing by the drinks tray. I rushed at Hardy. It all came back to me."

"What came back to you?"

"The training. My uncle Herbert and my father. When I was young they used to teach me self-preservation, army-style. How to kill before you were killed. I never thought I'd use such skills in earnest. But my fingers hadn't forgotten." He extended a pair of oarsman's hands, and Redfyre inspected the wide span and muscular thumbs. "My thumbs knew where to go. I'm pretty strong, Inspector, and I squeezed hard. It was surprisingly quick. Uncle Herbert taught me to count to thirty, to be sure. But by twenty, Hardy was sagging weightily against me, and I knew he was dead."

"And Dunne? What was he doing the while?"

"Trying to stop me! Shouting in my ear. When Hardy's body slumped down on the carpet, he put an arm under my shoulders and helped me into a chair. He found the drink I'd poured for myself just before this burst over us and made me drink it down. He told me it was all right, I'd done the right thing, the only thing. That the man I'd just killed was a verminous rat who deserved what he'd got several times over. If I hadn't done it, he would have. Either way, Hardy was not going to leave that room alive. 'Listen, lad,' he said, 'I've a story to tell you.' It wasn't the story I'd heard from my father, and I didn't believe the half of it, but after what's just happened in London . . . I know the captain had it right."

"What's just happened in London?" Redfyre hardly dared ask.

"My father died yesterday. You'll note I came as soon as I could."

"I've noted that you presented yourself for questioning twenty-four days after the murder occurred," Redfyre said coldly.

"Has it been that long? Really? Well, anyhow, I was with my father when he expired. No—don't slow me down with condolences that are neither required nor appropriate. You knew he was dying. That's why I went underground. I wanted to be sure that my father was dead and well beyond police attention before I spoke out. I wasn't having him drawing his last breath in a prison cell.

"I'd been suspicious of my father's business methods over the years and the way things always tipped magically in my favour. It seemed a callous thing to do to interrogate him on his deathbed, but I went for it. I had to know the truth before he slipped away. He admitted he'd been pulling the wool over everyone's eyes for the last few weeks concerning his state of health. He'd been bed-bound indeed, but lively enough to use the services of one of his secretaries who was allowed in every morning to 'complete my plans before I pop my clogs,' as he put it. When I pressed him, he admitted he'd paid an assassin he'd used on previous occasions to get rid of Fanshawe. 'The go-between, the know-it-all lightweight who could be the biggest menace of them all,' he said. 'He'd have you dangling on his watch chain forever more, my lad. You'd never be clear of the scandal.' He'd ordered Hardy to kill Fanshawe first, then deal with Dickie Dunne."

"Leaving Hardy at liberty?" Redfyre was incredulous. "Your father can't have been thinking very clearly."

"My father was sharp right to the last. It would have entertained him no end to envisage a man-to-man fight to the death between the two men he most hated. He had calculated that, as ever, the captain would beat the lieutenant. If that was the outcome, he was home and dry. Captain Dunne had known the truth for twenty-four years: the theft, the betrayal, the false witness . . . The scandal would have sunk my father, but it would especially, in his eyes, have ruined any prospects of a political career for me, or indeed any place in civilised society. Blackballing from clubs, cold shoulders, invitations refused . . . You can imagine. Yet Dunne had taken no steps to share his knowledge with anyone. He was no threat. I think my father probably had it right, judging by the size of the knuckle-duster Dunne was wearing on his right hand when he charged up to Hardy. He'd arrived prepared. Pity I hadn't known.

"The last thing my father did was hand me this. He lifted the shopping bag. 'You'll lack for nothing, son,' he said. 'But I want you to have this. There's a note inside.' A note that turned the world upside down for me! Would you like to see it, Inspector?"

Would he refuse?

Digby emptied the contents of the bag on to the desk. Out slid a battered red-and-gold commemoration tin bearing the head of Queen Victoria.

"Take the lid off," Digby told him.

On top was a folded sheet of paper, and underneath it, four chocolate bars. Not the original Fry's, but a later Cadbury's version of the queen's largesse. Solemnly, Digby passed Redfyre a penknife. "Will you do the honours?" he said.

"I believe this is how it's done," Redfyre said. He stripped the wrapper from the chocolate bar and sliced it from north to south down the long side. It fell apart, revealing an interesting filling. "Ah. Not nutty crunch, I believe."

"Now read the note."

With a sigh, Redfyre began to read the dying man's last words to his only son.

"'Just off now, son. Look after your mother, though Grace will get through. She's a tough woman and far too good for both of us! You needn't bother about that mad old bat of a granny—she's provided for. The businesses are yours. Ditch them if you like—it might not be what you'd want to add lustre to a political career. I only did it to give you a leg up. And I've always taken steps to smooth your path.

"'Just in case, I'm leaving you these reminders of my early army days. I told you the man I hated, Dickie Dunne, had done the dirty on us. Well, not quite true—I got the better of him! Thought he was so clever! But I was the one who got away with the diamonds. Hid them in a neat place, picked them up a year later when things had calmed down. I used the bugger's own crafty idea of a hiding place to get the stones back home in my kitbag. Who but Dickie Dunne would ever think of disembowelling a bloke's chocolate bars? Not that it did me that much good—if you ever have to shift rough diamonds, you'll find they're not worth a quarter of what people think. If needs be, go to your mother's cousin in Hatton Gardens in the Smoke. He'll do the best for you, but don't expect much. Farewell, Digby, and God bless you, my lad.'"

Redfyre sighed. "Well, as a confession it's not very specific, but it will have to do."

Digby Gisbourne bent his head to the list again and passed it back to Redfyre. "There. I think we're up to date. The first, the dancer, I've crossed out—nothing to do with me, Guv. The second, Ernest Jessup. The zealous accountant who started it all—I've ticked for him. I'd give him two ticks if I could. The general in the punt? I had no idea what had happened to that old fart! He crossed my father in a business deal, I remember. He was an obstacle to a land purchase. I'd better tick for him. Royston Chilvers? He was the Winter Icarus, wasn't he? I thought I'd heard the last of him. Didn't he fall off a tower?"

"No. Chilvers was cracked on the head whilst on the ground, then arranged to look interesting for the photographic record."

Digby's jaw sagged in astonishment. "I knew him. Chilvers was a Tory hopeful, about five years ahead of me in experience and age. When the local member of Parliament came down with pneumonia that winter, it was a disappointment for me. Too soon, you see. Chilvers would have gotten the nomination and been a fixture for the foreseeable ... But the MP recovered anyway."

"What a waste of talent. Tick?"

"Then there's Fanshawe. I've entered *him* on my father's account. And last, Hardy himself. I'm writing my name in that slot. There—I've initialled numbers two to five for Pa and signed for the last one myself. I hereby confess to killing Abel Hardy." He looked up from his scrawlings, puzzled and asked: "Look here, Redfyre—is this regular procedure?"

"Lord, no. It's very irregular. I'm taking no official notice at all." He smiled blandly. "Just helping you to clarify the events for yourself. You'll know it's regular when we put the handcuffs on you and get the Bible out. Now, just to dot the *is*, will you tell me how the pair of you managed the disposal of the body of Hardy?"

"I went down to the refectory, showed my face, forced down a bite of rice pudding and came away as soon as I could. Told everyone I'd be dashing in and out with an attack of the squitters. And Captain Dunne helped me dispose of the body."

"Mm. I worked out that it was a two-man job to get him down all those stairs, and one of them at least would have had to have a good knowledge of the building to find his way down through the master's lodge and into the graveyard."

"I knew the way down and where the key to the door was kept. I unlocked it, locked up afterward and threw the key away into the grass so that no one would venture into the graveyard for a while. Dunne knew the position of the tombstones on the other side. He'd often slept there himself in the summertime. He thought the body wouldn't be found for days," he finished accusingly. "We spent some time putting him into Dunne's greatcoat, fastening that ridiculous tie round his neck, emptying his pockets. At the last moment we noticed the shoes. Hardy had on a very nice pair, scarcely worn. They had to be swapped."

"We gathered as much. You've no idea how much time the men wasted doing a Prince Charming act. And you messed up the socks. It would have been a neat ending. Decayed body of tramp, later identified as Dunne. Hardy is buried under a false name and disappears completely, unmourned and not pursued too energetically by his wife. Edith wouldn't have wanted a close investigation into her husband's affairs. And 'Dickie Dunne,' on account of having kept a half crown in his pocket, is put into a marked grave. Two men off the face of the earth for good."

He turned his attention back to the list.

"We have a problem here," Redfyre said after a calculated moment's hesitation. "The number-six slot is already spoken for. We've had a prior confession for the murder of Hardy. Major—as we should properly call him—Richard Dunne confessed two days ago to the killing of his former comrade in arms. Ah, Constable! Thank you! Cup of tea, Gisbourne? Help yourself to sugar. Oh, and Jenkins, if anyone else appears at the desk confessing to the murder of Dr. Fanshawe, please tell them to join the queue."

"Popular bloke, was he?" Jenkins asked innocently.

CHAPTER 26

MacFarlane shuffled the interview sheets for the tenth time, failing again to see what he wanted to see in them. He sighed and looked suspiciously into the eyes of Redfyre, who was sitting opposite, shrugged his shoulders and conceded defeat.

"Right, lad. You win."

"Not me, sir. Justice, surely? Which is what we all signed up for. Besides, any other solution results, as we've both calculated, in defeat, derision—nay, contumely, even!" Redfyre smiled encouragingly. "You can imagine the headlines if we were to lose two cases, one after the other in court. 'Cack-handed police force, failing to control crime surge in the city' and all that. And we *would* lose. Gisbourne would employ the very best and smartest London lawyers and get away with it. I'm not sure, in any case, that his crime deserves an execution by hanging. But that's not mine to judge—or yours, sir. We might both agree that he did the world a favour, but you never know. English juries are a bit odd at times. I'd rather not risk it."

"So what *are* we to make of a joint hands-up from Dunne and Gisbourne? Bloody ridiculous! Are we quite certain that the two of them aren't colluding over their stories?"

Redfyre had hoped his boss wouldn't think so deeply into the matter. Again he had underrated him. "Colluding, sir?" He appeared to be giving the insight his full consideration. "No, I'm sure not. The two considered themselves enemies over past matters, if you remember, sir? And they wouldn't have so under-estimated the ability of the Cambridge CID to see through such a ploy, would they?"

It was clear to Redfyre, having gotten to know both self-confessed, synchronised stranglers during his interview sessions, that the two ingenious manipulators had certainly colluded with each other in the presentation of the body in the graveyard. They'd emptied pockets, removed shoes and socks, changed ties, planted a half crown and poured brandy down the dead man's throat. They'd plotted and planned together, all right. Plan A relied on police stupidity and inaction: vagrant, uniden-tified, death by natural causes. Bury in town plot. Plan B was in reserve place in case someone raised queries and an investi-gation was launched. And that was where Redfyre and Dr. Beaufort came onstage, asking questions and ferreting about in pockets and digestive tracts.

Most annoyingly, the pair had also colluded—in the most tactful way—with Redfyre himself. He was quite certain of that. They had saved themselves from a ramrod-straight police charge of first-degree murder by the subtle implication that they understood that he believed, as they did, in true justice. Plan C had been triggered. A double confession. And, most powerful of all, perhaps, before leaving the station, Gisbourne had notified him with the smiling triumph of a Parthian lining him up over his shoulder for a last shot of his readiness to marshal the forces of an extremely effective and expensive London defence lawyer.

A furrowed brow and a slow growl greeted Redfyre's tongue-in-cheek comment on the ability of the CID.

"If you say so, Inspector. Right. Let's take a last look at this fairy tale you've concocted before we sign our careers away. It all revolves around the victim, Hardy. The unknown element and late entrant to the party. Hardy is a man of the world, a sophisticate from London town, and it's he who catches on first to the infamous truth behind the gathering. All right so far?"

"That's correct. A tourist looking out for a good time in the sticks. But a reprobate—a gangster, fraudster and all-round scoundrel, as his wife will testify."

"This is the bit I don't hold with—the 'infamous truth,'" MacFarlane grumbled on. "Anyway, go on, dangle it in front of me again. I'll try to put myself into the skin of that puritanical windbag of a Prosecutor for a minute. Will he understand what you're getting at, Redfyre? It's a bit Machiavellian even for me, and I wasn't born yesterday."

"Well you'd better sharpen your elbow, and if he calls you up for an explanation, give him a dig in the ribs when the moment arrives. Hardy, our London sophisticate, turned up expecting a slap-up meal, perhaps to extend into one of the, er, lighter entertainments the town has to offer on a Friday night. At the very least, a round or two of bridge. Only to discover that he has been lured into a—shall we say, 'den of iniquity'? All the participants assembled are male. (Dig here.) Suggestions are made which make it clear that a scene of illegal activity is envisaged . . . Frolicking (another dig) of a masculine nature more associated with the bathhouses of ancient times than the groves of twentieth-century academe is anticipated. I say, sir— am I getting this right?"

"So far, so ambiguous. Go on. Nothing there yet to get me reaching for the carbolic that Jenkins's granny would prescribe."

"The realisation, perhaps the suggestion itself, whispered into his scandalised ear by Fanshawe, hits Hardy as he is standing at the drinks tray in front of the open window. Totally horrified by the prospect of the depravity that he now understands to be on the menu, with a "faugh!" of disgust, he takes hold of Fanshawe and begins to shake him. In the ensuing attempt by both Digby and Dunne to rescue Fanshawe, the poor chap, who, it will be remembered was of very light-limbed constitution, goes headfirst through the open window.

"Sir, here a reminder will not come amiss—that the master of St. Jude's has made it known that he will totally support this version given by the two impeccable witnesses: a Judesman who is engaged to his daughter, and a retired and much-decorated war hero, Major Richard Dunne, lately of the King's Own Yorkshire Light Infantry."

"Was he? Light-limbed, I mean. Fanshawe?"

"No idea," Redfyre said cheerfully. "But anyone who has evidence to the contrary will not want to advertise the knowledge. This is about sensibilities, after all."

"And are we clear as to who throttled Hardy?"

"Both would-be rescuers are uncertain whose grip it was that cut off the assailant's blood supply. Both were devastated by the outcome, and the two have jointly admitted the resulting manslaughter."

"Mm. At last, a bit of solid meat in this swirling Mulligatawny! 'Jointly'! That word does it! The word the judiciary authorities never want to hear. We all know how the Prosecution Service hates a 'joint' culpability charge . . . Never known one to succeed! Juries won't commit themselves to condemning two people to hang for the death of one. It goes against nature. They won't waste their time on it. You're right, Redfyre. They'll go for this fabrication of yours! You have my authority to set the jointly accused loose on bail with the usual precautions. No more disappearing acts."

"Thank you, sir. That's all taken care of. Mr. Gisbourne is not short of a bob or two, and he's come up with sufficient funds to bail them both out."

MacFarlane laughed and shook his head. "A tramp and a business magnate locked together in a three-legged race?"

"Oh, I think they've got a good step going, sir."

~⌐

"JENKINS! WILL YOU unlock the gentleman's shackle, please? And Constable, bring me the parcel I left in my locker."

Redfyre turned to the prisoner. "I'm setting you free, Major, now that I've heard your story. According to your once-commanding officer General Whitcliffe and half the population of Cambridge, to say nothing of the endorsement of my own dog, you are an innocent man. No, don't dispute what I have to say! I know you're not as straightforward as many think. In fact, I take you for a devious old bastard. And I know you to have form when it comes to the blame-taking business. You personally accepted a charge of looting all those years ago in South Africa and saved your men—none of whom, as far as I can see, had your trust or respect—from a nastier fate than the one doled out to them. And here you are, doing it again for the son of your would-be destroyer.

"What prompts you to do this? Self-sacrifice and martyrdom? Is it some religion you follow that imposes such behaviour?"

"I don't follow religion," Dunne said carefully. "Religion follows me. Hound, Harlot or Siren's voice of heaven—I've shaken them all off. But there's nothing wrong with setting my own human standards. That young Digby—he didn't commit murder. He reacted in an instinctive human way against evil when it reared its ugly, scaly head and made an attempt on his life. He's not a warrior, though I believe he has the stuffing for it. I was prepared to rid the world of a man who would have gone on adding infinitely to his shameful list of victims for cash. I had my knuckleduster on. I would cheerfully have rid the world of that preening, overconfident sod. So I'll take the blame. Yon Gisbourne impressed me. He must take after his mother. There's a physical family resemblance with his ghastly old pa, but if you can overlook that, you realise he's smart and has a conscience. Has a life in front of him—possibly an important one. Mine's worthless. I'm just trudging about, looking for death."

"Oh, spare me the Sydney Carton speech!" Redfyre snapped. "You sowed the seed for this outcome yourself, in my mind. One word was enough! 'Symposium.' Looked at from a particular angle, this crime becomes a hot potato for the Prosecution Service, bane of our lives! But you're lucky you spoke the word to someone who understood its dubious underlying meaning and could pick it up and run with it."

Dunne grinned. "I recognise fertile ground when I see it. Yon MacFarlane would have been slower on the uptake, but he'd have gotten there."

"Well, we're letting you loose. That is, when you've finished signing various legal documents."

Dunne, released from the chain, shot to his feet and looked about, a little disoriented and at a loss for words.

"You can go with Jenkins to pick up your bits and pieces below. But before you go," Redfyre said, "here you are. You'll be glad to be reunited with this, I expect." He handed him the brown paper parcel the constable had left on the desk.

Intrigued, the tramp tore off the wrappings. Out fell an army greatcoat bearing the label of a city laundry.

"I had it cleaned, so it's ready for the new season," Redfyre explained. "It stank of, well . . . better not think about it too closely, I suppose. They seem to have done a good job with it."

Dunne had slipped his old coat on with a cry of joy and broken into his marketplace Charlie Chaplin turn, goofing around the office and humming "Goodbye, Dolly Gray" when MacFarlane came in to hand him his release documents.

CHAPTER 27

A whirl of leaves hit Redfyre full in the face as he turned the corner into the lane. The blustery wind—the first of autumn—should have been reminder enough of the date, but it was the sight of the frail figure of his aunt Hetty holding onto her hat, standing on his doorstep with a parcel at her feet, that did the trick.

"I'm here, Aunt! Hang on to the doorknob!" he bellowed. "Here, let me take your parcel. Oh, for me?"

"You'd forgotten, hadn't you, Johnny?" she asked him, eyes twinkling over her china cup when they settled down to the tea table. "Your birthday?"

"It's always at an inconvenient time, Hetty. Beginning of the new term. Too many things to do. Though I do love September!"

He got up and went to the mantelpiece, pulling a coloured postcard from behind one of the porcelain lions he kept standing *gardant* there over his mail. "Everyone's flighting home, it seems. I received this card yesterday from Rosamund Wells. She's in Florence. She tells me she's returning to Jude's after all with her father, who's finally decided, and with much heel-dragging, to take on a further year as master." He gave his aunt a sharp look. "Though I don't imagine this is news to *you*?"

"No, I had a card, too." Hetty smiled innocently.

"I work things out because that's what they pay me to do,

Aunt, and I calculate that you knew about Cornelius Wells's decision to return before he even made it himself. In fact, it has occurred to me that his appointment in the first place and his task of cleansing the Augean stables that Jude's has become," he said evenly, holding her enquiring gaze, "was set in motion by you. Perhaps it was Uncle Gerald who was made the messenger? The one who sounded the alarm? He has entrée to the Army and Navy Club and other suchlike establishments, after all. The influential men in the London world—the Ks, the Ms, the Cs . . ."

"Oh, darling! The whole alphabet soup were at school with him," said Hetty comfortably.

Redfyre sensed that was as far as she would go for the moment in the way of an explanation for her involvement in the Jude's debacle. He would have to reconstruct the rest for himself. He was sure that Gerald had been steered by Hetty to exactly the right club-land after-dinner brandy drinker with his tale of woe. A tale triggered by the death of the tango dancer, perhaps? Information derived from Hetty's swarm of busy worker bees? It had even occurred to his suspicious mind that the glamorous Madame Dorine and her troupe of light-footed ladies could well be a fruitful source of information. Why not? After his recent discovery that Hetty's organisation extended to the brothels of the town, nothing could surprise him. Wherever women and men exchanged conversation or money, it seemed that Hetty had acquired recruits to her cause.

Waiting nervously in the King's Parade for the dance to begin, he hadn't failed to notice the mix of male characters performing for the crowd back in May. Along with the student contingent, some socially prominent men about town had taken part in the demonstration. Sportsmen all—and bless 'em! Not too proud to put on a pair of dance shoes and a show for the public. He'd recognised men who were in their professional

lives politicians, economists, scientists. Even a humble policeman and the policeman's dentist had stepped up and put their
reputation and dignity on the line.

"And with your new informant—little Pansy-Face—you
were on the inside of the bend," he persisted.

"I don't much like the word 'informant,' Johnny, though I
accept that it has a place in your policeman's vocabulary—along
with 'snitch,' perhaps. Rosamund is an intelligent young woman,
alert to the problems and injustices of her times. If she seeks
out or welcomes the company of like-minded, public-spirited
ladies, we will listen, support and advise her. Her father, Cornelius, was judged the ideal man to perform the diagnosis and
excision of the rot that had set in at a fine establishment. Now
you've met him, I'm sure you agree with that judgement. And
he was most ably assisted by his daughter, who managed to—"

He used her hesitation to supply mischievously: "Infiltrate?
Or does that have an uncomfortable flavour of 'plod parlance,'
too, Hetty?"

"You might say 'act as a stool-pigeon' for greater accuracy, if
you don't despise the vernacular. But I do. I was about to say,
'manage to get close to and distract one of the reprobates.' We
women do not falter when it comes to a little deception,
Johnny."

"I can't make my mind up, Aunt, whether your actions cut
off and exposed past disgraceful behaviour or led to further
bloody crimes."

"Certainly the first. Our involvement had foremost, and you
ought to know this, a *political* motive. Honestly, Johnny, I had
no idea about the other entanglement and won't be held responsible in any way. That appalling South African war business
you stepped into with both feet? Lost loot, ambition, revenge,
defenestrations . . . dear me! For a while, I thought I was review-
ing the Tory monthly digest." She dismissed a summer of

gut-wrenching work with her tone. Then she went on, suddenly earnest, "We've lived through dangerous times, these last few years. You, of all men, are well placed to know how near to the edge we've stepped—"

"Aunt, I felt the cliff edge crumbling under my foot."

"Then you would agree that this is no time to tolerate the demoralising philosophies that are being fomented in our seats of learning? The very places like Jude's and Trinity, which have always produced our brightest and most adventurous young men, are under clandestine attack from the barbarian in the east. And I can tell you, because it has at last been reported in our national newspapers, that the new communist empire, now rapidly building, is injecting vast amounts of cash into our universities and our press, as well as our unions and factories. This is not the time for our exhausted country to take its eyes off the ball, Johnny."

Looking with affection at the earnest, wise old face, Redfyre wondered whether to plunge into a string of comforting phrases praising the resilience of the young, stressing their need to experience argument, exhilaration, conviction and—yes—deception, to be able to judge what truly had value. And the absolute necessity for free and true speech in all this.

It would have been the easy response. But his aunt would have seen through him and sensed his own concern that the country he loved, though declared victorious, was enjoying no more than its halftime oranges. Though war-stressed and still grieving, they would yet have to keep a weather eye open on fresh rising powers eager to knock a punch-drunk old fighter off his pins.

In the end, he smiled and said simply, "Nor is it the time to throw away our swords, Hetty. I'm keeping mine bright and sharp. Who was it who said, 'Only the strong are able to bring about peace'?"

"Your Uncle Gerald. Last Tuesday, musing midcrumpet. Though it first could have been Aristotle, perhaps?"

"It was Gerald. Aristotle's advice, I believe, was, 'Make war that we may live in peace.' Unfortunately, the hotheaded youth he tutored, Alexander of Macedon, only heard the first half of the maxim. I have to say, it's a bit further than I would go, but I see from the unholy gleam in your eye that you, too, are a disciple, Aunt."

Redfyre smiled and tapped the postcard, not quite ready to let her off the hook yet. "Rosa says she's coming back. And speaking of tousle-headed young warriors, she's said nothing about her plans for wedded bliss with Digby Gisbourne."

"Ah yes. Pity! They were getting along so well. This was entirely unforeseen, but it's all come to nothing, apparently. The engagement's off. Rosa was rather looking forward to getting hitched to a rich man with a fine political career ahead of him. Perhaps eventually a knighthood? Sir Digby and Lady Gisbourne? She would have liked that, but—"

"Tell me. If you want a slice of chocolate cake."

"Digby has given up politics. Since he narrowly escaped a murder charge in the summer, he's changed. He's resigned from the party and left the college. Not only that—against all advice, he's selling off his father's grocery empire to some chaps called Sainsbury. The Drury Lane Sainsburys."

"Was it something I said?"

"I shouldn't think so, darling. I believe it was an old army officer from his father's past who inspired him to cleanse his soul and his bank account of the pollution of commerce. His co-accused in the murder charge, the Boer War captain, whom I'm sure you remember."

"Good Lord! Gisbourne's not taken to tramping the roads, has he? A vagrant's life and all that?"

Hetty gave a disparaging laugh. "Digby? Never think it! I

know John Clare's romantic view of vagabondage is very fashionable at the moment, but it ought not to be encouraged. On account of its message, as well as its clumping rhythm and jangling rhymes. She recited with mischievous relish:

> *"He eats (a moment's stoppage to his song)*
> *The stolen turnip as he goes along.*
> *He talks to none but wends his silent way*
> *And finds a hovel at the close of day.*

"No—Digby might well *steal* a turnip, but he would never eat it!" was Hetty's evaluation of the danger. "And in any case, it grieves me to say it, but Digby's present situation is much worse. You'll be horrified to hear of it, Johnny! He's applied for, and been given a post, at a . . . certain bureau at an address in Victoria Street in London, if you follow."

"No! Do you mean . . .? He can't have! Digby's joined the Secret Service? I knew they were recruiting, but—Digby! What on earth would they do with him?"

"The last I heard from a disgusted Rosa, they were finding him surprisingly effective. He's in the wilds of Dartmoor at the moment, learning fieldcraft. You know—tracking, shooting, skinning rabbits, killing people. Just their kind of man, apparently. Not such a hit with Rosa. She, I must say, sees no fun in introducing herself to the world as the wife of a—well, what exactly? No one's allowed to know!"

But even marriage to someone in a shady government office with a staff of three men and a cat in Victoria Street was preferable to being linked with a lowly police inspector, was Redfyre's grumpy conclusion.

His aunt read his thoughts, as she always had. "Cheer up, darling! Earwig's back from Berlin on Saturday, and the dancing school opens its doors next week for the new season. Dorine took quite a fancy to you, in spite of your being a little slow on your backward flicks. Or was that too fast on your progressive rocks? I expect she'll be able to help you work on both.

"Is she really French, you're wondering? Oh." Hetty sniffed, head to one side in consideration. "When she wants to be . . . or when *you* want her to be. So, have I earned my chocolate cake?"

31901065093199